Edward Behr has had a long career as a journalist and is currently *Newsweek International*'s cultural editor. His books include GETTING EVEN and ANYONE HERE BEEN RAPED AND SPEAKS ENGLISH? He lives in Paris

Also by Edward Behr

THE ALGERIAN PROBLEM
THE THIRTY-SIXTH WAY
ANYONE HERE BEEN RAPED AND SPEAKS ENGLISH?
GETTING EVEN

EDWARD BEHR

THE LAST EMPEROR

Futura

A Futura Book

Copyright © Recorded Picture Co (Productions) Ltd
and Screenframe Ltd 1987

First published in Great Britain in 1987
by Macdonald & Co (Publishers) Ltd
London & Sydney

ISBN 0 7088 3439 6

Typeset, printed and bound in Great Britain by
Hazell Watson & Viney Limited,
Member of the BPCC Group,
Aylesbury, Bucks

ERRATUM: In the captions to the colour photographs, the name
Keith Hampshire should read Keith Hamshere

Futura Publications
A Division of
Macdonald & Co (Publishers) Ltd
Greater London House
Hampstead Road
London NW1 7QX
A BPCC plc Company

Contents

THE CHING DYNASTY
(Emperors' names are in capitals)

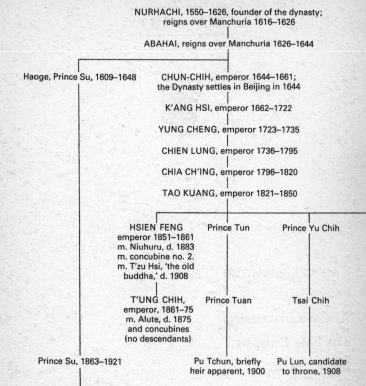

NURHACHI, 1550–1626, founder of the dynasty;
reigns over Manchuria 1616–1626

ABAHAI, reigns over Manchuria 1626–1644

Haoge, Prince Su, 1609–1648

CHUN-CHIH, emperor 1644–1661;
the Dynasty settles in Beijing in 1644

K'ANG HSI, emperor 1662–1722

YUNG CHENG, emperor 1723–1735

CHIEN LUNG, emperor 1736–1795

CHIA CH'ING, emperor 1796–1820

TAO KUANG, emperor 1821–1850

HSIEN FENG
emperor 1851–1861
m. Niuhuru, d. 1883
m. concubine no. 2.
m. T'zu Hsi, 'the old
buddha,' d. 1908

Prince Tun

Prince Yu Chih

T'UNG CHIH,
emperor, 1861–75
m. Alute, d. 1875
and concubines
(no descendants)

Prince Tuan

Tsai Chih

Prince Su, 1863–1921

Pu Tchun, briefly
heir apparent, 1900

Pu Lun, candidate
to throne, 1908

'Eastern Jewel'
1906–1948, aka as Yoshiko Kawashima
(exec. by Chiang kai-chek)

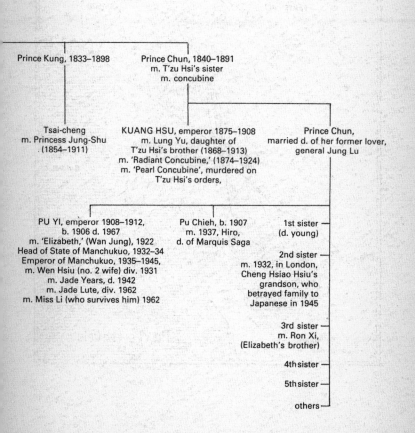

Prince Kung, 1833–1898

Prince Chun, 1840–1891
m. T'zu Hsi's sister
m. concubine

Tsai-cheng
m. Princess Jung-Shu
(1854–1911)

KUANG HSU, emperor 1875–1908
m. Lung Yu, daughter of
T'zu Hsi's brother (1868–1913)
m. 'Radiant Concubine,' (1874–1924)
m. 'Pearl Concubine', murdered on
T'zu Hsi's orders,

Prince Chun,
married d. of her former lover,
general Jung Lu

PU YI, emperor 1908–1912,
b. 1906 d. 1967
m. 'Elizabeth,' (Wan Jung), 1922
Head of State of Manchukuo, 1932–34
Emperor of Manchukuo, 1935–1945,
m. Wen Hsiu (no. 2 wife) div. 1931
m. Jade Years, d. 1942
m. Jade Lute, div. 1962
m. Miss Li (who survives him) 1962

Pu Chieh, b. 1907
m. 1937, Hiro,
d. of Marquis Saga

1st sister —
(d. young)

2nd sister —
m. 1932, in London,
Cheng Hsiao Hsiu's
grandson, who
betrayed family to
Japanese in 1945

3rd sister —
m. Ron Xi,
(Elizabeth's brother)

4th sister —

5th sister —

others —

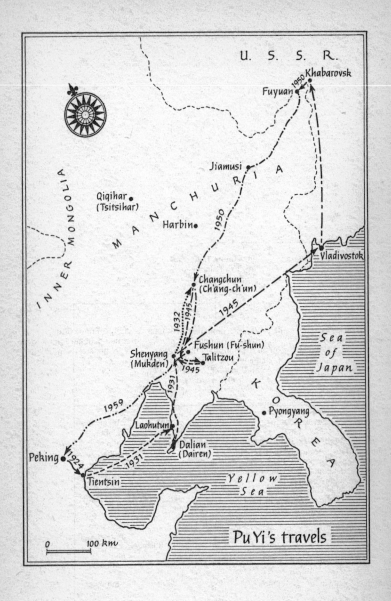

U. S. S. R.

1950 Khabarovsk

Fuyuan

Jiamusi

Qiqihar
(Tsitsihar)

MANCHURIA

Harbin

1950

Vladivostok

Changchun
(Ch'ang-ch'un)

1932

1945

1945

INNER MONGOLIA

Shenyang
(Mukden)

Fushun (Fu-shun)

Talitzou

1931

1945

Sea
of
Japan

1959

Pyongyang

Laohutun

K O R E A

Peking

1924

Dalian
(Dairen)

1931

Tientsin

Yellow
Sea

0   100 km

Pu Yi's travels

Chinese

ALUTE (1854–1875): Wife of Emperor Tung Chih. Dowager Empress Tzu-hsi (the 'Old Buddha') was strongly suspected of having caused her death.

AN TEH-HAI: Head eunuch at the court of Tzu-hsi, the 'Old Buddha'. Despite her friendship and protection, he was executed after exceeding his powers and assuming the lifestyle of a viceroy.

CHANG-HSUN, General: Known as the 'pig-tailed general', and a strong monarchist, he attempted to restore Pu Yi to the throne in 1917 in a short-lived, unsuccessful coup.

CHANG CHING-HUI: Shady businessman and even shadier politician, he became a leading pro-Japanese collaborator and Pu Yi's second Prime Minister. He died in captivity, a despised, senile figure, in the same prison where Pu Yi was undergoing 'remoulding' after being handed back to the Chinese authorities in 1950.

CHANG TSO-LIN (1875–1928): Manchuria's best-known Manchu warlord, a bitter enemy of Chiang Kai-chek. Murdered by the Japanese because they considered him an unreliable ally.

CHENG HSIAO-HSU: Confucian scholar, and one of Pu Yi's senior tutors, who became his political adviser and, later, his Prime Minister at the start of the 'Manchukuo' experiment. Resigned in 1935, and died a year later. Pu Yi – at the Asian war crimes trial in Tokyo – accused the Japanese of having killed him.

CHIANG KAI-CHEK (1887–1975): Leading nationalist leader of the Kuomingtang (KMT), both republican and anti-communist. After a brief flirtation with the Japanese he fought them following their invasion of China, and, after 1945, waged a series of losing battles against the Chinese communists, fleeing to Taiwan in 1949 where he set up a separate anti-communist Republic of China.

CHIEN-LUNG, Emperor (1711–96): One of the most prestigious emperors of the Ching dynasty.

CONFUCIUS (Kung-tzu) (551–479 BC): Philosopher and thinker whose writings and edicts influenced all successive imperial dynasties.

CHUN, first Prince (1840–91): One of the sons of Emperor Tao-kuang, and brother-in-law of Dowager Empress Tzu-hsi, whose sister he wedded. Their son became the prisoner-Emperor Kuang-hsu.

CHUN, second Prince (1840–91): A son of Prince Chun (the mother was a concubine). He married the daughter of Jung-lu, a famous Manchu general and former lover of Tzu-hsi, and the eldest son of that issue was Pu Yi, the last Emperor of China.

FENG YU-HSIANG, Emperor (1880–1948): The 'Christian general' who occupied Peking militarily in 1924 and compelled Pu Yi to leave the Forbidden City. Pro-communist at first, he ended up an ally of Chiang Kai-chek.

HUNG HSIU-CHUAN (1813-64): Unsuccessful candidate for the mandarinate exam, he became a convert to Protestantism, a visionary and the feared leader of the Taiping rebellion which almost brought the Ching dynasty to its knees before a series of defeats in 1864–5.

JADE LUTE (Li Yu-chin): Pu Yi's third concubine whom he left behind in Talitzou in 1945. She divorced him in 1958, while he was still in prison.

JADE YEARS (Tan Yu-ling): Pu Yi's second concubine, died in Manchukuo, at the age of twenty-two. At the Asian war crimes trial in Tokyo Pu Yi accused the Japanese of having engineered her death.

JUNG-LU (1836–1903): Manchu general and lover of Tzu-hsi.

JUNG-SHU, Princess (1854–1911): Adopted daughter of Tzu-hsi (originally one of her nieces). She was a daughter of Prince Kung, and after Tzu-hsi's death she became a leading dowager inside the Forbidden City. Pu Yi called her 'mother'.

KANG YU-WEI (1858–1927): Scholar and reformer, exiled by Tzu-hsi after persuading the prisoner-Emperor Kuang-hsu to adopt a sweeping reform plan which the 'Old Buddha' objected to.

KOO, Wellington: Born 1898. Lives in the USA. His name is an Americanized version of Ku Wei-chun. Became Chiang Kai-chek's chief foreign affairs adviser, cabinet minister and KMT lobbyist in the USA.

KUANG-HSU, Emperor (1871–1908): Dowager Empress Tzu-hsi made him Emperor at the age of five. In 1900 she scuppered his reform plan and put him under guard, a 'prisoner-Emperor' for the rest of his life.

KUNG, Prince (1833–98): Brother of Emperor Hsien feng, held the fort in Peking when his craven brother fled, later rallied to Tzu-hsi.

LI, 'BIG': Born in 1910. Pu Yi's personal servant from the age of fourteen.

LI TIEH-YU: Pu Yi's driver during the Manchukuo years. He became the lover of Empress Wan Jung (Elizabeth) and the father of her child, killed by the Japanese at birth. Died in Peking in 1985.

LI WENDA: Born 1922. Editor and Pu Yi's ghostwriter for *From Emperor to Citizen*.

LUSTROUS CONCUBINE (1874–1924): One of prison-Emperor Kuang-hsu's concubines. Later was one of the dowagers inside the Forbidden City in Pu Yi's time and one of Pu Yi's royal 'mothers'.

NIUHURU, Empress (1837–81): Wife of Emperor Hsien-feng. After his death, she became co-dowager with Tzu-hsi but was rapidly shunted aside. Tzu-hsi was widely believed to have caused her early death.

PEARL CONCUBINE (1876–1900): Prisoner-Emperor Kuang-hsu's favourite concubine and sister of Lustrous Concubine. Dowager Empress Tzu-hsi had her put to death in 1900, and later spread the rumour that she had committed 'patriotic suicide' rather than leave Peking during the Boxer Rebellion.

PU CHIEH: Born 1908. Lives in Peking. Pu Yi's younger brother.

PU YI (1906–67): The last Emperor.

SOONG, Mei-ling: Born 1897. Lives in USA. Chiang Kai-chek's second wife after his divorce. Became, as Madame Chiang Kai-chek, one of the most powerful women in Asia.

SOONG, T. V. (1894–1981): Mei-ling's younger brother, became Chiang Kai-chek's financial adviser, then Finance Minister.

SUN YAT-SEN: Chinese nationalist, died 1915.

Madame SUN YAT-SEN (1882–1981): One of the Soong sisters. After her husband's death she became a communist sympathizer and, under Mao, Vice-President of the People's Republic of China.

TEH-HING: Sister of Tzu-hsi, the 'Old Buddha'.

TZU-HSI, Dowager Empress (1835–1908): Presided over the decline of the Ching Dynasty. Her extravagant, cruel, corrupt and xenophobic misrule brought China to the verge of bankruptcy and anarchy. Two days before her death, she appointed the infant Pu Yi as her successor.

TUNG-CHIH, Emperor (1856–75): Son of Tzu-hsi, had a short reign and died young.

WAN JUNG, Empress (1915–46): Also known as 'Radiant Countenance' and as 'Elizabeth'. Pu Yi's first wife who followed him to Manchukuo where she became a recluse and drug addict.

WEN HSIU (1917–51): Pu Yi's first concubine, who divorced him in 1927.

YUAN SHI-KAI: Manchu general, briefly President, died 1916. He betrayed prisoner-Emperor Kuang-hsu and was known as the 'traitor general'.

European and American

BLAKENEY, Major Ben: U.S. Army Legal Department, defended Japanese accused at the Asian war crimes trial, Tokyo, 1946-7.

BORODIN, Michael: Soviet revolutionary and Komintern agent, US-born, adviser to Chinese Communist Party till 1927.

BURNETT-NUGENT, F. H.: Commander British garrison in Tientsin International Concession, 1928–31.

FLEMING, Peter: author and journalist, roving correspondent in China and Manchukuo in 1930s.

JOHNSTON, Sir Reginald: British colonial official, tutor to Pu Yi 1919–22, Governor of Weihawei (British enclave in China) and subsequently Professor of Chinese Literature at London University. Died 1938.

JORDAN, Sir John: Head of British diplomatic mission in Peking, 1910–12.

KASPE, Joseph: Owner of Hotel Moderne in Harbin. His son, a concert pianist of French nationality, was kidnapped, tortured and killed by a Japanese-protected gang in 1933.

KEENAN, Joseph: US Chief Prosecutor, Asian war crimes trial, Tokyo, 1946–7.

LYTTON, Lord: Headed the League of Nations enquiry into Manchukuo in 1932.

MORRISON, George (1862–1920): famous *Times* correspondent in China.

SNOW, Edgar: US journalist, China specialist and friend of Mao Tse-tung.

VESPA, Amleto: Born 1888. Italian-born double agent, forced to work for the Japanese after the creation of Manchukuo in 1931.

WEBB, Sir William: Australian judge and President of the International Military Tribunal at the Asian war crimes trial, Tokyo, 1946–7.

WOODHEAD, Henry: British journalist in Tientsin and Shanghai.

Japanese

AMAKASU, Masahiko: Member of Japanese secret police, posted to Manchuria where he became the head of the Manchukuo film industry and a close 'adviser' to Pu Yi. Committed suicide in August 1945.

ASAKA, Prince: Emperor Hirohito's uncle, played a crucial role in the 'rape of Nanking' in 1937.

CHICHIBU, Prince: Emperor Hirohito's younger brother, with special responsibility for Japanese-Manchukuo relations.

DAN, Baron: Banker, League of Nations counsellor, murdered in Tokyo in 1932.

DAISAKU, Colonel Komoto: One of the top intelligence chiefs in Manchuria, sentenced to death for war crimes by the International Military Tribunal in Tokyo, executed 1948.

EASTERN JEWEL (Yoshiko KAWASHIMA)(1906–49): Manchurian princess, and distant relative of Pu Yi. Japan's top spy in China from 1930 onwards. Executed by Chiang Kai-chek in 1949.

GIGA, Major: Military adviser to Chinese warlord Chang Tse-lin who was murdered by the Japanese secret service in 1928. Giga was killed by persons unknown in retaliation in Japan in 1938.

HIGASHIKUNI, Prince: Member of Japanese royal family, sent on a private mission to Peking in 1929 by Emperor Hirohito.

HIROHITO, Emperor: Born 1901. Became Emperor of Japan in 1926, since 1946 has been a constitutional monarch.

ISHIWARA, Kanji: Exceptionally talented Japanese staff officer, planned and masterminded the takeover of Manchuria by the Japanese in 1931. Promoted major-general, but never achieved top command because of his opposition to the Emperor's policies in pursuing war with the US.

ITAGAKI, Colenel Seishiro: Military intelligence officer in Manchuria and, later, Manchukuo.

MATSUI, General Iwane: Commander of the forces

advancing on Nanking in 1937; sentenced to death at the Asian war crimes trial in Tokyo for his role in the 'rape of Nanking' – though he did everything he could to prevent it.

NAKAJIMA, General Kesago: Responsible for the 'rape of Nanking'; he was never prosecuted.

SAGA, Hiro: Distant relative of the Japanese royal family, married Pu Chieh, Pu Yi's younger brother. Lives in Peking.

SHIMAMURA, Saburo: Japanese Gendarmerie general, arrested for war crimes, re-educated in prison with Pu Yi, wrote a book confessing his crimes.

TAKEMOTO, Colonel: Commanded the Japanese forces in Peking guarding the Japanese mission there in 1924. Played a crucial role in helping Pu Yi to take refuge inside the Japanese mission there.

TANAKA, Gi-ichi: Japanese Premier, died in 1929.

TANAKA, Takayoshi: Japanese agent in Shanghai, recruited Eastern Jewel and became both her 'case officer' and her lover; later became confidential adviser to US Prosecutor Keenan.

WATARI, Colonel Hisao: Member of the Japanese General Staff and one of the architects of 'Manchukuo'.

YAMASHITA, General Tomoyuki: One of the most brilliant Japanese field commanders in the Second World War, commander-in-chief of Japanese forces in Manchukuo, executed in 1948 for war crimes.

YOSHIOKA, General Yasunori: Special adviser to Pu Yi, 1931–45. Committed suicide shortly after his arrest by the Soviets in August 1945.

YOSHIZAWA, K: Head of the Japanese diplomatic mission in Peking, 1924.

FOREWORD

So far, he has been a mere footnote to history: Pu Yi, the last Emperor of China, inspired more mockery than hatred. Gangling, short-sighted, timorous and hopelessly absent-minded, he was a far cry from his tough Manchu ancestors who toppled the Ming dynasty in 1644 at the head of their Manchu and Mongol cavalrymen. It was no coincidence that Pu Yi's favourite film star was the silent comedy actor-director Harold Lloyd, also myopic and hopelessly clumsy. Time and again, the last Emperor of China acknowledged not only that he was no match for his forebears, but also that he was aware of the contempt and derision he provoked in others.

For all that, he was a formidable survivor. China, from the year of Pu Yi's birth (1906) onwards, was rarely at peace until 1949, when the Chinese Communist Party finally overcame the last pockets of Kuomingtang resistance, and Chiang Kai-chek fled to Taiwan. During these troubled years, Pu Yi survived the loss of his throne, expulsion from the Forbidden City, exile and various plots on his life, weathering his demeaning relationship with the

Japanese and, after nine years of 'remoulding' in Chinese prisons, ending up a respected citizen of communist China, seemingly more at peace with himself than ever before.

Such a record implies considerable toughness, determination and cunning. Pu Yi may have been the ultimate anti-hero, capable of appalling betrayals to save his own skin, but as my own perception of him deepened during my research into his character and life and times I realized that there was more to him than met the eye: the effete dandy who wallowed in self-abasement during his spell in prison adjusted extraordinarily quickly to his prisoner status. He also gained the grudging respect of men like Chou En-lai who were no mean judges of character. And in his convoluted way, when in the right mood, he could be humane and even generous to his enemies.

The frankness with which he admitted his failings was, of course, partly a feature of China's unique penitentiary system, with its emphasis on 'autocritique' and repentance. In Pu Yi's case, however, his lengthy confession of sins was a form of catharsis: he really did have a lot of past sins to account for, though intolerance was not one of them.

While I learned a lot about Pu Yi that surprised me in the course of interviewing surviving friends, relatives, former servants and prison officials, there was a part of him that was always elusive: post-Mao China, while slightly more tolerant than of old, remains, by Western standards, an extraordinarily puritanical country. Even today, there is still considerable unwillingness to talk about one's own or other people's emotional lives. Those who had known him best were extremely reluctant to talk about his sex life to strangers like myself.

The degree of diffidence is best illustrated by the behaviour of one of Pu Yi's last surviving eunuchs of the imperial court. After a brash French journalist had dared ask him what it felt like to be a eunuch, and whether after his operation he had still been able to experience sexual desire, the eunuch put an abrupt end to the interview and indicated he would meet no further members of the press.

I had similar questions that were never answered: Pu Yi had two wives and three official concubines during his lifetime, yet I was never able to ascertain, from those I talked to in Beijing, what his emotional relationships with them had really been. In the case of Elizabeth, his first wife, his physical encounters seem to have been a series of 'fiascos', and while his 'rapport' with his first concubine was, at least at first, less disastrous, she quickly left him; his later concubines were teenagers, and at one stage his attraction towards very young girls bordered on paedophilia.

From what I learned, there is no doubt in my mind that Pu Yi was bisexual, and – by his own admission – something of a sadist in his relationships with women. It could well be that his first wife's alienation, and his first concubine's departure, stemmed from his unacceptable behaviour.

All this, however, is only inferred in the diaries of Pu Yi's followers and in his own, highly selective autobiography. Time and again, as I pressed otherwise co-operative and even loquacious intimates of Pu Yi's life and times to tell me more, I inwardly raged at their protective discretion – while also, to some extent, sympathizing with it. Some of them may have been Pu Yi's occasional – and unwilling – sex partners in their own youth, and Chinese reserve is such that I knew I could not expect them to say so.

Purists may find my interpretation of Pu Yi's behaviour during his adult years too inferential, insufficiently backed by corroborative evidence, but I have tried to tell his story with as much regard for truth and accuracy as possible. There is no doubt in my mind that Pu Yi's awareness of his huge mistake in throwing in his lot with the Japanese from 1931 onwards resulted in a prolonged, and increasingly serious, nervous breakdown. One of the forms it took was in occasional sadistic sexual assaults on helpless, cringing adolescents of both sexes who, for several years, were his virtual prisoners inside the Salt Tax Palace in Changchun, the puppet capital of Manchukuo.

Yet this puppet-Emperor who moved as jerkily and clumsily as a real-life puppet was capable not only of acts of kindness, but also of real dignity, and even moral courage, as his attitude towards his first wife's lover attests. Throughout, he was conscious of the absurdity of his condition. At times, he displayed an onlooker's detachment, contemplating his own antics without any trace of complacency.

His predicament, of course, was that at an age when small boys are heavily dependent on a protective family environment and play at being astronauts or soldiers, he was catapulted onto the throne, treated as a living god, and deprived of any real affection. Only as a prisoner in a Chinese gaol did he start behaving like an ordinary human being. Until then, his relationships with all those around him – with the possible exception of his tutor, Reginald Johnston – had been on a completely artificial plane. But even Johnston idealized his royal pupil, and this quintessentially Scottish scholar was far too conventional, and too impressed by Pu Yi's royal status, to offer him any advice about his private, emotional life. As in other royal families, the fiction was maintained that the Emperor and his Empress were on perfectly harmonious terms – and Johnston helped maintain it, against all the evidence.

For all these reasons, no portrait of Pu Yi can be completely three-dimensional. Since none of the few aged, surviving members of Pu Yi's entourage are likely to unburden themselves completely, some shadows – especially surrounding his private life – will never be lifted.

There was a way out of such a problem, and that was to 'fictionalize' Pu Yi's story, by describing imaginary but likely events as though they were real – and the author an invisible fly on the wall. This technique has always irritated me in others – even when beautifully done, it is still a cop-out – and the temptation proved eminently resistible.

The events Pu Yi witnessed, and took part in, need no artifice, and the extraordinary ups and downs in his tragi-comic saga require no embellishments. Here is someone who began life as a medieval god-king, subjected to a daily royal routine that had changed little for the previous 2000 years. He lived through several wars and revolutions, both social and industrial, witnessed his country's transformation into a modern, totalitarian state, and eventually its entry into the small select club of major nuclear powers.

Towards the end of his life, Pu Yi must have looked back on his own past with baffled incredulity. It is as though the same person had spanned, in a short lifetime, the changes that took place between Louis XIV's France and de Gaulle's, or Tudor England's and Mrs Thatcher's, and lived to tell the tale.

It is hard to believe that we belong to the same century, or that he died, at sixty-two, only a decade ago.

ACKNOWLEDGEMENTS

During the 1984 Cannes Film Festival, I had a chance encounter with Jeremy Thomas, the British film producer. He told me that he had finally got Chinese permission to film *The Last Emperor* in China. I wished him luck. I knew he would need it.

Two Cannes Film Festivals later, we met at the very same table at the Carlton Bar. After a dozen journeys to China, some of them with director Bernardo Bertolucci and scriptwriter Mark Peploe, and endless negotiations there, Jeremy was about to start shooting *The Last Emperor* inside the Forbidden City – by far the most ambitious feature film project ever made by a foreign production company in China.

He asked me whether I would be interested in writing a book connected with the film. I said that rather than write a 'book of the film' I wanted to try my hand at a serious biography of Pu Yi and his life and times. This is the outcome of that talk.

My thanks are due, first and foremost, to Jeremy Thomas himself, for it was he who enabled me to meet the surviving *dramatis personae* in Pu Yi's life; without his daily help, in Beijing in 1986, I would never have been able to talk to them as I did, and probably would not have found them on my own.

I wish to thank Bernardo Bertolucci and Mark Peploe, too, for their counsels and suggestions. While all views expressed in the book are mine, their advice was precious: in the course of writing the script, they had been over much of the ground I was to cover, and made my research easier.

The entire Anglo-Italian team that made *The Last Emperor* in China under difficult conditions gave me their unstinted co-operation, as did the staff of Beijing's Number One Co-production Unit, and I thank them here.

The survivors of that fascinating, troubled period in Chinese history also deserve my special thanks. Pu Chieh, Pu Yi's younger brother, in his eighties but still in good health, with an excellent memory, saw me several times. So did Li Wenda, the distinguished editor who helped Pu Yi write *From Emperor to Citizen*, and probably knew him better than anyone alive. Jui Lon, Pu Yi's favourite nephew, Pu Ren, his half-brother, and Rong Qi, his brother-in-law, all gave me hours of their time. A special word of thanks for Rong Qi, who talked to me from his hospital bed where he was recovering from a heart attack.

Special thanks, too, to Jin Yuan, the retired Governor of Fushun prison, who devoted ten years of his life to Pu Yi's 'remoulding', and to Big Li, Pu Yi's lifelong servant and major-domo, who out of loyalty followed Pu Yi to prison, and answered all my questions patiently and sincerely.

It would have been impossible to get the flavour, as well as the substance, of their reminiscences without the help of a first-class interpreter. I was fortunate in Rachel Wang, a distinguished alumna of Wellesley College, and a bilingual American who entered into the spirit of my quest to such an extent that she was asking questions I should have thought of and had not; her enthusiasm, her tact and her knowledge of China and Beijing made my China research a joy.

The period spanning Pu Yi's life is a rich one as far as memoirs and histories are concerned. A primary source was, of course, Pu Yi's own *From Emperor to Citizen*, and, for the earlier chapters, Reginald Johnston's *Twilight in the Forbidden City* and Marina Warner's *The Dragon Empress*. For Chapters 12 to 16 I am hugely indebted to David Bergamini's monumental work *Japan's Imperialist Conspiracy*, an extraordinarily rich and detailed history of twentieth-century Japan. Our paths never crossed when we were both on the staff of *Life* magazine. I wish I had been able to meet him before his untimely death.

I wish also to thank the library staffs of the School of Oriental and African Studies and the Imperial War Museum in London for their unfailing kindness and co-operation, and *Newsweek*'s Ted Slate for unearthing rare, long-forgotten books and magazine articles. Thanks also to Ambassador Jacques Baeyens, Robert Elegant, Peter O'Toole and Jean Pasqualini and many other China experts for their help and advice.

Newsweek's editors were good enough to grant me a 'sabbatical' to work on *The Last Emperor*, and I thank them for their understanding and patience.

This book would never have been written without Ed Victor's initiative, encouragement and support. I suspect he planned the whole thing, down to my initial Cannes encounter with Jeremy Thomas. He was present at all stages of the preparation of the book – in Cannes, London and Paris, on the phone countless times to Beijing, read the initial draft, and, as always, made precious suggestions.

As soon as I began researching the project I understood why Ed Victor is such a great agent: he knows, sometimes better than his own friends and clients, where their interests lie.

Edward Behr
Paris, London, Beijing,
Ramatuelle, 1986–7

Because most of the people referred to in *The Last Emperor* were dead before the new 'Pin Yin' Chinese-to-English spelling system was adopted, I have used the old 'Wade' system throughout, both for names and places.

China's currency went through critical devaluation after devaluation during Pu Yi's lifetime, and experts are still divided on its worth in relation to Western currencies, then and now. A rule of thumb is that the Chinese dollar, in 1924, was worth roughly one-sixth of the US dollar. In later years it depreciated considerably, and the 'Manchu-kuo' dollar, in the closing stages of the war, became virtually worthless. Wherever possible, I have tried to relate currency values to their present equivalents.

CHAPTER ONE

The old man in a private ward inside Peking's Capital Hospital knew he was dying but at first had the good grace to pretend all was well and that he would soon be returning to his tiny, two-room apartment. Three years previously, in 1964, doctors had performed exploratory surgery, removed a kidney and told him he had cancer, which would probably spread. Since then he had been back in hospital twice, always a privileged, pampered patient.

Chinese hospitals are grim, efficient, overcrowded places. Doctors and nurses, underpaid and overworked, have no time for social niceties. Their handling of the sick is briskly impersonal. But in this case there was a difference. Premier Chou En-lai himself had phoned the Chief Hospital Administrator, and said: 'Look after him well.' It was the only call of its kind the staff could remember, and they were suitably awed. The cancer patient had the best of everything.

He had been easy to deal with, always thanking the staff for their small kindnesses, apologizing for causing them trouble – a model patient, except that he was always losing his glasses. He was, one nurse recalled, 'almost too humble, thanking everyone all the time'. At first his wife, herself a nurse at another hospital, had come to see him, but her visits became less frequent, and eventually ceased altogether.

The Cultural Revolution had started a year earlier, and she had a good excuse for not coming: the streets were no longer safe for most adults. In 1967, when the cancer patient was admitted to hospital for the third time, the movement was just fourteen months old – a disaster of almost unfathomable proportions, willed by Mao himself, which was to lead to some two million deaths, the deportation of some twenty million intellectuals, and bring China to an economic, political and intellectual standstill for ten years.

It was a time of chaos and blind cruelty. Gangs of Red Guard teenagers, hundreds of thousands of them pouring into Peking from outlying districts, roamed the streets, and their gang rule was law. It was a common sight to see adults with crude billboards delineating their 'crimes' pinned to them, front and rear, or wearing dunce caps, being spat at, insulted and beaten. Convoys of 'dunces' were paraded in requisitioned trucks on Peking's streets, taunted by cruel children drunk with their own power.

In 1967, the Cultural Revolution was only just getting into its stride. Understandably, adults lay low: a career in the party, a responsible job, singled one out for persecution at the hands of these angry, fanatical, unpredictable teenagers.

The man dying of cancer of the bladder in a private room of the Capital Hospital was only dimly aware of all this. All he knew was that because of some fresh turmoil, his family found it difficult to venture out to see him. He could hear the strange, unusual sounds outside – endless martial music of 'authorized' revolutionary tunes praising Mao, the 'Great Helmsman', relayed by loudspeakers day and night.

The dying man regarded himself as a loyal follower of

Chairman Mao, but there was a special place in his heart for Chou En-lai, not just because of his hospital kindness, but because of what had gone before. Now Chou, miraculously surviving the Cultural Revolution, was doing his best to limit the Red Guard madness, but with only partial success.

The sick man was utterly bewildered: he had boundless faith in Mao, in the Party and 'the masses', but could not understand why Party and masses were at each other's throats. It was his faith in the 'new society' that had enabled him to assume his illness with stoic composure. But as the days went by, and the Red Guards became noisier and more violent, his morale suffered. The pain increased steadily too. He wished his wife would come to see him one last time.

The visitors who burst into his room were absurdly young, vociferous and quite unimpressed by Chou En-lai. The corridor outside the sick man's room became first a raucous meeting place then a battleground, as Red Guards from the street, who had forced their way in, clashed with Red Guards stationed in the hospital itself. The former wanted to take the sick man away, punish him – perhaps even kill him. The hospital Red Guards – workers who had hastily slipped on red armbands to give themselves some kind of authority now that the Party apparatus was in shambles – protested they would be removing a dying man. With commendable courage, they defended their patient, first with words, then with their fists.

The invaders finally withdrew, threatening to return. They did score a minor victory. The old man, they said, had claimed in a recent book that he had become an ordinary citizen, so he should be treated like one. No more private rooms, special food or treatment. They would only leave, their leaders said, if he was put in a public ward, and treated like an ordinary patient.

The hospital Red Guards reluctantly complied. They carried him, as gently as they could, to a large, crowded ward on another floor. The old man was only dimly aware of what the commotion was all about. But once in the common ward he realized Chou En-lai's writ no longer ran everywhere: nurses ignored him, and pain-killing injections stopped. The pain got worse. He soiled his bed and no one came to clean up the mess.

Then, miraculously, another call from a furious Chou En-lai restored him to his old room. A relative who ran the Red Guard gauntlet to come and see him later recalled that the old man's body was now grotesquely swollen, and that his skin had a greenish hue. Pain-killing drugs resumed, but more haphazardly, as though the nurses were afraid that if they were too nice to him, they would fall foul of the Red Guards outside. And when a woman did come to see him, it was not his wife at all, but a ghost from the past – a former concubine he had not set eyes on for years.

This woman was still young, in her thirties, attractive, and very, very angry. She too wore a Red Guard armband, though certainly not entitled to one. It was simply a convenient disguise to move about more freely. She was accompanied by her sister-in-law, also masquerading as a Red Guard although she was in her forties at least. Both had made the trip to Peking by train all the way from Changchun, in Manchuria, and if they were shocked by the patient's appearance they did not show it. They shouted and nagged at the sick man, as though convinced he was shamming.

'You ruined my life,' the younger woman said. 'Everyone in Manchuria says that I'm an enemy of the people, simply because I was your concubine. You must write a confession saying I had nothing to do with what happened there during those years. Then maybe the Changchun Red Guards will leave me alone.'

The man mumbled he was too sick to write.

Li Yu-chin (Jade Lute) was not satisfied. 'That's not the only thing,' she shouted. 'You wrote a book. You mentioned me in it by name, you dragged me down with you. You owe me for that. How much money did you make, anyway?'

The man on the bed said it was not much, 'and anyway I gave most of it back to the state'. The two women did not believe him. 'You made money on the book. I'm entitled to my share,' the former concubine said.

They would have gone on harassing him, but another relative showed up. He was furious, and saw through them at once. 'You're not real Red Guards,' he told them. 'Those armbands are just a disguise to travel down here and harass a dying man. You want him punished so that people in Changchun will think you're real revolutionaries. I'll tell the Red Guards who you really are if you don't go away at once.'

The two women left after extorting 200 yuan (about £45) from the dying man. They said they would be back, but their bluff had been called, and they knew it. That was the last he saw of them.

His condition quickly deteriorated after that. A schoolboy great-nephew, himself sick with an injured spine and in the same hospital, came and held his hand, but the end was a lingering one. He was given no painkillers of any kind, nurses were scared to come near him, afraid of the Red Guards' reactions. All they wanted was for him to die, quickly. In the very final stages, the old man regained a modicum of peace, and the pain abated. But his last wife, whom he had married in 1962, never made it to the hospital in time.

'Look after him well,' Chou En-lai had said, but Chou's orders no longer carried any weight. After the old man died, things went from bad to worse. His body was cremated on the hospital premises, like that of a destitute with no family. The ashes were saved, but there was no ceremony of any kind. One of the dead man's relatives did brave the rampaging Red Guards, and carried the ashes for safekeeping to Chou En-lai's house.

Even in communist China, funeral rites are important. As his relatives put it, his soul would not rest until they had been performed. But the Cultural Revolution went on and on, followed by the 'terror' of the Gang of Four, and it was only in 1979 – three years after Chou En-lai's own death from cancer — that the dead man's family retrieved the ashes and held a formal burial ceremony. The remains were taken to the Eight Treasure Mountain cemetery thirty kilometres from Peking. This is a place where both prominent revolutionaries and ordinary people are buried, and the very fact that it was selected was proof that the dead man, though buried in the public section, had been not without honour in his country, at least in the last few years of his life.

His name was Pu Yi, and he had been, briefly, the last Emperor of China. Once he had been worshipped as a living god. Later he had been reviled as a traitor, given up for dead, and finally rehabilitated after fourteen years in detention, nine of them in a Chinese prison.

I met him once: making a TV documentary in China in 1964. I went to a reception given by the Chinese government after the inauguration of France's first Industrial Trade Fair in Peking. Only months before, de Gaulle had established diplomatic relations with Mao. In the crowded room, a gaunt, stooped figure, wearing thick pebble glasses, held up a glass, and smiled in my direction, a tired, wan smile. 'Kanpei,' he said. 'Cheers.' He was being observed by other guests with friendly curiosity. 'Who's that?' I asked Pierre Chayet, a French diplomat and personal friend since the Algerian War days. 'That's Pu Yi,' he said, 'the last Emperor of China. Just the person you need for your film.'

I searched the hall in a frenzy, but could not find him. I ran outside, but he had left. I tried to locate him, and failed. The officials whose help I enlisted either could not or would not get in touch with him.

Now, over twenty years later, it is as though we are meeting for the first time. Kanpei!

CHAPTER TWO

In 1793, Pu Yi's glorious ancestor, Emperor Chien-lung, the greatest of the Manchu (or Ching) dynasty warrior-kings, administered his famous rebuff to Lord Macartney, who had been sent by the British Government to establish relations with this 'Son of Heaven'. Chien-lung's high-handed dismissal, which put paid to any plans Britain might have had to develop a 'special relationship' with China, equated the British emissary with despised minor warlords who regularly kowtowed before him inside the Forbidden City.

'There are well-established regulations,' said Emperor Chien-lung, 'governing tributary envoys from the other States to Peking . . . As a matter of fact, the virtue and prestige of the Celestial Dynasty have spread far and wide, the kings of the myriad nations come by land and sea with all sorts of precious things. Consequently there is nothing we lack.'

Chinese emperors of the Ming (1368–1644) and Ching (1644–1911) dynasties believed that China's system of government was the best in the world because it was based on Confucian principles and owed nothing to the outside world.

The 'Analects' or teachings of Confucius (551–479 BC) were not so much a philosophy as a series of moral laws determining the relations between rulers and ruled, many of them admirable – and admirably suited to the hierarchically-minded emperors and their courtiers.

Confucius himself was a humanitarian aristocrat, a pacifist who loathed not only the warrior but the commercial classes, a scholar who firmly believed that social differences were divinely ordained, but that rulers had a moral duty to behave responsibly and generously towards their inferiors. The hymn, 'The rich man in his castle, the poor man at his gate', would have had his wholehearted approval. Some of his precepts have a distinct 'Moral Rearmament', 'Oxford Group' flavour.

It was Confucius's respect for knowledge and the intellect that was responsible for the Chinese meritocracy system that put scholars (mandarins) in charge of provinces, and restricted the top echelons of the administration to a tiny elitist minority which had proved its brainpower in gruelling examinations. The system bore some resemblance to the narrow governing 'Oxbridge' elite in Britain and even more to the French *Grandes Ecoles* 'mandarinate' that restricts the entire top stratum of government and university bureaucracies to a tiny group that has successfully weathered the gruelling entry exams into *Polytechnique*, the *Ecole Normale Supérieure* or the *Ecole Nationale d'Administration*.

What made the Chinese system unique was the fact that its intellectual elite was at the service of an imperial dynasty which clung to a medieval view of the world – a view very few of the highly intelligent, highly educated mandarins in key positions dared question. The insularity of China's rulers went hand in hand with a taste for secrecy (to this day Peking is a city of walled compounds, not just inside the Forbidden City) and a passion for intrigue.

It is difficult to say, in the almost constant series of conflicts that marked relations between China and the outside world just before Pu Yi's birth, which side behaved worst: racist, absurdly conservative imperial China, arrogantly convinced that it had nothing to learn from the 'red-haired barbarians', or the Western powers – and Japan – whose cynical, predatory immorality in that heyday of nineteenth-century imperialism still shocks. Britain fought China in the Opium War of 1839–42 to ensure the free export of India-cultivated opium to China after a Manchu dynasty emperor had banned its import. Japan behaved disgracefully throughout. Western attitudes towards China are best reflected in Lord Palmerston's extraordinarily racist outburst. He wrote in 1855:

> The Time is fast coming when we shall be obliged to strike another blow for China. These half-civilized governments such as those in China, Portugal and Spanish America all require a Dressing every eight to ten years to keep them in order.
> Their minds are too shallow to receive an Impression that will last longer than some such Period, and warning is of little use. They care little for words and they must not only see the stick but actually feel it on their shoulders before they yield.

China felt the stick a year later, when Palmerston mounted an expedition after an incident involving the British merchant vessel *Arrow* in Canton harbour. Lord Elgin, son of the British aristocrat with a passion for Greek statuary, embarked on a 'mission to Peking' to demand retribution – and request the presence of a permanent British ambassador accredited to the Manchu Court. The Elgin Mission, delayed by the outbreak of the 1857 Indian Mutiny, eventually led to a second war, involving French gunboats and marines as well as a fully-fledged British and Indian army expeditionary force, the sacking of the Summer Palace and the establishment of foreign concessions on a scale that the late Emperor Chien-lung had always resisted.

It was ironic – and evidence of Chinese imperial insularity at its most absurd – that the main reason why China fought so fiercely to prevent Lord Elgin from entering Peking was that the imperial court simply could not believe that foreign powers would mount such an expedition just to exchange ambassadors and further trade. The Manchu warriors had come down from their Tartar fastnesses in the north-east to conquer and remove the Ming dynasty. The Manchu court – in 1860 – firmly believed that Lord Elgin, like its own Manchu forebears, had the same goal, that the 'big-nosed hairy ones' intended to sit on the throne themselves. Only gradually did the imperial advisers realize that the British and French 'barbarians' merely sought trade – and a permanent diplomatic presence in Peking. Had they understood this earlier, thousands of lives, and the inestimable treasures of the Summer Palace, might have been saved.

As it was, the Elgin expedition marked the start of China's 'colonization' and territorial encroachment – a process that was to continue throughout the nineteenth century and right up to the end of the Second World War. No sooner had Lord Elgin obtained an embassy in Peking than Russia seized Haishenwei harbour, more commonly known today as Vladivostok. The Japanese, some years later, would annex Formosa, the French Annam, Britain Burma. All along the Chinese coast, Japan, France, Germany, Russia and Britain established foreign 'concessions' with the hated privilege of extraterritoriality. Whereas Emperor Chien-lung had confined foreigners to tiny enclaves in Canton, denying them even the right to enter Canton's walled city, by the time of Pu Yi's birth (in 1906) every foreigner living in one of the many concessions China enjoyed the equivalent of diplomatic privileges of freedom from arrest or trial in Chinese courts, and the British, French, German and Japanese enclaves on Chinese soil had become microcosms of their respective countries. Of all the major powers only the USA failed to enter the 'concession' race – refusing to copy the Europeans' colonial pattern because of their own experience as a colony. As time went on, however, Americans flocked to the foreign concession enclaves, and in their wake – following the European example of sending elite troops to protect their national minorities – came the United States Marines.

Because the nineteenth-century Manchu emperors regarded China as their own private possession, this only made the 'foreign devils' more eager to lay hands on parts of it. 'It was the instinctive, unwavering aim of Manchu statecraft to keep the people in purdah,' wrote Paul H. Clements, author of *The Boxer Rebellion*. 'The Manchurian conquerors of one of the most favoured regions of the globe were not slow in realizing that, being relatively few in numbers, it was to their interests, as overlords of an intelligent and law-abiding though passive race constituting one-fourth of the world family, to interdict all efforts at change, to seal the country so that a repetition of their own exploit, or disaffection with their own rule resulting from outside influences, would be impossible.'

No one typified this spirit more than Dowager Empress Tzu-hsi (her name, 'Motherly and Auspicious', was but one of many, including 'Perfect', 'Reverent', 'Illustrious', that she acquired with age), the wicked 'Old Buddha' born in 1835 who dominated China from 1860 to her death in 1908 and placed Pu Yi on the throne two days before she died.

Tzu-hsi was one of the most ruthless, cunning and unprincipled rulers of her time. She is an integral part of our story because, without her, China would have become a different country, and Pu Yi almost certainly would never have become Emperor. She was the incarnation of almost everything that was wrong with China's leadership in the nineteenth century. At the same time, her force of character, her manipulative skills, and – especially – her ability to get out of tight corners compel admiration. In her political manoeuvrings and juggling powerbroker skills she resembled the late Indira Gandhi. There was something Gaullian about her stubborn nationalism. And her dark side makes both Messalina and the Borgias look positively bourgeois.

Tzu-hsi started life with a distinct advantage: she was a

Manchu – that is to say, she was a member, by birth, of the ruling tribe, only five million strong, which dominated China from 1644 onwards. Marina Warner, whose excellent book *The Dragon Empress* remains the best and most authoritative biography about her, says: 'Tzu-hsi's family was not rich; in China that probably meant her father was honest.' He was a junior mandarin of the Civil Appointments Board. Later he became Intendant, or Commissioner, of Anhwei, a green and pleasant part of China on the mighty Yang-tse River. The family had aristocratic antecedents: her Yehe Nara clan included a 'royal', a young girl who had married Nurhaci, founder of the Ching (Manchu) dynasty, some 250 years before Tzu-hsi's own birth. Since then, her family had gone down in the world. At the time of her birth in 1835 Lan Kueu (Little Orchid), as she was known before acquiring her 'imperial' title, was just another well-born Manchu girl in a middle-ranking civil servant family.

There are no early photographs of Tzu-hsi. In her later years, the sepia photos, though carefully posed, give her a positively simian look. She was tiny, and in her youth must have had considerable *fausse laide* charm. 'A lot of people were jealous of me, because I was considered to be a beautiful woman at the time,' her sister Teh-hing quotes her as saying. What distinguished her from most other Manchu girls of her age was her precocious intelligence and – even in her teens – her overweening ambition.

Manchu women started life with one built-in advantage over well-born 'Han' (Chinese) girls: their feet were not bound. They were not subjected to this protracted form of torture that made Chinese courtesans hobble on three-inch stumps – the 'lotus feet' that were supposed to galvanize Chinese men into sexual frenzy, and prevent Chinese women from leading normal lives.

Because she was so small, her feet were tiny without any form of artifice: in later life, when she met foreign women, she could not help staring in horror at their huge, ungainly shoes. Perhaps it was her appearance – tiny feet included – that caused the royal 'talent scouts' to select her when, after a suitable period of mourning for his father, the young Emperor Hsien-feng (1831–61), whose name meant 'Universal Plenty', began looking for wives and concubines.

She was ordered, along with her sister, to appear before the court inside the Forbidden City in 1851. Tzu-hsi was one of sixty selected Manchu girls of good family so summoned, in a ceremony that owed something to ancient Chinese ritual, something to a banal beauty contest, and a great deal to astrology. She was sixteen at the time, and after a careful screening by the Emperor's mother (Hsien-feng himself had no say in the matter) she was appointed 'Honourable Person', a concubine of the fifth rank. Her sister failed the test. The astrological data, satisfactory in Tzu-hsi's case, were inauspicious. They were, however, compatible with another bachelor 'royal'. Tzu-hsi's sister married one of the Emperor's younger brothers, Prince Chun.

The Forbidden City was a town within a town, a community of tens of thousands set down in a maze of palaces, temples, courtyards and gardens. To this day, to pass through the Wumen, or Midday, Gate, set in its high ochre walls (in former times solely for the Emperor's own use – his subjects used side entrances), is to enter a world unlike any other: the buildings – mostly made of wood, and painted in bright colours – have an informality which is a constant source of visual delight. Even in today's noisy, traffic-congested Peking, the outside world seems to exist not at all.

The Forbidden City was not simply the palace of the Emperor. It was the source of all government, with offices, temples, bank vaults, theatres, armouries, schools, kennels and even prisons and 'punishment rooms' for recalcitrant courtiers and disobedient concubines.

The imperial palace, surrounded by a ten-metre wall and a fifty-metre moat, stands at the entrance to the Forbidden City. It was supposed to have 9,999 rooms, though an official count by museum officials in 1958 showed there were only 8,886. The palace is not the single structure typical of Western-style building, but rather a series of interlocking towers, courtyards and pavilions. At its centre is a tower with a double roof covered by glazed yellow tiles – made exclusively for the Emperor. One of the pavilions inside the imperial palace is the Tower of the Five Phoenixes. The phoenix, in Chinese mythology, symbolizes good fortune, and the roof of the Phoenix Pavilion is covered with their effigies.

The palace is connected by a white marble bridge, the Gold Water Bridge, to the rest of the Forbidden City, and only the Emperor could walk down its central portion. It leads to the Gate of Supreme Harmony, opening onto a huge paved courtyard, almost as large as a football stadium, with enough room for 90,000 standing people. Here the imperial guards and officials gathered to pay their respects to the Emperor on formal occasions.

Within the walled grounds of the Forbidden City there are nineteen other palaces. Some, like the Six Western Palaces and the Six Eastern Palaces are more like stately homes. In Pu Yi's time, they were the private living quarters of empresses, concubines and eunuchs. During the Ming dynasty more than a thousand eunuchs lived there. When Pu Yi became Emperor, their number was down to about two hundred.

Each one of the other palaces served a special function. The Hall of Supreme Harmony, with its seventy-two vermilion supporting columns, housed the imperial throne: it was rarely used except for coronations, and the most formal court ceremonies. The Emperor relaxed in the smaller Hall of Complete Harmony where he held informal meetings with his courtiers, listened to music or rested. It contained a smaller throne.

Banquets were held in the Hall of Preserving Harmony, as were state exams for aspiring mandarins. Connected by marble staircases and terraces is the Gate of Heavenly Purity, with four gilded bronze lions mounting symbolic guard over the Emperor's privacy – his private living quarters, the Palace of Heavenly Purity. Next door is the Palace of Union where the Empresses were crowned and where the ladies of the court cultivated silkworms. Adjoining this is the Palace of Earthly Tranquillity with its special 'red room' where imperial wedding nights were spent. Red is an auspicious colour in China, and the room is decorated with golden-embroidered phoenixes. The only piece of furniture in this room was a huge four-poster bed. Dowager Empress Tzu-hsi, as she became, preferred the small, exquisite Hall of Mental Cultivation, probabaly because it was closest to the imperial garden, with its stone landscapes, pines, cypresses, ponds and flowerbeds. She was inordinately fond of gardening, and spent whole days there.

Today, the whole of the Forbidden City is a vast museum, complete with jewels, ceremonial clothing, amber seals and cooking utensils. It is still possible to wander along its narrow lanes and imagine that one is back in imperial times. Unlike Versailles, which is best seen from the air if one is to be aware of its extraordinary symmetry, it is impossible to get an overall view of the Forbidden City, though it is possible to see the imperial palace from Coal Hill, a small rise at the rear of the Forbidden City, once used for storing coal. Inside the city walls, the eye is constantly dazzled by Chinese flying buttresses, gilded carvings, statuary of all kinds, and the exquisitely shaped yellow, green and red roofs. It is a place full of surprises: narrow doors lead to spacious quadrangles, marble steps to small, delicate temples. Without a detailed map, it is easy to get lost in this delicate maze.

In Ming dynasty times, as many as 100,000 eunuchs served the Emperor. Some – a tiny minority – became as influential as ministers, but most were practically slaves, to be beaten and even executed at will. Despite the penalties involved, it was well known that the eunuchs robbed the Emperor blind: this was their understandable revenge for their despised, abject condition. During Tzu-hsi's time the eunuchs were notoriously corrupt. They were only following Tzu-hsi's own example: one of her characteristics was a lifelong passion for riches. Even at the height of her power and fame, she squirrelled away vast quantities of jewellery, money, antiques and bullion, making little distinction between the revenues of the state and her own. The famous 'marble boat' which is one of the more unusual, and tasteless, treasures of the Summer Palace (rebuilt to her specifications after its destruction in 1860) was constructed with funds diverted from allocations meant to rebuild the Chinese navy.

A concubine of the fifth rank – which was what Tzu-hsi became in 1854 – was not necessarily an intimate of the Emperor, and Tzu-hsi quickly realized that she needed the complicity of eunuchs to gain admittance to the royal bedchamber. The new Emperor, Hsien-feng, was in any case a singularly *fin de race* individual: weak, dissolute, cowardly, he had, since puberty, been an assiduous client of Peking's brothels – male and female.

The legitimate sexual pleasures of the court he found boringly conventional. Twelfth-century erotic Taoist textbooks – bedside reading for Chinese aristocrats – left nothing to the imagination, though everything was couched in suitably flowery language: fellatio was 'the jade girl playing the flute'; sodomy 'playing with the flower in the back garden'. How the diminutive vivacious but not outstandingly handsome (by classical Chinese standards, at least) Tzu-hsi wormed her way into the young Emperor's bed is not known. Palace gossip, later, had it that she bribed the chief eunuch to suggest her name to the Emperor. In any event, her name showed up on the jade tablet – a kind of stud book – containing the names of the Emperor's night-time companions.

According to time-honoured ritual, which had more to do with security than eroticism (Manchu, and Ming emperors before them, had morbid fears of assassination), one night the eunuch came, stripped her naked, wrapped her in the scarlet rug and carried her across his shoulders to the royal bed. For breeding purposes, the date of her intercourse was registered and signed with the imperial seal. The Emperor may have been charmed not only by her sexuality but by her wit and pleasing singing voice. Her name cropped up with increasing frequency on the jade tablet, and in April 1856, at twenty, she gave birth to a son.

The Emperor already had a daughter by another concubine, but girls were of little account: Tung-chih was to be the Emperor's only male child. As a result, overnight, Tzu-hsi's status changed. She became a concubine of the second rank. Already, as courtiers and eunuchs knew, she had a will of steel, and had set her sights on the highest goal attainable for women, the status of Dowager Empress. Without the calamities experienced in China just as she was gaining the Emperor's sexual favours, she would not have stood a chance.

The year Tzu-hsi became one of many imperial concubines coincided with some of the most calamitous events in China's history: an inspired convert to Protestantism who had failed his mandarin exams, Hung Hsiu-chuan, proclaimed himself a rival 'Heavenly King' and declared holy war on the Manchu 'usurpers'.

From his Kwangsi Province, his followers gathered strength, moving south and west. They overran Anhwei, Tzu-hsi's home base, took control of Nanking, the capital of South China, and soon threatened Peking itself. The rebel Heavenly King's peasant army was a well-disciplined, fanatical force. The Taiping Rebellion, as this episode was called, was a curious mixture of puritanism, crudely adapted Protestantism and primitive communism. Over-taxed farmers, longtime supporters of the overthrown Ming dynasty, southerners who regarded the Manchus as alien Tartar invaders, all rallied to this Heavenly King's cause.

By any standards the young Emperor, Hsien-feng, behaved disgracefully. When the Taiping forces reached the outskirts of Tientsin, the coastal city only 100 kilometres south of Peking, he panicked. Only his entourage prevented him from ignominiously leaving the Forbidden City for a palace in Jehol (Chengde), in the north, on the pretext of an 'annual tour of inspection'.

Luckily for him, the rebel Heavenly King rapidly began showing signs of dementia, and at the time that Tzu-hsi's visits to the royal bedchamber were increasing, the Emperor's armies started winning victories over the Taiping rebels. By the time she gave birth to a son, some of the danger to the throne was past, but the cost had been heavy: China was a devastated land, and the tide was not to turn decisively against the Taipings until 1860. This was the year the Franco-British expedition, led by Lord Elgin, marched on Peking. With British and French troops at the gates of the Forbidden City, the Emperor panicked again, and this time he did flee to Jehol, moving most of his court into the royal hunting lodges there. Tzu-hsi and her newborn son came too. The Emperor's more courageous brother, Prince Kung, remained behind to deal with the Anglo-French 'barbarians'.

The news of the foreign armies' occupation of his capital, and their sack of the Summer Palace, plunged the Emperor into depression, from which he emerged only to drown his sorrows in drink, drugs and debauchery. Tzu-hsi was excluded: by now she openly despised the 29-year-old rake, preferring the company of eunuchs for their wit, and officers of the palace guard for their virility.

The rumour-mongering, gossipy court was quick to report her infidelities, and she was relegated to the status of a lowly palace hanger-on. Had the Emperor been fully in control of the situation, she might well have been put to death. But he had other, more pressing, problems than the infidelity of one of his concubines. His exile dragged on – and on. It was now 1861, the Anglo-French forces were still garrisoned in and around Peking, and food was so scarce and inflation so rife in the capital that the customary Chinese reverence for royalty was replaced by contempt and hatred: shopkeepers flung handfuls of bills, made worthless by inflation, at palace officials. There was open scorn for the craven, debauched Emperor, too scared to face the barbarian invaders.

He was dying anyway – of dropsy, drink and depression. And just before his death Tzu-hsi displayed some of the mettle that was to make her the most powerful woman in China.

'The Emperor being practically unconscious of what was taking place around him,' she told her sister Teh-hing, 'I took my son to his bedside and asked him what he was going to do about his successor to the throne. He made no reply to this, but, as had always been the case in emergencies, I was equal to the occasion, and I said to him: "Here is your son"; on hearing which he immediately opened his eyes and said: "Of course he will succeed to the throne." I naturally felt relieved when this was settled for once and all. These words were practically the last he spoke.'

Legend, and posthumous hatred of Tzu-hsi, naturally provide another version of the succession. It is now believed that she bribed a eunuch to steal the imperial seal proclaiming her son Emperor, and that she burnt an imperial decree telling the eight Regents named to oversee the new Emperor's reign to 'put Tzu-hsi to death if she gives any trouble'.

By this time Tzu-hsi was a brilliant manipulator, and in the uneasy court atmosphere in Jehol, with the Emperor's body lying in a coffin waiting for the astrologically favourable moment to begin the journey back to Peking, she quickly gained the upper hand. The late Emperor's good-natured but childless 'number one' wife, the Empress Niuhuru, was charmed by Tzu-hsi's deferential, helpful manner. Almost illiterate, completely baffled by her new responsibilities, Niuhuru readily acceded to Tzu-hsi's suggestion that both women should become co-reigning Empress Dowagers, with powers exceeding those of the eight Regents.

By the time the dead Emperor's coffin reached Peking, Tzu-hsi was within an ace of the supreme power she had coveted from the start.

She quickly showed her Machiavellian side. No sooner had the funeral procession reached Peking than she struck out, using Prince Kung and another imperial brother, Prince Chun (who had married her sister) as allies: the Regents were dismissed for having bungled negotiations with the invading 'barbarians'; history was rewritten, for Tzu-hsi now claimed that the late Emperor, the father of

45

her child, had been 'forced, greatly against his will, to seek refuge in Jehol'. Three more princes, including one who was thought to have plotted her death, were arrested for subversion. Two were 'permitted to commit suicide', and the third was beheaded like a common criminal. They were the first of many, many deaths at the hands of the 'Old Buddha', and soon her superior intellect turned her co-Dowager Empress into a willing cipher. Tzu-hsi started making all major decisions on behalf of her infant son, negotiating with the barbarians: their armies helped defeat the remaining bands of Taiping rebels before leaving China. The foreigners were mostly gone by 1863, but a few hundred British and French troops stayed on to protect the newly opened legations in Peking's new 'Legation Quarter'.

Tzu-hsi soon showed that loyalty was the least of her qualities: in 1885, she accused Prince Kung of attempting to molest her during an audience, and while she later 'forgave' him, she downgraded him to the post of 'adviser', promoting the more malleable Prince Chun – Pu Yi's grandfather – instead.

She was gradually embarking on a course that was to lead China to both economic and moral bankruptcy: when she needed funds for her extravagances, she sold the right to the offices of magistrate or prefect. Her Forbidden City expenditure rose astronomically. Her costly palace pleasures were in the hands of her favourite eunuch, An Teh-hai, later executed for behaving like a king himself.

Tzu-hsi knew that once her son came of age, she would no longer, as the formula went, 'lower the screen and attend to state business'. Women, even dowager empresses, were not officially allowed to conduct state business from the throne room except behind a yellow screen.

Luckily for her, her son, Tung-chih, proved to be almost as feckless as his father. Tzu-hsi treated him with the utmost indulgence. Inevitably, in time, critics would accuse her of deliberately fostering his innate tendency towards drink and debauchery. Certainly, she made no

46

effort to put a stop to his expeditions to brothels in Peking. He enjoyed the company of transvestites, was almost certainly bisexual, and may have contracted syphilis. Married at sixteen to a beautiful Manchu aristocrat (daughter of one of the officials compelled to commit suicide – the match was supposed to heal a clan rift), he failed to mend his ways. Meanwhile, aware that if her son had a male child she herself would in time lose her considerable power and prestige (for if anything happened to her son, her daughter-in-law, Alute, would in turn become Regent) Tzu-hsi did everything in her power to humiliate the girl.

Again, events conspired to Tzu-hsi's advantage. The young Emperor died of smallpox in 1875, aged nineteen, Alute committed suicide shortly afterwards (encouraged to do so, critics alleged, by the Dowager Empress herself) and Tzu-hsi once more became the uncontested ruler of China. She herself claimed that, after her son's death, 'all happiness was over'.

Tzu-hsi lost no time: the day her son died, she held an emergency meeting to determine the succession, and to no one's surprise the court endorsed her choice: her brother-in-law Prince Chun's three-year-old son, promptly named Kuang-hsu, 'of glorious succession'.

It was an arbitrary, illegal and highly criticized choice, even if, by now, her courtiers were reluctant to do anything to provoke her terrible temper. The Emperor was not only the temporal but the spiritual ruler of China. An important part of his duties involved ancestor-worship and sacrifices at the graves of his forebears. Only a male heir of the next, younger, generation could perform such ceremonies. As a cousin of the late Emperor, Kuang-hsu was unable to perform such rites with any validity. Tzu-hsi promptly adopted him to put things right, but her callous indifference to tradition when it suited her caused at least one distinguished mandarin to commit suicide, and when Prince Chun heard the news of his son's succession, he wept.

Many years later, Pu Yi, recalling visits to his grandfather's home, saw 'many scrolls in my grandfather's own handwriting hanging in the rooms of his sons and grand-sons. There was a pair which read: "Wealth and Fortune breed more Fortune, Royal Favours bring more Favours." '

Prince Chun may have been a right royal toady, as the scrolls suggest, but he knew enough about Tzu-hsi by now to fear her. With a child again on the throne, Tzu-hsi was all set for another spell 'behind the yellow screen'. This time, it was to end in murder and revolution – and one of the blackest periods in Chinese history.

CHAPTER THREE

For all the slide into corruption, anarchy and – eventually – revolution, the first years of Dowager Empress Tzu-hsi's stewardship, the 1880s and 1890s, were at first perceived by China's growing foreign community as years of progress and harmony.

Her co-Dowager, Niuhuru, though officially of equal rank, took no part in the running of state business, and after her untimely death in 1818, aged forty-four, Tzu-hsi reigned supreme in name as well as in practice. Inevitably, but probably with good reason, palace gossip maintained that Tzu-hsi had had Niuhuru poisoned.

Tzu-hsi never changed her attitude towards the hated 'barbarians'. But the old Chinese adage 'Use the barbarians to control the barbarians', came into its own. For the first time, foreigners other than Jesuits (who had practically assumed Chinese nationality along with its customs) came to China in large numbers – as boatbuilders, mercenaries, administrators on contract, translators. Certain sections of the bureaucracy – Customs and Excise in particular – became foreign (predominantly British) preserves. Tzu-hsi rightly assumed that well-paid foreigners would be more honest than mandarins. She even began entrusting certain Chinese diplomatic missions to foreigners.

But just as it appeared that unprecedentedly harmonious relations might lead to a new era of trust, the huge influx of foreign missionaries of all kinds led to new tension – and confirmed Tzu-hsi in her view that all foreigners were, at heart, 'devils'.

Some of these new missionaries behaved, in their way, just as brutally as Palmerston: they requisitioned Buddhist temples – and turned them into Christian churches. Some of the new 'rice Christians' were often transparent rogues, hiding behind their new religion to evade Chinese justice, and this irritated Chinese officials. Anti-Christian pamphlets began to proliferate, along with Chinese equivalents of the 'Protocols of the Elders of Zion', accusing Christians of everything from cannibalism to drinking menstrual blood. And when some forty babies in a Sisters of St Vincent of Paul convent in Tientsin died of smallpox in 1870, after a sick child had been brought into the convent and baptized, the local community rose up against the missionaries, convinced they had indulged in human sacrifices. Hot-headed French diplomats behaved with their customary blustering arrogance – and were torn to pieces by an angry mob. The Sisters had been guilty of nothing more serious than religious zeal combined with statistical pride. In their enthusiasm to swell the numbers of babies baptized, they habitually took in the dying – and even, without knowing it, accepted kidnapped children provided by a corrupt doorman. Gunboat diplomacy became the order of the day once more as French warships moved close to the shore near Tientsin and opened fire at random and without warning, killing several innocent Chinese.

Tzu-hsi knew China could not hope to win a military victory against any Western power, so she ordered her Viceroy in Tientsin to punish those who had massacred the nuns and the French diplomats. Eight ringleaders were executed, twenty-five more sentenced to long prison terms, and the families of the French dead received financial compensation. It was by no means sure that France regarded this as sufficient, and there were rumours that Napoleon III intended mounting a punitive expedition there, using the pretext of the French deaths to gain more concessions. Luckily for China, the Franco-Prussian War of 1870 soon diverted French priorities elsewhere, and his plans were dropped.

Finally, unable to prolong her Dowager mandate beyond young Emperor Kuang-hsu's eighteenth birthday, Tzu-hsi resigned her duties gracefully enough. By this time, she had such a network of spies inside the Forbidden City that nothing could occur there without her being instantly informed. She resorted to petty tricks – like walling up the Emperor's access to both the Empress's and the imperial concubines' quarters, so that Kuang-hsu had to pass her own quarters (the floorboards creaked) whenever he visited them. The new Empress was in any case a natural Tzu-hsi ally – one of her own nieces.

With age, Tzu-hsi's greed and building splurges increased. From bribes, presents, and graft of all kinds she had accumulated a huge personal fortune, and talked to London banks about stashing away some eight and a half million pounds sterling (in gold and bullion) 'in a safe stronghold'. The various palaces, gardens, temples and lakes, built at the nation's expense at Tzu-hsi's express command, are a delight to today's tourists, but they were hugely extravagant, for China was bankrupt and incapable of defending herself against her predatory neighbours: in 1887 the French occupied the Chinese protectorate of what is now Indochina. Japan, already set on her expansionist course, in 1894 annexed Korea, then a strategically important Chinese protectorate, after clobbering China's forces on land and sea. What upset Tzu-hsi as much as the military loss was the fact that she was compelled, because of China's defeat, to cancel her elaborate sixtieth birthday celebrations.

Japan's victory was the signal for another mad scramble among the major powers for more Chinese territory: Germany moved into Kiachow, in Shantung Province, after the murder of two German missionaries there in 1897; Britain (in Hong Kong, Canton and Weihawei) and Russia (in Manchuria and Mongolia) had already carved out huge 'zones of influence'.

One country that failed to get its pound of Chinese flesh was Italy. In 1899, an Italian diplomat, De Martino, was dispatched from Rome to demand that China surrender San-men Bay in Chekiang. Italy had no sizeable navy, and no real means of resorting to gunboat diplomacy should the demand fail. For once, China stood firm, abruptly refused to give up any territory and called Italy's bluff. De Martino left China that same year a much humiliated man. Part of his trouble, noted George Morrison, the famous London *Times* correspondent in Peking, was that the Chinese failed to understand De Martino's incompetent translator and could not find any place on the map that corresponded to the Italian demand. Also, Chinese mandarins scornfully told him, De Martino had proved his illiteracy by referring, in a note demanding a permanent Italian concession, to the 'European concert of nations' using a Chinese ideogram 'commonly used for theatrical performances'.

But just a few months before De Martino's ill-fated 1899 mission, Tzu-hsi was back in power once more – and had locked up the young Emperor, Kuang-hsu, on an improvised island prison in the Summer Palace grounds. Kuang-hsu's disgrace was to have enormous repercussions in China, setting the seal on the end of the Manchu dynasty, and ensuring that whoever succeded Tzu-hsi would not be Emperor for long.

As the young Emperor gradually took stock of China's disastrous state, he became increasingly appalled. He promptly fell under the spell of a small group of 'reformers', of whom the most prominent was a scholar called Kang Yu-wei, who, while remaining a loyal monarchist, had set his heart on bringing about sweeping change.

Emperor Kuang-hsu started reading Kang's memos – and acting on them. And in 1886, for a heady 'hundred days', sweeping reform edicts, carrying the Emperor's seal, flooded ministries, provinces and army headquarters all over China. One decree established Peking University; another made the more progressive city of Nanking the capital of all China; foreign travel was to be encouraged, technical schools set up throughout China, and village temples turned into schools. Chinese traditional dress was to be scrapped in favour of Western clothing, the army Westernized, and journalists encouraged to write about politics; old-fashioned mandarin scholarship tests which determined access to key posts were abolished, and many office-bearers declared redundant.

In the avalanche of measures there were many that were admirable, overdue even. But at times the Emperor's indiscriminate enthusiasm for change – and utter contempt for the consequences of his actions – smacked of Evelyn Waugh's Oxford-educated African hero Seth in *Black Mischief*, with Kang Yu-wei as his Basil Seal. Not only was there no effort to prepare the country, the hostile court or the huge vested interests in favour of the status quo for change, but their implementation was left vague – the responsibility of local officials who nearly all ignored their contents. Tzu-hsi, like a shrewd angler, played the Emperor like a fish on the end of a long line. At the end of the 'hundred days', she struck.

The Emperor, conscious of his utter isolation inside the Forbidden City, thought he had the support of the one apparently reform-minded general in China, Yuan Shi-kai. Yuan had distinguished himself in Korea and commanded the best troops in the land. Emperor Kuang-hsu summoned him to Peking. At the same time he sent his reform advisers a pathetic note. 'In view of the present difficult situation, I have found that only reforms can save China, and that reforms can only be achieved through the discharge of the conservative and ignorant ministers and the appointment of the intelligent and brave scholars. Her Graceful Majesty, the Empress Dowager, however, did not agree. I have tried again and again to persuade her, only to find Her Majesty more angry. You . . . should

53

deliberate immediately to find some ways to save me. With extreme worries and earnest hopes.'

At first Yuan Shi-kai played along. He seems, at one stage, to have become a genuine reformer himself. But among the Emperor's advisers were radicals, openly advocating Tzu-hsi's removal ('The old rotten . . . must be got rid of, or our country will perish'). Personal loyalty to the Manchu dynasty was a sacred duty among Manchu 'bannermen' – as the tribal followers of China's ruling family were called. Yuan Shi-kai, a leading bannerman and one of the most influential at court, went straight to one of Tzu-hsi's henchmen to warn her of what was afoot.

The old Empress, now sixty-four, stormed into the Emperor's quarters. 'Do you know the law of the Imperial Household for one who raises his hand against his mother?' she screamed, and struck him.

Palace guards loyal to her took the Emperor away to a small island on the south side of Sea Palaces. 'There was nothing I could say,' Kuang-hsu told an aunt later. He was to remain Tzu-hsi's prisoner until his death, ten years later. The ill-prepared coup collapsed, Yuan Shi-kai's soldiers moved into Peking, six leading reformers (but not Kang Yu-wei, who escaped) were beheaded, all reform decrees annulled, and Tzu-hsi was formally restored to power for a final, disastrous stretch.

As Reginald Johnston, later Pu Yi's tutor and a close friend of Kang Yu-wei, was to write in *Twilight in the Forbidden City*, the Emperor 'would have been saved ten years of misery and degradation had he shared the fate of the six martyrs'. As it was, he was compelled to affix his own seal on decrees annulling every one of his reforms, as well as on the death sentences of his friends. The public announcement from the palace simply said: 'The Emperor being ill, the Empress Dowager has resumed the regency.'

Perhaps it was Italy's humiliation – once De Martino had decamped from Peking without China's surrendering any new territorial concession – that led the 'Old Buddha', once more in total command, to believe the time had come to take a stronger line against the 'foreign devils'. Perhaps, with age, her political sense was no longer as acute. Now the Emperor was her prisoner, Tzu-hsi looked forward to 'lowering the yellow curtain' for the rest of her life.

She seems to have had no sense of foreboding, no sense of being on the brink of yet another violent upheaval that would deliver the Manchu dynasty its near-fatal blow, and when it broke she seemed blind to its consequences. She saw in it only the possibility of driving out the hated, arrogant 'foreign devils' for good, putting the clock back and heralding a new Chinese Golden Age of splendid isolation.

The Boxer Rebellion, like the Taiping Rebellion half a century earlier, stemmed from a provincial, grassroots movement. Unlike the Taipings, however, the Boxers were firm supporters of the monarchy. Their leaders genuinely believed that Empress Tzu-hsi could only be saved from the hated 'foreign devils' with their help. They were also singularly innocent in other ways: amulets and charms, they believed, were adequate protection against foreign bullets.

While the Boxer Rebellion was gathering strength, with Tzu-hsi's tacit approval, she took out an additional insurance policy: she announced, by imperial decree, that henceforth her heir apparent would be Pu-chun, a raffish teenager and son of her kinsman, Prince Tuan, who had married one of her own nieces. Tuan had long been a palace favourite, a swashbuckling ape of a man who reminded her of those dashing officers she had favoured as an obscure, disgraced concubine in Jehol. What is more, he was a good soldier, loyal, without a trace of dangerous intellect, and he shared her views of foreigners, while his reputation for corruption and greed made him her docile pawn: he was unlikely to turn against her or press for 'reforms'.

But Tzu-hsi was not the only one to believe, as she told her court at this time, that 'the foreigners are the only curse of China today'. The 'Righteous Harmony Boxing' movement, anti-Christian, anti-foreign, fanatically devoted to the Manchu dynasty, might have remained just another arcane secret society with its pagan rites and rituals, like hundreds of others that had flourished throughout China for centuries, had it not been for the debts, humiliations and misery that had spread throughout China after the Sino-Japanese War. Like the Taiping rebels, the Boxers swept all before them, murdering foreigners indiscriminately, preaching holy war, claiming supernatural powers. They grew into a formidable force.

It was Tzu-hsi's last disservice to China that she believed she could use the Boxers to her own advantage, to rid her of the foreigners and swell the ranks of her armed supporters. The Boxers did not even have to be paid – no mean advantage at a time when China was deep in debt for 'reparations' to Germany, France and Japan.

The Boxer Rebellion has spawned dozens of books and at least one involuntarily hilarious film, *Fifty-Five Days in Peking*, with Ava Gardner. How the Boxers marched on Peking, gained Tzu-hsi's support, laid siege to the Legation Quarter, and were finally scattered by a multinational force of relieving American, British, French and Japanese troops – with the Kaiser's Imperial Guard arriving too late for the fighting but not for the looting, has become one of the mythic events of this century, attracting, at the time, an enormous amount of media coverage, spawning quantities of eye-witness accounts, and stimulating a new and unprecedented interest in twentieth-century China.

Empress Tzu-hsi's meandering, mendacious course – arming and encouraging the young Boxers, while at the same time indulging in a handwringing exercise to convince the West she was a victim of, and not a party to, the siege of Peking by the ragtag Boxer rebel armies, scarcely fooled her siege victims. The 'sorcerer's apprentice' Boxers earned her fawning thanks while they appeared to be winning. She clearly hoped, at one stage, that they would kill the besieged foreigners to the last woman and child, to avoid any eye-witness reports of her two-faced villainy.

As soon as it was apparent that the foreign, British-led rescue column mounted to relieve the besieged foreigners in Peking was bound to win, she changed her tune. It had all been a mistake, she whined. The Boxers had been rebels, not patriots. She had done her best to protect the foreigners, had herself been near death several times.

Her assertions were belied by her behaviour once it was clear the Boxer rebels had lost their final battle. She decided to leave Peking, fearing reprisals by the 'foreign devils'. Before fleeing the Forbidden City the 'Old Buddha' struck out blindly, in an almost insane burst of temper. She had some aides, who had been brave enough to denounce her pro-Boxer policy, beheaded. And when Pearl Concubine, the prisoner-Emperor's favourite, begged her not to disgrace her Manchu ancestors by flight, Tzu-hsi ordered her eunuch bodyguards to throw her into the north-east courtyard well. The prisoner-Emperor was forced to watch the murder of his beloved concubine. Later her death was officially recorded as 'patriotic suicide'.

With her six-inch fingernails cut short (shaking hands with Tzu-hsi, one diplomat had remarked, had been like 'holding a clutch of pencils'), and looking, in her disguise, very much a squat, dumpy peasant woman, Tzu-hsi's sorry column wended its way south-west to Shansi Province, while the European soldiers who had lifted the Peking siege looted the Forbidden City, scrawled obscenities on the walls of the royal bedchamber inside the Hall of Mental Cultivation, and the Western powers devised new ways of making China pay.

Tzu-hsi's exile lasted two years, first in Hsian, then in Kaifeng. During this time her ministers, left behind in Peking, did their best to placate the occupying Western commanders. In return for huge financial reparations, the invaders decided to let bygones be bygones, finally allowing Tzu-hsi to resume the throne.

It was an extraordinary comeback. The major powers, after toying with China's occupation or an enforced change of dynastic rule, decided in the interests of stability to allow the Ching dynasty to continue. In exchange for large sums of money (payments were theoretically due until 1940), more concessions and some scapegoat executions, all was forgiven – and the resilient Dowager Empress returned to Peking in state. The foreign powers cynically accepted the fiction of a 'rebellion' against the throne, which had occurred against her will. Some of her ministers obligingly agreed to hang themselves. Other, lesser leaders were either beheaded or executed by the occupying forces. Prince Tuan, who had encouraged her to throw in her lot with the Boxers, was disgraced but allowed to go into exile. The decree making his son the heir was annulled. That part of the family was disbarred from the throne for all time, and a further decree deprived them of all their noble titles.

Never at a loss, Tzu-hsi now turned to another of her soldier favourites for assistance. General Jung-lu had been one of those dashing officers at Jehol who had befriended Tzu-hsi in the old days, and it was common knowledge they had been lovers in her youth. One of his daughters had married into the imperial clan. Jung-lu had played an equivocal role during the siege of Peking, appearing to side with the Boxers but in fact doing everything in his power to prevent them from winning a decisive victory. Renegade Yuan Shi-kai, the 'traitor' who had betrayed his Emperor's reform plans to Tzu-hsi, had been another opponent of the Empress's pro-Boxer policy: he too now gained favour.

Tzu-hsi made her return to Peking first in a ceremonial train provided by the Belgians (who had built the line), in a coach hung with royal yellow silk, then in a hand-carried ceremonial chair bedecked with peacock feathers. Prisoner-Emperor Kuang-hsu knelt in front of her at the South Gate of the Forbidden City, slavishly welcoming her back. The foreign community, some of whose members she had done her best to starve, kill and set fire to over fifty-five days, stood and watched, and when she gave them a shy, little-girl smile, bowing towards them in a demure gesture of obeisance, her palms together, they broke into a round of applause. She had turned her blackest day into a personal triumph.

It was a brief but remarkable comeback. She received the diplomats, with the silent, cowed Emperor at her side. She gave a tea party for foreign ladies, with lavish presents. She even sobbed as she held their hands and told them how ghastly things had been during the troubles. 'The Boxers for a time overpowered the Government,' she said, 'and even brought their guns in and placed them on the walls of the palace. Such a thing will never occur again.' She presented her guests with some of her Pekingese puppies, and the awed recipients only later noted that they had been doctored so that none of them would ever breed.

Tzu-hsi even began implementing some of the reforms that had led to the Emperor's disgrace, reorganizing the legal system, streamlining the bureaucracy, abolishing torture, suppressing the opium traffic, encouraging her staff to travel abroad, even – in 1906 – announcing her belief in a constitutional monarchy.

She seemed, amazed diplomats said, to have turned over a new leaf. But despite the crippling sums the foreign powers continued to demand in the form of reparation she never once volunteered to contribute part of her personal fortune, now estimated at over £23 million in gold, towards the cost of paying for her failed policies. China was now a passive onlooker even when, in 1904-5, Japan and Russia went to war on Chinese soil over Manchuria, and Russia was badly beaten. Japan obtained huge territorial and railroad concessions in Manchuria. The 'Old Buddha' accepted this fresh humiliation with apparent equanimity, spending more time than ever on amateur theatricals, carefully planning the ceremonial of her birthdays, delighting in the extravagant gifts her officials showered on her (paid for, as usual, by bone-poor overtaxed peasants).

As she felt more secure, so her treatment of the prisoner-Emperor took a turn for the worse. Briefly, in the first few months after her return, she had relaxed her hold on him; she even, on occasion, went through the motions of asking his advice. But soon she discovered the 'foreign devils' would not, as she had feared, compel her to give him back his freedom, and she resumed her old ways. Kuang-hsu, prematurely aged, sick, his will broken, was now the butt of cruel jokes played on him by insolent eunuchs. Electric light was installed in the Forbidden City in 1903, but not in Kuang-hsu's quarters. When she did allow him to return to his former apartment inside the Forbidden City, she made sure the windows were walled up, so he had no view, and remained conscious at all times of being her prisoner.

The 'Old Buddha' had always been a prodigious eater, and in 1907 she fell seriously ill with dysentery. Kuang-hsu, tubercular, depressed, suffering from Bright's disease, was also bedridden. Intimations of mortality compelled Tzu-hsi to look around, a third time, for a suitable heir. Her choice reflected her current loyalties – and her determination, even in death, to ensure that no successor would ever assume her charisma.

There were several candidates for the succession – and for the regency. One was a young prince, Pu Lun. General Yuan Shi-kai believed that he stood a good chance of acting as his Regent, and even hinted that this was the succession team the 'Old Buddha' had picked. And there was Prince Chun the Second, another son of the toady Prince Chun who had wept when she had selected his son – the ill-fated Kuang-hsu – to be Emperor.

This Prince Chun was a mediocre, muddle-headed, weak-willed conservative who would certainly never measure up to her. What is more, he had married a daughter of her old friend and ex-lover General Jung-lu, and had a three-year-old son, Pu Yi. There were other candidates, but most palace insiders felt that Yuan Shi-kai and Pu Lun were on the inside track. The 'Old Buddha' consistently refused to make her decision known, until the very last minute.

On 14 November 1908, the prisoner-Emperor died.

His death, at thirty-four, was not unexpected, for he had seemingly lost the will to live. But the manner of his death came as a surprise. A court doctor, who had examined him three days previously, reported the dying prisoner-Emperor exhibited symptoms more akin to acute poisoning than to either tuberculosis or Bright's disease. 'He could not sleep, he could not urinate, his heartbeat grew faster, his face burnt purple, his tongue had turned yellow,' the doctor who examined him wrote. Though he dared not say so outright, it is clear he believed the Emperor had been murdered.

There were several possible suspects: the Dowager Empress, fearful that if he outlived her he might tell his appalling story, could well have ordered her eunuchs to poison his food. 'Traitor' Yuan Shi-kai, scared that after Tzu-hsi's death the Emperor might exact a terrible revenge, also had good grounds to do away with him, and sufficient friends at court to do so; and the court eunuchs, who knew their jobs were at risk if he lived and carried through his threatened reforms, may well have killed him themselves. The truth will never be known.

The following day (15 November 1908) the 'Old Buddha' herself was dead, of dysentery, after rashly indulging in one last gigantic dish of crab apples and cream, and – finally – choosing the Emperor of her choice.

CHAPTER FOUR

It was already dark on 13 November 1908 when an unusual procession left the Forbidden City through the ceremonial Wumen Gate and began wending its way through the city. It consisted of marching men and richly uniformed cavalry. At its centre was a palanquin, borne aloft by some of the imperial palace's strongest eunuchs. Their escort was a squad of imperial guards, preceded by the palace chamberlain and other dignitaries, all on horseback.

The cortège took about half an hour to reach its destination: the lakeside Northern Mansion, home of Prince Chun the Second and his two wives. There was no advance notice of any kind – there were no telephones in Peking at the time – and the procession had been hastily assembled: the 'Old Buddha' was clearly dying, and it was imperative that her successor be summoned as quickly as possible.

The procession halted at the lakeside, where most of the cavalrymen remained. The gates of Northern Mansion swung open, the eunuchs bearing the palanquin entered, along with court officials. It was only then that Prince Chun realized that his elder son, Pu Yi, had been chosen to become the next Emperor, and that they had come to take him away.

The tiny three-year-old was playing with his wet nurse, Mrs Wang (Wan Chao), when the palanquin swung into the family yard. A headstrong child, he invariably resisted all efforts to put him to bed at a reasonable hour. The house was full of relatives, servants, hangers-on. The palace officials' arrival threw the household into turmoil. The chamberlain shouted to 'get the child dressed' and into the palanquin as fast as possible, but the sudden, frightening apparition of so many strangers in strange robes scared the small Pu Yi out of his wits. He hid in his nurse's arms. When they tried to grab him, he scuttled away into a hiding place – a cupboard used for hide-and-seek games with his nurse. Smiling, obsequious eunuchs tried to tempt him out of there. Palace officials ordered the eunuchs to pick him up. Pu Yi clawed at them, wriggled away, sobbing and screaming. It was an inauspicious start to any reign.

Prince Chun's aged mother fainted in the middle of this embarrassing scene, and had to be carried to her room. The palace chamberlain expected Prince Chun to take command and assert himself as Regent, but he just sat, overcome by the sudden news, unable to move.

It was the chamberlain who finally took command. 'The nurse. Get the nurse!' he shouted. Mrs Wang, the 21 year-old wet nurse, was the only person with any influence over the small Pu Yi. She knew what to do: she went up to him, bared her breast, and offered it for him to suck. The effect was immediate. His cries subsided and he settled into her arms, secure in the soft cradle provided by her warm young body. She carried him out without a word, climbed into the palanquin, and the two of them were borne off to the imperial palace, leaving Northern Mansion in uproar. Pu Yi was not to see his real mother again for over six years.

Pu Yi's own memories of that day are understandably

hazy. When the time came to write his autobiography, however, some of the eye witnesses to that scene were still alive. Pu Yi sought them out. He was also lucky: the man who helped him write and research his autobiography, Li Wenda, an experienced journalist and editor, indefatigably tracked them down.

Nowhere in Pu Yi's book, *From Emperor to Citizen*, does Li's name appear. Like all good ghostwriters, he minimizes his role. But all of Pu Yi's surviving relatives and former retainers agree that Pu Yi would have been incapable of writing the book unaided. It was Li Wenda who filled in for me many of the gaps in Pu Yi's story. He admitted he did a great deal of legwork, tracking down distant relatives, courtiers and surviving eunuchs and cross-questioning them about Pu Yi's early years.

Li Wenda is a man with impeccable revolutionary credentials. From 1944 onwards he served in the 4th (Communist) Route Army, first against the Japanese, then against Chiang Kai-chek's Kuomingtang (KMT) forces. He left the army in 1949 to become a journalist. Before that, he had been in charge of his unit's newsletter, a cyclo-styled sheet regularly printed just behind the front lines, usually under exceedingly hazardous conditions. Later, he worked for a newspaper and a state publishing house, which hired him to supervise the Pu Yi autobiography, a project which had Chou En-lai's blessing. Thanks to Li Wenda, we know a great deal about Pu Yi's early days inside the Forbidden City.

Overnight, Pu Yi found himself treated like a God, unable to behave as a child, except with his wet nurse. He was carried everywhere on a palanquin by eunuchs, for it was considered demeaning for an emperor to walk. Wherever he went, other eunuchs and attendants kowtowed, kneeling and knocking their heads nine times on the ground as he went by. Only his nights were secure: he slept inside the Palace of Heavenly Purity on a huge 'kang', or platform bed, in the arms of his faithful nurse.

Only hours after leaving his family home, Pu Yi was

taken to the Hall of Mental Cultivation to see the 'Old Buddha'.

'I still have a dim recollection of this meeting,' Pu Yi wrote many years later, 'the shock of which left a deep impression on my memory. I remember suddenly finding myself surrounded by strangers, while before me was hung a drab curtain through which I could see an emaciated and terrifyingly hideous face. This was Tzu-hsi. It is said that I burst out into loud howls at the sight and started to tremble uncontrollably.

'Tzu-hsi,' Pu Yi continued, 'told someone to give me some sweets, but I threw them on the floor and yelled: "I want nanny, I want nanny", to her great displeasure. "What a naughty child," she said. "Take him away to play." ' She died two days later.

Tzu-hsi's death was marked by only formal mourning. As the news spread, many wealthy Chinese flocked to singsong girl houses (as brothels were euphemistically called) and openly rejoiced. Two weeks later, on 2 December, Pu Yi was crowned.

The coronation ceremony was both religious and secular: musicians, eunuchs and priests packed into the Hall of Supreme Harmony where Pu Yi was perched frighteningly high on his throne. It was a cold day, that 2 December, and Pu Yi shivered with cold as well as fright, as a succession of palace guard officers and ministers paraded before him, one by one, to swear allegiance. Though Nurse Wang was the only person who could control him, and with whom he felt at ease, she was excluded from the ceremony. Protocol demanded that Prince Chun, father and Regent, should be the one to attend him during this lengthy, awesome ceremony, utterly incomprehensible to any three-year-old.

'I found it all long and tiresome,' Pu Yi wrote. 'It was so cold that when they carried me into the Hall and perched me on the high and enormous throne I could bear it no longer. My father, who was kneeling below the throne and supporting me, told me not to fidget, but I struggled and cried: "I don't like it here. I want to go home." My father grew so desperate he was pouring with sweat. As the officials went on kowtowing to me my cries grew louder and louder. My father tried to soothe me by saying, "Don't cry, it'll soon be over." His words, meant to be soothing, had a deplorable effect on the palace staff, who saw them as a gloomy, prophetic omen.'

Pu Yi settled down to a protocol-bound existence, without any companions of his own age. His courtiers treated him with the deference due to a living god. From time to time, when he became too obstreperous, the eunuchs looking after his daily needs locked him inside a small, barren room, until he calmed down. Nurse Wang was his one link with the past, and she continued to breastfeed him, and share his bed, for the next five years.

It was important for the Emperor to develop the traditional skills of a calligraphist, and his eunuch companions first taught him to read and write, getting him to memorize the basic set of Chinese characters required to recognize his name on the imperial seals. Nurse Wang, like nearly all country girls of that time, was illiterate, and the court officials both despised and feared her. They regarded this selfless, devoted woman with suspicion because they feared that if she remained inside the Forbidden City, she would, in time, wield inordinate influence over the new Emperor. For the moment, there was little they could do: as soon as Pu Yi was separated from her, he became a fractious little boy, subject to uncontrollable fits of rage. Besides, they had other, more serious problems confronting them.

The year Pu Yi ascended to the throne, China was in chaos. Ever since the Boxer Rebellion, there had been simmering, intermittent civil war in the country. In the south, the imperial writ no longer ran: Canton and the whole of Kwangtung Province seethed with republican fervour, led by Dr Sun Yat-sen, founder of the Kuomingtang (Alliance) party, who had been exiled and had just staged his ninth unsuccessful coup to overthrow the monarchy. But whereas in the early days of the KMT his support had come mainly from overseas Chinese and from some

Japanese secret societies, now the opposition within China had grown to include officials, army officers, merchants and even Confucian scholars, all convinced the Manchus must go. The virtual collapse of the administration made the advent of the republic inevitable – a matter of months rather than years – even as Pu Yi was being proclaimed Emperor.

Ironically, it was Prince Chun, one of the most incompetent Regents in the history of China, who virtually ensured its demise by sacking the one man who might have kept it going for a little longer.

Yuan Shi-kai, who had betrayed the reformists to Tzu-hsi's arch-conservative camp in 1898, was, at the time of Pu Yi's accession, Commander-in-Chief of the Chinese army. Whatever his moral failings, he was a competent soldier, a disciplinarian who inspired confidence in his men. Prince Chun promptly had him fired.

The terms of his dismissal were deliberately insulting. According to the imperial decree, signed by the infant Pu Yi:

. . . Yuan Shi-kai is now suffering from an affliction of the foot, he has difficulty in walking and it is hardly possible for him to discharge his duties adequately. We command Yuan Shi-kai to resign his office (of Commander-in-Chief) at once and to return to his native place to treat and to convalesce from the ailment. It is our resolution to show consideration and compassion.

Yuan Shi-kai had long been a favourite of the Europeans – especially the British community in Peking, who saw him as the proverbial 'strong man' who would keep China stable, on Europe's side, and in a position to meet its huge reparation debts.

'Why can't Yuan Shi-kai put himself at the head of 10,000 men and sweep the lot out?' Sir John Jordan, British Minister in Peking, undiplomatically asked Morrison of the *Times*. In fact Yuan Shi-kai had already begun, through intermediaries, to sound out the republicans on their intentions. His dismissal was providential: it allowed him to sit back and simply let events take their course.

The end came for the Ching dynasty on 10 October 1911, but not, surprisingly, at the hands of Sun Yat-sen's KMT republicans. Instead, in Wuhan, a group of young army officers mutinied, turning against their corrupt generals and demanding widespread reforms. The demoralized imperial army sided with the rebels. No troops could be found to defend the moribund regime. Governors fled, and soldiers fraternized with the mutineers. These, however, had no clear political designs. Sun Yat-sen's republicans did have, and they took over the leadership of the movement. From Wuhan the rebellion spread over most of the country. China's bankers, entrepreneurs, shopkeepers and tiny middle class openly sided with the republicans, demanding the end of the hopelessly archaic, inefficient Ching dynasty.

Morrison telegraphed the London *Times*: 'The Manchu dynasty is in danger. The sympathies of the immense mass of educated Chinese are all with the revolutionaries. Little sympathy is expressed for the corrupt and effete Manchu dynasty with its eunuchs and other barbaric surroundings. The Court is in great anxiety and the outlook for the throne ominous.'

In desperation, Prince Chun now called on Yuan Shi-kai to return to Peking and deal with the hopeless situation. Yuan blandly replied that his foot still hurt. Meanwhile, he was plotting with the revolutionaries, who had offered to make him China's first republican President. 'Traitor' Yuan had always had immense ambitions of his own. Now convinced his hour had come, he took command of the imperial forces, but made certain the republicans would nowhere be decisively crushed. Secretly, he was negotiating with some of their leaders – but not with Sun Yat-sen, who was still in exile. Morrison of the *Times* visited Yuan Shi-kai in Hankow where he was going through the motions of defending the dying Manchu dynasty, and came away convinced that 'China is indifferent whether Yuan Shi-kai makes himself President or Emperor; the Manchus must go. There seems absolute unanimity about this.'

In December 1911 Prince Chun resigned as Regent, and the Dowager Empress, Jung-shu, who had always shown a good understanding of political issues, authorized Yuan Shi-kai to work out a compromise with the republicans. From that moment onwards, Yuan Shi-kai was in full command of events. Within a year he had had Sun Yat-sen shunted aside and become China's first republican President.

Though he was only five years old at the time, Pu Yi did witness what must have been one final, crucial meeting between Dowager Empress Jung-shu and the shifty Yuan Shi-kai. This is how he described the scene:

> The Dowager Empress was sitting on a 'kang' [plat-form bed] in a side room of the Mind Nurture Palace, wiping her eyes with a handkerchief while a fat old man [Yuan] knelt on a red cushion before her, tears rolling down his face. I was sitting to the right of the Dowager and wondering why the two adults were crying. There was nobody in the room besides us three and it was very quiet; the fat man was sniffing loudly while he talked and I could not understand what he was saying . . . This was the occasion Yuan directly brought up the question of abdication.

By any standards, the 'Articles providing for Favour-able Treatment of the Great Ching Emperor after his Abdication' were extraordinarily generous: the Emperor retained his title ('the Republic of China will treat him with the courtesy due to a foreign sovereign'), a huge privy purse, continued residence in the Forbidden City (for an undetermined period of time), and his personal fortune. The palace guard would continue to serve the ex-Emperor, the only difference being that henceforth they would – for accounting purposes – be regarded as regular members of the armed forces. And though the new

Chinese republic established its own orders and decorations, the Emperor was still empowered to distribute his own awards – his own personal imperial 'Honours List' with all its attendant pomp and snobbery. Just about the only change in the Emperor's lifestyle was that no more eunuchs would be engaged, but the security of tenure of all existing palace employees was guaranteed.

The terms were so generous because, for all the republicanism of China's 'advanced' elite, there was still considerable respect for the notion of monarchy among the Chinese peasants and farmers – and they made up eighty per cent of the population. For them, it was unthinkable to make a clean break with the past. Foreign governments with Chinese interests were also in favour of a compromise. Japan, itself an imperial power, was against any harsh treatment of the Chinese royal family; so were most Western powers, intent on preserving Chinese stability so that the reparations extorted from Tzu-hsi after the collapse of the Boxer Rebellion would continue to be paid.

It was because the agreement between the court and the new republican leaders was so favourable to the Ching dynasty that Pu Yi, at five, had no inkling of what had happened. The protocol and ritual governing the young Emperor's life remained unchanged. In fact, life at court became more make-believe and Pirandellian than ever. Lacking any real powers of government, court ritual, court tradition and court intrigue were now all that the thousands of palace employees had left. The Forbidden City was sufficiently self-contained for them to believe it was the real world.

For Pu Yi, it was the first of his many prisons.

CHAPTER FIVE

In the earliest photographs of Pu Yi a solemn little boy stares back at the camera, thinking secret thoughts. He looks sad but composed. There is a stillness to him, and a trace of haughty contempt in his fixed stare.

Chinese parents are extremely indulgent where their very small children are concerned. Up to the age of five or six, they are rarely punished, no matter how badly they behave. Extreme indulgence goes hand in hand with parental warmth and concern. Even Mao's Cultural Revolution failed to change this order of things in any durable way. As a result Chinese children feel extraordinarily protected within their immediate family circle.

Overnight, after his move into the Forbidden City and his coronation, the three-year-old Pu Yi was suddenly deprived of the security of his immediate family. His one link with the past was his wet nurse, Mrs Wang. Apart from her, all were strangers, remote, grown-up, always bowing and scraping in his direction.

Their very deference was frightening. Wherever he went within the palace grown men either knelt down and hit their heads on the floor in a ritual kowtow, or else turned their backs on him. Only 'eunuchs of the Imperial Presence' were allowed to look at the boy king. The others had to face the wall, or stare down at the ground.

From the moment Pu Yi got up in the morning till the moment he fell asleep, mercifully in the arms of his wet nurse, sucking at her breast, everything was done for him by selected 'eunuchs of the Imperial Presence', strange, beardless men with pigtails (queues) and high-pitched voices. They washed him, emptied his chamberpot, cleaned his behind, dressed him, played with him, carried him about the place in ceremonial chairs or palanquins. They deferred to him constantly. Pu Yi had only to say 'I'm hungry' and a huge buffet was set up wherever he happened to be. He could relieve himself at any time – a eunuch was constantly in attendance with the royal chamberpot.

The Forbidden City was almost exclusively male, and almost all the males living there were eunuchs. This state of affairs had come about during the previous Ming dynasty, when emperors had feared for the virtue of the numerous concubines. In Tzu-hsi's time, over a thousand eunuchs had attended her. When Pu Yi became Emperor, there were some two hundred eunuchs left, including only a few teenagers, at his personal service. Some of them were well educated. They were, he wrote later, 'my first teachers' – and practically his only companions from the age of three onwards.

It was relatively easy to become a eunuch: the operation was ridiculously cheap (about 70 pence) and those who performed it were so skilful that only four to five per cent of their patients died.

It helped to have relatives already working inside the Forbidden City. Mostly, recruitment was by co-optation: eunuchs recruited each other, and though most of those working inside the Forbidden City were despised menials – sweepers, kitchen hands, refuse collectors, gardeners and handymen – there were considerable opportunities for advancement. Educated eunuchs became clerks, those with good singing voices or a pleasing wit were expected to put on shows – and often became the confidants of palace officials in high places.

Since Confucian traditions required that a body be buried whole to attain heaven, eunuchs were careful to keep their severed testicles pickled in brine in tiny jars about their person – and in theory at least they were liable to inspection. There was a lucrative black market trade in these grim relics. A few eunuchs set up luxurious households in Peking with adopted or real families (for some underwent emasculation in adult life, after raising families). A few eunuchs were even thought to be not eunuchs at all, but charlatans who took advantage of the fortunes to be made within the Forbidden City to pose as eunuchs, and fool the imperial household controllers. One of Tzu-hsi's eunuchs had become as powerful as any viceroy.

Financial rewards could indeed be huge: since the eunuchs largely ran the Forbidden City, opportunities for graft (squeeze, as old China hands called it) were endless. The eunuchs were not the only ones to divert palace household expenses to their own use, but the scale of corruption was such that almost every eunuch inside the Forbidden City augmented his income in some way or other – sometimes by outright begging. From his earliest age, Pu Yi became used to scattering coins to fawning, servile men who regarded such largesse as their due.

In theory, any eunuch caught stealing was liable to instant beheading, but such executions, by the time Pu Yi became Emperor, were exceedingly rare. Instead, eunuchs were beaten, thrashed on their bare behinds at the slightest provocation. Pu Yi soon got used to the sight of one eunuch using the paddle, or the cane, on another. Tzu-hsi had habitually had dozens of eunuchs beaten daily: she claimed they enjoyed it. Pu Yi rapidly followed her example. Records show it was not unusual for him to have several eunuchs thrashed in a single day, for real or imagined offences – often simply for the sheer perverse spectacle of it. An entry for 21 February 1913 in one of his tutor's diaries reads: 'His Majesty frequently beats the eunuchs, he has had seventeen flogged recently for minor offences . . . His subject [the diarist] remonstrated but His Majesty did not accept his advice.' Pu Yi himself noted that, as a child, 'flogging eunuchs was part of my daily routine. My cruelty and love of wielding power were already too firmly set for persuasion to have any effect on me.'

A privileged coterie of eunuchs became Pu Yi's constant attendants. One of them, Chang Chieng-lo, became almost a foster father in those early years, teaching the Emperor to read and write, and delighting him with children's stories. Pu Yi was genuinely fond of him. But though a small group of eunuchs played daily with the 'Son of Heaven', they were not immune from punishment. In a tantrum, even during a game, Pu Yi sometimes had his grown-up playmates flogged. He also childishly – and wilfully – tested his power and authority over them, as 'Lord of Ten Thousand Years', to see how far he could go. 'Once,' he wrote, 'I had a brainwave. I wanted to see whether those servile eunuchs were really obedient to the "Divine Son of Heaven". I picked on one of them and pointed to a piece of dirt on the floor. "Eat that for me," I ordered, and he knelt down and ate it.'

His wet nurse was the only person who could restrain the little boy. One of his eunuchs regularly put on a puppet show which delighted the small Pu Yi. To reward the eunuch, Pu Yi decided to present him with a cake, but ordered his nurse to put iron filings in it. 'I want to see what he looks like when he eats it,' Pu Yi said. With difficulty, the wet nurse got him to substitute dried beans for iron filings. But she never did manage to prevent him from using the eunuchs as target practice for his air gun. On rare occasions (but only up to the age of four) his eunuch companions would lock him inside a bare palace room when his temper tantrums became too violent. But no one, from the age of five onwards – not even his wet nurse – had any real authority over him. The Emperor was Divine. He could not be remonstrated with, or punished. He could only be deferentially advised against ill-treating innocent eunuchs, and if he chose to fire air-gun pellets at them, that was his prerogative.

Perhaps young Pu Yi's fits of cruelty came from his impatience at his complete lack of privacy. 'Every time I went to my schoolroom to study, or for a stroll in the garden, I was always followed by a large retinue,' he wrote.

In front went a eunuch whose function was roughly that of a motor horn; he walked twenty or thirty yards ahead of the party intoning the sound . . . 'chir . . . chir . . .' as a warning to anyone who might be waiting in the vicinity to go away at once. Next came two Chief Eunuchs advancing crabwise on either side of the path; ten paces behind them came the centre of the procession. If I was being carried in a chair there would be two junior eunuchs walking beside me to attend to my wants at any moment; if I was walking they would be supporting me. Next came a eunuch with a large silk canopy followed by a large group of eunuchs, some empty-handed, others holding all sorts of things: a seat in case I wanted to rest, changes of clothing, umbrellas and parasols.

After these eunuchs of the Imperial Presence came eunuchs of the Imperial tea bureau with boxes of various kinds of cakes and delicacies . . . They were followed by eunuchs of the Imperial dispensary . . . at the end of the procession came the eunuchs who carried commodes and chamberpots. If I was walking, a sedan-chair, open or covered according to the season, would bring up the rear. This motley procession of several dozen people would proceed in perfect silence and order.

One of Pu Yi's ritual daily visits was to the five women who lived in the Eastern Palaces – and whom he called mother' though he felt nothing but hostility towards them.

These were all widows or former concubines of the two

preceding Emperors, and they had lived inside the Forbidden City all their adult lives. Empress Dowager Jung-shu was their acknowledged leader. She had been the 'number one' wife of the prisoner-Emperor Kuang-hsu. More important, she was the 'Old Buddha's' niece, and by the time Pu Yi became Emperor she had become almost as tradition-minded and autocratic as her formidable aunt. Palace officials and eunuchs alike were terrified of her.

Three of the other four old ladies were Dowager Consorts – widow-concubines of Kuang-hsu's predecessor, Tung-chih, the debauched young man 'adopted' by Tzu-hsi and selected as Emperor in 1874 so that she could continue as Dowager Empress. The fourth was Lustrous Concubine, sister of Pearl Concubine, the prisoner-Emperor's favourite, whom Tzu-hsi had had put to death just before the collapse of the Boxer Rebellion.

Pu Yi's special hatred was for Jung-shu, who believed small boys should be half-starved to keep them in good health. He had to report to each one of them every day, however, and they would ritually ask him if he was in good health. 'Although I had so many mothers,' wrote Pu Yi, 'I never knew any motherly love.'

He soon had an additional reason for loathing them: when he turned eight, they conspired to get rid of his wet nurse. Mrs Wang was made to pack her bags and leave, without even being allowed to say goodbye to her adored charge. Pu Yi learned of her departure only after it had occurred. After she left, he cried himself to sleep, night after night, in his huge, empty bed.

The Dowager Consorts were overwhelmingly concerned with their status, and mostly blind to the changes taking place outside the walls of the Forbidden City. They treated Pu Yi's mother, Prince Chun's 'number one' wife, with considerable contempt, not allowing her to visit the boy Emperor regularly until he was thirteen.

Each of the Dowagers had large numbers of servants and hangers-on. All, without exception, robbed the women blind. Eunuchs were superstitious, always making religious sacrifices, consulting fortune-tellers, praying to a whole range of household gods, but essentially theirs was a thieving 'below stairs' mentality: almost all of them were 'on the take'. They had a fine sense of hierarchy, unerringly knew which visitors were important and which could be 'squeezed'. One trick they often practised was to wait till an important official was about to have an audience with one of the Dowagers, and then tip a bucket of water over his sable jacket. To keep the Dowagers waiting was unthinkable, so the official was compelled to rent suitable ceremonial clothing from the eunuch for a sizable fee. 'The eunuchs,' Pu Yi wrote, 'always kept a complete range of clothing to be hired out at short notice by officials.'

By far the biggest 'perk', as far as the eunuchs were concerned, was food. The same absurd ritual that turned every walk into a procession governed mealtimes. In the days of the 'Old Buddha', meals had been served whenever she felt like it – there were no fixed hours. Marina Warner, in *The Dragon Empress*, noted:

> Lunch and dinner always consisted of the same hundreds of dishes, from which she picked and chose her favourites. As these remained constant the cooks pocketed a good part of the table d'hôte allowance by serving up day after day the same dishes she never sampled till the weevils were crawling in them visibly.

When Pu Yi was a small boy, the same routine prevailed. Every mealtime mobilized dozens of eunuchs from several different household departments. They set up a huge buffet, but it was all for show: the food in the imperial yellow porcelain with dragon designs inscribed with the words 'ten thousand long lives without limit' was never actually eaten – though it was all, very probably, carried away by the eunuchs for their own consumption or sold. Pu Yi actually ate only food prepared in the kitchens of the four 'High Consorts'.

Imperial household accounts of this period survive, and the cost of food within the Forbidden City was phenomenal.

In one month in 1909, Pu Yi alone is shown to have eaten nearly 200 pounds of meat and 240 ducks and chickens. He was four at the time. This amount was quite distinct from that earmarked for the court, which was also unrealistically high. Pilfering was on a gigantic scale.

'Just as food was cooked in huge quantities and not eaten, so was a vast amount of clothing made which was never worn,' Pu Yi wrote. Custom required that everything the boy-Emperor wore in his childhood had to be new. Once worn, clothes were disposed of, almost certainly sold. Records exist of the scores of silk tunics, sable jackets, fur-lined coats and padded waistcoats specially made for Pu Yi during the course of a single month. The number was astronomical. The four High Consorts had their own equally extravagant and wasteful establishments, with peculation on a similar scale.

Education was another part of Pu Yi's life that was totally mismanaged, at least until Reginald Johnston, his Scottish tutor, appeared on the scene in 1919. Apart from learning to read and write (an arduous process for all Chinese, who have to master thousands of ideograms and practise calligraphy for hours every day), Pu Yi's tutors concentrated on Chinese classics and Confucian texts. In his early years, Pu Yi wrote, 'I learnt nothing of mathematics, let alone science, and for a long time I had no idea where Peking was situated.'

The awe the small Pu Yi was held in by tutors and eunuchs alike meant that his progress was never tested in either examinations or compositions. In theory, all emperors had to be fluent in Manchu – a language very different from Chinese – but Pu Yi never mastered it. At the age of eight, however, his tutors decided to establish a small palace schoolroom, where Pu Yi would enjoy the company, and the emulation, of a small number of aristocratic children of his own age. Among them was Pu Chieh, his younger brother by three years, who was to remain a close member of Pu Yi's household for the rest of his life.

As Pu Chieh tells it, the awe surrounding a Chinese

emperor was such that Prince Chun never referred to Pu Yi, at home, as 'your elder brother'. He knew he had an elder brother and that he was the Emperor, but he had no idea that this 'living God' was a boy only three years older than himself. 'I had imagined a venerable old man with a beard,' said Pu Chieh. 'I couldn't believe it when I saw this boy in yellow robes sitting solemnly on the throne.'

Pu Yi was formally introduced to his new school companion in the presence of the four High Consorts and Pu Yi's own parents, who kowtowed solemnly before him. By this time Pu Yi had forgotten what his mother had looked like, and did not recognize her. As Pu Chieh recalls it, 'One of the Consorts said: this is your older brother. He is the Emperor so if you play with him don't fight with him.' They played hide-and-seek, a game Pu Yi had played previously only with his eunuchs, and Pu Yi threw a tantrum when he discovered that his younger brother's sleeve lining was yellow – a colour reserved for the Emperor himself.

After this somewhat inauspicious first encounter, Pu Chieh was one of three boys brought into the Forbidden City daily to attend school classes with Pu Yi. Pu Chieh remembers that he and Pu Yi would sometimes make their way together to the classroom. 'Every time we came to a door, it had to be unlocked by a eunuch, who had to be tipped. There are hundreds of doors inside the Forbidden City, and each one was guarded by a different eunuch.' (Traditions die hard in China: Bertolucci found just as many door guardians – no longer eunuchs, of course – while filming *The Last Emperor* inside the Forbidden City, and each one had to be bribed or cajoled into opening his door.)

The presence of hand-picked school companions in no way altered the totally artificial life led by Pu Yi. An emperor could not be reprimanded in any way, for laziness, for unruly classroom behaviour. The device used by his tutors was to select a convenient whipping-boy from among his companions, and punish him in lieu of the Emperor. Seen from today's vantage point, the whole of

Pu Yi's childhood virtually ensured that he would grow up with a host of psychological problems. Emotionally deprived, forced to treat the old royal Dowagers as 'mother', trea ed with absurd respect, waited on hand and foot by eunuchs whom he ordered to be beaten for the slightest fault, Pu Yi's early life was a classic recipe for neurosis. When his real mother died, shortly after getting to know him again, Pu Yi's emotional deprivation was complete.

CHAPTER SIX

By the time he was seven, Pu Yi was adept at living in two worlds: the childish one of games with eunuchs and the puppet shows and entertainments (including dog fights) they put on to keep him from being bored, and nights spent cuddling up to his wet nurse Mrs Wang; and the very different official world, focusing on the chores and pageantry of playing at Emperor, that took up more and more of his time.

Prince Chun, Pu Yi's father, had been one of the least efficient, most indecisive Regents in Chinese history. For this reason he had never been able to explain to Pu Yi the nature of the revolution that had occurred in China in 1911. Pu Yi was dimly aware that, outside the Forbidden City walls, something had changed. But nothing was done to make him aware of the fact that while he might still play at being Emperor within the palace grounds, China had become a republic, nor was he made to grasp the implications of such a change.

On his seventh birthday, one of the imperial eunuchs gave him the childhood panoply of a general's uniform, complete with toy sword and plumed hat. Little Pu Yi swaggered around the palace, pleased as punch. He was unwise enough to show his present off to the old Dowager Consorts. They immediately spotted that this was the hated uniform of a republican general. They shrieked at him to take it off at once and put on his traditional imperial robes. An enquiry was held. The eunuch who had presented Pu Yi with the uniform was given two hundred strokes of the rod, and permanently banished from the imperial presence.

In the make-believe atmosphere of the Forbidden City, Pu Yi was compelled to behave like a real Emperor still. Supervised by his tutors and palace chamberlains, he had to put his imperial seal on documents submitted to him at long, boring court ceremonies during which he remained perched on his oversized throne and had to listen for hours to droning voices speaking of matters he did not understand. It did not matter, to his tutors, that the documents presented to him for signature were not matters of state at all, but court circulars or household directives dealing with staff promotions, or the dates when trees should be transplanted, or the eunuchs made to change from their winter to their summer uniforms. What concerned them was not the content of such imperial decrees, but the ritual involved.

There were religious ceremonies, too, for the Emperor played an important role in the ancestor worship of his Manchu emperor forebears. Pu Yi did not fully understand the meaning of these rites either, but very quickly came to realize that he was, inside the Forbidden City, which was the only world he knew, an absolute monarch still. And because his tutors also lived in the make-believe world they were intent on prolonging, and could not accept the reality of a changing world beyond the Forbidden City walls, they not only encouraged Pu Yi to think of himself as a real Emperor, but made him a party to their intrigues and restoration plots.

Pu Yi's chief tutor was Chen Pao-shen, a learned Confucian scholar with a wispy beard who gave himself the inflated title of 'Political Director'. Chen was a dyed-in-the-wool conservative, a fervent royalist who genuinely believed that the hated republic would not last. He used every conceivable opportunity to impose his views on the seven-year-old Pu Yi.

To mark the break between the monarchy and the republic, the Chinese government, whose President was still Yuan Shi-kai, had decided to abandon the old Chinese calendar and celebrate not only Chinese New Year but the Western one as well. A senior presidential aide called on Pu Yi on 31 December 1911 to present his respects for the coming New Year. Dressed up 'in full regalia of golden dragon coat and gown, hat with a pearl button, pearl necklace . . . I sat solemnly on the throne of the Cloudless Heaven Palace,' Pu Yi wrote, 'surrounded by Ministers, Companions of the Presence and sword-bearing Imperial Guards.' Yuan's representative bowed, took a few steps forward and bowed again, came closer, bowed a third time – almost a kowtow – then expressed his congratulations and best wishes.

Tutor Chen later explained to Pu Yi how important this ceremony had been, and how 'even that President of theirs can't flout' the Articles of Favoured Treatment, now stored in China's National Archives.

Soon afterwards on Pu Yi's birthday (14 February), Yuan Shi-kai again sent his official congratulations. The rest of the capital took its cue from the President – and all of a sudden it became fashionable to flaunt one's connections with the Ching dynasty court. Pu Yi wrote that 'former Ching officials who had been lying low throughout the first years of the Republic now proudly wore their distinctive Court regalia – red hats and peacock feathers . . . Some even revived the practice of having outriders to clear the way and a retinue crowding around them when they went through the streets.' Earlier, to avoid attracting attention, palace officials had changed into their ceremonial court clothes only after entering the Forbidden City. Now, wrote Pu Yi, 'they dared to go along the street in full Imperial costume'.

That same year, 1912, the senior Dowager, Empress Jung-shu, died, and Tutor Chen again told Pu Yi how significant it was that the President had ordered an official twenty-seven-day mourning period, and that all the hated republican flags were flown at half-mast. President Yuan Shi-kai himself wore a black armband, and called on Pu Yi to pay his respects. Pu Yi's tutors told him that this could only mean that big changes were afoot. Inside the Forbidden City, there was much wailing as eunuchs intoned funeral chants and prepared for the lengthy burial ceremonies – but the grief was purely formal: jubilation prevailed throughout the Forbidden City, and Pu Yi himself was aware of the new, expectant mood.

Peking had never been a bastion of republicanism: it was a city that owed much of its prosperity to the court's extravagant spending. Many Western observers felt, at this time, that there was a strong undercurrent in favour of the restoration of the monarchy. There was – and President Yuan Shi-kai saw this as *his* opportunity, not Pu Yi's, and encouraged the movement.

The Presidential palace was opposite the main entrance to the Forbidden City. The first inkling Pu Yi had of Yuan's own designs on the monarchy was when the wily old President started spending huge funds on its embellishment. He also introduced a curious, and – imperial palace officials felt – ominous custom: army bands were brought in to serenade him at mealtimes. Pu Yi stared, for hours, at the presidential building, from a window high up in the imperial palace, and listened to the martial music. His tutors could talk of nothing but the President's rumoured longing to become king. Pu Yi recalled that the entire court kept a daily watch on the work in progress. 'We felt,' said Pu Yi, 'that our own fate was bound up in it.' Pu Yi advanced what he thought was a compelling argument: 'He can't become Emperor,' he told his tutors. 'After all, the Imperial Seals are mine. We can always hide them.' Deferentially, his tutors replied that 'traitor' Yuan would probably have new ones made.

Yuan Shi-kai's ambitions even affected the way his

tutors behaved towards Pu Yi in the palace schoolroom. One of his 'royal' classmates was a boy called Yu Chung, son of Prince Pu Lun who had been – briefly – a rumoured heir apparent both in 1876 and in 1908. Prince Pu Lun had never taken kindly to being passed over in favour of Pu Yi and became one of Yuan Shi-kai's closest supporters, urging him to form his own new dynasty.

Yu Chung was the classroom scapegoat – he was the one the tutors would punish whenever Pu Yi did anything wrong – but 'suddenly', Pu Yi noted, 'they became very polite to him'. They did not want to antagonize a family that might soon be playing an important role alongside a new emperor.

For 'traitor' Yuan Shi-kai lived up to his reputation: after toying with the notion of restoring Pu Yi to the throne, he finally (in 1915) organized a plebiscite and had himself proclaimed Emperor.

It was the shortest reign in the history of China, lasting only a few weeks: Yuan had powerful enemies, including some senior army officers. After a brief series of skirmishes, he had to 'postpone' his enthronement ceremonies, for which he had already had coins minted and plans made down to the last detail. In a volte-face of quite astonishing bad faith, he resumed the title of President of the Republic, announcing that he only wanted to 'obey the law of the people' and would hence-forward 'devote the rest of my life to the maintenance of the Republic'. Six months later – by June 1916 – he was dead.

Understandably enough, Yuan's death led to great rejoicing within the Forbidden City. For Pu Yi, who still saw these court intrigues and palace coups through the prism of childhood, the most important consequence was that the palace tutors reverted to their former deference, and Yu Chung to the role of whipping-boy.

A year later, at the height of the First World War, another 'coup' occurred, this time with more serious consequences for Pu Yi. Decades later, a prisoner of the ruling communist Chinese regime, he was still being called to account for his role in the 1917 restoration attempt.

By 1917 Pu Yi was eleven years old. He now had greater understanding of his ambiguous status. His tutors allowed him to read certain selected Peking newspapers, and eunuchs smuggled in the brasher, illustrated magazines, which frequently carried articles about the court – and the possibilities of Pu Yi's own restoration.

The man who initiated the ill-fated 1917 attempt to restore the Ching dynasty to its former position of power and splendour was a general, Chang-hsun, known in the press as the 'pig-tailed general' because, out of loyalty to the Ching dynasty, he had always refused to cut off his queue – the traditional hairstyle the Manchus had introduced to China in the seventeenth century. Courtiers, and Pu Yi himself, still wore queues. The 'pig-tailed general' insisted that troops under his command also wear them, and the 'pig-tailed army' had the reputation of being the best-disciplined, most efficient fighting force in China. Pig-tailed Chang-hsun, who had won many of Yuan's battles for him, had the distinction of being both pro-Yuan and pro-monarchy. He seems to have been a bluff, straightforward, law-and-order soldier, without much wider political understanding. At the time of the 'coup' he was 'viceroy' of Kiangsu province, and in control of China's strategically most vital area – Tientsin and the Tientsin–Peking railroad. As a sound military man, he was naturally concerned both by the wave of dissident movements in the north-east and the even more disquieting situation in the south, where radical movements were openly defying the central authority of Peking.

As Pu Yi tells it, Tutor Chen (now promoted to 'Grand Guardian') arranged for Pu Yi's special audience with the 'pig-tailed general' in the Hall of Mental Cultivation, which Pu Yi now used as his personal quarters.

The scenario had clearly been worked out in advance between the general and the court, but Pu Yi, only aware that the general was 'a loyal subject', was simply told to 'make it very clear' he was 'interested in him'. 'Chang-hsun is bound to praise Your Majesty,' his tutor told him. 'You must remember to reply modestly so as to display Your Majesty's Divine Virtue.'

Tradition required that Pu Yi be alone to receive outsiders. The 'pig-tailed general' kowtowed, and Pu Yi told him to sit. 'I was somewhat disappointed at the appearance of this "loyal subject" of mine,' Pu Yi recalled later. 'His face was ruddy, with very bushy eyebrows, and he was fat. The sight of his short neck made me think that but for his whiskers he would have looked like one of the eunuch cooks . . . I looked carefully to see whether he had a queue and indeed he did: a mottled grey one.'

The meeting was short, and only banalities were exchanged. But a fortnight later, Pu Yi's tutors announced: 'Chang-hsun is here.'

'Has he come to pay his respects?' Pu Yi asked.

'No. All preparations have been made and everything settled. He has come to bring Your Majesty back and restore the Great Ching.'

As Pu Yi tells it, 'I was stunned by this completely unexpected good news.'

Tutor Chen briefed him once more on how to behave. 'There is no need to say much. All you have to do is accept. But not at once. You must refuse at first and finally say, "if things are so then I must force myself to do it".'

Chang-hsun then appeared, kowtowed again, and read a prepared speech. There was a mandate from the people, he said. 'A republic does not suit our country. Only Your Majesty's restoration will save the people.'

While he 'droned on', Pu Yi suddenly wondered what would happen to the President of the Republic, Li Yuan-hung, who had succeeded Yuan.

'He has already memorialized [i.e. formally requested the Emperor] asking that he be allowed to resign,' said the general.

A eunuch promptly appeared with a pile of imperial edicts already prepared by the palace tutors. Pu Yi duly apposed his seals. One edict appointed a Regency Board, including, hardly surprisingly, both tutor Chen Pao-shen and the 'pig-tailed general'. To his very considerable annoyance, however, Pu Yi's own father was not among the Board members.

The news was quickly relayed to the outside world, and President Li Yuan-hung promptly took refuge inside the Legation Quarter, where Chang-hsun's soldiers could not pursue him.

As Pu Yi tells it:

Ching clothes that had not been seen for years reappeared on the streets . . . Shops did a booming trade . . . Tailors sold Ching dragon flags as fast as they could make them . . . theatrical costumiers were crowded with people begging them to make false queues out of horsehair. I still remember how the Forbidden City was crowded with men wearing Court robes with mandarins' buttons and peacock feathers in their hats . . .

Just how real was the restoration fervour? In Peking, at any rate, Chang-hsun had considerable support among shopkeepers, who hung out flags with the imperial dragon emblem on them to show where their preferences lay. But the Chinese, the diplomats said, were always ready to fly flags – to avoid fines or property destruction – and their support did not count for much.

The court's euphoria lasted less than two weeks. Chang-hsun had grossly underestimated the republican sentiments of some of the other powerful army commanders, and the personal mistrust of him of others. There was a widespread feeling in the army that Chang-hsun had stolen a march on his associates, that the movement failed not because it lacked sympathizers but because some of the principal participators were selfish, ambitious, and jealous of one another, and because Chang-hsun had none of the essential qualities of statesmanship.

The twelve-day 'midsummer madness', as Peking's *corps diplomatique* called the attempted coup (another name for it was the 'Restoration Comedy'), ended abruptly when a small plane piloted by a republican officer dropped three small bombs onto the Forbidden City, wounding a sedan-chair carrier and scattering a crowd of panic-stricken, twittering eunuchs who were gambling in a Forbidden City alleyway. The High Consorts hid under tables and beds. Eunuchs hustled Pu Yi to an improvised shelter in his bedroom. The 'pig-tailed general' took refuge in the Dutch Legation, and soon Peking's streets were littered with castaway pigtails.

In the circumstances, republican China's authorities behaved with admirable restraint. Not only were the Articles of Favourable Treatment not amended, but Chang-hsun was allowed to go relatively unpunished into honourable retirement. Pu Yi's tutors remained at their posts. The only real casualty, apart from the unfortunate sedan-chair carrier, was President Li Yuan-hung himself. He had 'lost face' by abandoning his post and dismissing parliament at Chang-hsun's request. He was promptly replaced by Feng Kuo-chang, a conservative aristocrat. A new parliament was convened, which declared war on Germany – a sop to the monarchists, who were pro-war, and a rebuff to Dr Sun Yat-sen, who was violently opposed to Chinese involvement. It was also a shrewd financial move: as a condition for entering the Allied camp, China's reparation payments were cancelled.

The 'midsummer madness' was to have lasting adverse consequences for Pu Yi. Not only was he to be directly blamed, later, for encouraging the coup, but growing radical hostility towards the central government was to focus on its almost inexplicably lenient attitude towards the court. Republican critics said it showed how pro-monarchist even republican politicians could be.

Pu Yi's tutors learned nothing from either fiasco. They encouraged him to believe that a strong pro-restoration body of opinion existed throughout the country. The court began playing politics, financing pro-restoration politicians out of its privy purse, distributing titles, honours and other privileges – such as the right to wear imperial yellow jackets, or ride a horse into the Forbidden

City. From 1917 onwards the feeling grew among young Chinese intellectuals, who began playing an increasingly important role both in government and in the various 'revolutionary' movements that were popping up all over the country, that neither Pu Yi nor his court could be trusted to respect their side of the Articles of Favourable Treatment bargain.

It was a feeling that Pu Yi himself, as he moved from childhood to adolescence, did nothing to dispel.

CHAPTER SEVEN

Reginald Johnston first set foot inside the Forbidden City on 3 March 1919. He owed his new job – as Pu Yi's English-language teacher – to one of the court's tutors, Chen Pao-shen, who respected him as an outstanding Chinese linguist, and to the Chinese republican government. Born in 1874, and a former 'Hong Kong cadet' in the British Colonial Service, Johnston had been a civil servant in Hong Kong and in Weihawei, then one of the oldest British-owned Chinese colonies after Hong Kong. He had travelled extensively throughout China and was a noted Chinese poet and calligraphist. At forty-five he was tall, corpulent, with blue eyes, a ruddy complexion and a shock of grey hair. To Pu Yi this confirmed bachelor looked like 'an old man'. The palace paid for his services, and provided him with a rent-free mansion which he furnished in traditional Chinese style.

Johnston's *Twilight in the Forbidden City* is a mine of information about Pu Yi from 1919 to 1924. Johnston wrote the book after leaving Peking to take up his new appointment as Commissioner of the British Concession of Weihawei. It was not published until 1934, by which time he was about to become Sir Reginald and take up a Professorship of Chinese at London University. Like Pu Yi's own autobiography, it is highly selective in its presentation of facts. It reads (as his film incarnation, Peter O'Toole, points out) very much like the heavy, rhetorical nineteenth-century prose of Thackeray and the *Edinburgh Review*, and is full of respect for the monarchy – any monarchy.

A conservative, with a great deal of respect for the arch-disciplined Japanese and a blind belief in the superiority of the British Empire over any other system of government, Johnston immediately felt a liking for Pu Yi, whom he depicted throughout his book as a perfect little gentleman. He did, however, recoil from the blinkered, venal Manchu court he got to know so well from the inside. His book corroborates much of Pu Yi's own memories of it, as a place of absurd extravagance, grotesque waste, endless and futile intrigue, and total irrelevance to China and the outside world. To Johnston's credit, he did try and reform the system, but in the end corruption prevailed, and he failed.

From 1919 onward, until Pu Yi's marriage in 1922, Johnston visited the palace daily, spending at least two hours a day with Pu Yi. Officially he had been hired solely as a language teacher, but Johnston's self-appointed task was to make his young pupil aware of the world at large, introduce him to Western values, and teach him the rudiments of 'civilized Western' behaviour. Even after Pu Yi was married, and Johnston's formal studies ended, the teacher continued to see Pu Yi almost daily. He became, briefly, a functionary of the court again in 1924, when Pu Yi appointed him 'Imperial Commissioner in charge of the Summer Palace'.

Johnston was neither a martinet nor a narrow-minded 'imperialist', for all his empire-building views, but was convinced that China was 'not ripe' for republicanism and that its best interests lay in a constitutional British-style monarchy. Unlike most British diplomats in Peking, he had been no admirer of 'traitor' Yuan Shi-kai. In this respect, he was far shrewder than *Times* correspondent George Morrison, who had displayed such a bias in the general's favour that his Peking dispatches became totally unreliable and should have led to his immediate recall to London.

While Johnston was convinced most Chinese were in favour of the restoration of the monarchy, he did not let his bias interfere with his account of the events he witnessed from 1919 to 1924. He was an excellent and accurate reporter. Though his Confucianism makes him sound, at times, like a tediously moralizing old bore, he is never patronizing where Pu Yi is concerned. If he has a fault, it is that, as his book shows, he was an unbridled snob. His new appointment filled him with delight. In his house, he prominently displayed those marks of respect and favour accorded to him by the court – his promotions in the mandarinate hierarchy, the occasional letters sent to him by Pu Yi. In *Twilight* he writes endlessly – and tediously – about the various court rituals he attended, first as a 'junior mandarin' entitled to entry into the Forbidden City in a sedan chair, then as a 'grade two' mandarin entitled to wear a sable robe, and finally as a 'Chinese mandarin of the highest order', able to ride around the Forbidden City on horseback, a right he exercised constantly with enormous gusto.

Johnston was also proud of the many gifts and other marks of esteem he received from the imperial family – porcelain, old manuscripts, paintings, jade, ginseng, as well as fruit and cakes from the Dowagers. Though he only rarely wore his court clothes, appearing at official ceremonies in a morning coat, and was excused from kowtowing, he wrote he would have done so with pleasure, but 'to kowtow with the ease and grace which seemed to come naturally to the Chinese and Manchus would be almost an impossibility for the untrained Europeans'.

Johnston's interests were exclusively literary, historical and political. Unlike his contemporary, Morrison, he never indulged in any love affairs, or visited Peking's many 'singsong houses'. Though there was nothing effeminate about Johnston, his sex drive appears to have been completely sublimated.

Without any marked disapproval, he noted that all major events governing court life were determined by astrologers, including the date of his own appointment as tutor. The traditionalist in him was clearly delighted to enter through the Gate of Heavenly Purity into 'a new world of space and time . . . old before the foundation of Rome', where the date was still calculated in terms of the years of Pu Yi's 'reign', and where all court events, from royal audiences to the change from winter to summer hats for the palace guard and court officials, was recorded in a daily court circular restricted to a privileged few, and penned by a court calligraphist.

That Johnston constantly had British interests at heart in his talks with Pu Yi is certain. With some naivety, he admits as much in *Twilight*. Nor is there any doubt that Johnston served Britain well, maintaining close relations with the British Legation in Peking at all times.

This has given rise to the legend of Johnston as 'secret agent', one of those empire-building adventurers in remote places in the John Buchan mould. It is an enticing notion, but almost certainly a false one, for there was nothing secret about Johnston: everything he learned, everything he saw, he immediately, and somewhat boastingly, communicated to his friends in the British Legation – including his first impressions of Pu Yi.

Everyone inside the Forbidden City was aware of this: tutors, courtiers – and later Pu Yi himself – used Johnston as a conduit to relay information back to the British government. In turn, Johnston loyally and on the whole accurately briefed the court on what he thought the British government had in mind for China. Johnston's 'old boy' relationship with British diplomats on the one hand and Pu Yi and his following on the other was a privileged one, but it never determined or even influenced British policy. Indeed, to many Peking diplomats, Johnston was too steeped in Confucian learning, too 'Chinese' to be completely reliable. As Daniele Varè, writer and diplomat in Peking at this time, put it in his book *Laughing Diplomat*, the Peking-based diplomatic corps 'lived a life of complete detachment from that of the Chinese, in a kind of mountain-fastness'.

Twilight in the Forbidden City is a remarkable document, but, again like Pu Yi's own autobiography, it is almost as fascinating for its omissions as for its revelations.

In his account of daily life at the court of Pu Yi, there are almost no references to the adolescent Emperor's tantrums or mood swings, his indifferent scholarship, or to the savage beatings he inflicted on eunuchs. There is nothing, either, about Pu Yi's private life. In his effort to show Pu Yi in the best possible light, Johnston even allows the boy Emperor to take credit for initiatives Johnston himself proposed. It was Johnston, for example, who suggested to Pu Yi, at the time of his marriage, that he throw a party for foreign guests to introduce his bride – or, rather, brides. Johnston, with his customary discretion, describes the event as though the idea had been Pu Yi's own.

Johnston is also completely silent on the subject of Pu Yi's sexuality. Like most conventional Britons of the time, he regarded the whole topic as taboo. In *Twilight* there are a few references to Pu Yi's bride, 'Elizabeth', whom he both knew and liked, but no hint that the relationship between them was anything other than ideal.

Immediately after his first meeting with Pu Yi, Johnston sat down and, in his ponderous, Thackerayan prose, dashed off a 'memorandum' to the 'British authorities' – presumably the British Minister in Peking, Sir John Jones:

The young emperor has no knowledge whatever of English or any other European language, but seems anxious to learn and is mentally active. He is allowed to read the Chinese newspapers, and evidently takes an intelligent interest in the news of the day, especially in politics, both domestic and foreign. He has a good knowledge of geography, and is interested in travel and exploration. He understands something of the present state of Europe and the results of the Great War, and seems to be free from false or exaggerated notions about the political position and relative importance of China.

He appears to be physically robust and well-developed for his age.

He is a very 'human' boy, with vivacity, intelligence and a keen sense of humour. Moreover, he has excellent manners and is entirely free from arrogance. . . He has no chance of associating with other boys except on the rare occasions when his younger brother and two or three other youthful members of the imperial clan are allowed to pay him short visits. . . Even his daily visits to the schoolroom are made the occasion of a kind of state procession. He is carried there in a large chair draped in imperial yellow, and is accompanied by a large retinue of attendants.

Johnson added that 'although he does not appear to have been spoilt, as yet, by the follies and futilities of his surroundings', there was 'little hope that he will come through unscathed' unless he was quickly withdrawn from the 'hordes of eunuchs and other useless functionaries who are now almost his only associates'.

Johnston felt that Pu Yi would benefit from an immediate transfer to the 'less debilitating' Summer Palace, where he would 'live a much less artificial and much happier life', with 'ample space for physical exercise' – without eunuchs.

Though he failed to mention it in his report, the first thing that happened to Johnston after his formal introduction to Pu Yi was that the court eunuchs crowded round him, congratulating him on his new appointment – and demanding money on this auspicious occasion. Johnston, like the canny Scot he was, promptly asked them for a receipt. They backed away, but he had made them his enemies for life.

Pu Yi's meeting with Johnston had a lifelong effect.

Before 3 March 1919, Pu Yi had seen foreigners only from afar, at a reception staged by Dowager Empress Jung-shu. He wrote that 'their strange clothes and their hair and eyes of so many colours were both ugly and frightening'. He had seen pictures of foreigners in smuggled illustrated magazines. 'They wore moustaches on their upper lips; there was always a straight line down the legs of their trousers; they invariably carried sticks.' Pu Yi's eunuchs had filled him with comic misconceptions about the 'foreign devils'! their moustaches were so stiff that lanterns could be hung on them. Their legs did not bend. They used their sticks to hit people.

Pu Yi recalled that Johnston's piercing blue eyes and grey hair 'made me feel uneasy. . . I found him very intimidating and studied English with him like a good boy, not daring to talk about other things when I got bored. . . as I did with my other Chinese tutors'. Very soon, Pu Yi's other tutors were asking Johnston to use his influence with the Emperor to get things done which they on their own could not persuade Pu Yi to do.

Johnston initiated a series of informal 'current affairs' sessions, either alone with Pu Yi or with just one other boy in attandance. When Johnston started teaching Pu Yi English, he found a much-thumbed copy of *Alice in Wonderland* in the schoolroom – but neither Pu Yi nor any of the other boys in the royal schoolroom (Johnston erred in his initial report when he stated that Pu Yi had no school companions) could understand a word of it. Johnston taught Pu Yi the rudiments of world history (including British history) and used British newspapers and magazines to illustrate his language sessions. Among them were articles about the First World War, and Johnston rightly believed Pu Yi would be fascinated by pictures of tanks, guns and trenches. As Pu Yi shrewdly noted, 'teaching me English was not so important in Johnston's eyes as training me to be like the English gentlemen he was always talking about'.

At this time Pu Yi had never left the Forbidden City, except for a rare state visit to the Summer Palace. He had never wandered the streets of Peking, shopped or seen ordinary street traffic. Nor had he expressed much desire to do so. According to his younger brother Pu Chieh, 'he felt that, as Emperor, the kind of ceremonial routine laid down for him was inevitable, and pre-ordained. He was strangely resigned to it, at least at thirteen.'

For Pu Yi lived vicariously, through his eunuchs. Whenever he wanted something, they procured it for him – at a price. At fourteen Pu Yi decided he would become, at least outwardly, the little English gentleman Johnston so clearly wanted him to be. He sent his eunuchs out to buy him 'large quantities of Western clothing'. 'When I went to the schoolroom, Johnston quivered with anger and told me to go back and take them off at once.' The clothes, bought from a theatrical costumier in Peking, had been loud, ill-fitting, grotesque. The next day Johnston came to the palace with one of Peking's best-known Western tailors. 'If you wear clothes from a second-hand shop you won't be a gentleman, you'll be. . .' He spluttered, and words failed him, Pu Yi noted.

Johnston also instructed Pu Yi in table manners – how to drink tea Western-fashion (the Chinese drink it noisily, to show their appreciation, just as the Chinese postprandial belch is a tribute to one's host's excellent food), how to nibble delicately at biscuits, how to use a knife and fork, how to make small talk. From his own account of those first few years with Johnston, it is clear Pu Yi went through a childish, but understandable, pro-Western phase. He ordered Western clothes in large quantities, also rings, tiepins, cuff links, neckties. He instructed his eunuchs to buy him European-style furniture. He even took to calling himself Henry (Henry VIII seemed to him a good example of rumbustious kingship). Pu Chieh became William. Later, he called his bride Elizabeth. He even started speaking a mixture of English and Chinese in his everyday conversation, a kind of Chinglish, though his progress in the English language was, at best, slow.

In his quiet, reserved way, Pu Yi started hero-worshipping Johnston. 'I thought everything about him was first-rate,' he wrote. 'He made me feel that Westerners were the most intelligent and civilized people in the world and that he was the most learned of Westerners.' By the time his formal studies ended – with marriage – 'Johnston,' he wrote, 'had become the major part of my soul.'

It was because Johnston disapproved of queues that Pu Yi decided to cut his off – a gesture as sacriligious as a Brahmin severing his sacred thread. It is proof of Johnston's extraordinary prestige and usefulness to the court that he was not fired for encouraging Pu Yi to do this. The Dowager Consorts screeched their shame and displeasure, and so terrified were the eunuchs that none would perform the operation for him – Pu Yi had to do it himself. The pigtail was more than a political symbol – it was the one Manchu custom that had acquired quasi-religious significance, and traditionalists saw the passing of the queue as putting paid to any chance of survival of the Manchu dynasty. They had lobbied in favour of its retention for years – not least by arguing that the pigtail was a badge of Manchu office, a useful way of determining who should be allowed in and out of the Forbidden City. After Pu Yi's bold act, thousands of courtiers followed suit. Only Pu Yi's Chinese tutors and a few of the most conservative court officials clung to theirs.

Younger brother Pu Chieh was one of the members of his entourage who was torn between a longing to emulate Pu Yi and fear of his family's wrath if he did so. Three-quarters of a century later, sitting in his tiny living room, a shrivelled yet imposing figure with a strong hand-grip and a surprisingly youthful voice, Pu Chieh described to me how he had rushed home after class and told his grandmother he wanted it off. 'She said: "I don't suppose there's anything I can do, now the Emperor has cut his off." But she was very upset and from that day onwards she made me wear a hat inside the house. "You're never to take it off in my presence," she said. And I never did.'

Johnston was responsible for several other dramatic changes in Pu Yi's adolescent lifestyle. Shocked by the way he was carried everywhere in sedan chairs and palanquins, he encouraged him to walk, and introduced the first bicycle to the Forbidden City. Pu Yi was so delighted by this new mode of transport he ordered all the gate and door flanges levelled so he could cross them without dismounting. Pu Yi bought bicycles for Pu Chieh, and for some of the more athletic eunuchs. Giggling eunuchs on bicycles did considerable damage to Forbidden City flowerbeds and rose gardens as they teetered uncontrollably all over the place, for the royal brothers had to have attendants, wherever they were, and as many as ten eunuchs careened along behind Pu Yi and Pu Chieh, trying to keep up with them, and usually falling off.

Another revolution encouraged by Johnston was the installation of telephones inside the Forbidden City. In 1919 Prince Chun, Pu Yi's father, had just had one installed in his home, the Northern Mansion where Pu Chieh lived, and Pu Chieh told Pu Yi about this magic toy. Pu Yi ordered one installed. His imperial household staff was horrified. 'There is no precedent for such foreign contraptions in the ancestral code,' his courtiers argued. Pu Yi said the Forbidden City was already full of 'foreign contraptions' – pianos, electric light, chiming clocks. What was wrong with a telephone? The imperial tutors fell back on another line of argument. 'If outsiders can make phone calls will they not offend the Celestial Countenance?'

Their real fear, of course, was that a telephone would be Pu Yi's lifeline to the outside world, that he would escape their control. Prince Chun, whose sole concern was for the continued payment, by the Republic, of the privy purse, sided with the anti-phone lobby, but finally he gave in, reluctantly.

As soon as the telephone was installed, Pu Yi, 'in a high state of excitement', started making his first calls. ' I rang up a Peking opera actor and an acrobat and hung up before saying who I was. I called up a restaurant and ordered a meal to be sent round to a false address.' Even after the novelty had worn off, Pu Yi became an inveterate phone user, carrying on interminable conversations with Johnston.

Emboldened by his phone victory, Pu Yi decided the Forbidden City should have its own fleet of cars, and these were used for the first time when he went to pay his respects to his dead mother in her home in North Peking on 30 September 1921. It was his first outing – barring a trip or two to the Summer Palace – and the main Imperial City gate was thrown open for the royal cortège – another sign, courtiers noted, that the Articles of Favourable Treatment were being observed to the letter. For months, Pu Yi had been pestering his tutors, and his court, for permission to take a drive through Peking's streets. Johnston was all for it, but the answer had been an unequivocal no, on security grounds. Now troops and police lined the streets, packed with bystanders who showed immense curiosity, but no hostility, towards their ex-Emperor.

Privately, court officials told Johnston the sheer cost of allowing Pu Yi out on Peking's streets was prohibitive: the army and police had to be bribed to turn out, 'largesse on a fantastic scale' had to be distributed. Johnston suggested he and Pu Yi should simply walk the streets incognito. 'The suggestion,' says Johnston, 'was regarded as unworthy of serious discussion.'

Pu Yi did get his way once or twice – driving out in a palace car to visit one of his sick tutors – but again in a highly visible, unnecessary cortège which included uniformed police and army officers to see he drove straight there and back, without stopping off on the way to meet with diplomats in the 'Tartar City' – the Legation Quarter.

Perhaps the most absurd battle Johnston had to fight on his student Emperor's behalf was the struggle for the royal glasses. It had become clear to Johnston that Pu Yi was short-sighted, and that this explained his frequent headaches, bouts of irritation and spells of inattention. The Emperor needed spectacles, badly.

Out of the question, said the Dowager Consorts. The Emperor's eyes were far too precious to be entrusted to foreign doctors, and, besides, 'the wearing of spectacles by emperors is just not done'. Even Pu Yi's father, Prince Chun, felt the dignity of the Emperor's office would be seriously impaired by such a step. Johnston had to put his job on the line. In the last resort, Pu Yi put his foot down and demanded glasses – but Dowager Consort Tuan Kang was not told until Pu Yi had actually started wearing them: a frightened court official told Johnston that, had she known in advance, she might well have committed suicide.

Johnston also did his best to stimulate his pupil's intellectual curiosity by staging various 'bridge parties' (as E. M. Forster called them) with leading Chinese writers and poets, but this was only a partial success: accepting an invitation to the Forbidden City was regarded as a political act, and an automatic endorsement of the pro-monarchy establishment.

Last but not least, Pu Yi discovered the movies: the Chinese government itself, as a wedding gift, installed a projection room for him inside the Forbidden City and soon there were weekly screenings – again to the scandal of diehard court officials and Dowager Consorts. To be singled out for an evening's cinema entertainment was almost as sought after as a princely title – or being given the right to ride through the Forbidden City on horseback.

But for all the progress of his royal pupil, and his new freedom, Johnston was not entirely satisfied. Pu Yi, he wrote, had a 'frivolous' side. 'At first I ascribed this to youthful irresponsibility [but] there were times when I seemed to detect signs in his nature of something like a permanent cleavage, almost suggesting the existence within him of two warring personalities.' Pu Chieh recalls his mood swings: 'When he was in a good mood, everything was fine, and he was a charming companion. If something upset him, his dark side would emerge.'

It may have been a family trait; more probably it was the inevitable consequence of being waited on, hand and foot, by cringing, fawning courtiers.

'He was now terribly bored,' Pu Chieh recalled, many

years later, 'and felt trapped.' Pu Yi wanted out, and telephones, cars, Western clothes and magazines were becoming unsatisfactory surrogates.

With Pu Chieh's connivance, Pu Yi started making plans to escape from his gilded prison. Sensing their livelihood at risk, the elderly Dowager Consorts, normally at such loggerheads with one another that they were scarcely on speaking terms, conspired together to reduce Johnston's growing influence, and keep Pu Yi in their power, for ever doomed to live the life of a puppet emperor in a make-believe but highly remunerative court.

They decided to get him married as soon as possible.

CHAPTER EIGHT

Pu Yi's autobiography paints an appalling, and probably accurate, picture of the state of his court in his adolescent years but says almost nothing about his private, emotional life.

The reason is, of course, that his book had a very definite aim – to contrast the 'bad old days' with Mao's 'new society'. To underline this, Pu Yi emphasized those character traits which he knew would excuse him in his readers' eyes – and also amuse them, portraying himself as an immature, childish, spoilt buffoon. He may not have blackened himself unduly, but he certainly failed to mention what Johnston was at pains to reveal – that he took an intelligent interest in China's almost permanent state of crisis during those adolescent years and that he quickly became an astute and sophisticated, albeit passive, witness to the near-collapse of China during this period.

Pu Yi never became as fluent in English as Johnston had hoped, but he was an avid reader of newspapers – both English and Chinese. Because of the importance of China's British concessions, there was a flourishing

English-language press. Chinese papers represented all varieties of opinion, from arrant conservatism to extreme revolutionary views. Outside the capital, many local correspondents of the foreign-language newspapers were missionaries, and many of these were pro-republican. Johnston often complained to Pu Yi that he spent far too much time reading the papers. But from Johnston's own memoirs, it is clear that the Scottish Confucian moralist and the adolescent Emperor spent hours talking politics, about which Pu Yi knew far more than he infers in his book.

Pu Yi was thirteen at the time of the '4 May Movement' – the huge student rally that took place in 1919 on Tien An Men square, close to the Forbidden City, to protest the Versailles Treaty decision which gave Germany's Tiengtsao Concession over to Japan as its reward for entering the First World War on the side of the Allies.

It was an immoral, unjust and arrogant decision, which understandably alienated China from the West for many years. The 4 May Movement was to become the mythic basis for all subsequent 'revolutionary' movements. When the time came for Bertolucci to film 4 May students in action outside the Forbidden City during the making of *The Last Emperor*, there was no lack of volunteers: in present-day China's history curriculum, the 4 May Movement is seen as the precursor of them all.

There are only two brief references in Pu Yi's book to 4 May, and he claims he learned about it from talking to Johnston (though he can hardly have failed to hear the students' clamour from within the Forbidden City walls). According to Johnston, both the 4 May and other revolutionary movements 'were followed by the Emperor with the closest interest'. But what interested both men far more than the aftermath of the 4 May Movement were the continuing rumours of restoration coups and endless newspaper debate about their chances of success.

Even after his ignominious 1917 failure, the 'pig-tailed general', Chang-hsun, continued his plotting, along with the famous Manchu warlord Chang Tso-lin, the peasant boy who had become an all-powerful warlord, virtually in control of both Manchuria and Mongolia. In his book, Johnston quotes extensively from English-language editorials from 1919 to 1924, which Pu Yi read with considerable attention, and while Johnston's selection is arbitrary it is clear that the eventuality of a restoration was both openly debated and even regarded as probable. Johnston quotes the *Peking and Tientsin Times* of 19 March 1921 as saying that 'it is probably a moderate estimate to suggest that ninety per cent of the population would favour the return of the Emperor'. ('I believe this was no exaggeration,' Johnston characteristically added.) To give such a claim substance, he also quoted from a republican paper, *Shu Kuang*, also in 1921, deploring that in the countryside 'the illiterate . . . obtuse [population] have no conception whatever of the meaning of liberty, political rights and government . . . One comes across people who ask questions like: "How is the Emperor? Who is now ruling in the Imperial Palace?" '

'No monarchist plans were discussed in the palace, and the Emperor himself was not a party to any of the plots,' Johnston claimed. 'The subject was scrupulously avoided by his Chinese tutors and by myself, as we were all anxious that he should not be personally involved in anything that might be interpreted as a conspiracy against the Republic.'

But Johnston was quite prepared to answer any of Pu Yi's questions about his chances of restoration and Pu Yi, Johnston inferred, asked often enough. When he did, 'I did not hesitate to express my own opinion with all the force with which I was capable,' which was that 'any conspiracy of the 1917 type should be scrupulously avoided . . . and that the Emperor should refuse to listen to any invitation to resume the throne unless it came to him in the form of a genuine and spontaneous appeal from the freely elected representatives of the people.' Johnston added that he felt such an eventuality, given Chinese circumstances, was 'very remote', even if – were such a free vote to occur – it was his opinion that 'the majority in favour of monarchy would be enormous'.

The inference was that Pu Yi was doomed to remain a virtual prisoner inside the Forbidden City until such time as the Republic collapsed of its own accord. Even if this occurred, there was no certainty of restoration – for there was a plurality of rival restoration movements, all at each other's throats, and by no means all of Pu Yi's aristocratic relatives were in favour of having him back on the throne. In other words, Pu Yi's prospects were grim, for all the luxury he wallowed in. And even the extravagances had begun to pall: the Republic had begun reneging on its privy purse grants. The royal family was running up huge bills, and the incompetent ex-Regent Chun, Pu Yi's father, had begun selling off palace treasures in ever-increasing quantities to keep the court in the state to which it was accustomed.

Such was the climate inside the Forbidden City when the Dowager Consorts started looking for a wife for Pu Yi. Needless to say, he was not consulted. There were many shrill disputes before their choice was narrowed down to four – and early in 1922 Pu Yi was handed four photographs and asked to choose.

As Pu Yi pathetically put it:

> To me the girls seemed much the same and their bodies looked as shapeless as tubes in the dresses. Their faces were very small in the pictures and I couldn't see whether they were beauties or not . . . It did not occur to me at the time that this was one of the great events of my life, and I had no standards to guide me. I casually drew a circle on a pretty picture.

The girl he selected was Wen Hsiu. She was thirteen years old, flat-faced, stocky and a member of an aristocratic but impoverished Manchu family. She had been included, one suspects, to 'pad' the list. Pu Yi's choice led to consternation among the Dowagers.

He could have Wen Hsiu as a 'secondary consort' (i.e. a concubine), the Dowagers determined. But Wen Hsiu was quite unsuitable to be an empress, and he was told to try again.

Showing less determination than over the issues of bicycles, telephones and spectacles, Pu Yi obediently did as he was told. This time he picked out Wan Jung (Beautiful Countenance), sixteen, a member of one of Manchuria's most prominent, richest families, currently based in Tientsin, where she had been educated at an American missionary school. The Dowagers beamed. They then tried to persuade Pu Yi to pick out further 'secondary consorts' (traditionally an emperor had four concubines, at least), but Pu Yi put his foot down, and the Dowagers demurred.

Wan Jung's picture makes her out to be an opulent, sensual beauty, an Oriental Claudia Cardinale, full-lipped, tall, with huge eyes and a melancholy expression. She was highly educated (like Pu Yi, she had an English-language tutor) and used to having things her own way.

Pu Yi, as was the imperial custom, was not to set eyes on her until his wedding day, which climaxed in a series of complicated processions and rituals which Johnston spells out in his book with considerable relish – and at interminable length. First the betrothal announcement appeared on 15 March 1922 in Johnston's beloved *Court Gazette*. On 17 March Beautiful Countenance was brought to Peking by special train, where she was ceremonially greeted by court dignitaries, republican officials and an army guard of honour, and taken to a special house, the Mansion of the Empress (outside the Forbidden City) to be 'trained in court etiquette'. On 6 April Pu Yi – again with an escort of courtiers – went to his ancestors' shrine to inform them of his impending marriage.

And on 4 June, without anyone other than his brother Pu Chieh and Johnston being aware of it, Pu Yi desperately tried to extricate himself from the whole business and flee the country.

What happened was that Pu Yi had taken seriously Johnston's idle talk of his, one day, studying at Oxford. Pu Chieh remembers this time well. 'Pu Yi constantly talked about going to England, and becoming an Oxford student, like Johnston,' he told me. 'This went on for months. We didn't want anyone to know, certainly not father. Whenever we could, we would steal something of value lying around the palaces – a painting, or porcelain antique, anything that I could carry without being seen. I had friends who could get a good price for such things, and little by little we accumulated a nest-egg, and these same friends stored away the money in Tientsin.'

Did this mean, I asked, that Pu Yi did not want to go through with the wedding?

'Pu Yi's decision had nothing to do with the impending marriage,' Pu Chieh said. 'He felt cooped up, and wanted out.'

Pu Yi clearly hoped that Johnston, who had waxed so eloquent about Oxford, would encourage his plan. But when the crucial moment came, he backed down. Johnston himself recorded the whole incident in detail, revealing not only Pu Yi's desperation but the British government's highly ambiguous attitude at the time towards the unfortunate ex-Emperor.

As Johnston tells it, he received a confidential note from Pu Yi to be at the Palace at 3 p.m. on 3 June 1922, with two cars. Johnston hired a car, with driver, from a garage and, driving his own car, led the small convoy inside the Forbidden City. Once inside, Pu Yi called him into his office, made sure no eunuchs were listening, and outlined his plan. Johnston was to drive him, his luggage and a personal servant to the British Legation that afternoon. Once in the safety of the Legation, he intended to draft an open letter to 'the people of China', renouncing his imperial title, his privy purse and all his other privileges. Immediately afterwards, he intended to leave China – and hoped that Oxford University would accept him as an undergraduate.

Johnston, taken aback, gave Pu Yi three reasons why he should do no such thing – none of them convincing. The first was that the new pro-monarchist President of China, Hsu Shi-chang, had resigned the day before, and public opinion – and the press – would infer that 'they had been engaged in political intrigue together'. The second was that, by giving up his subsidies, he would leave himself open to the charge that they were about to be taken away from him anyway (which was not the case) and that he would be accused of trying to 'save face' by 'giving up voluntarily what would in any case be taken away from him by force'.

The third reason was, quite simply, that Johnston said he doubted whether Pu Yi would be welcome, even temporarily, inside the British Legation.

'But you promised!' the distraught Pu Yi said.

Johnston had a reply ready for that one too. The British Legation had indeed, through Johnston, told Pu Yi that if his life were in danger, he would be welcome. But 'no actual danger threatened the Emperor's person'. Moreover, said Johnston, China was currently without either President or parliament – so who would have the power to acknowledge his renunciation?

Reluctantly, almost tearfully, Pu Yi dismissed Johnston, unpacked his bags – and told his brother that the scheme had failed, that the British, in the last resort, had let him down.

In his report on the affair, Johnston claimed that Pu Yi had been motivated by 'growing disgust with the corruption which he knows is rife throughout the palace'. Pu Chieh knew otherwise; as he told me, Pu Yi had desperately wanted to break out of his palace to try and start living a normal life.

Johnston's motivations, in turning Pu Yi down, were of course far less high-minded than he made them out to be. The main reason why he flatly refused to take Pu Yi back to the British Legation was that the British government, not for the first time in its inglorious diplomatic history, 'didn't want to get involved'. Johnston admitted as much to Pu Yi, arguing that his taking refuge inside the British Legation 'might easily be construed, however unjustly' as 'unwarrantable interference in China's internal concerns'. As Johnston himself commented later, had the

British Minister agreed to play host to Pu Yi, 'all his subsequent activities would have been traced to British intrigue. I myself would unquestionably have become the victim of slander and denunciation.'

Such scruples were absurd: Peking's foreign legations at this time – and later – were rather like the inviolate havens in a child's game of 'touch'. Chinese presidents, warlords and cabinet ministers, when in desperate trouble, used the different legations as sanctuaries just as Latin American cabinet ministers, later, were to use each other's embassies after *putsches* against them. Britain, at the time, was one of the major powers in Asia, if not the major power, and could well have weathered any of the crises outlined by Johnston, had they arisen.

One of his subsidiary arguments had been that the young Emperor should put his financial house in order before taking such a desperate, final step. But the uncharitable inference drawn is that Johnston's negative reflex was motivated by other, far less high-minded considerations: Johnston, one assumes, enjoyed his role as imperial tutor and high-ranking mandarin far too much to risk jeopardizing it. And some of his delight in ancient court ritual permeates his account of Pu Yi's wedding, which took place seven months later, and which Johnston wrote about exclusively for *Country Life* and the *Times*, 'no foreigner beside myself', he proudly noted, 'being present'.

The wedding itself was preceded by more court ritual, all of it determined by astrologers, and everything took place as though Pu Yi's pathetic attempt to escape from his stifling routine – and his arranged marriages – had never occurred.

On 21 October 'betrothal presents' were assembled and carried over to the princess: two saddled horses, eighteen sheep, forty pieces of satin and eighty rolls of cloth. The bizarre procession wended its way through Peking's streets escorted by palace guards, court musicians and a loaned detachment of Chinese republican cavalry.

This was a symbolic dowry in the Manchu tradition. Real gifts followed later: large quantities of gold and silver, precious porcelain, bolts of satin, more saddled horses. There were similar gifts for the bride-elect's parents and brothers. The bride's servants, Johnston noted, received £70 each.

On the wedding day itself – or rather wedding night, for according to Manchu tradition everything had to take place by moonlight – a huge procession, with palace guards, republican soldiers, and both Chinese and European-style brass bands, paraded through Peking once more, this time escorting the Empress-to-be from her temporary home to the Forbidden City itself. The princess travelled in a specially prepared ceremonial sedan chair, called the 'Phoenix Chair' (the mythical animal symbolizing happiness and good fortune), decorated with silver birds, and held high by twenty-two servants.

At the gates of the Forbidden City, the procession halted, the Phoenix Chair carriers were replaced by eunuchs, and the princess – alone – was carried into the Forbidden City and into her new life. Court musicians, using rare musical instruments only brought out on special occasions, intoned their weird melodies. Inside the Palace of Earthly Peace, all princes, relatives (the bride's parents and brothers had been elevated to princely rank or to dukedoms in the phantom court order) and principal courtiers kowtowed interminably before Pu Yi, perched on his Dragon Throne. Then, in the Empress's new residence, she herself knelt and then bowed six times before the Emperor and his court as the imperial decree celebrating the marriage was read out.

Shortly afterwards, around 4 a.m., a similar, slightly less elaborate ceremony took place to welcome Secondary Consort Wen Hsiu. Two days later, a huge, formal reception took place in the Palace of Cloudless Heaven attended by republican cabinet ministers and high officials, and that same evening Pu Yi and his bride hosted a less official party for some two hundred prominent foreigners – a discreet Johnston initiative, this. Johnston proudly noted that he was one of four specially chosen Court officials called upon to announce the names of guests to the Emperor and his bride as they arrived.

A suitably coached Pu Yi made a short speech in English: 'It is a great pleasure to us to see here today so many distinguished visitors from all parts of the world. We thank you for coming and wish you all health and prosperity.' Bowing to the assembled guests, he toasted them in champagne. The foreigners burst into applause. On leaving the Forbidden City, all were handed a small remembrance gift – cloisonné ashtrays for the men, silver trinkets for the ladies.

Outwardly, Pu Yi went through these ceremonies with suitable aplomb. He was seventeen, by his own account totally inexperienced sexually, and nothing in his previous years had prepared him for marriage, or female companionship of any kind. Suddenly he found himself saddled with two wives. As he describes it, 'I [had] hardly thought about marriage and family. It was only when the Empress came into my field of vision with a crimson satin cloth embroidered with a dragon and a phoenix over her head that I felt at all curious about what she looked like.'

The wedding night, or what was left of it after the arrival of the Secondary Consort, was spent, according to Manchu dynasty tradition, in the bridal chamber of the Palace of Earthly Tranquillity. It was, Pu Yi recalled, 'a rather peculiar room – unfurnished except for the bed-platform that filled a quarter of it, and everything about it except the floor was red'. The bed itself, the 'Dragon-Phoenix couch', was a huge fourposter with red and gold curtains, also embroidered with dragons and phoenixes. From its photograph, it looks rather like the bed in the famous 'Chinese room' in the One Two Two, the celebrated pre-war bordello much patronized by Edward VII on his visits to Paris.

'When we had drunk the nuptial cup and eaten "sons and grandsons" cakes,' wrote Pu Yi, 'I felt stifled. The bride sat on the bed, her head bent down. I looked around me and saw everything was red: red bed-curtains, red pillows, a red dress, a red skirt, red flowers, and a red face . . . it all looked like a melted wax candle. I did not know whether to stand or sit, decided that I preferred the Hall of Mental Cultivation [his boyhood quarters], and went back there.

'How did Wan Jung feel, abandoned in the bridal chamber? What was Wen Hsiu, not yet fourteen, thinking? These questions never even occurred to me.' Pu Yi would have us believe that, at this very moment, his thoughts revolved exclusively around his future as Emperor. 'I thought: if there had been no revolution I would now be starting to rule with full powers. I must recover my ancestral heritage.'

This is at total variance with the sentiments he had expressed during his harrowing encounter with Johnston a mere seven months previously.

What is far more likely, that traumatic dawn, is that he was obsessed by shameful proof of his sexual inadequacy. For he knew that his premature flight from the Palace of Earthly Peace would be reported by the omnipresent, malicious, gossipy eunuchs – and that such behaviour, in Chinese folklore terms, was both risible and profoundly humiliating.

It was perhaps too much to expect an adolescent, permanently surrounded by eunuchs, to show the sexual maturity of a normal seventeen-year-old. Neither the Dowager consorts nor Johnston himself had given him any advice on sexual matters – this sort of thing simply was not done, where emperors were concerned; it would have been an appalling breach of protocol. But the fact remains that even a totally inexperienced, over-sheltered adolescent, if normal, could hardly have failed to be aroused by Wan Jung's unusual, sensual beauty. The inference is, of course, that Pu Yi was either impotent, extraordinarily immature sexually, or already aware of his homosexual tendencies.

The taboos surrounding homosexuality in China today are so strong that try as I might, in conversation with Pu Yi's surviving relatives, I found no way of getting them to discuss this, except in the vaguest, most allusive terms.

The nearest I came to it was when Pu Chieh told me – in response to the deliberately innocent question: 'Why did Pu Yi never have any children?' – that, many years later, 'the ex-Emperor was found to be biologically incapable of reproduction'.

Pu Yi's description of his wedding night is practically the only reference in his book to his relationship with Beautiful Countenance (or Elizabeth, as he soon started calling her). About Wen Hsiu, his Secondary Consort, there is nothing at all. Pu Chieh remembers the three of them – the two brothers and Pu Yi's bride – laughing, cycling around the palace grounds, 'playing games like children'.

Wan Jung was no uneducated doll-like creature. Her parents, in sophisticated, Western-oriented Tientsin, had brought her up as a relatively 'modern' girl. She could read and write English fluently. She was fond of jazz, and could even two-step. Rong Qi, her younger brother, remembers her as a 'high-spirited, independent-minded, headstrong girl, a typical princess'.

Rong Qi was only ten at the time of the wedding, but he too remembers Pu Yi and Wan Jung, shortly after their marriage, racing their bicycles through the alleys of the Forbidden City, scattering eunuchs, cornering each other, indulging in mock fights like children. 'There was a lot of laughter, she and Pu Yi seemed to get on well, they were like kids together.'

The light-hearted companionship did not last. A few months after the wedding, Wan Jung was spending more and more time alone, in her own quarters, increasingly moody and bored.

San Tao, one of her young eunuchs, today a crotchety 85-year-old and one of the two surviving eunuchs of this era, is reluctant to talk about those days. A nut-brown, wizened old man with crew-cut white hair, a querulous – but not markedly high-pitched – voice and a permanent sense of grievance at his ruined life (later he became a small-time antique dealer, smuggler and petty criminal and now lives in an old people's home), he behaves like someone entrusted with secrets far too important to be imparted to strangers. When San Tao was taken on as a young eunuch in the Empress's household, he was twenty-one, and in mortal fear of Pu Yi, who once, in jest, pursued him through his bride's palace with a revolver. Pu Yi was only re-enacting a scene in a Western but San Tao, unaware of this, believed that Pu Yi, for no reason that he could think of, wanted to kill him.

After much beating about the bush, deliberately avoiding the subject and rambling on about palace events that had no bearing on the questions put to him, he slyly acknowledged the unusual relationship between Pu Yi and his bride. 'The Emperor,' he said, 'would come over to the nuptial apartments about once every three months, and spend the night there.' And then? More rambling, more reminiscences about his later life. Very interesting, but how did the Emperor feel?

'He would leave early in the morning on the following day,' San Tao said, 'and for the rest of that day he would invariably be in a very filthy temper indeed.'

CHAPTER NINE

One of 'Old Buddha's' less endearing characteristics had been her habit of sending those she wished to ruin hugely expensive, useless presents. The recipients, according to custom, were compelled to return the compliment even more lavishly, or risk losing face to an unacceptable, fatal degree.

Pu Yi's court never indulged in such tactics: Prince Chun, the ex-Emperor's venal, weak Regent father, would probably have found the idea attractive enough, but by the time he was in charge of the royal finances it was no longer feasible: to keep the House of Ching afloat, despite its annual subsidy from the Republic of 4·5 million Chinese dollars (about £750,000 in current values), the imperial court was compelled to mortgage or sell off, piecemeal, some of the inestimable treasures accumulated over the centuries by the Ming and Ching dynasties.

As Pu Yi grew into manhood, his financial situation went from bad to worse. In theory, he was one of China's richest men. In practice the imperial finances were like a huge block of ice melting under the hot sun: there seemed no way of stemming the melting process.

Pu Yi's wedding had been immensely costly, and the presents he had received – some of them in cash – certainly did not match the expenditure. Many gifts were in the form of statues, porcelain, jade or ancient manuscripts, valuable, certainly, but not readily marketable, and some had symbolic value only. Pu Yi's bride came from a wealthy family, with extensive property holdings in Tientsin, but Pu Yi, with two wives to maintain, found that the running costs of two new households were heavy.

What really caused the privy purse to melt, though, was neither Pu Yi's personal extravagance nor the sudden demands on him by the two women. The Imperial House-hold Bureau, which administered the Emperor's fortune and that of his relatives, was both corrupt and inefficient – and one of the worst culprits was none other than Regent Chun himself, who was well aware that the 'squeeze' on the royal family amounted to strangulation but was per-fectly amenable to letting the process continue – as long as he obtained his share of it. Reginald Johnston's portrait of him is devastating:

> He is well-intentioned . . . tries in his languid and ineffectual way to please everyone, succeeds in pleas-ing no-one, shrinks from responsibility, is thoroughly unbusinesslike, is disastrously deficient in energy, will-power and grit, and there is reason to believe he lacks both physical and moral courage. He is helpless in an emergency, has no original ideas, and is liable to be swayed by any smooth talker.

A suitable rule of thumb, as far as Prince Chun was concerned, Johnston added, was to ask him which course to follow, and then take the one he advised against. Prince Chun had large amounts of Forbidden City artefacts sold off to pay the palace debts, but was so inept even in his corrupt practices that he was systematically robbed in the process.

The treasures of the Ching dynasty, at the time of Pu Yi's enthronement, were incalculable: in the years Pu Yi lived inside the Forbidden City, he was constantly coming across storerooms full of antiques, scrolls and gold ornaments. These treasures apart, Pu Yi had inherited vast amounts of antiques from the Ching palaces in Mukden and Jehol, some of which had been brought to the Forbidden City and forgotten; his family also owned estates, farmlands, family mansions in Peking, Tientsin and Manchuria. As Johnston discovered, no inventory of the imperial family's wealth had ever been made.

The thrifty Scot was scandalized and, as soon as he was on informal terms with his royal pupil, began urging him to take a closer interest in his belongings and inheritance. Like a loyal family accountant, he even went to the trouble of itemizing those portions of the Mukden and Jehol treasure troves which, in his opinion, belonged to the family and not to the Republic.

But he failed to attract Pu Yi's interest until too late: mathematics was a 'despised science' reserved for the inferior shopkeeper class. Money matters, Johnston noted, 'were beneath the notice of a scholar and a gentleman'. No princeling Johnston ever came across, save one, was able to operate an abacus, and while an abacus, as Johnston somewhat pedantically pointed out, could produce results with great accuracy and speed, it had 'the signal disadvantage of not being able to work backwards in search of a fault'. That was Pu Yi's problem, too: by the time he became aware the court was becoming bankrupt, it was too late to discover what faults had caused the Ching dynasty's ruin.

Johnston's simple explanation was that the system itself was at fault. In the old days, the Manchu princes had never had to bother about their finances. They had stewards to look after their interests, and even if the stewards were corrupt, or put their own families on the payroll, there was so much money available, and the cost of living for nobles was so cheap, that the princes never had to worry.

After the 1911 'revolution', the Manchus no longer

directly raised taxes. This became the prerogative of the republicans, which, in some parts of China at least, meant the warlords who had carved out autonomous fiefdoms of their own. The Ching dynasty had to make do with its privy purse. Its annual subsidy from the Republic of £750,000 was an astronomical sum, but the stewards of the Imperial Household Bureau who ran the Manchus' finances for them were both incompetent and corrupt, and had become adept at 'creative accounting'.

Johnston saw an early example of this when Pu Yi donated £8,000 for the repair of Legation Street in Peking. By the time the Imperial Household Bureau and their business accomplices had taken their cuts, the amount available for its actual repair had been reduced to £80.

The Forbidden City's household expenses continued to be a crying scandal. It was common knowledge that some of the senior eunuchs lived in palatial splendour in Peking or Tientsin. Because the graft filtered all the way down to the humblest eunuchs, no one, least of all Pu Yi's Chinese tutors, would blow the gaff. And when the Republic, itself in a near-bankrupt state during all the years of Pu Yi's adolescence, started witholding some of his privy purse, the situation worsened dramatically – for pilfering represented only a small percentage of the enormous sums syphoned off by Pu Yi's court officials.

The big money was in the sale of antiques, gold ornaments and ancient scrolls sold off by officials (and Prince Chun himself) to meet current expenses. The treasures, Johnston wrote, 'were disposed of in a ruinously corrupt and wasteful manner', sold, with the connivance of palace officials, to an 'exclusive ring of dealers' with close family ties to the Imperial Household Bureau. 'The prices paid,' Johnston wrote, 'were far in excess of the amounts entered in the palace accounts, but far below the market value of the articles sold.' Ornaments and statues in solid gold were often sold off by weight. Hardly surprisingly, luxurious antique shops sprang up all over Peking, many of them owned by friends and relatives of the Imperial Household

Bureau staff, and by eunuchs. Pu Yi did not care, Johnston added. 'He had never been taught the value of money.'

The first major scandal to come to Pu Yi's attention occurred with the death of Chuang-ho, one of the Dowager Consorts, in 1921. No sooner had she breathed her last, Johnston wrote, 'than her staff of eunuchs proceeded to strip her palace of its jewellery and treasures'. This was not in itself a scandal, he noted – such practices were taken for granted – but 'the thieves struggled among themselves for the booty and caused an unseemly uproar in the death chamber'. No one was punished, he added. Had they been, it would have caused the old lady's soul to 'lose face'.

Robbery occurred inside the Forbidden City on such a scale that after his marriage even Pu Yi started becoming aware of what he described as this 'orgy of looting'. 'The techniques varied,' Pu Yi wrote. 'Some people forced locks and stole secretly, while others used legal methods and stole in broad daylight.' A diamond ring he had bought for £18,000 unaccountably disappeared; the pearls and jade in the Empress's ceremonial crown were stolen, and replaced by paste.

At Johnston's instigation, Pu Yi, in early June 1923, finally ordered an inventory in the Hall of Supreme Harmony where a huge cache of golden ornaments and antiques was stored. On the night of 26 June, a fire swept through this palace, and despite the speedy arrival on the scene of the Italian Legation's fire brigade, it was burnt to the ground – along with its priceless contents.

On the morning of 27 June, Johnston 'found the Emperor and Empress standing on a heap of charred wood, sadly contemplating the spectacle'. Some of the imperial household officials, he wrote, 'were fussily doing their best to instruct the well-disciplined Italian firemen in the art of how not to extinguish fires'. The area was crowded with foreigners, some still in evening clothes, who had heard about the fire during the night, and left their dinner parties to scour the debris for souvenirs.

The imperial household ghouls even managed to turn this calamity to their advantage: as Pu Yi noted, 'the gold merchants were invited by the Household Bureau to submit tenders and one of them bought the right to dispose of the ashes for £60,000.' The lost treasures included 2,685 gold statues of Buddha, 1,675 altar ornaments in solid gold, 435 priceless porcelain antiques, thousands of old manuscripts and 31 boxes containing sable furs and imperial robes. The inference, of course, was that many of these items had been sold off – and the thieves needed to cover their tracks. Though some eunuchs and palace servants were arrested, none was brought to justice. But the fire did at last galvanize Pu Yi into action that Johnston had been urging for years. Eighteen days after the fire, he expelled the eunuchs from the Forbidden City *manu militari*, without giving them time even to pack.

He resolved to do so, he wrote later, because he had belatedly realized the situation inside the Forbidden City had become completely out of hand. Eavesdropping on some whispering eunuchs outside his window, Pu Yi heard them discussing him, complaining 'my temper was getting worse' and concocting a story to the effect that Pu Yi himself had set fire to the Hall of Supreme Harmony. And when a eunuch, punished for some minor offence, threw lime into a servant's eyes and stabbed him, Pu Yi recalled how he had ordered eunuchs beaten for minor offences, 'and I wondered whether they might not make some such attack on me'. The culprit was at large somewhere in the palace grounds, and no one could – or would – turn him in.

Pu Yi made one of his rare trips to his old family home, the Northern Mansion, and told his father he had decided to expel the eunuchs without warning. Temporizing as usual, Prince Chun begged him either to reconsider the matter, or at least give them time to pack. Pu Yi said that if he did so, the eunuchs might well put the entire Forbidden City to the torch – they were completely out of control. 'Unless they are expelled immediately and without any prior warning,' Pu Yi told his father, 'I'll never return to the Forbidden City.' As a result, Johnston wrote later, Prince Chun 'was in a state bordering on hysteria'.

To get them out, Pu Yi enlisted the help of the republican army. A general with a hand-picked unit of crack troops entered the Forbidden City while all the eunuchs were being summoned to a mass meeting in its main yard. They were told to leave then and there, under the supervision of the army. Days later, disconsolate eunuchs were still encamped outside the Forbidden City walls, seeking readmission to collect their belongings and back pay. Though Johnston had nothing to do with Pu Yi's decision to expel the eunuchs, they believed he was responsible. He began receiving a flood of letters. Some eunuchs begged for his intercession. Others sent him death threats. China's press applauded the decision – as a sign of the ex-Emperor's growing maturity.

The Dowager Consorts were as surprised by the expulsion as the eunuchs themselves: suddenly, they found themselves almost servantless. They raged, wept and finally begged Pu Yi to let them have their eunuchs back. He finally gave in, and a select group – fifty in all – were allowed back into the Forbidden City.

Johnston turned the flat expanse that had once been the Hall of Supreme Harmony into a tennis court. Both Pu Yi and the Empress, he noted, took to the game with enthusiasm. The court was inaugurated with a foursome – Pu Yi and the Empress playing against Johnston and Rong Qi, the Empress's young brother. Johnston and Rong Qi won.

In 1986, Rong Qi recalled that when the tennis court area was not being used for tennis, the Emperor and Empress used it as a bicycle stadium, staging races and even cycle hockey matches. 'But after the eunuchs went,' he added, 'many of the palaces inside the Forbidden City were closed down, and the place took on a desolate, abandoned air.'

Pu Yi was gradually discovering the extent of the Imperial Household Bureau's criminal activities. Unaccountably, he noted, despite the eunuchs' departure and other household economies, the budget for the For-bidden City's annual expenses continued to spiral: in 1923 it was more than double what it had been under the spend-thrift, extravagant 'Old Buddha', Tzu-hsi. Pu Yi was now aware that his own father, and his new father-in-law Jung Kuan, also known as Prince Su, were both 'on the take', and that some of the Manchu princes in his entourage were conniving with the Household Bureau. His reaction, his relatives revealed years later, was to fly into violent rages – but his attention span was short.

There were some expenses that were incompressible, involving 'face'. Typical of these was Pu Yi's contribution to the 'disaster fund' set up after the 1923 Tokyo earth-quake, which had wiped out most of that city. Pu Yi, by this time chronically short of ready cash, gifted £33,000 worth of valuable antiques. The Japanese government, to prevent them from being dispersed, acquired them and housed them in a special museum.

The gift led to fulsome Japanese thanks – and an official Japanese delegation made the trip to Peking to thank Pu Yi personally. The Japanese politico-military establish-ment, by 1923, had already set its sights on Pu Yi as a possible pawn in a carefully prepared plan to extend its zone of influence in north-east China, though Pu Yi him-self was as yet unaware of the fact. Johnston, tempera-mentally pro-Japanese, was on excellent terms with the Japanese Legation in Peking. After Pu Yi had made over a small but luxurious villa inside the Forbidden City to Johnston to use as an office, Japanese diplomats were fre-quent visitors there and began meeting Pu Yi at Johnston's instigation.

Johnston, at this time, was no longer simply an ex-tutor: he had set himself up as Pu Yi's unofficial public relations adviser. The private luncheon parties in his villa were attended not only by the ex-Emperor and his bride, and certain selected Japanese, but also by distinguished foreign visitors of all sorts – British admirals, the Governor of Hong Kong, a few selected non-Japanese diplomats and visiting scholars known to be favourably disposed to Pu

Yi. Johnston wrote later that he was swamped by begging letters from prominent Chinese asking to meet the ex-Emperor informally, but he turned most of them over to the Imperial Household Bureau. He was, however, actively concerning himself with Pu Yi's immediate prospects. The ex-Emperor seemed to have forgotten his disappointment at Johnston's negative reaction to his plea for help shortly before his wedding; and with China in turmoil, and both monarchists and leftists increasingly encroaching on the shrinking authority of a discredited republican government, Johnston was aware that Pu Yi's future was, to say the least, precarious.

With Pu Yi's financial interests ostensibly in mind, he returned to the idea he had outlined to the British government immediately after his first meeting with his royal pupil, in 1919: Pu Yi, he told the ex-Emperor and all those advisers he thought he could trust, should immediately make plans to abandon the Forbidden City once and for all and move to the Summer Palace, ten miles' distant, where he would be both physically less at risk and be able to cut household expenses drastically. Inevitably, the imperial household officials fought a protracted rearguard action to prevent this from happening – aided, hardly surprisingly, by Prince Chun and Pu Yi's father-in-law Jung Kuan.

Johnston's advice was sound: the Articles of Favourable Treatment had never granted Pu Yi security of tenure in the Forbidden City. He was there 'temporarily'. Theoretically, the Republic could compel Pu Yi to vacate it at a moment's notice: his permanent abode, according to the Articles, had always been the Summer Palace, which Pu Yi himself had visited only once or twice, and which his Household Bureau had allowed to fall into disrepair. With growing left-wing sentiment in China, Johnston argued, it would only be a matter of time before the weak Republic would be compelled to ask him to move out.

The Household Bureau, of course, objected that the Summer Palace was far too small to accommodate Pu Yi and his staff in the manner to which they were accustomed. What the officials really meant, of course, was that they feared that if such a move took place, hundreds of redundant hangers-on battening on the imperial privy purse would be sacked – which was what Johnston had in mind.

Their other argument, carrying far more weight with Pu Yi, was that should such a move occur, most of the remaining treasures of the Forbidden City would have to be left behind – and would, inevitably, fall into the hands of the Republic.

Some of Pu Yi's closest Chinese advisers, including his former senior tutors, told Johnston privately that Pu Yi needed everything he could lay his hands on to make up a 'war chest' with which to begin a full-scale restoration campaign. They told Pu Yi (in a confidential report Johnston may not have seen) that 'the most important thing today is to plan a restoration. To carry out this great enterprise of changing the world there are many things to do. The first priority is to consolidate the base by protecting the court; the next most important task is to put the imperial property in order so as to secure our finances. For it is necessary to have the wherewithal to support and protect ourselves; only then can we plan a restoration.'

Johnston, always a careful man, did not want to be involved in any overt pro-restoration intrigue, but he did point out to the 'plotters' that it was better to work out a compromise with the republican authorities while there was still time, to determine what Pu Yi might keep and what rightly belonged to the Republic.

Pu Yi sided with Johnston. He made two appointments which filled his Household Bureau with apprehension: a non-Manchu official, Cheng Hsiao-hsu, known for his integrity, was given the impossible task of reforming the Household Bureau, and Johnston himself was made Commissioner in charge of the Summer Palace, to prepare it for Pu Yi's permanent occupation.

Johnston set about his task with Scottish practicality: his intention was to make the Summer Palace pay for itself, in the later manner of British 'stately homes', by opening part of it up to the public, selling not only entrance tickets but fish from the lake, and licensing hotels and shops. He found the place in better repair than he had expected, and endured one more example of the venality of the Household Bureau: contractors engaged by the Bureau submitted estimates so outrageously high that he turned to Peking contractors for sealed, competitive bids. Theirs were seven times lower than those of the firms 'recommended' by the palace officials.

But while Johnston was succeeding, the unfortunate 'reformer' Cheng Hsiao-hsu was meeting with almost complete failure: he did reduce the palace staff, eliminating hundreds of non-jobs held by officials' protégés. But the threatened Household Bureau, headed by Shao Ying, fought back, using the weapon of total, palace-wide non-cooperation. As Pu Yi wrote: 'If he [Cheng] wanted money, there was no money and accounts in black and white proved it. If he wanted some object nobody knew where it was stored.' Three months after taking on the imperial household vultures, Cheng resigned, allegedly for 'health reasons', in fact totally discouraged – not least by Pu Yi's own father's intrigues against him.

The reforms had come too late: within months of his attempt to sweep the Forbidden City clean, Pu Yi himself was out of it for good. It was an even more inglorious departure than the one he had envisioned (and Johnston had vetoed) shortly before his reluctant marriage to a glamorous but unwanted wife and an equally unwanted – and neglected – concubine.

CHAPTER TEN

The Grand Hotel des Wagons-lits in Peking's Legation Quarter was almost as fine an example of rococo architecture as the celebrated restaurant in Paris's Gare de Lyon. Its spacious, high-ceilinged rooms and immense, brass-tapped bathrooms were a monument to French *fin-de-siècle* notions of comfort and British standards of plumbing. The hotel, and the nearby Peking Club which nearly all diplomats and well-heeled foreign residents belonged to, were privileged rumour mills in a pre-television, pre-transistor radio age, places where news of all sorts was spread – about politics, endemic civil wars, the sex lives of prominent Chinese statesmen and Western diplomats, and the latest news from home.

The Grand Hotel des Wagons-lits fulfilled another, essential, role. It was where wealthy Chinese families checked in whenever trouble threatened in the rest of the city. The Legation Quarter was patrolled not by Chinese policemen, but by the different peace-keeping forces – British marines, French *fusiliers-marins*, Japanese security guards. In the game of 'touch' that Chinese politicians and generals indulged in during all the years Pu Yi spent inside the Forbidden City, the Wagons-lits Hotel was almost as inviolate as a legation building. The sudden rush to book rooms there presaged trouble – like hordes of correspondents descending on Beirut's Commodore Hotel in Beirut in the early eighties. Often, the first inkling Peking-based diplomats had of impending catastrophe was when its French manager reported all rooms suddenly and inexplicably booked.

The Wagons-lits Hotel put up its *complet* sign on 23 October 1924 – and that, along with the cutting of Johnston's phone line, was the first inkling he had of a crisis. At first he thought some local troops had mutinied, 'a not infrequent occurrence', as he put it. He was wrong.

China, at the time, was at war – but that in itself was nothing new: two warlords slugging it out in the northeast was a familiar story. Only this time one of the warlords concerned had set his sights on Peking. The so-called 'Christian general', Feng Yu-hsiang ('that huge benevolent whale', Christopher Isherwood called him), who had joined forces with another warlord, Wu Pei-fu, to teach the Manchurian General Chang Tso-lin a lesson, had unexpectedly changed his mind. Abandoning his erstwhile ally, he had left the battlefield with his troops (legend had it he baptized them with a firehose) and marched instead on Peking, set on becoming its military and political boss.

His troops had moved into the city, his supporters were freeing left-wing political prisoners and whipping up the radical Peking students and intellectuals into a frenzy. Since Feng Yu-hsiang was known to be in favour of a drastic revision of the Articles of Favourable Treatment, and since their abrogation would be a popular, cost-free move, Johnston at once knew that his protégé was in trouble.

Inside the Forbidden City, what remained of the House of Ching was busy coping with another kind of crisis. The second of the old Dowager Consorts had just died, and this required an elaborate, protracted series of ritual prayers, ceremonies and vigils. There were no eunuchs left to rob the old lady of her many possessions, but Pu Yi, as head of the family, was required to officiate at her bedside in the death chamber.

Pu Yi, Johnston reported, suspected something was up, having already spotted troop movements on Prospect Hill beyond the Forbidden City. Peering through binoculars, he calmly pointed out to Johnston that their uniforms were unfamiliar. The head of his Imperial Household Bureau, Shao Ying, had already sent out tea and cakes to them. They had scoffed the lot, Pu Yi said with a grin, and had politely asked for more.

Johnston then had lunch with Pu Yi, and left after promising to keep in touch.

While Johnston went back and forth from the palace to the Peking Club to the legations and the Wagons-lits Hotel in search of news, the 'Christian general' showed an unexpected, distinctly Cromwellian streak: he had the presidential treasurer beheaded for corruption, and from the terrified President Tsao Kun, a much discredited politician who had spent a fortune to get himself elected after Hsu Shi-chang resigned, Feng extracted a presidential order dissolving parliament. He also forced Tsao Kun's resignation from the presidency. Tsao Kun promptly headed for Tientsin's International Concession, taking with him the presidential seals with which he intended to revoke all orders promulgated under duress.

He was unwise enough to travel by train, and in a farcical interlude the train was stopped, he was relieved of his seals and allowed to continue his journey. Meanwhile his ministers, advisers and erstwhile political supporters vanished into the various sanctuaries at their disposal – some to friendly legations, others to faraway foreign concessions, and by 5 November the 'Christian general's' coup was a complete success.

By 2 November Feng's troops had surrounded the Forbidden City, but Johnston could still go in and out. He left that day with 'articles of value' belonging to Pu Yi which he deposited in the Hong Kong and Shanghai Bank.

He then returned to the palace, where Pu Yi showed him the jewels the dead Dowager had left behind. 'They would have all been stolen if they had been left in her palace,' he said, and asked Johnston to take one 'in memory of her'. Johnston selected 'an exquisite green jade ring'. Forbidden City staff and servants were leaving like rats from a sinking ship, and Johnston noted its 'ghostly, forlorn appearance'.

On 4 November Johnston returned to the Forbidden City and met with both Pu Yi and the Empress. He planned to smuggle the royal couple out, using his car, the following day.

Feng's troops got there first: early on 5 November, Johnston had a distraught call from one of Pu Yi's uncles (telephone lines had been restored). The 'Christian general's' troops had not only ringed the Forbidden City but were allowing no one in or out – and all phone lines to the palace had been cut again. Johnston and the princely uncle made an attempt to enter the Forbidden City gates – Johnston flourishing his palace pass – but were turned back.

Unknown to Johnston, Pu Yi had already been escorted out of the Forbidden City and was at that very moment a virtual prisoner inside the Northern Mansion, Prince Chun's family house, overlooking the lake known as the 'Back Sea'. An emissary of Feng had entered the Forbidden City early that morning demanding that Pu Yi sign the document he flourished. It was the long-awaited 'revision of the Articles of Favourable Treatment', turning Pu Yi into a private citizen, reducing his privy purse from £750,000 to around £95,000 enjoining him to leave the Forbidden City and guaranteeing his freedom of movement and the protection of the state. 'The Ching House will retain its private property,' the document added, but 'all public property will belong to the Republic.'

'Frankly speaking,' Pu Yi wrote many years later, the revised Articles 'weren't nearly as bad as I had expected'. While Pu Yi was reading them, his father Prince Chun arrived and, true to form, staged a dramatic, hysterical collapse.

What upset Pu Yi more than the substance of the ulti-matum was Feng's insistence that he vacate the Forbidden City within three hours. One Dowager Consort was lying dead in her palace, with the funeral rites as yet unfinished, and the two remaining old royals steadfastly refused to move, threatening to poison themselves with opium over-doses if compelled to leave their quarters. Pu Yi was understandably in a quandary. 'Call Johnston,' he ordered. But Johnston could not be reached. The phone lines were still down.

The head of the imperial household Shiao Ying, ashen-faced, told Pu Yi that if they were not out of the Forbidden City on time, the 'Christian general' would order his artil-lery to start shelling the palaces. The threat increased Prince Chun's panic, and Pu Yi's father-in-law scurried out into the open to look for a place to hide.

A last-minute compromise was worked out with Feng's emissary: the two old ladies could stay inside the Forbid-den City 'for the time being', and the funeral rites for the dead Dowager would be carried out according to plan. But Pu Yi had to leave right now. Within three hours he and the Empress were in a five-car army-escorted convoy on their way to the Northern Mansion. As he was about to step into his car, the general's emissary came up to him.

'Mr Pu Yi, do you intend to be an emperor in future, or will you be an ordinary citizen?' he asked.

'From today onwards I want to be an ordinary citizen.'

'Good,' he said. 'In that case we shall protect you. As a citizen, you'll have the right to vote and to stand for elec-tion. Who knows,' he added with a smile, 'you could even be elected President some day.'

Remembering his abortive attempt to escape two years previously, Pu Yi replied: 'I have felt for a long time that I did not need the Articles of Favourable Treatment. I am pleased to see them annulled. I had no freedom as an emperor. Now I have found my freedom.'

Feng's soldiers burst into a round of applause.

Pu Yi had managed his exit as gracefully as the 'Old Buddha' her return to the Forbidden City in 1902 after the

Boxer Rebellion. Unlike the 'Old Buddha', however, he was to have no respite: arriving under armed escort at the Northern Mansion, he found himself not only a prisoner of Feng's troops, but also a bone of contention between rival courtiers and advisers. Pu Yi was in an unprecedentedly embarrassing position: his friends fought among themselves over him as though he were a highly valuable but passive piece of property.

His father-in-law and his wife Elizabeth saw the situation differently. Far from being a source of revenue, the Emperor turned private citizen now looked like being a possible financial burden. Pu Yi's relations with his in-laws, never really cordial, became increasingly strained. Secondary Consort Wen Hsiu, still only fifteen, less educated than her senior bride, was totally bewildered by the move.

For Pu Yi himself, used to being waited on hand and foot, the Northern Mansion was little more than a slum, which he hoped to vacate as quickly as possible, especially since his father, utterly shaken by his son's expulsion from the Forbidden City, was displaying all the signs of a serious nervous breakdown.

The building, today the headquarters of Peking's Public Health Bureau, is a large, not particularly attractive house with pointed roofs and large courtyards front and rear. It lies next to the huge walled property later made over to Madame Sun Yat-sen, the widow of the republican leader, who was to become Vice-President of the Chinese People's Republic under Mao. These days a huge chimney stack, belching black smoke from an adjacent factory, disfigures an otherwise graceful skyline. Outside the house, then and now, Chinese anglers fish for tiny minnows in the Back Sea. For Pu Yi, used to the splendid isolation of the Forbidden City and its multiplicity of palaces, it was distinctly cramped – especially since it was soon packed, day and night, with hordes of relatives, followers, advisers and hangers-on, all proposing different, and mutually contradictory, plans of action. That first afternoon, Johnston managed to slip into the Northern Mansion where he found Pu Yi 'the least agitated' of all those present, 'full of dignity and self-possession', displaying 'amused contempt at the alarm and bewilderment shown by others' – especially his own, incoherent, father. Johnston brought good news: the British, Dutch and Japanese Legation heads had formally protested to the new Chinese government (hastily convened by Feng) at the way Pu Yi had been expelled from the Forbidden City. They had demanded – and obtained – guarantees for his continued safety and freedom.

This put new heart into Pu Yi's frightened, gabbling followers – but not for long. The next twenty days were full of conflicting rumours and growing confusion – and everyone inside the Northern Mansion, including Pu Yi, became fearful of what might happen next. Far from guaranteeing his 'personal freedom', the new, ephemeral government kept him a virtual prisoner inside the Northern Mansion. 'People could go in but not out,' Pu Yi wrote, except for foreigners, who were kept away (this was to keep Johnston from seeing Pu Yi). For all his other failings Johnston was a level-headed, well-informed, shrewd Scot, who might have quelled some of the wilder rumours spreading through the town (including the report that the communists intended putting Pu Yi on trial, that the 'Christian general' was planning to introduce 'people's self-rule' and march into the Legation Quarter), but until 25 November he and all other foreigners were banned from the Mansion.

As Pu Yi put it, many years later, 'the storm . . . dropped me at the crossroads. Three roads stretched out before me. One was to do what the revised Articles suggested: to abandon the imperial title and my old ambitions and become an enormously wealthy and landed "common citizen". Another was to try and get the help of my sympathizers to restore the old Articles, to regain my title and to return to the palace to continue to live my old life. The third possible course was the most tortuous: first to go abroad, and then to return to the Forbidden City as it had been before 1911. In the words of the time, this course was: using foreign power to plan a restoration.'

Both Pu Chieh, an alert and observant witness of the scene, and Rong Qi, Pu Yi's brother-in-law, told me that Pu Yi at this time seriously considered a fourth option – a dignified exit to enable him to fulfil Johnston's goal and become a genuine Oxford-educated Anglo-Chinese aristocrat. But Johnston was temporarily inaccessible and Pu Yi's divided supporters could agree on only one thing: the first option was a non-starter. For the rest, they had in mind not what they could do for Pu Yi but what Pu Yi could do for them. The result was to be disastrous for all concerned.

CHAPTER ELEVEN

Until Feng forcibly removed Pu Yi to his father's mansion, the ex-Emperor had lived in a vacuum. The Forbidden City had been a protective cocoon: none of the intrigues and plots devised by his imperial household staff, tutors and well-wishers had been of any real consequence. Suddenly, despite his virtual imprisonment inside the Northern Mansion, he became aware of the world around him and of the forces impinging on him, intent on using him as an instrument of their *realpolitik*. Nothing in Pu Yi's later behaviour can be either excused or even understood without a brief overview of these different, conflicting and quite formidable entities.

In 1924 China, the 'sick giant of Asia', was in a state of near-permanent anarchy: in the south the uneasy Kuomingtang-communist alliance still operated, though Dr Sun Yat-sen was about to leave his Shanghai base to enter a Peking clinic, terminally ill with cancer. (He was to die there a year later.) On the island of Whampoa, near Canton, the KMT's rising star, Chiang Kai-chek, was still commandant of the revolutionary Military Academy

Top: Water gate at Peking (POPPER).
Bottom: Marble barge in Summer Palace (POPPER).

Top: Empress Palace Suite (POPPER). Left: Dowager Empress (TOPHAM).
Right: Dowager Empress and GT Eunuch (PICTORIAL PRESS).

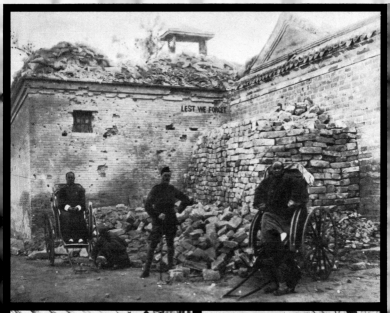

Top: British Legation 1900 (HULTON).
Left: Empress waving during Boxer Rebellion (HULTON).
Right: Sikhs leading Boxer prisoners (HULTON).

Young Pu Yi (HULTON).

P'ou lou son of Prince Boxer (PICTORIAL PRESS)

Top: Sun Yat Sen visiting Ming Emperor tombs in 1911 (ALDUS).
Bottom: Yuan Shi-Kai after inauguration 1912 (HULTON).

Top : Pu Yi's first wife
(HULTON).
Bottom: Pu Yi's first wife
(KEYSTONE).

there, breeding-ground of later revolutionaries and KMT generals. He was about to secure the services of a recently returned young Chinese communist aristocrat from France, Chou En-lai, as lecturer and political commissar. The communists were a growing force in Canton, 'the cradle of the revolution', and Mikhail Borodin, Stalin's Komintern agent and ex-American labour organizer, was busy organizing the growing Chinese Communist Party along orthodox Stalinist lines – and finding the Chinese very, very different from the Russians.

In the north-east, Russians and Japanese uneasily co-existed, the Russians in the north, the Japanese in the southern portion of Manchuria. After Russia's defeat in the Russo-Japanese War of 1904-5, the Japanese had obtained hugely advantageous concessions in Manchuria, including a huge stake in the previously Russian-owned and -operated railway system. With it the Japanese acquired the right to open hotels, and bring in railway troops to guard their line, on the Russian model. The Japanese also increased the size of the enclaves under their control and acquired new concessions in Mukden (now Shenyang) which was then Manchuria's capital, and Port Arthur. They also increased the size of their garrison in Manchuria, a force known as the 'Kwangtung army'.

But neither the Japanese nor the Russians had things entirely their own way in Manchuria, which remained an integral part of China: both were wary of General Chang Tso-lin, the Manchurian warlord who had flirted both with the Japanese and Sun Yat-sen, but was tough enough – and wily enough – to play his own game.

Foreign concessions dotted the whole of the Chinese coastline, and their influence, and arrogant aloofness from Chinese-administered territories had never been greater. The British, in particular, with Hong Kong and Weihawei as secure 'colonial' bases and a network of powerful banks in every concession enclave, regarded China almost as a British protectorate; officially, the USA and Europe went through the motions of considering China as a sovereign country, a full member of the League of Nations and –

already – a huge potential market for their goods. But respect for China in the world's capitals was scant. Events since the 1911 'revolution' had done nothing to enhance China's international standing: republican governments and presidents came and went, members of the parliament (when there was a parliament, which was not often) openly bought their seats, politicians of all hues emulated the gross corruption of Pu Yi's own imperial household vultures. Warlords indulged in war games rather than full-scale wars, profitable for themselves but ruinous for the country. Their allegiances were always temporary, their loyalty for sale to the highest bidder. Millions of drug addicts fuelled a huge, barely clandestine traffic in morphine, heroin and opium. The political instability of Peking's central government, in the two years immediately following Pu Yi's flight from the Forbidden City, was such that Professor James E. Sheridan, the leading expert on Chinese political history of the twenties, was to write that 'cabinets had no more substance than a ruler in a motion picture'.

Pu Yi, the legitimate if deposed descendant of the Ching dynasty, suddenly became another wild card in this complicated, barely comprehensible game.

Alone among the major powers, one country knew perfectly well not only how to exploit this wild card, but what its long-term policy regarding China should be: Japan, which from Pu Yi's birth had seen him as a possible sleeping asset, now entered the picture. From the moment Pu Yi uneasily settled in the Northern Mansion, determined to make his stay there as short as possible, the Japanese began wooing him. As David Bergamini, in his masterly life's work *Japan's Imperial Conspiracy*, showed, Pu Yi was but a minor pawn in a Japanese grand design which was to lead to Japan's invasion of China and its tentacular conquest of almost all of South-East Asia, in a well-thought-out, utterly ruthless long-term policy of world conquest.

While Pu Yi was fretting about the 'Christian general's' soldiers at his gate in 1924, Hirohito was still officially

Crown Prince of Japan but had to all intents and purposes been the country's effective ruling Emperor for some years, standing in for his incapacitated father as Regent since November 1921. Behind the smokescreen of Japan's politico-military establishment, it was Hirohito, as Berga-mini revealed in his epochal and unjustly forgotten book, who both called the shots and ruthlessly disposed of those Japanese generals and officials who opposed his policies.

At the time, the full extent of Japan's threat either to China or to the rest of Asia was perceived by few: rather, Japan was considered by the protagonists of the struggle for China as a useful, sympathetic base. Chiang Kai-chek had been partly educated there, both as a revolutionary and as a soldier. He was to marry there, and – before full-scale war engulfed both countries – return there fre-quently, on easy terms with politicians, financiers and the famous Black Dragon secret society bosses. Sun Yat-sen, early on in his revolutionary career, had spent some time in Kobe, where he had been treated with kindness and respect. Britain in particular saw Japan as a potential ally in Asia, especially after the Soviet takeover in 1917.

Johnston's pro-Japanese sentiments were not entirely idiosyncratic – they reflected the cosy, after-dinner con-versations at British Legation dinner tables, after the ladies had left and the port and brandy had circulated freely. As Edgar Snow was to write later in his *Battle for Asia* 'many of the British and French governing class sincerely believed Japan had a legitimate right to expand . . . some of the most influential British peers believed that Japanese control of Manchuria . . . might not be injurious to the interests of empire. They were perhaps not unaware of the contradiction in their own position in denying empire to Japan. A little room at the expense of China could not seriously harm anyone. It would build a needed barrier against the spread of bolshevism in the North . . .' Snow added that most French and British government leaders 'genuinely believed that the Japanese, once they had removed the bolshevik menace from its frontiers, would restore the peace, order and security of investment: re-division of territory might render both China and Japan better markets for capital'.

Long before Hirohito started playing any role as youthful Regent, Japan had shown, in various ways, its huge priority interest in China – including, especially, Manchuria. When Japan declared war on Germany on the side of Britain and France in August 1914, the object had not been to help the Allies but – as Foreign Minister Kanji Kato put it – to 'silence in advance any British objections to Japanese moves on China'. Also in 1914, Baron Shimpei Goto, one of Japan's leading administrators and ex-Governor of Taiwan, had addressed the Saiwai Club, an organ of the Japanese House of Peers, in these terms: 'Our emigration policy,' he said, should be a form of 'peacefully disguised military preparedness . . . Permanent victory in Manchuria largely depends on an increase in the population of Japanese colonizers. German inhabitants of Alsace-Lorraine played no small part in winning these areas over for Germany in the Franco-Prussian war of 1870. If Japan had 500,000 immigrants [in Manchuria] they would be of great use in case of war . . . and if a war opportunity is unfavourable, they can be used to maintain strongholds for negotiated peace.'

Goto said all Japanese hospitals built in Manchuria 'should be planned as military hospitals, with large verandahs for wounded soldiers'. Railway employees in Manchuria 'should be military officers, and the railway should be ready for military emergencies'. The port officials (at the Japanese Port Arthur concession) 'should be Navy men'.

While Pu Yi was still a child, at the start of the First World War, Japan spelled out the trade-off it expected from its lukewarm participation in the war. This included railroad rights and a takeover of the German concession of Tsingtao, ninety-nine-year leases over parts of Manchuria and 'first option' rights there in its economic development. The 4 May Movement was the result of the deal Japan forced through at Versailles, and during the short-lived Allied attempt to help White Russian movements holding out against the Soviet Red Army in the wake of the 1917 Revolution, some 30,000 Japanese troops were moved through Manchuria to reinforce the 'whites'. There were Japanese troops stationed in Siberia until 1922, and at no time did Japan ever consider Manchuria an integral part of China.

In spite of all this, Japanese modesty, discretion and extreme reserve encouraged British illusions about the viability of a Japanese partnership. Crown Prince Hirohito himself, even at this early period of his life, was presented as a diffident, scholarly young man, with a penchant for military history and marine biology, a happily married, monogamous, upright aristocrat whose private life contrasted favourably with China's debauched princely families, with their eunuchs, teenaged concubines and dubious morals.

The truth was something else. Crown Prince Hirohito's personal life was indeed irreproachable, but it was not so much marine biology that was his *violon d'Ingres* as the kind of biology that makes germ warfare possible. The Japanese army was denigrated by Western spit-and-polish advocates, but they were not to know that some of Japan's top military theorists had deliberately ordered Japanese soldiers to look scruffy and unshaven in order to fool experts into believing they were also incompetent soldiers. But these were minor matters compared to the all-important Japanese military will to conquer. The year before Pu Yi went through his elaborate wedding ceremony, there occurred an event that was never reported until David Bergamini stumbled across it in the course of his research. In 1921, a group of Japanese military attachés met in Baden-Baden – almost certainly with a close relative of Hirohito's, Prince Higashikuni, manipulating events from the wings – and there the top three leaders of the ultra-secret meeting, known later as the 'three crows', worked out a blueprint to make Japan's armed forces the most efficient, most up-to-date in the world.

Their first priority was to appoint a sub-committee, another group of up-and-coming officers, the 'eleven reliable men', to implement this programme, and these 'eleven reliable men' were in time to become key figures in the Japanese master plan. Three of the 'reliable men' were to be hanged as war criminals in 1948. All three were Manchurian specialists, and were later active there, two of them as top military intelligence officers, and the third, Tojo, as head of the Japanese Gendarmerie.

By the time Pu Yi was married, an active Japanese secret service was at work in Europe. Before Pu Yi had even begun fighting his losing battle against his imperial household rogues, Crown Prince Hirohito, in 1921, had set up his 'Social Problems Research Institute', otherwise known as the 'University Lodging House', in the shadow of the imperial palace, on the site of what had once been a meteorological observatory. Here, in Bergamini's words, was established 'a security-shrouded indoctrination center for young men who wished to play a part in his dreams for Japan. Here, in the precincts of the palace, were made the first rough plans for Japan's attempt to conquer half the world.'

Many of the graduates of this 'by invitation only' ultra-secret think-tank would also end up later in Japanese-occupied Manchuria – for whether Japan's strategists belonged to the 'strike North' school (against the Soviet Union's Siberian conquests) or the 'strike South' school (China and South-East Asia), Manchuria was the key; and Manchuria was the cradle of the Ching dynasty, the homeland of Pu Yi, though he had never set foot in it.

The head of the University Lodging House, an ultra-nationalist called Dr Shumei Okawa, had spent ten years in China as a Japanese spy. His illuminated tenet was that Japan had a 'divine mission' to 'free the universe'. Many years later, at the Asian war crimes trial of 1946, he successfully simulated madness, was declared unfit to plead – and shortly afterwards miraculously recovered his sanity, dying in his bed of a stroke in 1957. He had close links with the Black Dragon Society, which was not, at least at first, an underworld gang but a patriotic 'club' of nationalists determined to resist non-Asian invaders. It was named after the Amur (meaning Black Dragon) River which separated Manchuria from Siberia, and it stood for extreme hostility, first towards Russia, then towards the Soviet Union. Sun Yat-sen's 1911 'revolution' which overthrew the Ching dynasty had been partly financed by it.

By the time Pu Yi left the Forbidden City, nominally a private citizen, part of the Manchurian homeland he had never seen was in effect a Japanese colony. In South Manchuria, the Japanese concession, or 'Kwangtung leased territory', was, as Professor Albert Feuerwerker wrote in *The Cambridge History of China*, 'an island of Japanese society and culture on the Chinese mainland'. Through the Japanese-run South Manchurian Railway Company, the Japanese controlled communications, though their writ was a narrow one, extending no further than each side of the railroad tracks. Though Japanese immigrants were given financial incentives to settle in Manchuria, they did so, from Japan's point of view, in disappointingly small numbers until 1931.

This was the lie of the land while Pu Yi was brooding about his options inside the Northern Mansion, and though he was certainly not aware of the secret Japanese plans for the conquest of China – part of its master plan for conquering half the world – he could not have been unaware of the extent of Japanese influence in his ancestral Manchurian homeland, and ever since he had been a toddler he had heard his bannermen talk about the possibility of Manchuria breaking away from China and becoming a sovereign monarchy once more.

Johnston wrote at length, and highly sympathetically, about these monarchist dreams, rejecting them not because he felt Pu Yi had no moral right to break his agreement with republican China once the Articles of Favourable Treatment had been accepted, but because such a move, in his opinion, simply would not work. As he put it (referring to plots afoot in 1919) 'it was no longer true to say that if the Emperor fled to Manchuria he would be allowed to take peaceable possession of his throne . . . a monarchist movement in Manchuria would lead to civil war'.

'This was recognized by most of the monarchist party,' Johnston added, and led them to think that nothing should be attempted 'until the Republic perished through its own inward rottenness . . . or until something should happen in Manchuria which would lead to foreign intervention. What this "something" might be, no one knew; but there were many who felt convinced that the day would come, sooner or later, when Japan would find herself forced to take active steps to protect against Chinese encroachment the vast interests acquired by her in Manchuria as a result of the wars she had fought on Manchurian soil. A conflict between Japan and the Chinese Republic . . . would, thought these monarchists, give them the opportunity they desired.'

After the abrogation of the Articles of Favourable Treatment in 1924, the monarchists around Pu Yi had another argument: the Manchus, Johnston wrote, were officially still 'aliens', though nominally Manchuria was part of the Chinese Republic, and 'an alien race or family owed no allegiance to China'.

These were some of the issues so heatedly discussed inside the 'Northern Mansion' after Pu Yi's ejection from the Forbidden City. Pu Yi's uppermost consideration, understandably, was for his own safety, for Feng's soldiers were unreliable, the left-wing students and political radicals were in uproar, and there were constant rumours that the KMT might leave its southern base and march on Peking.

Then, overnight, in one of those volte-faces that the Chinese had come to accept and that made China such a difficult country to understand and report, the situation dramatically changed.

A few weeks after Pu Yi's removal from the Forbidden City, Chang Tso-lin, the Manchurian warlord, entered Peking with only a small bodyguard force, forcing out his erstwhile ally the 'Christian general' without firing a shot, and putting in his place a 'moderate', Marshal Tuan Chi-jui, as 'provisional Chief Executive'. The guard around the Northern Mansion was withdrawn. Not only was Johnston allowed access to Pu Yi once more, but Chang Tso-lin sent word to Johnston he wished to see him.

Chang Tso-lin, a hugely powerful warlord whose writ ran over most of Manchuria (with the exception of the Japanese railroad enclaves and concessions) and most of Chinese Mongolia as well, was one of the most colourful, ruthless adventurers of his age. His mother had been a seamstress, and they were so poor young Chang hunted hares in the Manchurian desert to keep the family alive. One day, out hunting, he spotted a straggling, wounded bandit on horseback, killed him, took his horse, and, in typical Wild West fashion, became a bandit himself. He soon acquired a private army of his own, and something of a Robin Hood reputation. During the Russo-Japanese War he fought on Japan's side for a hefty fee, terrorizing the Russians by his daring cavalry tactics. He then – again for a sizeable cash prize – accepted incorporation in the regular Chinese army.

From then on his relations with the Republic, the growing KMT movement in the south and the Japanese were marked by Chang's determination to keep his Manchu army under his personal control, and Manchuria free from foreign domination. He had flirted with Dr Sun Yat-sen, but not for long. In 1916, the Japanese tried to kill him, hiring an assassin to throw a bomb into his horse-drawn carriage while he was escorting some Japanese dignitaries to a dinner party in Mukden. Chang Tso-lin survived to drive the Japanese out of Mukden along with the Japanese-backed Mongols with whom they had hoped to occupy the city. He was a man of infinite resource, fond of expeditious justice – instant beheadings were his speciality – and, if such a term can have any meaning in the China of the 1920s – a patriot, whose rough-and-ready Manchurian administration was the least corrupt and most efficient in the whole of China. His name had frequently been mentioned as one of the possible contenders for a revived Manchurian dynasty, and there were even those who thought that if Chang Tso-lin had really wanted to, he could have supplanted the House of Ching and become Emperor of China himself. But this self-taught soldier of fortune, who in later life sported otter-lined greatcoats, acquired a taste for chic teenage concubines and compared himself to Napoleon, was too active and restless an adventurer to settle down.

Chang Tso-lin's attitude towards Pu Yi had been, at all times, respectfully cordial. At the time of his wedding, he sent him £1,600 in cash – an important token both of loyalty and esteem. When he heard what Feng had done to Pu Yi, he flew into a violent rage, not just because he had not been forewarned, but because, as Johnston put it, 'he probably felt that if the treasures of the Forbidden City had to pass out of imperial custody, he himself would make quite as suitable a custodian of them as anyone else'.

This was the man who summoned Johnston – on Pu Yi's behalf – after his arrival in Peking on 23 November, 1924. Johnston arrived bearing gifts from Pu Yi – a signed photograph and a topaz and diamond ring. Chang accepted the photograph, but not the ring, and proceeded to give Johnston a brief lecture on the situation as he saw it.

He deplored the 'Christian general's' clumsy move, but felt that he himself could not intervene overtly to restore Pu Yi to his former splendour inside the Forbidden City without laying himself open to the charge of favouring the Manchu separatist cause at the expense of the Chinese Republic, to which he remained loyal, at least on paper. His main purpose, in seeing Johnston, was to use him to reassure the foreign legations that Pu Yi would be in no danger, and that he favoured some quiet way of restoring the Articles of Favourable Treatment without seeming to act as kingmaker.

Johnston reported this good news back to Pu Yi, also spreading the word, as Chang Tso-lin had intended, to the legation diplomats. But the ex-Emperor was not entirely reassured. One of Chang's characteristics, Johnston noted, was boundless self-confidence, which explained why he had shown up in Peking with only a token force, leaving the bulk of his army behind. Feng's troops were still in Peking, armed and restless. Johnston – himself a prey to rumours by now – feared a coup and advised Pu Yi to find a safer place to live than the Northern Mansion, which was at least five kilometres from the safety of the Legation Quarter. Johnston told Pu Yi he must move – immediately, and without informing any of his entourage, including his own wife (who would follow later) or the excitable Prince Chun.

What followed was a Mack Sennett-like chase that took Johnston, Pu Yi and his fourteen-year-old servant, Big Li, all over town in an effort to prevent any Chinese secret servicemen who might be keeping a discreet eye on him from finding out where they were heading. But it was also designed to fool Prince Chun's own servants, who would undoubtedly have told their master about the escapade.

Johnston, Pu Yi and Big Li got into Pu Yi's chauffeur-driven car, with Johnston giving the driver directions. Johnston's own car followed, his driver at the wheel. As both cars were about to set off for the Legation Quarter, one of Prince Chun's aides rushed out of the house and asked where they were going. 'Just for a short drive,' Pu Yi said.

The aide clearly had instructions from Pu Yi's father never to lose sight of him. 'I'll come too,' he said, and got into Pu Yi's car. With Johnston's car following, the small convoy left the Northern Mansion. As they departed two policemen jumped on the running-boards of Pu Yi's car, and there was nothing anyone could do to prevent them from remaining aboard. Johnston whispered instructions to Pu Yi's driver, taking them through a maze of streets, doubling back on their tracks – his ultimate destination the German Hospital in the Legation Quarter where he knew Pu Yi would be welcome, at least temporarily. There was a violent sandstorm, with so much dust in the air that he could only see a few feet ahead of him.

To give some credibility to Pu Yi's 'short drive' pretext, Johnston's first stop, after buying a gold wristwatch in a jeweller's shop, was in front of a well-known, German-owned photography store inside the Legation Quarter called Hartung's. Pu Yi and Johnston went inside and pretended to look at some photographs. By the time they left the shop, a small crowd had gathered, and Pu Yi had been recognized. The two cars were allowed to leave, however, and now Johnston told the driver to make for the German Hospital. Once inside, he asked for a friend of his, a Dr Dipper. Pu Yi and Johnston sat in the hospital waiting room while Prince Chun's aide waited outside in the car. The German doctor agreed to provide Pu Yi with a room, and Johnston left him there, returning to his own car. By now Prince Chun's aide realized he had, quite literally, been taken for a ride, and furiously ordered Pu Yi's driver to take him back to the Northern Mansion. The two policemen stayed at the hospital. As for Johnston, he made straight for the Japanese Legation. This was where, all along, he had planned that Pu Yi should stay 'until the situation had been clarified'.

Johnston's appointment was with K. Yoshizawa, the Japanese Minister in charge of the legation – with whom Pu Yi had negotiated the dispatch of antiques as part of the Tokyo earthquake disaster fund. Yoshizawa told Johnston, after some hesitation, that Pu Yi would be welcome as a guest of the Japanese Legation. Johnston then returned to the German Hospital, but to his intense astonishment – and brief alarm – Pu Yi had disappeared.

In the race to claim Pu Yi, the head of the Japanese Legation guard, Colonel Takemoto, had pre-empted his superior. Through a trusted Pu Yi aide, the Japanese colonel had arranged for Pu Yi's immediate transfer to the Japanese Legation in a horse-drawn carriage which picked up Pu Yi at the hospital even as Johnston was parleying with the Japanese Minister. In the sandstorm, the carriage strayed briefly from the Legation Quarter by mistake. Pu Yi was horrified that he might again be recognized and, this time, arrested. But the coachman found his way again, and Pu Yi slipped into the Japanese compound unseen.

It was an interesting example of a Japanese military decision overriding civilian scruples: officially, the commandant of the legation guard was subordinate to the Japanese Minister, but in fact the officer corps, with its privileged lines of communication to the imperial palace, called the shots.

The unfortunate Chinese policemen who had jumped on the running boards of Pu Yi's car at the start of the escapade had stayed with Pu Yi all this time. Realizing their mistake in not preventing him from entering the German Hospital, and fearing for their lives if they returned to the Northern Mansion without Pu Yi, they begged to become part of his retinue. Pu Yi agreed, and from that day on they were on his private payroll.

The comic adventure through Peking's streets, leading to Pu Yi's refuge inside the Japanese Legation, was the last major service rendered by Johnston to his former pupil. Years later, going through the events of that fateful day with Pu Chieh, Pu Yi's younger brother, I asked him whether he had any awareness at the time of the consequences of this decision. 'There was a British camp, and there was a Japanese camp,' he said. 'The Japanese won.'

Johnston's initiative, however, was a personal one. The British too feared for Pu Yi's life at this time, and consequently there would have been no objections had Pu Yi ended up in the British, instead of the Japanese, Legation. Had he done so, his life might have taken a completely different course. Johnston either remained unaware of the far-reaching effects of his decision, or else chose to disregard them. His pro-Japanese bias never weakened. In his preface to *Twilight in the Forbidden City*, he refers to 'the twilight of dawn as well as a twilight of evening . . . it may well be that the night which swallowed up the twilight described in these pages will be followed in due time by another twilight which will brighten into a new day of radiant sunshine.' The obvious allusion, Pamela Atwell noted in her introduction to a new edition of his book in 1985, was to the 'Land of the Rising Sun'. Johnston died in 1938, his illusions about the Japanese intact.

CHAPTER TWELVE

The Japanese Legation – almost opposite the British Legation compound where Johnston now moved to in order to be close to Pu Yi – consisted of several small buildings, none of them comparable, in size, to the Northern Mansion. For the first few days, Pu Yi was loaned the three-room apartment normally occupied by Minister Yoshizawa and his wife. This soon proved far too small, and Pu Yi was given one of the Japanese Legation houses inside the compound, a combination of living quarters for himself and his two wives, office and improvised court.

Following Pu Yi's escape, the police guard around the Northern Mansion was reinforced. When Empress Elizabeth, in a car driven by a junior Japanese attaché, tried to leave the building she was turned back. Yoshizawa's personal intervention was required to secure her transfer, as well as that of Pu Yi's young concubine, Wen Hsiu.

Later, one of Pu Yi's distant relatives, recalling the scene inside the small Japanese Legation house, described the atmosphere as 'not at all royal' – a bit of a mess, in fact, with Pu Yi surrounded by suitcases, crates and papers and his two wives quarrelling over who should occupy the larger of the several bedrooms. And even the hospitable Yoshizawas were secretly dismayed by the way their hitherto quiet legation, furnished in the traditional Japanese style, was taken over by Pu Yi's loud, ill-mannered, quarrelling followers. Johnston himself, who is surprisingly discreet about this short interlude in Pu Yi's life, also appears to have been upset at the way they behaved.

One faction of his court, headed by his own father, urged Pu Yi to return to the Northern Mansion. Among this group were those, like 'reformer' Cheng Hsiao-hsu, who felt Pu Yi was making a big mistake putting himself in the debt of the Japanese. Cheng, whose loyalty to Pu Yi stemmed from his belief in the sacredness of royalty (he was not even of Manchurian descent), observed the struggle among Pu Yi's followers with high-minded detachment. He despised many of the extreme monarchists for their unsophisticated, blatant sponging on what was left of court largesse. Having attempted, and failed, to reform the royal finances, he knew how venal some of Pu Yi's most vocal supporters really were. Prince Chun himself had lost all credibility with Pu Yi: he had behaved with hysterical cowardice throughout his ordeal, and appeared to have only one consideration in mind – money. For this reason alone, Pu Yi was disinclined to listen to him, or to those who wanted him back inside the Northern Mansion.

Others viewed the Japanese Legation as a kind of Trojan Horse which would eventually lead Pu Yi to Manchuria, and make him king again. If this happened, they believed, their princely titles would no longer be pieces of paper but enable them once more to become feudal, tax-levying lordlings, rich and powerful. These were the uncouth, loud-mouthed bannermen who shocked the Japanese by their bad manners – and Pu Yi by their unsubtle financial claims on him.

These could not have occurred at a worse time, for the Chinese and foreign-language press, after Pu Yi's eviction from the Forbidden City, was full of stories about the way 'national treasures' stored there had mysteriously disappeared. The infamous Imperial Household Bureau, and not Pu Yi, had been responsible, but public opinion was unaware of this. Meanwhile, the shaky Chinese government temporarily in place not only had no cash for Pu Yi's reduced stipend, but was perilously short of funds to run what parts of the country remained under its nominal authority.

The central government's control over its finances, wrote Professor Albert Feuerwerker in Volume 12 of *The Cambridge History of China*, had 'almost evaporated'. As Professor Sheridan put it (in the same volume), 'the minister of finance had no money, the minister of communications regulated no railways because they were all in the hands of the military commanders . . . and all government schools were closed because utility bills had not been paid and teachers received no salaries'. It was hardly the time for Pu Yi to ask for what remained of his privy purse, especially now that he had fled to the Japanese Legation, implicitly rejecting the authority of the Chinese government.

A more sophisticated, more sinister individual now began playing an increasingly important role in Pu Yi's life. Lo Chen-yu had been a bannerman in the *ancien régime*, who had come to Pu Yi's attention in 1922. He had a veneer of scholarship, but his real interest was in antiques. A familiar figure at court from Pu Yi's wedding onwards, he had been the indispensable middleman when the time came for the Imperial Household Bureau to start selling off the treasures of the House of Ching. A highly venal man, now in his fifties, Lo Chen-yu quickly quarrelled with 'reformer' Cheng Hsiao-hsu who spotted him for what he was – a corrupt, fast-talking con man with a shrewd eye for the value of antiques of all kinds and a reputation as a forger of 'ancient' scrolls. In disgust, Cheng Hsiao-hu packed his bags and retired, temporarily, to Shanghai.

In this miniature, fake court, Pu Yi began showing increasing signs of the kind of weakness his tutors had observed as a child: he took up a subject with immense enthusiasm, only to lose interest in it and revert to the one topic that really interested him – entomology and, in particular, the study of ants, about which he knew a great deal.

Lo Chen-yu, during those three months Pu Yi spent inside the Japanese Legation, ingratiated himself to a dangerous degree – and Pu Yi's new mentor, either temperamentally or because he was secretly paid for his services by the Japanese, became the first of a series of pro-Japanese 'fifth columnists' within the much-reduced imperial court. It was Lo Chen-yu who, day in, day out, urged Pu Yi to leave China – not, as Johnston would have liked, for Oxford, but for Japan. He did not succeed, but he was responsible for Pu Yi's next move – to Tientsin.

Just before he left, Pu Yi held his first court reception since his eviction from the Forbidden City. The occasion was his nineteenth birthday (by Chinese reckoning it was his twentieth, for in China a baby is one on the day of its birth) and the Japanese Legation reception room was turned, for the day, into an improvised throne room. Japanese servants brought in splendid carpets, a yellow armchair to symbolize a throne and plenty of yellow cushions and paper ornaments. The monarchists attended in their finery – Ching bonnets with red tassels, Mandarin buttons, sable robes. Diplomats also attended, in frock coats. Altogether, Pu Yi reckoned, there were some five hundred guests.

The speech Pu Yi made – later reported in the press – was both dignified and melancholy. He reminded them he was speaking as a guest 'under a stranger's roof', and 'as I am only a young man of twenty it is not right I should be celebrating "long life" '. His youth inside the Forbidden City (the 'Great Within', as he called it), 'had been', he told them, 'that of a prisoner' and he did not regret its end. The manner of it had been painful, though, because while he would happily have been a party to the abrogation of the Articles of Favourable Treatment, 'the sending of troops to the palace was a violent act . . . I have long had a sincere wish not to use that empty title, but being compelled to drop it by armed force has made me most unhappy'. The suddenness of it all was also humiliating. 'Even if [the 'Christian general'] had been justified in driving me out, why did he impound all the clothes, vessels, calligraphy and books left by my ancestors? Why did he not allow us to take away rice bowls, tea cups and kitchen utensils in daily use? Was this a case of "preserving antiques"? I do not think he would have acted so harshly even in dealing with bandits.'

Pu Yi gave no hint of what his future might be, beyond a pledge to stay out of politics: 'I will never agree to any proposal that I should seek foreign intervention on my behalf: I could never use foreign power to intervene in domestic Chinese politics.'

The guests gave him an ovation. That week, Pu Yi, with his young servant Big Li, cycled out of the Japanese Legation for a brief spin as far as the Forbidden City. It was another melancholy occasion, and Pu Yi rode away at high speed.

The Japanese diplomats were furious at this outing. When he tried, a few days later, to repeat it, the legation guards refused to open the gates. The Japanese Minister said these were security measures for Pu Yi's own good: he feared for his life in the anarchy that followed the 'Christian general's' overthrow. The feeling that he was a prisoner once more now made Pu Yi more responsive to Lo Chen-yu's plan that he should leave Peking altogether, for safer, less expensive Tientsin. There is a proverb, both Czech and Chinese: 'A fish, and a guest, begin to stink after the third day.' Pu Yi had been a guest of the Japanese Legation for three months.

The Yoshizawas expressed their formal, excessively polite regrets, and told him he was free to stay as long as he liked. Secretly, they were relieved to see him go – and may have talked Lo Chen-yu into proposing the move, which Lo himself supervised. A special train was hired on the Peking–Tientsin railway, and on 23 February 1925 Pu Yi made a quick, furtive trip to Peking's railway station.

He wore Chinese dress for the occasion – a black gown and skullcap, and his favourite Harold Lloyd glasses.

Johnston made the trip too. It was to be one of his last, leisurely conversations with Pu Yi, for his Ching interlude, which had made such an indelible mark on his life, was over: he was about to resume his Colonial Service career, as Commissioner of Weihawei, and the train journey was part of a protracted series of goodbyes. In any case, Pu Yi, at this stage, was no longer of major concern to the British government (Chiang Kai-chek was becoming the man to watch now) and Pu Yi lacked the funds to keep Johnston on his payroll.

Tientsin (or Tianjin, as it is now called) was, at this time, China's most cosmopolitan city after Shanghai, a prototype of the international concessions China had been compelled to recognize under growing foreign pressure. It had a large British, French, German and Japanese community – and each of these foreign concessions was a miniature colony. There were three 'English' municipalities, five foreign churches, eight tennis clubs, five Masonic lodges, seven social clubs (all out of bounds to Chinese), hockey, cricket and golf clubs, swimming pools (for foreigners), and a huge racecourse – burnt down during the Boxer Rebellion, later rebuilt with an imposing grandstand. It boasted four foreign daily newspapers – the *Peking and Tientsin Times*, *L'Echo de Tientsin*, a Japanese paper called the *Tenshin Nichi-Nichi Shimbun* and the German *Tientsin Tageblatt*. There were small Belgian and Italian communities, and thousands of now stateless White Russians. As Isherwood wrote in *Journey to a War*:

> You see two or three of them behind every bar – a fat, defeated tribe who lead a melancholy indoor life of gossip, mah-jongg, drink and bridge. They have all drifted here somehow . . . and here they must stop; nobody else will receive them. They have established an insecure right to exist – on nansen passports, Chinese nationality-papers of doubtful validity, obsolete Tsarist identity-certificates as big as table-

cloths, or simply their mere impoverished presence. Their great pallid faces look out into the future, above innumerable cigarettes and tea-glasses, without pity or hope. 'Their clocks,' says Auden, 'stopped in 1917. It has been tea-time ever since.'

Gordon Hall (named after 'Chinese' Gordon, the British general killed at Khartoum) was the British civic centre where expatriates enjoyed communal activities, but life revolved around the many foreign restaurants, cafés and nightclubs. There were foreign-owned hotels and cinemas, too, and a large, flourishing brothel and opium den area in Dublin Road.

The atmosphere was that of a small-time colony, tempered by the proximity of a large, and largely ignored, Chinese city. There were an English-style Victoria Park, German cafés with orchestras, dingy Russian restaurants and chic British stores. Whiteway and Laidlaw, the Harrods of Tientsin, had an international reputation for well-cut British tweeds and memsahibs' 'sensible shoes'. As in all such small, claustrophobic colonies far from home, middle-class morality, petty jealousies and club gossip assumed an absurd importance – and Pu Yi's arrival was treated as a major social event.

The colonial atmosphere was, however, special, not only more cosmopolitan than similar communities in British India or Africa, but also less secure: the European merchants, bankers and civil servants and their families were well aware that theirs was a highly artificial haven of law and order set down in a vast, anarchic country. This meant that national differences were less important than the unifying racial factor: even during the First World War, the British, French and German communities in Tientsin had felt more united – as members of a superior, 'advanced' civilization – than temporarily divided by war.

Henry Woodhead, editor of the *Tientsin and Peking Times*, wrote about this highly artificial colonial enclave in his *Adventures in Far Eastern Journalism*. He became Pu Yi's occasional, privileged companion – his paper ran a

daily 'Court Circular' chronicling his day-to-day outings –
and because of Pu Yi's intermittent news value, Woodhead
became a sought-after 'stringer' for other publications. 'I
was on intimate terms with the Emperor,' he boasted. A
somewhat narrow-minded, conventional English empire-
builder, Woodhead, a drop-out from Brighton College,
had none of Johnston's intellect. He was typical of the
middle-class Englishmen who sought adventure in the
remoter parts of Empire not for gain but as a means of
escaping the narrow British class distinctions of the
period. He epitomized the Englishman abroad – the kind
Somerset Maugham wrote about with a mixture of loathing and fascination.

Woodhead, in his reporter's capacity, was on hand
when Pu Yi arrived at Tientsin station in his special train,
flanked by Johnston and a large number of plainclothes
Japanese policemen. A Japanese guard of honour presented
arms, and Pu Yi was whisked away to Tientsin's Japanese
Concession.

Lo Chen-yu had picked out the place for him to stay,
the 'Chang Garden', a large, walled estate belonging to a
loyal bannerman who had promised Pu Yi he could stay
there as long as he liked, rent-free. From the Japanese point
of view, it was admirably situated – not only was it well
inside the Japanese Concession, on Asahi Road, but it also
faced Kasuga House, the headquarters of the Japanese
secret service in Tientsin. But the house was not ready,
and Pu Yi spent his first night in a Japanese-owned hotel.

According to Woodhead, Pu Yi already owned a large
house of his own in the British Concession. The reason he
did not consider moving into it, Woodhead learned later,
was that Pu Yi had asked for police protection, which the
British-run Municipality had refused.

As soon as the Chang Garden house was adequately
furnished, Pu Yi's two wives followed him to Tientsin.
Once more, there were disputes about rooms and prece-
dence. In his reminiscences of everyday life in Tientsin,
Woodhead recalls the Pu Yi household 'ambiance' primar-
ily as a doggy paradise. There were Empress Elizabeth's

many Pekingese, never adequately house-trained, constantly yapping; there were Pu Yi's two mean-looking English mastiffs, 'Mr and Mrs Ponto', who roamed the Chang Garden grounds at night. Pu Yi promised Woodhead an offspring, should they mate, but Woodhead turned the offer down: he did not know how long he would be staying in Tientsin, and he feared the dog's food bill would be huge. The animals were tolerated at garden parties because of the social distinction of their owners. But Pu Yi left their handling to his servants, and they – and the Empress – spoilt the Pekingese outrageously. Because Empress Elizabeth had Pekingese, Wen Hsiu wanted some too. The vicious fights among the dogs mirrored the almost equally raucous, high-pitched quarrels that would break out, later, between Empress and concubine. For the time being, in those early days in Tientsin, Woodhead noted that Elizabeth ('a lovely girl who resembled a piece of delicate porcelain') and Wen Hsiu seemed to get on well enough, 'like sisters'.

Pu Yi enjoyed the relative informality of those early months in Tientsin. He was freer in his movements than ever before. Though – again for his security – Japanese bodyguards followed him everywhere, he became quite a man about town: he and his Empress attended the annual ball of the Scottish St Andrew's Society, causing a minor problem for its organizers when it was discovered that Chang Tso-lin's son, who was no friend of Pu Yi's, had also been invited. (The problem was resolved: they both came, but at separate times.) Woodhead says Pu Yi was always dressed in style – the Johnston legacy had borne fruit. Pu Yi bought two motorcycles, which he rode only within his house compound, and Woodhead recalls a hilarious afternoon when Pu Yi insisted that the visiting Johnston try and ride one, the nervous Scotsman taking off and weaving shakily around the courtyard, while Pu Yi laughed.

Some of the English-language editorials Johnston had used inside the Forbidden City to teach his pupil English had been written by Woodhead, and one day Pu Yi told the British journalist he wanted to visit the *Peking and Tientsin Times* printing office. He would do so, he added, under his usual alias, 'Mr Wang'.

One afternoon, a Chinese clerk rushed into Woodhead's office saying, 'The Emperor is here.' 'No, no,' Woodhead said, 'that's Mr Wang.' Pu Yi spent a long time in the paper's offices, delighted to learn how it was 'put to bed'. Afterwards, a Chinese typographer told Woodhead that the armchair in which 'Mr Wang' had sat should be put under glass. 'The Emperor has sat on it!' There was at least one firm monarchist among the paper's Chinese staff.

Woodhead also introduced Pu Yi to a small informal bridge club, the Tripehundverein, which had English and German members (no one knew how the club had got its name, which means 'association of ne'er-do-wells in German slang). Pu Yi accepted his membership in a ceremonial presentation of a scroll with an impressive-looking crest of arms.

While Pu Yi was socializing with the leading members of Tientsin's small-time diplomatic corps and business elite, drinking chocolate in Herr Bader's café, listening to the band of the Royal Scots after its Sunday church parade, ordering suit after suit at Whiteway and Laidlaw's, and, according to Woodhead, indulging in his favourite sports – tennis, skating and motoring – China itself was going through one of its periodic crises. In many ways, Pu Yi's retreat to Tientsin made sense, for Peking was almost without any form of government during the first eighteen months of his stay, full of students and undisciplined soldiers roaming the city at will. In Tientsin, Pu Yi was far from the cut and thrust of day-to-day politics, physically safe – and out of trouble.

Rival warlords dominated powerless governments composed largely of their own nominees, but these came and went with bewildering speed. The 'Christian general' and Chang Tso-lin slugged it out again in 1925 – the prize again being Peking. Pu Yi watched the ebb and flow of inconclusive battles with interest, for his advisers had persuaded him that the warlords held the key to his future:

whoever won would – they believed – restore the Articles of Favourable Treatment and their by now badly needed cash flow.

Of all the contenders, Marshal Chang Tso-lin looked like the most reliable horse to back. One day in June 1925 Pu Yi's father-in-law Jung Yuan, still the House of Ching's money-man despite his obvious failings, brought Pu Yi great news: Chang Tso-lin had pledged £70,000 to what was left of Pu Yi's imperial household 'war chest'. The pay-off was that 'Generalissimo' Chang, as he now called himself, requested an informal meeting with Pu Yi – just the two of them, and not in any foreign concession. Without informing the Japanese – but a Japanese secret serviceman followed him anyway – Pu Yi slipped out one night and met Chang Tso-lin in a secluded house in the Chinese city. It was ringed by Chang's personal body-guard – six-footers in grey uniforms of the generalissimo's own design.

The man who formally kowtowed to Pu Yi inside the mansion was not Pu Yi's idea of a warlord at all: slight, wearing civilian clothes, with a pencil moustache, Chang Tso-lin, from his photographs of this period, looked a little like a Chinese Clark Gable, and like him had a flashing smile and immense charm. Woodhead, who knew him well, described him as 'a slender, delicate-looking man with extraordinarily small hands' who chain-smoked incessantly.

Sitting side by side, the two men exchanged compliments: Pu Yi, as he later wrote, 'was in very good spirits' because the warlord's formal kowtow had dispelled 'my uneasy feeling that I had lowered my dignity by coming to see him'. Pu Yi thanked Chang Tso-lin for maintaining the House of Ching palaces in perfect condition in Manchuria and other areas under his control. There had been no looting, Chang agreed. He cursed the 'Christian general' for his barbarous behaviour the year before. Pu Yi pointed out that it was because of Feng and his plundering troops that he had moved to Tientsin in the first place. Pu Yi gave Chang a wry description of his empty, petty socializing life in Tientsin with second-rate Europeans. Chang sympathized. 'If you need anything,' he said, 'just let me know.'

A junior aide, hovering in an ante-room, came in: 'The Chief of Staff wants to see you, sir.' 'There's no hurry,' Chang Tso-lin said. 'Tell him to wait a moment.' Pu Yi rose. The talk, he felt, was at an end. As he stood he caught sight of a ravishingly beautiful young Chinese girl – obviously the generalissimo's latest concubine, impatiently awaiting his attentions.

Chang Tso-lin escorted Pu Yi to his waiting car. Observing the Japanese secret serviceman standing next to it, Chang Tso-lin said, in a loud voice, meant to be overheard: 'If those Japanese lay a finger on you, let me know and I'll sort them out.'

The next day the Japanese Consul-General rebuked Pu Yi for the meeting: if it occurred again, he said, using extremely polite language and bowing repeatedly, Japan 'will no longer be able to guarantee Your Majesty's safety'.

Pu Yi's advisers were jubilant, especially since, shortly afterwards, Chang Tso-lin swung into action, routed Feng's forces and, in June 1927, was formally in control of Peking, where he proclaimed a military government. The 'Christian general' fled to the Soviet Union, an 'honoured guest' of the Soviets, but his five-month stay there failed to impress him: he left the Soviet Union a far more lukewarm communist sympathizer than he had been on his arrival.

Had Pu Yi – after his ambiguous meeting with Chang Tso-lin, who clearly intended, in a roundabout way, to warn him against involvement with the Japanese – exploited this friendship, and acted boldly, he might well have returned to Peking, protected by his troops, and maybe able to press for some kind of a durable revision of his status. The trouble was that, either through inaction in his Tientsin backwater and a consequent thirst for intrigue, or the contradictory advice of his meddling 'court', Pu Yi dabbled in a whole slough of rival, and fickle, warlords. One of these, Chang Tsung-chang, variously known as the 'dogmeat general' (because of his unsavoury origins) or as the 'long-legged general' (because of his habit of avoiding any personal risk in battle) had once been a colleague of Chang Tso-lin's. Now he had a small fiefdom of his own, and a true con man's gift of the gab. Pu Yi saw a lot of him in his Chang Garden home, fascinated by his tales of derring-do, and – one suspects – because he was bored. Another, even more dubious war-lord temporarily on Pu Yi's limited payroll was a former Cossack general, Semenov, whom he met, briefly, in 1925. Semenov was busy raising an 'anti-Bolshevik league' with the help of Tientsin's White Russian com-munity – but his protection rackets made him a feared and loathed Mafioso figure as far as most Tientsin-based White Russians were concerned. What money he did raise he spent on himself and his Cossack hooligans.

Pu Yi was interested, for at this time Feng was still in control of Peking and entertained strong communist sympathies. An even more persuasive liar than the 'dog-meat general', Semenov used a well-worn con man's ploy: he did not really need the money, his supporters had already pledged 300 million roubles, and US, British and Japanese banks held huge funds at his disposal; the Hong Kong and Shanghai Bank alone had £50 million on deposit for him, he claimed, remitted by the 'British Secret Ser-vice', – part of Britain's long-term plan to topple the Soviet Union. Only a temporary cash flow problem made him come to Pu Yi in the first place. Once his well-financed, highly motivated Cossack-trained armies had gone into action, Pu Yi's restoration to the Manchu throne would be practically a *fait accompli*. It would be a pity to miss out on such a promising venture. Pu Yi gave him £5,000.

Another self-styled public relations specialist, Liu Feng-chih, claimed he was uniquely qualified to bribe members of Chang Tso-lin's entourage to ensure that Pu Yi would return to the Forbidden City as Emperor. This particular swindler suggested that pearls would do the trick. They were duly handed over. From Liu in Peking came the news that more was needed – preferably in cash. Pu Yi started to get suspicious. 'I realized that something was wrong,' Pu Yi wrote later, 'when he came in tears to tell me about his poverty: this time he only asked for ten dollars.'

The drain on Pu Yi's 'war chest' had been considerable – without much to show for his muddled intrigues. Had any of them been successful, however, they would have been short-lived. For suddenly, in 1928, events began to move fast. Chiang Kai-chek began his 'grand design' to establish his authority over the whole of China, and as he started challenging all rival warlords, their interest in Pu Yi's restoration faded, and his own hopes crumbled. 'With their fronts disintegrating,' Pu Yi wrote later, 'the Northern generals had no inclination to worry about [my] Articles of Favourable Treatment.'

CHAPTER THIRTEEN

Chang Tso-lin had made his name with the Japanese as the leader of a daring force of ex-bandit 'irregulars' and had helped them crush the Russians in Manchuria during the Russo-Japanese War of 1904–5.

Since then he had experienced the Japanese both as friends and enemies: they had tried to murder him in 1916, but had bankrolled him in 1924. Since both Chang Tso-lin and the Japanese believed the communist threat from southern China was the major danger to Asian stability, he was confident an 'objective' alliance existed between them. The newly appointed Japanese Premier Gi-ichi Tanaka wished him well.

Tanaka's government, however, was not where Japan's policies were decided, for the country's affairs were handled on two different, and sometimes conflicting, levels. On the one hand there was a formal civilian government. But major policies and long-term strategy were independently determined by Emperor Hirohito through a series of intelligence and military networks, working in absolute secrecy and with virtually unlimited means at their disposal.

In 1927, while Pu Yi was fretting in Tientsin and flirting with Chang Tso-lin, Emperor Hirohito was already planning the neutralization of Chang Tso-lin and the takeover of Manchuria. Prime Minister Tanaka was unaware of this. Though an ex-military man, he was not part of the Emperor's inner circle of conspirators – the 'three crows' and 'eleven reliable men' who had begun planning Japan's military conquests as far back as 1921 in Baden-Baden.

All Tanaka suspected from garbled, incomplete intelligence reports was that some army hotheads among the Japanese Kwangtung army stationed in Japanese-controlled Manchurian enclaves might be intent on 'destabilizing' Chang Tso-lin. Tanaka was in favour of supporting both Chang Tso-lin *and* his KMT rival, Chiang Kai-chek. 'We negotiate with Chang Tso-lin so long as he prevails in the North and with Chiang Kai-chek so long as he is in control of the South,' he said.

Tanaka advised Chang Tso-lin to stick to Manchuria – and pull his armies back north of the Great Wall. But Chang Tso-lin refused. 'I have advanced on Peking and am waging war on communist influences,' he told Tanaka. Chang Tso-lin marched south, engaged Chiang Kai-chek's forces in a series of inconclusive battles, then returned to Peking.

His Japanese advisers then came up with an extraordinary piece of information. The Soviet Embassy in Peking, they told Chang Tso-lin, harboured some fascinating documents which, if published, would radically alter the balance of power in China. Chang Tso-lin had his men break into the Embassy, in defiance of all diplomatic conventions, and carry away all the documents they could find. Among them were directives from Stalin's Komintern outlining the Soviet Union's long-term plans to penetrate the KMT and use the Chinese Communist Party to bring about a Marxist revolution in China, with detailed blueprints for the penetration of the KMT through its Komintern agents and its gradual takeover by Chinese communists.

Chang Tso-lin, the staunch anti-communist who had

always been convinced that Chiang Kai-chek was a prisoner of his communist allies, was delighted to see his theories confirmed – and to expose the Soviet Union in its true colours, as a sinister power intent on exporting world revolution.

But the sensational raid (it was front-page news everywhere) also suited Chiang Kai-chek, giving him the pretext he needed both to gain Japan's approval and to break dramatically with the communists, which he had already promised the Japanese he would do. On 17 April 1927, 'Black Tuesday' in the annals of the Chinese Communist Party, Chiang turned on his communist allies; they were butchered without warning. Five thousand were beheaded. Chou En-lai, who had just become Shanghai's communist mayor, escaped, but the communists were temporarily removed from China's political map altogether. Borodin returned to the Soviet Union, and some erstwhile communist sympathizers, like Feng Yu-hsiang, the 'Christian general', threw in their lot with the KMT.

Chiang Kai-chek then quarrelled with his own KMT associates and announced his 'retirement'. Some weeks later he was in Japan, ostensibly to court Mei-ling Soong, the daughter of the millionaire Shanghai banker whose other daughter had married Sun Yat-sen, become both a communist and his respected widow – and narrowly escaped strangulation at the hands of Chang Tso-lin, buying her freedom for a £125,000 ransom.

While in Japan for those fateful three months, Chiang Kai-chek not only wooed Mei-ling but made a secret deal with the Japanese. Working through the tight-knit, unofficial Hirohito 'net', he briefed the Emperor – through trusted intermediaries – on his future strategy: he would eliminate what was left of his communist allies, and, with the support of all but the diehard 'northern generals' who would have nothing to do with him (he had Chang Tso-lin clearly in mind), would become overall ruler of China up to and including the Great Wall in the north.

Chiang Kai-chek added that he knew that 'pacification' would be a long and costly operation. The communists were on the run, but they would surely reorganize. In return for Japanese support – i.e. non-belligerence – during what he foresaw would be a protracted struggle against them, Chiang Kai-chek was prepared to let both Mongolia and Manchuria fall under Japanese control. He knew he had more than enough on his plate without having to take on these traditionally 'difficult' territories.

Hirohito sent his close associate and relative Prince Higashikuni to China as observer, to keep a close watch on the situation – and to report back directly, without going through official Japanese diplomatic channels. This was the same Prince Higashikuni who had masterminded the Baden–Baden meeting of the 'three crows' in 1921, and the co-opting of the 'eleven reliable men' sworn to fulfil Emperor Hirohito's dream of conquest.

Back in China once more, Chiang Kai-chek launched his 'Northern Expedition' to regain control of China up to and including the Great Wall north of Peking. Pu Yi, from the safety of Tientsin, saw the whole confused civil war as a struggle between rival warlords, and prepared to make a deal with whoever came out on top. But something happened which was to make him Chiang's enemy for life – and thus, when the time came later for a Japan-KMT showdown, to motivate him to side with Japan against Chiang Kai-chek.

In Hupei Province, Chiang's advancing armies profaned the sacred Ching tombs containing the remains of Emperor Chien Lung, the most famous of all the Chings, as well as those of the 'Old Buddha'. The mausolea were broken into, the skeletons dragged out into the open and picked clean of the priceless jewels buried with them.

It was an affront Pu Yi could neither forgive nor forget, and it was to have a profound effect on all his later behaviour. The plunderers were never punished, and there were unfounded but persistent reports that some of the mausolea jewels ended up on the shoe buckles of Mei-ling Soong, Chiang Kai-chek's new bride.

As Chiang Kai-chek's troops advanced northward in

1927, Japan started to fulfil its part of its bargain with him. As usual, nothing was left to chance.

In December 1927 (the same month Chiang Kai-chek finally married Mei-ling Soong, in Nagasaki), a small railway bridge was blown up by 'bandits' on a railway line in Manchuria – or so all the newspapers reported. In fact the explosion had been the work of a Japanese colonel, Komoto Daisaku, permanently based in Port Arthur in the Japanese enclave there. Hardly coincidentally, Daisaku had been one of the 'eleven reliable men' co-opted by the 'three crows' at the 1921 Baden-Baden meeting.

It was, as David Bergamini noted in *Japan's Imperialist Conspiracy*, 'a dry run . . . He repeated the experiment several times on several different bridges in the months that followed. The reaction was always the same: bandits.' The stage was set for Chang Tso-lin's unattributable murder.

Chiang Kai-chek's Northern Expedition, meanwhile, gathered strength in the first six months of 1928 and turned into a disaster for Chang Tso-lin, whose armies had to beat a painful retreat north. Chang decided the tide had turned against him, temporarily, and that he could not remain in Peking. Although he had heard rumours of a Japanese plot against him, he still regarded the Japanese garrisons in their Manchurian enclaves as potential allies, and he himself habitually travelled with three Japanese military advisers, with whom he was, outwardly, on exceedingly friendly terms.

Near Mukden, on the Peking–Mukden railroad line, at a point where it ran under the Japanese-owned Darien–Mukden line, Daisaku planted explosives and began a vigil near the track. Three Manchurian soldiers hostile to Chang Tso-lin, mounted guard on this vital rail crossing.

As a security precaution, Chang Tso-lin sent a 'decoy' train off first. This seven-carriage train contained his favourite 'number five' concubine, the beautiful young woman Pu Yi had caught sight of in Tientsin.

Seven hours later, on the night of 2 June 1928, his own

Pu Yi, aged 3 (Richard Vuu) in Tzu Hsi's bedroom two days before her death (ANGELO NOVI)

Pu Yi (Tijger Tsou) with his wetnurse (played by Jade Go) (ANGELO NOVI)

Right: Pu Yi (Tiger Tsou) on the Imperial Throne. (KEITH HAMPSHIRE)
Below: The emperor's younger brother, Pu Chieh (Henry Kyi) watches the Republican army invade the Forbidden City (KEITH HAMPSHIRE)

Eunuchs carrying trays of food for the emperor's picnic meal (ANGELO NOVI)

The assembled court on the day of Pu Yi's wedding to Wan Jung, the empress and to his 'secondary consort' Wen Hsiu (ANGELO NOVI)

Above: Concubine Wen Hsiu (centre, played by Wu Jun) being attended by Manchurian bridesmaids at her wedding to Pu Yi
(KEITH HAMPSHIRE)
Left: Wen Hsiu (Wu Jun) in bridal attire
(KEITH HAMPSHIRE)

Above: The adolescent Pu Yi (Wu Tao) riding a bicycle inside the Palace grounds (ANGELO NOVI)

Left: Reginald Johnston, Pu Yi's tutor (Peter O'Toole), referees a tennis game inside the Forbidden City (ANGELO NOVI)

Left: Pu Yi (John Lone) as Chief of State of Manchukuo, the puppet Japanese-dominated state
(FRANK CONNOR)

Below: Eastern Jewel (Maggie Han), the famous pro-Japanese spy who became close to the Royal couple
(ANGELO NOVI)

Manchukuo emperor Pu Yi (John Lone) attending an official ceremony (ANGELO NOVI)

Empress Elizabeth (Joan Chen) ravaged by drugs, and about to flee the Manchukuo capital in August 1945 (ANGELO NOVI)

armoured train steamed out of Peking station. Daisaku heard about the decoy train just in time – and waited.

Chang Tso-lin sat in his carriage most of the night with one of his Japanese advisers, a Major Giga. He felt safe as long as Giga stayed in the compartment. They played mah-jong and drank beer together most of the night. A few miles from Mukden station, Major Giga said he had to attend to his luggage. He rushed to the rear platform of the last carriage, curled up in a blanket – and hoped for the best. Minutes later, a terrific explosion tore up the track, telescoping the carriages, killing Chang Tso-lin and six-teen other passengers.

Major Giga survived, shaken but unhurt. Dead men tell no tales, and Daisaku's Japanese explosives experts promptly bayoneted the three Manchurian guards – but one of them escaped, only slightly wounded.

The Japanese had all along hoped that Chang Tso-lin's son, Chang Hsueh-liang, would become their docile Manchurian puppet. He was an opium addict, and lacked his father's charisma. But the son turned out to be unex-pectedly determined: overcoming his addiction, he was to become known as the 'Young Marshal', Chiang Kai-chek's conscience, henchman and, finally, prisoner.

The Japanese, of course, tried to spread the story that 'bandits' hostile to Chang Tso-lin had blown up his train, but the son soon learned from the surviving guard how the Japanese had killed his father. His reaction upset the Japanese calculations: the outrage convinced Chang Hsueh-liang that Japan – and not Chinese communism – was China's real enemy. In time, in an uneasy, temporary alliance with the KMT-communist military, he was to swing the remnants of his father's defeated army into the struggle against Japan. He also, many years later, took his revenge: in 1938 Major Giga was murdered in Japan, almost certainly by a Manchu 'hit squad' acting on Chang Hsueh-liang's behalf.

The Young Marshal not only showed that he himself would not collaborate with the Japanese, he refused to tolerate collaboration in others: learning, shortly after his father's death, that a Manchurian general, Yung Yu-tang, and the civilian head of the Manchurian railways had secretly begun plotting with the Japanese to set up a Japanese puppet Manchurian state, he invited them to play mah-jong with him, and gunned them down in his mansion. Shortly afterwards he joined up with Chiang Kai-chek's forces south of the Great Wall. Manchuria, Emperor Hirohito discovered, was going to be a more difficult nut to crack than expected.

Chang Tso-lin's murder shocked Pu Yi, but at the time he was unaware of the extent of Japanese participation in it. Chang Tso-lin had been only one of many potentially useful warlords. His death was a blow, but not a fatal one.

Pu Yi, at this time, was still highly favourably impressed by the Japanese. In Tientsin he was a minor celebrity. At official dinners, consuls called him 'Your Imperial Majesty', and he was a frequent guest at receptions, parades and national days. But when he went to hear British army bands play in Victoria Park he did so as an ordinary, and increasingly bored, private citizen.

The Japanese were the only people to take him seriously: they piped him aboard their naval vessels on the Pai River, organized formal visits to Japanese Concession schools, and on Hirohito's birthday he was guest of honour at their garrison army parade, taking the salute like a head of state. Japanese officers briefed him on the military situation in China. It was only later that Pu Yi discovered they also had spies inside his home, and knew everything that went on there.

He was dimly aware that all Japanese were not equally impressed by him. The Japanese officers of the Tientsin garrison repeatedly urged him to visit Japan, or at least the Japanese-occupied parts of Manchuria. The Japanese Consul-General urged him to stay put.

Disinformation was now used to put Pu Yi into a suitable frame of mind. Lo Chen-yu, the sinister antiques dealer, came to Pu Yi almost every day with 'evidence' of republican plots, including assassination attempts, being prepared against him. One night Pu Yi's residence came under fire from a sniper in the middle of the night. Pu Yi's own guards caught the culprit – and were surprised to find he was a Japanese *agent provocateur*. Shortly afterwards, Lo Chen-yu's star faded, and he left Pu Yi's court to pursue a more profitable career elsewhere as a dealer in antiques.

In spite of such evidence of Japanese skulduggery, Pu Yi had sufficient faith in the Japanese to urge his younger brother, Pu Chieh, not only to learn the language, but to go to Japan to complete his education. In March 1929, he left for the Peers' School in Tokyo – where Hirohito had been educated. After graduation, he was to enter the Military Cadets Academy. It was a substantial Japanese propaganda victory. Meanwhile, those closest to Emperor Hirohito knew that another scheme was afoot, far more elaborate and effective than Chang Tso-lin's murder.

Shortly after Pu Chieh left for Japan in 1929, some Japanese 'sightseeing tourists' crisscrossed Manchuria by train, complete with notebooks and binoculars. They were the advance elements of the Emperor's personal Manchurian fifth column. Their head was one of the most brilliant, ambitious officers in the Japanese Army, Lieutenant-Colonel Kanji Ishiwara. He had been in Manchuria since 1928, and his task was to deliver the Emperor a blueprint for the seizure of Manchuria.

Ishiwara was not one of the 'eleven reliable men', but he had been a highly successful Japanese spy in Europe in the mid-1920s and was one of Japan's top intelligence operatives. At forty he was one of the handful of officers singled out for a distinguished general's career. He had been a founding member of a secret study group handpicked for the Manchurian operation a year before. His father was an important leader of a Buddhist sect, the Nichiren, with a large following throughout Japan. Ishiwara was also an ideologue, in favour of the long-term fusion of Japan, China and Manchuria into an Oriental superpower as a prerequisite to an all-out war between the 'yellow' and 'white' races. That such a war would come in his lifetime was one of Ishiwara's intimate convictions, as was his belief that the Soviet Union should be the first of the white races to feel the overwhelming might of the Orientals. The Western capitalist nations' hatred of communism, he argued, would keep them neutral during this first, preliminary war.

Ishiwara was, during his Manchurian assignment, writing a book about all this: he knew that many Japanese staff officers, and some of Hirohito's own advisers, regarded him as a somewhat maverick visionary, but there was a brilliance in his plan which showed he was an officer of the highest intelligence, resource and imagination.

The report that finally ended up on Emperor Hirohito's desk was a classic recipe for the takeover of a foreign country from the inside, using deception, disinformation, terror and a minimum of force – a technique used to such effect later on that when, generations afterwards, historians started debating the origins of the Second World War, the case could be made that it began not with Hitler's invasion of Poland in 1939, nor his occupation of Austria or the Sudetenland, but with Ishiwara's Manchurian blueprint.

CHAPTER FOURTEEN

When the Young Marshal, Chang Tso-lin's son, decided to make peace with his old enemy Chiang Kai-chek and rallied to him with his defeated but still impressive Manchurian army, it was not only the Japanese who looked foolish: Pu Yi himself suddenly felt out-flanked. He was relatively secure at Chang Garden inside Tientsin's well-policed Japanese Concession; with British, French and Japanese troops in the town to protect their own nationals it was unlikely that any marauding Chinese KMT troops would enter this privileged foreign zone. What saddened him was that most of his local Manchu monarchist supporters vanished into thin air, as did the blood-sucking warlords on his payroll.

With the help of the Young Marshal, Chiang Kai-chek was not, as he had expected, restricted to 'classical' China south of the Great Wall. His forces were able to move north, into Chinese Mongolia and Manchuria. The Japanese troops in their concession-like enclaves in Port Arthur and Mukden had no orders, at this stage, to start a full-scale war: Chiang Kai-chek still had privileged access to Hirohito's special envoy, Prince Higashikuni. Besides, it was by no means certain that Japan's sixteen battalions in Manchuria would gain the upper hand.

Pu Yi's morale was low, and made worse by a deteriorating climate at home – both financial and emotional. The Empress's father, Jung Yuan, was still in charge of Pu Yi's money matters, and though there were fewer opportunities, now, for him to indulge in his own private 'squeeze', expenses outstripped revenue in Micawberish fashion – and he seems to have been mean, as well as corrupt, for while in Tientsin Pu Yi received a desperate letter from the Empress's mother, begging for money 'for rice to eat'. The couple had formally separated, and Jung Yuan had simply stopped his payments to his wife. In 1934 she was to turn up in Peking in comfortable circumstances: Pu Yi paid her a pension regularly from the time he received her letter.

The list of claims on Pu Yi's fortune was endless. There were his small but expensive liaison office in Peking, the cost of maintaining Ching dynasty mausolea all over China, the 'Imperial Clan Bureau' (for impoverished members of the Ching family) and daily supplicants: eunuchs from the Forbidden City down on their luck; unscrupulous journalists ready to insert pro-monarchist articles in their papers for a suitable fee; bannermen who in exchange for their kowtows had to be sent on their way with small cash presents. Because his was an empty, frivolous existence, Pu Yi saw them all. He had always been a soft touch, genuinely moved by poverty. His visitors knew this, and made the most of it.

The Chinese extended family system meant that Pu Yi was compelled to feed and look after a score of young relatives who had no real business being in Tientsin. As a gesture of loyalty, impoverished cousins sent him their young sons to feed, educate and bring up as loyal Ching dynasty subjects. Pu Yi could not refuse them without losing face. For this reason, in Tientsin, the Chang Garden house was full of what most foreigners assumed were servants. Pu Yi's 'court' referred to them, pompously, as 'page boys'.

In fact there were fewer real servants inside the house than most visitors imagined, and paying their wages was becoming a problem. Pu Yi, painting himself as usual in the worst possible light, wrote in his memoirs that he never tired of 'buying pianos, watches, clocks, radios, Western clothes, leather shoes and spectacles'.

Those who actually remember the Tientsin days – his half-brother Pu Ren who visited him occasionally, and his brother-in-law Rong Qi, told me in Peking in 1986 that they felt Pu Yi slightly overstated things. There was a piano, Pu Yi had several pairs of glasses (he was always losing them, even then) and he had separate Chinese and European wardrobes. But the food, they added, was plain, and everyone – Pu Yi included – became money conscious.

Worse than the downward turn in finances was the sad alienation of his two wives. As Pu Yi remembers it, both Empress Elizabeth and his concubine Wen Hsiu failed to adapt to their new straitened circumstances.

'Wan Jung (Beautiful Countenance) had been a young lady of Tientsin, so she knew even more ways of wasting money on useless objects than I did,' he wrote. 'Whatever she bought for herself Wen Hsiu would want too.' Pu Yi complained that the Empress was well aware of her 'imperial' status, and had no idea of the value of money: household costs escalated as his wives vied with each other.

The local 'tout-Tientsin' was naturally agog: at official functions, Pu Yi usually appeared in Elizabeth's company; he took Wen Hsiu to cafés, tea rooms and the cinema. Foreigners remarked on Elizabeth's spectacular beauty, but also on her bored, withdrawn look.

Opium, in China, has always been a medicine as well as a scourge, and the Dowager Consorts in the Forbidden City regularly had eunuchs prepare pipes for them. As anyone who has ever smoked opium knows, it is, compared to other drugs, a singularly civilized, satisfactory experience. The number of hale, hearty, wizened old opium-smokers with parchment skins in Hong Kong is proof that it is rarely fatal, if taken in moderation. Old-fashioned Chinese matrons, even in today's Hong Kong, recommend it for a whole variety of women's ailments. It is especially effective, they say, in cases of post-parturition blues.

In Tientsin, Elizabeth started smoking opium, and because she was a headstrong, independent-minded girl, only nineteen at the time, there was little Pu Yi could do. It cost almost nothing, and made her less ill-tempered. At first it was not even a habit, just something to do to pass the time of day, for she was bored in 'provincial' Tientsin, cooped up all day, unable to live her life freely, bored with Pu Yi, whom she had started to despise.

Pu Yi was an honorary member of the Tientsin Club (he was a 'special Chinese', there were no other non-European members) and at first Elizabeth played tennis there, but the light-hearted early days inside the Forbidden City were gone for good, and she faced the complaints of the more conservative members of Pu Yi's tiny court who claimed she should behave with Empress-like reserve.

She and Pu Yi started living increasingly separate lives, says her brother, Rong Qi. They would see each other at mealtimes, and, if invited out together, appearances would be preserved. But the marriage – such as it was – was over. She blamed Pu Yi for everything – for her narrow life, for money worries, for not being able to move around Tientsin with the freedom of her girlhood days, for Pu Yi's refusal to allow her to dance the two-step in public or enjoy herself as a teenager. She had all the burdens of an empress without any of its advantages. This was hardly the life she had imagined for herself.

The scenes between Elizabeth and Pu Yi were painful to witness. And there was at least one person who witnessed them as a duty: the Japanese had 'infiltrated' a full-time spy into Chang Garden. He was a Japanese butler, and he reported back to his masters on an almost daily basis. He was to remain with Pu Yi for years. One report described how the couple screamed at each other in the garden one afternoon. Among the insults Elizabeth spat at Pu Yi was the expression: 'You eunuch!' But it is difficult to know whether she was savaging him for his sexual or political inadequacy: Elizabeth had never liked the Japanese. She and Wen Hsiu had that, at least, in common.

But whereas Elizabeth, despising Pu Yi and hating her life, took refuge in opium and passivity, Wen Hsiu did something about her predicament: one day she simply walked out of the house, never to return. China, in 1928, was a surprisingly liberal country in some respects. Divorce by consent was possible without court proceedings. But Pu Yi, under pressure from his advisers, baulked at this: it was unprecedented for the concubine of a Ching dynasty emperor, even a deposed one, to do such a thing. Chang Garden buzzed with excitement as the indignant courtiers scornfully snubbed her family members and haggled with their lawyers. It was only when Pu Yi's courtiers heard that she was about to file divorce proceedings in a local Tientsin court that Pu Yi agreed to divorce by consent. She was paid off with £5,200 alimony. There was ill feeling towards Wen Hsiu on all sides: some of her own relatives cursed her for moving out because they had acquired status through her, even if Pu Yi's fortunes were at their lowest ebb. One of her brothers refused to talk to her, and accused her, in an open letter to a local paper, of 'dishonouring the family name'. She herself, Pu Yi noted with compassion, obtained very little of the alimony after the lawyers and family had taken their cuts.

Concession gossip, of course, was that Elizabeth had forced out a rival. This was not strictly true, for Wen Hsiu was scarcely a rival for Pu Yi's affections: as far as his two wives were concerned, he himself admitted he had none.

He was preoccupied by the turn of events, the world's indifference to his plight, the fact that there seemed to be no way out of his predicament. It was too late, now, to hope for Oxford and a Westernized life of leisure. Johnston had assured him that 'the gate to London was always open', but Pu Yi now felt he was too old in life to become an Oxford undergraduate. He was still a young man, but life was passing him by. The petty jealousies and rivalries within the parochial Tientsin concession were reflected in his own domestic unhappiness. What upset him most of all, a close relative recalled in Peking over fifty years later, was that 'he had no place to go'.

His only move, in fact, reminded him of his growing predicament: the loyal, wealthy bannerman who had loaned him the Chang Garden mansion died, and his son demanded rent. To save money, Pu Yi's court moved to a smaller house inside the Japanese Concession, 'Quiet Garden', almost next to the Japanese army barracks. It was common knowledge, among the concession foreigners, that Pu Yi was having a hard time of it. The 'colonials' reacted in different ways: the shopkeepers became less fawning, but some of the other residents, the British in particular, 'felt sorry for the old boy'.

With the dignity of impoverished noble families, Pu Yi's older courtiers tried to keep up appearances, and took refuge in empty court ritual as a means of overcoming hard times. One of his faithful aides, in these dark days, was Cheng Hsiao-hsu, the non-Manchu scholar who had tried, and failed, to reform the palace finances in the old days. Cheng had returned from his Shanghai home to Tientsin after his rival, Lo Chen-yu, had left. Cheng was in his spry seventies, the epitome of the Confucian moralist, for whom spiritual wealth alone counted: his loyalty was touching, his integrity legendary. He did not lighten the atmosphere, though. The grimmer the circumstances, he explained, the more necessary it was for Pu Yi to assume a dignified, royal mantle.

To please him, Pu Yi stopped going to cafés and night-clubs, and went to the cinema less often. On Elizabeth's nineteenth (by Chinese counting, twentieth) birthday, Pu Yi had promised her a party, with a jazz orchestra, foreign guests, and a Western-style buffet as well as a Chinese banquet. Out of the question, Cheng Hsiao-hsu insisted, and the party was cancelled.

During this dismal period, Pu Yi's nearest equivalent to

the regretted Johnston was Kenji Doihara, who was to play a key role, soon, in events leading up to Japan's disguised annexation of Manchuria. Doihara had been one of the 'eleven reliables', handpicked back in 1921 to fulfil the Emperor's dream: appointed to a key Intelligence role, he was an 'old China hand' with excellent Chinese contacts in Manchuria. He had known Chang Tsu-lin, and was thoroughly experienced in subversion techniques: he knew which corrupt Chinese politicians to bribe with money, which ones preferred women or opium. The Japanese compared him, wrongly, to Lawrence of Arabia, for he was more secret agent than combatant.

Doihara was but the first of a number of presentable, wordly officers deliberately brought into contact with Pu Yi. From 1935 onwards, the one who was to consistently fulfil this role – part go-between, part ADC, part military mentor – was Yasunori Yoshioka, a charming, Chinese-speaking career officer, who was to stay with Pu Yi for practically the rest of his life. He was regularly promoted, despite his 'detachment' and eventually attained the rank of major-general.

As Pu Yi was to find out later, these sophisticated, highly intelligent men were part of the Japanese master-plan for the subjugation of China, specially picked for their social skills. Their mundane, easy-going manner was a veneer: like all the Japanese officers hand-picked for the Manchurian takeover operation, they were utterly ruthless and fanatically obedient to the Japanese military code of honour. Devotion to the Emperor among the military was, at this time, on a scale few non-Japanese could even begin to understand.

It was Doihara who cleverly began convincing Pu Yi that the time would shortly come when he must begin to play an active role again – first as ruler of Manchuria, then as emperor of the whole of China. It was Doihara, too, in his carefully prepared briefings showing the relative dispositions of Japanese, KMT and communist forces, who convinced him that Chiang Kai-chek did not stand a chance. For, true to form, the Japanese had not the least intention of allowing Chiang Kai-chek to pacify China and rid it of communist 'bandits' while sticking to their promise of non-belligerence: on the contrary, the master plan involved the conquest of China – or at least, its reduction to the status of a Korea-type colony, useful for its manpower, rice and raw materials. This, however, was still the privileged secret of Emperor Hirohito and his tiny charmed circle.

In fact, at this time things were going well for Chiang Kai-chek: his forces were on the offensive against the communists and he was greatly helped by the Young Marshal's army. Even in Manchuria, the situation looked more promising for Chiang Kai-chek than he had dared to hope: an anti-Japanese resistance leader, General Ma, was harassing Japanese lines of communication. Some genuine Manchurian bandits also kept the Japanese garrison armies on their toes, and there were even White Russian adventurers among them.

Another unusually talented Japanese officer now enters the picture. With Doihara, he was to make the Ishiwara blueprint one of the most successful Japanese feats of arms of this pre-war period. Major Takayoshi Tanaka was an experienced secret service operative with almost as many crimes on his conscience as Doihara, but he was to have a very different fate. While Doihara was sentenced to death, and hanged, after the war by the International Military Tribunal for the far East, Tanaka was to end up as the privileged aide and boon companion of the Tribunal's chief American Prosecutor, Joseph Keenan. During the Tientsin period, however, Doihara and Tanaka were to make a formidable team.

By 31 May 1931 most of the plan drawn up by Ishiwara was complete. Vital to its success was the construction of a swimming pool for a Japanese officers' club in Mukden. The 'swimming pool' was in fact a concrete emplacement for two huge 9.2 inch Japanese artillery pieces, trucked into Mukden under conditions of utmost secrecy and set up in the 'swimming pool' emplacement, hidden from prying eyes by fences, tarpaulin and a wooden shed.

The two guns were manned by a squad of crack Japanese artillerymen sworn to secrecy. One gun was trained on the main Chinese constabulary barracks, the other on the Young Marshal's small air force base at Mukden airport. Even within the Japanese garrison in Mukden, few Japanese knew of this lethal secret weapon. None of the Chinese did. Most of the Young Marshal's forces were in any case fighting 'bandits' (i.e. communists) in the south, on Chiang Kai-chek's behalf, and Chiang himself was about to enter Peking's Rockefeller Hospital for another opium withdrawal cure.

Another of Ishiwara's ruses was to have some Korean labourers brought in from the nearby Korean border and, under Japanese supervision, put to digging irrigation ditches which, hardly coincidentally, ran through Chinese farmland in south-westernmost Manchuria. The farmers protested, as Ishiwara knew they would, and attacked the Koreans. Suddenly imbued with humanitarian zeal (for Korean labourers were habitually treated like sub-humans) Japanese troops from the concession garrison quickly came to 'protect them'.

Ishiwara's final trump card was a fake derailment on the Japanese-owned South Manchuria Railroad north of Mukden itself. Special Service Organ agents planted explosives – near enough to make impressive craters, far enough away from the track to do no real damage at all.

The Chinese were accused of trying to derail a Japanese train and Japanese troops moved in to cordon off the whole area. An additional, unplanned, incident made Ishiwara's task easier: a real-life Japanese spy was caught and shot by the Chinese in south Manchuria. This, too, provided the Japanese with an excuse to intervene in Manchurian affairs, should they need it.

As David Bergamini, author of *Japan's Imperial Conspiracy*, showed in his hour-by-hour chronology of events in both Manchuria and Tokyo, the ultimate deception was that the whole Japanese invasion, euphemistically called the 'Mukden Incident', was engineered without the formal approval of the Japanese government: the fiction was, all along, that some nationalist hotheads in the Japanese army had overstepped their responsibilities – but that the government, and the Emperor, were forced, by the course of events, to underwrite and accept responsibility for their actions. The whole affair slightly resembled the famous Gaullist 13 May 1958 'coup' in Algiers – except that, unlike de Gaulle, Emperor Hirohito had approved the whole plan himself, down to its last details.

On the night of 18 September, 1931, everything went as planned. Colonel Doihara, aware of all the preparations, was ostensibly out on the town with Chinese cronies, establishing his alibi, and preparing to become Mayor of Mukden thanks to the support of his venal Chinese political cronies.

On the morning of 19 September the two huge artillery pieces opened up on the Chinese garrison in Mukden. Shells destroyed the Young Marshal's small air force in a few minutes, and the Chinese constabulary fled from their burning barracks, fighting a rearguard action. There were sporadic battles against Japanese units, which appeared out of the woodwork all over south Manchuria, but all the Chinese troops in Manchuria were either irregulars or raw conscripts, no match for the Japanese crack troops. All the most experienced units were down in the south with the bulk of Chiang Kai-chek's armies.

By nightfall on 19 September 1931, it was all over, at the cost of five hundred Chinese and only two Japanese dead. All of south Manchuria was in Japanese hands. International reaction was suitably indignant, and the League of Nations alerted. Japanese propaganda, of course, reacted with expected disclaimers and pained sorrow at being misunderstood: their small forces (20,000 against 200,000 Chinese) had simply reacted to 'provocations'.

Doihara used the Mukden Incident to intensify his own disinformation campaign. The fact that the Chinese troops and constabulary had put up such a poor fight was clear proof, he told Pu Yi, that in their hearts they remained loyal to 'Your Imperial Majesty'. Ever since Chang Tso-lin's murder, all Japanese intelligence departments had organized a campaign denigrating both Chang Tso-lin and his son for their 'misgovernment' of Manchuria. It was a blatant lie: for all his swashbuckling, brutal methods, Chang Tso-lin's Manchuria had been the one part of China where drug trafficking and grosser forms of corruption had been sporadically suppressed. Pu Yi, in his Tientsin enclave, was unaware of this. He even, at first, believed the Japanese version of events, as did much of the outside world. The Japanese were highly skilled in the use of the 'big lie'.

The antique dealer and scroll forger, Lo Chen-yu, now made an unexpected reappearance – at a meeting convened by the commander of the Japanese garrison in Tientsin. Lo Chen-yu, now scarcely bothering to conceal that he was on the Japanese payroll, produced 'documents' from important Manchu notables in now Japanese-occupied Manchuria 'proving' that a popular consensus existed for Pu Yi's return there. 'He begged me,' wrote Pu Yi, 'not to miss this opportunity and to come at once to the "land where our ancestors rose up" [against the faltering Ming dynasty].'

Once in Mukden, Lo Chen-yu said, Pu Yi would be proclaimed Emperor 'by popular acclamation'. A Japanese general then put in a word or two. With the KMT forces in disarray, he respectfully suggested to His Imperial Majesty, it was likely they might try and do something rash – like murdering Pu Yi. He also produced articles from the by now Japanese-supervised Manchurian newspapers proving both his and Lo Chen-yu's points.

Pu Yi returned to the Quiet Garden house a puzzled, undecided man. He called in his longtime advisers, among them the honest, austere Cheng Hsiao-hsu. Cheng advised caution. His dislike of Lo Chen-yu made him distrust any plan that involved him. He begged Pu Yi to stay put.

But the pressures on Pu Yi were immense, and various. Two personal initiatives encouraged Pu Yi, wrongly, to think that Britain, too, was officially backing him as the new Emperor of Manchuria: the local British garrison commander in Tientsin, Brigadier F. H. Burnett-Nugent, called to offer his 'personal congratulations' on the 'opportunities' open to Pu Yi after the Mukden Incident. He was merely reflecting the private prejudices of many British expatriates who believed that, with the rest of China in turmoil, Pu Yi had every right to establish his own kingdom in Manchuria, with Japanese support, to keep it out of the turmoil affecting the rest of China. And Johnston also made an appearance, on a private visit, which Pu Yi construed as 'Foreign Office business'.

Johnston too was excited by the implications of the Mukden Incident. He had just finished writing his book, *Twilight in the Forbidden City*, but told Pu Yi he would delay publication to add a chapter entitled 'The Dragon Goes Home' – a clear indication of Johnston's own, wholehearted approval of the Japanese-inspired plan. Johnston – like Burnett-Nugent – was in favour of Pu Yi returning to the land of his ancestors and establishing his kingdom there. (In later years, he was to fly the flag of 'Manchukuo', Pu Yi's puppet state, from a flagpole in the garden of his Scottish island retreat.)

The real reason for Johnston's Tientsin visit was to ask Pu Yi to contribute a brief preface to his book. Pu Yi did so, acknowledging Johnston's key role. 'In 1924,' it read in part, 'after leaving the residence of Prince Chun, I took refuge in the Japanese Legation. It was Johnston, my tutor, who was chiefly instrumental in rescuing me from peril.'

In his usual somewhat prissy way, Johnston noted that the preface had been 'actually transcribed' by the Emperor's 'devoted servant the famous poet, statesman and calligraphist Cheng Hsiao-hsu, about a week before they both left for Manchuria, to become Chief Executive, and Prime Minister, respectively, of the new State.' (The preface – and the book – were to be the subject of considerable debate at the 1946–7 International War Crimes Tribunal.) As a farewell present, Pu Yi gave Johnston a valuable painted fan, inscribed with a personal token of his esteem.

The Japanese now stepped up their pressure on Pu Yi, using Colonel Doihara for the purpose. Doihara met Pu

Yi repeatedly, without interpreters, Doihara speaking Chinese which, he recalled, was 'nothing marvellous'. Pu Yi was however favourably impressed by his apparent sincerity. His talent, Pu Yi wrote, lay in making one feel 'that every word he spoke was completely reliable'. The Japanese army, Doihara told Pu Yi, had no real designs on Manchuria. It 'sincerely wants to help the Manchurian people to set up their own independent state'. This new state's sovereignty would be guaranteed by Japan, but, Pu Yi wrote, 'as head of this state I would be able to take charge of everything'.

Would it be a republic or a monarchy? Pu Yi was anxious to know, and Colonel Doihara was clearly not prepared for this question. 'It will be independent and autonomous, and entirely under Your Majesty's control,' he said. 'That's not what I asked,' Pu Yi said with unaccustomed bluntness.

'This problem will be solved after you come to Mukden,' said Doihara. Not good enough, Pu Yi replied.

'Of course it will be a monarchy; there's no question of that,' Doihara said with a winning smile.

'Very well. If it is a monarchy I will go.'

The Tientsin press was now well aware of the stepped-up visits by prominent Japanese to the Quiet Garden. Rumours that Pu Yi was about to reclaim the Manchurian throne reached Chiang Kai-chek, and a trusted emissary showed up, offering to revive the Articles of Favourable Treatment, or grant Pu Yi a yearly stipend, 'or anything else I might ask in return for my living anywhere except in Japan or the North-east.'

'I remembered the desecration of the tombs,' Pu Yi wrote, and suspected that Chiang Kai-chek was 'only trying to lure me south . . . Once in his power I would be helpless.' Pu Yi gave the emissary 'a non-committal answer'.

Chiang Kai-chek was to make one last attempt to persuade Pu Yi to change his mind. On 10 November, on his way back to Britain, Johnston was passing through Shanghai. T. V. Soong, brother of both Sun Yat-sen's widow and of Madame Chiang Kai-chek, was at this time Chiang Kai-chek's Finance and acting Foreign Minister. Soong asked Johnston over, told him Pu Yi was 'in danger and in need of my help'. 'It was apparently hoped,' Johnston scornfully wrote, 'that I would return to Tientsin and make an effort to dissuade him from embarking on the Manchurian adventure.' In polite but unequivocal terms, Johnston told T. V. Soong he would do no such thing.

One final hurdle had to be overcome: since Pu Yi was to be a Manchurian monarch, his Empress could hardly be left behind. Colonel Doihara now called on his henchman, Major Tanaka, and his partner in crime. She was a Manchu princess turned Japanese agent, a beautiful, amoral tomboy who should, by rights, be far more famous than Mata Hari. Her name was Eastern Jewel and she happened to be an acquaintance of Pu Yi's Empress, and a distant relative.

Theirs was a twin task: by any means, fair or foul, Pu Yi and his Empress had to be persuaded to leave Tientsin. And afterwards the two Japanese agents were to focus news media attention away from Manchuria – on something that would make dramatic front-page headlines elsewhere.

Because Prince Su was always on the move, and mostly broke after 1916, he had no compunction about farming out some of his many girl children to his friends. At eight, he sent her to Japan to be 'adopted' by one of his former Japanese advisers, a member of a prominent Japanese family. From then on, Eastern Jewel became a loyal citizen of Japan. She assumed her 'protector's' family name (she became known, in Tokyo, as Hoshiko Kawashima) and soon shocked Tokyo by her utter contempt for social conventions of all kinds. As her later mentor and co-conspirator, Major Tanaka, recalled in the '50s, both in articles and interviews, she boasted that she had slept at the age of fifteen with the elder Kawashima (her foster-father and her own father's bosom friend) and a year later with his son. Briefly married to a Mongol prince (the marriage was an arranged one, and Eastern Jewel claimed it was never consummated), she left him for a bohemian student life in Tokyo, then for a whole series of rich lovers with whom she travelled extensively.

Her life had its ups and downs. In chatty letters to friends, in her early twenties, she described with great humour her bohemian days in Peking, living in the YWCA and in shady hotels alongside prostitutes and gangsters. In 1928, during one of her penniless spells, she had parleyed her royal Manchu blood into an invitation to Tientsin, as a houseguest of Pu Yi and the Empress. Elizabeth had taken to her immediately. The two young women came from identical, patrician Manchu backgrounds. Both were the daughters of raffish, unscrupulous fathers. During her adolescence, as a prim convent schoolgirl, Elizabeth had heard a great deal of gossip about Eastern Jewel: how she slept with any man she fancied, how she lived to please only herself, how she mixed, on easy terms, with aristocrats and 'singsong' girls, respectable businessmen and members of the Tokyo and Shanghai underworlds. To Elizabeth, Eastern Jewel was the perfect example of the 'liberated' modern woman she had once aspired to be – before succumbing to the lure of a glamorous marriage that had failed to live up to expectations.

In Tientsin in 1928, Eastern Jewel had been Elizabeth's houseguest for several weeks, far prolonging her intended stay of a few days. Pu Yi and his Empress had taken her to parties and shown her something of Tientsin's nightlife – staid in comparison to the Shanghai and Tokyo scenes she talked about so amusingly. Her uninhibited lifestyle and unusual vitality and zest for living had made a deep impression on Elizabeth; the two women had kept in touch ever since.

In Shanghai, at a party, shortly after her return from Tientsin, Eastern Jewel met Major Tanaka, a bull of a man whom she immediately tried to seduce. He was already working as a Japanese spy, and drew heavily on his secret funds to keep her in her accustomed style. She may, at first, have been in love, but her sexuality was masculine: she enjoyed seducing strong, powerful men and then leaving them – preferably with depleted bank balances. Major Tanaka found her an irresistible foil. He himself was not the jealous type, and while they remained sexual partners for years, he was quite happy for her to use her charms on others – men or women, it made no difference to him. He was delighted not only with her sexuality, her amoral approach to life, but also respected her for her brains, her daring, her dashing 'I'll try anything once' approach (so different from that of most Japanese girls), her habit of dressing up as a man. He was also delighted to discover the extent of her aristocratic connections, invaluable in a spy. As Bergamini wrote: 'Being a Chinese princess she could move in Chinese circles closed to any other [spies] . . . being a Manchu princess she looked down upon the Chinese masses with a fanatic contempt beyond Chinese understanding.' Tanaka paid for her English lessons, and made her his fully fledged partner. Her friendship with Pu Yi and Elizabeth, he realized, must soon become a tangible asset.

By the time Major Tanaka and Eastern Jewel had become a practised team of spies, in 1931, Pu Yi had finally overcome his earlier hesitations and was now determined to become Manchuria's Emperor, should the circumstance arise and the Japanese make him a formal offer. But things were not going entirely their way. In the north the Japanese were meeting with unexpected resistance from the heroic General Ma.

So another part of the Ishiwara blueprint was brought into play: specially paid Chinese 'agitators', recruited by the Japanese secret police, attacked Japanese shopkeepers in Harbin, giving Japanese troops a pretext to take over the city.

The Japanese finally established control over the north by mid-November, but now Pu Yi was showing signs of last-minute nerves. Empress Elizabeth was refusing to leave Tientsin, and some of his advisers used her unexpected stubbornness to get him to refuse all Japanese offers. Colonel Doihara sent Eastern Jewel an urgent message to leave Shanghai and report to him at once in Tientsin.

She put on one of her many disguises (this time a traditional male Chinese robe), got one of her occasional boyfriends, a Japanese pilot, to fly her to Tientsin, and reported for duty at Doihara's office.

Characteristically, she did so with her usual sense of theatre, still in male disguise, refusing to give her name to the clerk in Doihara's office. He suspected a plot and put his revolver on his desk. 'You speak like a eunuch,' Doihara said. 'Are you one of Pu Yi's men?' Eastern Jewel laughed. As Doihara later told friends (they, in turn, told Bergamini), Doihara grabbed his sword. 'Very well then, if you won't tell me who you are, let's see what you are,' he told her. Drawing his razor-sharp samurai sword, he nicked the top of her robe. She didn't move, smiling provocatively. He flicked open the Chinese gentleman's robe, and 'with a guttural samurai yell' suddenly severed the silk scarf she had used to bind and conceal her breasts. 'I saw that she was a woman, so I conducted a thorough investigation and determined that I had not put even the smallest scratch on any part of her white skin.'

The next day Eastern Jewel called on Elizabeth at the Quiet Garden house. She reported back to Doihara that the Empress had been delighted to see her, and that they had gossiped for hours. The Empress was overjoyed to listen to the latest Peking and Shanghai gossip, and to the latest stories of Eastern Jewel's own love-life, though she had been careful, of course, to conceal her Japanese connections. She knew that Elizabeth hated and despised the Japanese, and had consistently warned her husband against them; it had been yet another reason for the rift between them. It was highly unlikely, Eastern Jewel told Colonel Doihara, that she would leave Tientsin of her own accord. Strong-arm methods would have to be brought into play. Doihara, ably seconded by Eastern Jewel, set about frightening Pu Yi out of his wits.

In a few days, they succeeded: a café waiter was bribed to 'confess' to Pu Yi that a contract was out on his life, financed by the Young Marshal. Eastern Jewel slipped a couple of lethal-looking snakes into his bed. Pu Yi received a mysterious basket of fruit from an unknown admirer, and in it were two time-bombs. These were immediately handed over to Japanese security specialists who, after cursory examination, told Pu Yi they came from the Young Marshal's arsenal.

The following day (8 November 1931) Doihara decided on tougher measures altogether: he organized anti-Pu Yi riots in Tientsin on a huge scale.

As a later (March 1932) Tientsin municipal government report was to show, the violence was carefully planned and masterminded by Japanese secret police, backed by elements of the local Japanese army Concession garrison, using a hard core of 500 Chinese professional agitators who were well paid for their services. The riots, ostensibly left-wing, led to the destruction of Chinese property worth £3.5 million. Several Chinese policemen were killed, scores wounded – and, as the report showed, all recovered arms, ammunition and spent cartridges were of Japanese make. Those arrested confessed they had been armed and paid by Japanese agents to create disorder.

The initial contingent of demonstrators, set on mayhem, gathered first in the police barracks of the Japanese concession to be briefed by Japanese ringleaders. Their initial targets were Chinese police stations in the Chinese part of Tientsin, and only slight damage, or loss of life, occurred within Tientsin's foreign concessions.

The riots went on for three days. Japanese armoured cars fired random shots into the Chinese part of the city, stories were circulated blaming the Young Marshal, and Pu Yi genuinely believed that the mob was out to get him. By this time, he was virtually a prisoner of the Japanese inside his compound. There was a natural tendency to believe the Japanese version of what was happening outside. By this time, Woodhead had left for Shanghai, so there was no immediate way of finding out the truth from an independent observer. Besides, Japanese disinformation tactics were brilliant: many foreigners genuinely believed the Japanese version of events.

Having provoked the riots, the Japanese used them as a pretext to declare martial law inside the Japanese Concession. Doihara told Pu Yi his life was in serious danger. Eastern Jewel, by now a constant visitor, showed some of her consummate acting skills. She begged him to leave, to save his life, even if this meant leaving his Empress behind for the time being. Thoroughly demoralized by now, Pu Yi agreed.

It was a humiliating exit. As Pu Yi tells it, his valet, 21-year-old Big Li – the same young Manchu servant who had accompanied him to the German Hospital in Peking back in 1924 – tried to open the garage door of Quiet Garden, and found this impossible. It had not been used for such a long time, Pu Yi noted, that it was 'pasted over with advertisements'.

To avoid being seen, Pu Yi waited until the dead of night. Then a car was brought round to the front door. Big Li opened the trunk of the car: Pu Yi leapt in, curled up in a foetal position, and off it drove, with his driver at the wheel and his Japanese interpreter, fully aware of the scheme, in the front seat. So apprehensive was the driver that he reversed into a telegraph pole, denting the car –

and badly stunning Pu Yi.

Inside a Japanese restaurant courtyard a dazed Emperor was helped out of the trunk, given a Japanese greatcoat and taken by Japanese staff car to a waiting launch. In it, waiting for Pu Yi, was the faithful Cheng Hsiao-hsu and two other members of Pu Yi's 'court'. Despite his earlier misgivings, Cheng had decided to follow his Emperor.

Down the River Pai the launch went, challenged once by a Chinese navy patrol boat. The Japanese crew pretended to obey the navy order to stop, then gunned the engine into action and roared away into the dark night. The patrol boat gave chase but the Japanese boat was faster. Pu Yi later learned that the escape plan included a lethal 'fail-safe' device: one of his Japanese escorts, in an article written long after the Second World War for the Japanese magazine *Bungei Shunju*, revealed that a large drum of petrol on deck – right next to Pu Yi – had been placed there for a sinister purpose. He had orders to blow up the boat, all hands included, if they were stopped.

Pu Yi was lifted aboard the Japanese merchant ship *Awaji Maru*. All night he stayed put in a small cabin. The weather was rough and he was abominably seasick. The following morning at Yingkow the Emperor and his small party were put ashore.

There were, Pu Yi recalled, 'no crowds, no flags. The handful of people there to meet me were all Japanese.' It was in fact a humiliatingly low-level delegation, including a secret policeman called Masahiko Amakasu who had achieved some notoriety, back in Tokyo in 1923, for strangling a left-wing activist, his wife and small child, with his bare hands. As Bergamini noted, 'It was a foretaste of the kind of court that would surround his puppet throne in the years ahead.'

The Japanese escorted Pu Yi to a train, and hours later Pu Yi found himself at Tangkangtzu, a local spa, in a luxurious suite inside the Tuitsuike Hotel, an establishdcıment owned by the Japanese-controlled South Manchuria Railway Company before the takeover and reserved for Japanese VIPs. Here he found the sinister antiques expert

Lo Chen-yu waiting for him. Lo Chen-yu explained that the reason for the secrecy, and the absence of welcoming crowds, had been that last-minute discussions were still proceeding among the Japanese on the way the news of his arrival should be handled. Pu Yi ate an elaborate Japanese meal and, exhausted, went to sleep.

The next day, Pu Yi decided to take an early-morning stroll. A worried aide told him this was not possible.

'Why not?' he asked. 'Who said so? Go downstairs and ask.'

'They won't even let us downstairs.'

A furious Pu Yi summoned Lo Chen-yu, but he had vanished. The entire party was to be held incommunicado, a Japanese secret policeman told them with much bowing, until orders had been received from a Colonel Itagaki.

It was Seishiro Itagaki, another member of the 1921 'eleven reliable men' cabal, who had masterminded the Mukden Incident, working hand in glove with Ishiwara. Affable, back-slapping, with top connections, he was to play a leading role in Japanese-occupied Manchuria, and in China, for the next few years. Later, an intimate of Emperor Hirohito, he was to become War Minister, eventually sharing Doihara's fate, one of the eight Japanese war criminals hanged in 1948.

Pu Yi belatedly realized he was a prisoner once more, with far less cards to play than in Tientsin. The Japanese were treating him far less respectfully than he had expected. Itagaki would not even come to see him: they spoke by telephone. Cheng Hsiao-hsu now wore an 'I told you so' expression, but was too loyal to express his thoughts out loud. It was all very different from the rosy picture painted by Colonel Doihara, and Pu Yi realized, by stages, that he was not even going to be allowed a 'triumphal return' into Mukden, Manchuria's capital. After letting him kick his heels for a week in the railroad hotel, Itagaki informed him curtly on the phone that he would be taken to Port Arthur instead.

Port Arthur was the headquarters of the old-established Japanese-leased territory ceded by China since the 1904–5

Russo–Japanese War. Although Pu Yi did not realize it at the time, frantic discussions over his status were going on within the Japanese military establishment: the Kwangtung army did not want a monarchy, even a puppet monarchy, rashly conceded by Doihara. The Japanese experts on Manchuria, who had worked hard to win over prominent Manchurian civilian 'collaborators', felt that a 'parachuted' outsider like Pu Yi would destroy years of valuable work, and seriously weaken their contacts with the local élite. Not that the Japanese were in any way concerned with human rights, or intended to allow Manchurians any real local political autonomy. They were simply aware that Chiang Kai-chek's KMT government was preparing to lodge a formal protest at the rape of Manchuria before the Geneva-based League of Nations, and wanted to be in the strongest possible position to counter its charges and show that the Manchurian breakaway had popular grassroots support.

Pu Yi, unaware of any of this, saw the move to Port Arthur as a step in the right direction. But in the Japanese-owned Yamato Hotel, he was a prisoner again, not allowed downstairs from his VIP suite, and visits were still severely restricted. Officially, the Japanese line remained that they wanted to keep his arrival secret 'for the time being'.

Meanwhile, back in Tientsin, Elizabeth was still being regularly visited by Eastern Jewel, who brought the Empress reassuring news. Eastern Jewel's family owned a house in Port Arthur, and here, she told Elizabeth, she would soon be reunited with Pu Yi. The Japanese had rented it, and were establishing it as a half-way house for him before preparing an official ceremony to celebrate his return according to his exalted rank. Eastern Jewel was still fazed by Elizabeth's refusal to believe that Pu Yi's decision had been anything but a huge mistake, that the Japanese had fooled him all along, and that their promises meant nothing.

Elizabeth might, had she been as independent-minded as Wen Hsiu or as free as Eastern Jewel, have made the decision to break with Pu Yi there and then. An empress did not sue for divorce, though, and her own father – hoping to become Pu Yi's money-man again if he did become Emperor of puppet Manchuria, had considerable influence over her. What is more, for all their drifting apart in Tientsin, she seems, at this time, to have been genuinely fond of Pu Yi still. Lacking Eastern Jewel's spirit, she was also probably scared she might simply be cast aside as an unwanted wife, as her mother had been, and left without any resources at all. For when Elizabeth heard garbled reports that Pu Yi was under arrest in Port Arthur, she changed her mind, stormed and ranted, shed hysterical tears, and demanded to be reunited with him.

About six weeks after the inglorious escape in the boot of a car, they were together again, in the waterfront house belonging to Eastern Jewel's family. Eastern Jewel herself was back in Shanghai, not a moment too soon, for Major Tanaka had several other jobs for her: she was to be a leading *agent provocateur* in the localized war that would break out in Shanghai between China and Japan the following month, to draw attention away from the situation in Manchuria. And she acquired two more lovers, both extraordinarily valuable sources of information for Major Tanaka: from the pillow talk of a British military attaché in Shanghai, she relayed the news that for all Britain's verbal condemnation of Japan's Manchurian aggression, there would be no tough practical measures taken against Japan. Her other lover was none other than Sun Fo, Sun Yat-sen's son. For the entire duration of the Sino-Japanese clash in Shanghai, which was to lead to thousands of deaths and the first indiscriminate bombing of civilians by (Japanese) planes, Eastern Jewel was able to relay to Tanaka precious titbits of information straight from the privileged centre of the KMT camp.

As a spy, Eastern Jewel was to go from strength to strength, and by 1937, when the Japanese had finally over-run northern China and installed a puppet Chinese government in Peking, she was to return there in state, no longer concealing the fact that she was a leading Japanese collaborator. She used her influence with the top Japanese establishment to blackmail wealthy Chinese, threatening to report them to the Japanese secret police for anti-national activities unless they paid her huge sums of money. She moved into a palatial Japanese-requisitioned building. Losing her looks (she became wrinkled, fat and looked more and more masculine), she had to rely on different wiles to take young men to bed: a famous Peking actor who refused to make love to her found himself in prison, accused of stealing her purse. She became increasingly bisexual, sleeping with the singsong girls she also continued to provide for Tanaka, who remained her friend. But even he was to tell Bergamini later that her behaviour went 'beyond common sense'. After Japan's collapse, she refused to escape to Japan, but it was another three years before she was caught – by Chiang Kai-chek – and beheaded. As Bergamini reported, 'her judge . . . condemned her most of all for having ridden in Japanese airplanes and looked down in contempt – she, a woman – on the good earth of China'.

While Eastern Jewel, still young and beautiful, was sleeping with her two new lovers, and Japan was preparing for an armed showdown with China in Shanghai, Colonel Itagaki flew back to Tokyo from Manchuria to brief the Emperor on the situation there. The audience was not concerned so much with Pu Yi as with the broader aspects of Japanese policy in Manchuria, and the need to establish a Japanese-controlled puppet state there while avoiding the charge of outright annexation of Chinese territory, attempting to convince international public opinion that it was a fully independent, sovereign state.

Bergamini, years later, obtained an account of the meeting. Itagaki told Hirohito that 'the new puppet state would preserve a façade of independence and self-rule', but that Japanese 'advisers' would in fact be in full control. To fool the foreign powers, however, these advisers would masquerade as Manchurians, assume Manchurian names and have temporary Manchurian citizenship. Hirohito asked whether there were any precedents for such dual nationality. Itagaki said the practice was quite common.

The Shanghai provocations that were to lead to full-scale war started a week later. And while the war was still raging, with some 20,000 Japanese troops due in Shanghai to overcome the unexpected, heroic resistance of the 19th Route Army, Colonel Itagaki was back in Manchuria, having his first major face-to-face talk with Pu Yi, and spelling out what was in store for him.

Itagaki spoke not with the smooth charm of Colonel Doihara, but with the authority of someone who had been briefed by Emperor Hirohito himself. He was blunt and to the point: there would be no 'empire', at least not for the foreseeable future; the new state would be called the 'Republic of Manchukuo', and Pu Yi would be its Chief Executive. The capital would not be Mukden but Changchun, in northern Manchuria, a grim, industrial town 500 miles north of Port Arthur. Itagaki produced from his briefcase the 'Declaration of Independence of the Manchu and Mongol People' and a facsimile of its new flag, a white expanse with five coloured lines in a small rectangle symbolizing the 'five races' of Manchuria – Manchurians, Chinese, Mongols, Japanese and Koreans.

Pu Yi indignantly pushed away the flag and the declaration. 'What sort of state is this? It certainly isn't the great Ching Empire,' he said, indignantly.

Of course not, Itagaki said patiently, as though reasoning with a child. This was a new state, sanctioned by the 'Administrative Committee for the North-East', the collaborator body the Manchurian specialists had worked on so effectively. 'It has passed a unanimous resolution acclaiming Your Excellency head of state.'

Pu Yi was quick to note he was no longer being called Your Imperial Majesty. 'I was so worked up,' he wrote later, 'I could hardly sit still.'

'I cannot accept such a system,' Pu Yi told the colonel. 'The imperial title has been handed down to me by my ancestors, and were I to abandon it I would be lacking in loyalty and filial piety.'

It would only be a temporary arrangement, Itagaki

countered. The new National Assembly would surely, in time, revive the imperial system.

This was the first Pu Yi had heard of a Manchurian parliament and he was furious. The discussion was getting nowhere. Itagaki picked up his briefcase. 'Your Excellency should think it over carefully,' he said. 'We will continue our discussions tomorrow.'

The next day Itagaki told Pu Yi even more bluntly that there could be no alternative to the Japanese proposals. The ex-Emperor's entourage advised him to accept them. Cheng Hsiao-hsu himself, who had done his utmost to prevent Pu Yi from leaving Tientsin, seemed by now resigned to the situation. Besides, if Pu Yi was to be head of state, Cheng would be Prime Minister, and he was vain enough to brighten at the thought.

Quite apart from the Kwangtung army's view that local collaborators should have their puppet parliament and be given some material rewards for their Japanese collaboration, there was another vital reason why Itagaki, under the firm guidance of the Japanese imperial palace, had produced this particular blueprint: though the League of Nations had fallen short of imposing effective sanctions on Japan for its annexation of Manchuria, it had appointed an investigating commission to assess the Manchurian situation at first hand, and it was more urgent than ever to show the world that 'Manchukuo' had at least some of the trappings of an independent, normal state.

A week after Itagaki's meeting with Pu Yi – on 29 February 1932, a leap year – the Lytton Commission appointed by the League of Nations arrived in Tokyo on the first leg of its fact-finding mission.

concerned so much with Pu Yi as with the broader aspects

CHAPTER SIXTEEN

To Americans and Europeans alike, Manchuria is at the other end of the world, at the Tartar confines of easternmost Siberia and northernmost China, as remote as the Galapagos or Easter Islands.

To the Russians, Japanese and Chinese, it was – and remains – a highly important industrial and agricultural country in a strategically important part of the world. It is across the River Amur, which marks the boundary between Manchuria and the USSR, that Chinese and Soviet troops and missiles today still keep up their costly vigil.

Japan's determination, in the 1920s, to take over Manchuria and install a Japanese-controlled puppet government there can only be understood in an overall strategic and economic context, which was even more important then than it is today. Manchuria, with only 9 per cent of China's total population, was – despite its rugged climate, hot in summer, icily cold in winter – potentially the richest part of China in the troubled, anarchic 'twenties. It had – and still has – huge mineral and coal reserves. Its soil is

Top: Japanese Chinese war in Manchuria (TOPHAM).
Bottom: Chinese communists v. Japan (CAMERA PRESS).

Top: Pu Yi in Manchuria
1938 (HULTON).
Right: Emperor of
Manchukuo (POPPER).

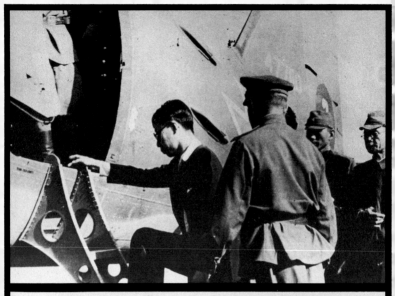

Top: Arrest by Russians of Pu Yi (KEYSTONE)
Bottom: Forbidden City 1949 (POPPER)

Top: Dohiara and Itagaki on trial (HULTON/BETTMANN).
Bottom: Pu Yi on trial 1946 (POPPER).

Top: Pu Yi preparing
confession (CAMERA PRESS).
Bottom: Pu Yi's brother in
Peking 1981 (TOPHAM).

Jin Yuan, former governor of Fushon jail

Top: Li Wenda, Pu Yi's ghost writer
Bottom: Pu Ren, Pu Yi's half brother

perfect for soya bean and barley. Its horseback-riding farmers are among the hardiest, most industrious in the world (from their ranks came the tough Manchu cavalry warriors who conquered China for the Ching dynasty in the seventeenth century), and its economic development, long before the Mukden Incident, outstripped the rest of China – partly because of the sound administration of the murdered 'generalissimo' Chang Tso-lin. In every respect it was way ahead of China in food production, income and railroad infrastructure. In 1933, at a time when Japanese occupation was not yet fully under way, it accounted for 14.3 per cent of all of China's industrial output, 12 per cent of its industrial labour force, and between 1913 and 1930 it increased its agricultural production by 70 per cent.

One of the reasons why Chang Tso-lin became such a formidable figure was that he fully grasped from the start, even as a minor warlord, the importance to China of railroad communications. Despite the fact that, as a result of the Russo-Japanese War of 1904-5, the Japanese had taken over some of the Russian-built, Russian-operated railroads in the area and created their own, powerful, Japanese-owned South Manchuria Railroad Company, Chang Tso-lin had had the foresight to set up his own railway company – which explained why he was travelling in his own, armour-plated train when he was killed. Before his death, he had also acted as a go-between over competing Japanese and Soviet interests in Manchuria, for the Soviets, especially in the first decade after the October 1917 Revolution, were never free of the suspicion that the British and Japanese might combine to attack Russia on its Manchurian border in order to destabilize the admittedly shaky and economically bankrupt regime.

Even after Chang Tso-lin's death, both Soviet- and Japanese-operated trains continued to run in Manchuria with separate armies of Soviet and Japanese 'railway troops'. Manchuria's railroad tracks accounted for more than 30 per cent of China's total rail infrastructure. Between 1928 and 1937 it grew by 4,500 kilometres, double the increase in the whole of the rest of China.

By any standards, in the twenties, Manchuria was a valued prize, a hugely profitable land waiting for development: for pre-Second World War Japan, especially, Manchuria was an essential source of raw materials and factories. Without Manchuria's resources, Japan could probably not have embarked on its policy of conquest over the rest of South-East Asia (beginning with China) nor taken the risk of bombing Pearl Harbor in 1941, thereby compelling the United States to enter the Second World War. Manchuria became Japan's Ruhr, fuelling its war economy – including its increasingly important war-related industries. And because Manchuria, compared to the rest of war-torn China, enjoyed such an economic boom, its population increased, from 18 million in 1910 to 38 million in 1940 – a sudden and spectacular leap occurring after the 1931 Mukden Incident. This was the country that was about to become 'Manchukuo', with Pu Yi as its 'Chief Executive'.

It was also to become, after 1931, one of the most brutally run countries in the world – a textbook example of colonialism, albeit of the Oriental kind. In Manchukuo's first few years the brutality was mainly confined to the Manchu, Chinese and White Russian population of Manchuria, so the outcry was far more muted than in the case of the later Nazi occupation of Europe after the start of the Second World War. These were still the days when American, British, French or Italian passports afforded their holders real protection. And the innate, and often unconscious, racism of foreign observers was such that they tended to take for granted the exactions inflicted by Orientals on Orientals, or on other despised human beings like the stateless Russians, then several hundred thousand strong in Manchuria.

British journalist-explorer Peter Fleming described how, on a Manchurian train, the Japanese took his friend Kini for a White Russian and routinely beat her up, until they discovered she was Swiss, and apologized profusely. As Fleming put it in his book *News From Tartary*, 'you can beat White Russians up till you are blue in the face, because they are people without a status in the world, citizens of nowhere'. Such routine brutality was totally unsurprising to him and to other Western observers.

The overt random cruelty witnessed by Western travellers was only part of a systematic reign of terror, imposed from on high in Tokyo, incorporating both fascist and colonialist features, designed not only to terrorize the local population but to turn the thinly disguised Japanese occupation into a profitable operation.

Under barely disguised colonial rule, emigration to Manchuria was to surpass Japan's wildest expectations. There were 240,000 Japanese in Manchuria in 1931. By 1939 the figure had risen to 837,000, which represented a quarter of the population of the new capital of Manchukuo, Changchun. The Mukden Incident put an end to any restraint on immigration or property acquisition, allowing the Japanese to 'develop' the area with a completely free hand.

There is no doubt that, in time, Japan intended to turn Manchukuo into an official Japanese dependency: in August 1935, the Japanese government officially announced its immigration plan for Manchuria, designed to settle five million people there between 1936 and 1956. The purpose was not merely strategic, but to relieve the then considerable problem of Japanese agricultural over-population at home. Between 1938 and 1942 a force of 200,000 young farm workers volunteered to go to Manchuria and were settled on farms (most of them expropriated from their rightful Manchu owners), which were turned into 'strategic hamlets'.

Bachelor volunteers apart, 20,000 families a year moved to Manchuria from 1936 onwards, until – by the middle of the Second World War – Japan started losing the command of the seas and was no longer able to ship them out in such numbers.

Japanese governments, from 1931 on, saw in Manchuria a huge potential for feeding Japan. Official Japanese propaganda had it that these farm volunteers and retired servicemen were sent to previously uncultivated, barren areas of Manchuria.

The facts were very different. For all its vastness (more than twice the total area of France and pre-war Germany combined) it simply was not true that huge tracts of land were lying fallow, awaiting the industrious Japanese colonists. The new Japanese agricultural settlements were bitterly resented and many were under constant threat of attack. Hundreds of thousands of Manchu farmers were dispossessed – or worse. There exists an appalling Japanese eye-witness account, by a former agricultural volunteer, of Manchurian farmers rounded up and turned over to Japanese conscripts with instructions that these were freshly captured 'bandits' to be used for bayonet practice. Understandably, many of the now landless farmers swelled the ranks of the anti-Japanese guerrilla armies and became real bandits. Others flocked to the towns, where work was assured.

For Manchuria, from 1931 onwards, became an industrial powerhouse. Japanese bauxite was in short supply, so Manchurian alumina shale was developed on a vast scale; from 1932 onwards, the Japanese invested hugely in Manchuria in iron, steel, fertilizer, explosives, chemical, machine tool, electrical engineering, boilermaking industries. There was an equally startling construction boom. With American help, the Japanese set up a fledgling automobile industry (Dowa Company) in 1934, and even a small aircraft industry (the Manchurian Airplane Company), first for light engines, later for the aircraft themselves. On a *Saturday Evening Post* assignment, Edgar Snow wrote that 'change becomes apparent when the Border is crossed, even before one enters the big cities, where a phenomenal building boom is rapidly altering the face of Manchuria'. He contrasted China's dirty trains with Japanese 'ordered cleanliness and service'. 'Manchukuo', a visiting American businessman told him, should really be called 'Japanchukuo'.

Professor F. C. Jones, an expert on Manchuria whose book *Manchuria After 1931* remains the most authoritative work on the subject, wrote that 'the Japanese built up, in Manchuria, an industrial potential far ahead of anything which existed elsewhere in eastern Asia exclusive of Japan and the USSR', but, in every case, 'integrated the Manchurian economy to their own ends'. In the classic colonial pattern, Manchuria produced either raw materials or semi-finished goods, with the finishing process taking place in Japan. 'It was a typical colonial structure,' Jones wrote. 'The managers and technicians were exclusively Japanese.'

Typically colonialist, too, was Japan's education policy in Manchuria. After the Mukden Incident all the old Chinese universities in Manchuria closed down. The Japanese encouraged the establishment of new colleges, but eradicated humanities from the curriculum because, as Jones put it, their teaching was 'liable to have undesirable political consequences'. A London *Times* reporter, visiting newly-established Manchukuo in December 1932, quoted a Japanese officer. 'Manchuria needs work,' he said, 'not the high-collar youths with half-baked notions who swarm in Japan.'

This was recognized in the publications issued by the Manchukuo government, which were designed to prove that the country was fully independent. In Volume 3 of *Contemporary Manchuria* (January 1939), the author of the 'Education' section boasted there was 'no undue emphasis on mental training'. The Japanese required obedient industrial workers and foremen, and designed the Manchukuo educational system to make sure they got an adequate supply.

In most countries, the industrial proletariat has the edge over its agricultural equivalent in terms of salaries, housing and purchasing power, but in Manchukuo tight Japanese control over the local economy meant that its workers produced capital, not consumer, goods – and a stringent import policy meant that even essential consumer items like clothing, and even food, were in short supply – and worsened by the year. There was an effort made to house the influx of badly needed industrial workers, and the Japanese-built housing still stands today. But inside these buildings, wrote Jones, 'were people whose health had been largely undermined by malnutrition and overlong factory hours'.

There was another side to the Japanese occupation of Manchuria, and it is documented in a remarkable, long forgotten book by an Italian adventurer with the unlikely name of Amleto Vespa.

Vespa, born in 1888, settled in Harbin during the First World War after an adventurous youth in the service of the Mexican revolution. A fluent Chinese and Japanese linguist, he became, during the First World War, a freelance intelligence agent in China, on the side of the Allies. During these years, he became friendly with Chang Tso-lin who put him on his payroll and made him a senior officer in his own, personal secret police. From then until Chang Tso-lin's death, Vespa, a short, stocky man with a distinct physical resemblance to Mussolini (a man he much admired), became a highly effective agent, with a remarkable record for putting gun-runners, pimps and drug traffickers behind bars. Because the Italians disapproved of his activities, he took out Chinese citizenship – an act he was later to regret, since this put him, after the Mukden Incident, on a par with the despised Chinese and Manchus as far as the Japanese were concerned.

In 1931 Colonel Doihara threatened to kill Vespa's Italian wife and child unless he became a Japanese secret agent. With no recourse, Vespa agreed to work for them. At the same time, he did his best to thwart them, becoming a successful double agent. Until he was able to flee Manchuria in 1936, he observed the Japanese at work, in Harbin and elsewhere, at extremely close quarters, and his book, *Secret Agent of Japan*, is an extraordinary record of this little-known period.

So sensational was the book when it first appeared in 1938 that some critics believed Vespa had made most of it up. But both Edgar Snow and H. J. Timperly, then China correspondent of the *Manchester Guardian*, who knew Manchuria well, vouched for its accuracy. So, later, did a number of other experts who were able to check Vespa's account of his life in Manchukuo in the thirties – and found it tallied with Japanese documents in their possession.

As Vespa tells it, Colonel Doihara summoned him to meet the head of the Japanese secret service in Manchuria, a man of immense sophistication, who spoke perfect English, and whose name Vespa never discovered. He may have been a Japanese prince of the royal blood, for no one except an intimate of the Emperor, Bergamini wrote, would have dared to speak with such cynical contempt of his subordinates and of foreigners in general, and so openly –,and knowledgeably – of Japan's world design.

The mysterious secret service chief told Vespa what his duties would be. The occupation of Manchuria must be made to pay for itself. After all, this was the way all colonial powers had traditionally behaved, and 'we Japanese are a very poor people. . . In one way or another, therefore, the Chinese of Manchuria must foot the whole bill.' They would do so, the intelligence chief told Vespa, in a number of ways: through monopolies, ransoms, kidnappings and the deliberate sabotage of the 'Eastern railway' which the Soviets operated at the expense of the Japanese-owned South Manchuria Railway Company. Among the monopolies to be set up, special attention was to be paid to the manufacture and sale of opium, to gambling and to prostitution. 'Those who have been granted monopoly concessions have to pay very heavy sums,' the Japanese intelligence chief told Vespa. 'They are entitled to our protection.' Japanese-owned monopolies, operating under Japanese protection, were in time to cover almost every aspect of Manchuria's day-to-day economy – there was even a chimneysweep monopoly, owned by a Japanese businessman and 'protected' by ten members of the Japanese Gendarmes.

Vespa was to become the leader of a squad of 'hit men' and act both as enforcer and go-between on behalf of the Japanese secret service.

The strong-arm squad was to be used in a multitude of ways, Vespa was told. One Japanese priority was to compel all goods to be transported not on the Soviet-controlled railroad, but on the Japanese-owned South Manchuria line, and one of Vespa's tasks was to 'interfere with the running of the Harbin–Vladivostok railway, and stop it altogether. . . There are going to be many wrecks, one wreck after another, until the Russians find themselves obliged to ship their goods over our line to Dairen [Dalian]. There are also going to be frequent wrecks on other lines controlled by the Soviets, and, for the sake of appearances, a few on the Japanese line.'

The senior Japanese official also planned kidnappings on a large scale, with big ransom money being demanded from those who could afford it; special attention was to be paid to the 7,000 Russian Jews still living in Manchuria. Many of them, Vespa was told, 'have been able to become naturalized citizens of other countries. . . most foreign firms are represented by them. We cannot attack them openly and directly, especially those who have acquired passports of countries with extraterritoriality rights. But indirectly we will make things tough for them. . . we can very well touch all those who seek to do business with them.'

There should be occasional fake attacks on Chinese villages, with Vespa's strong-arm men fleeing on the arrival of Japanese troops, 'so we may thus gain the gratitude of the Chinese', and also fake attacks on Japanese soldiers, 'giving us pretexts for punitive expeditions and for withdrawing the inhabitants of those areas we wish to give to Japanese colonists'. In all these schemes, mercenary-minded White Russian émigrés could be usefully enlisted as hit-men along with the Manchurian and Chinese 'bandits' Vespa was to recruit. Every organization, Manchu or foreign, 'which is not sincerely friendly to the Japanese', must be eliminated, the official said.

One problem Vespa was to face in carrying out Japanese orders (which he did, but in such a way, he claims, that the tables were often turned on them) was that the hated Japanese gendarmerie itself indulged in protection rackets, often of 'unauthorized' gambling-den, opium-parlour or brothel entrepreneurs who were not paying their dues to the Japanese authorities. In Harbin, where Vespa lived, a live-and-let-live policy was instituted: the Gendarmerie was allowed to keep five brothels, five opium parlours, one gambling shop and one hard-drugs narcotics shop. 'A small number,' Vespa noted, 'when one considers that in Harbin alone there were 172 brothels, 56 opium-dens and 194 narcotics shops.' These, he adds, were not really shops at all. 'The morphine or heroin addict simply knocks at the door, a small peep-hole opens, through which he thrusts his bare arm and hand with twenty cents in it. The money is taken and he gets a shot in the arm.'

From 1932 onwards, Vespa reported, the Japanese hugely increased areas under opium poppy cultivation. After 1937, 'shipments of opium to China,' he wrote, were made 'daily under the guise of Japanese military supplies. In places where there is no Japanese military command the opium is shipped to the Japanese Consulate. Japanese warships transport opium along the Chinese coast, and Japanese gunboats perform the same service on all the large rivers of China.' Drugs remained strictly forbidden to the Japanese themselves, however. Vespa quoted from a booklet distributed to all Japanese troops by the Japanese Military Command, which read: 'The use of narcotics is unworthy of a superior race like the Japanese. Only inferior races, races that are decadent like the Chinese, the Europeans and the East Indians, are addicted to the use of narcotics. This is why they are destined to become our servants and eventually disappear. A Japanese soldier guilty of using narcotics becomes unworthy of wearing the uniform of the Imperial Japanese Army and of venerating our divine Emperor.'

Vespa's account of his dealings with the Japanese secret police and his gangs of Chinese and White Russian toughs – and the way he managed, in fact, to become a double agent, informing his victims in advance whenever he could of what was about to happen to them – not only makes sensational reading but also shows that kidnapping, either for ransom or for reasons of political intimidation, was as rife in Manchuria from 1932 onwards as it was to become, later, in Lebanon. In his book, Vespa published long lists of names of Chinese and stateless foreigners who were kidnapped, and often killed.

One case, involving the popular Russian Jewish owner of Harbin's Hotel Moderne, was reported internationally because it was so horrible. Joseph Kaspe had made a sizeable fortune in Manchuria. He owned not only the town's leading hotel, but also a jewellery shop and a chain of cinemas. He had become a naturalized French citizen, and one of his sons, Simeon, a talented pianist, was a graduate of the Paris Conservatoire and a budding concert pianist of repute. In 1933, Simeon visited Asia for a series of concerts, and came to stay, briefly, with his father. He was kidnapped on 23 August 1933 by a gang of White Russians working hand in glove with the Japanese Gendarmerie. The kidnappers demanded a huge ransom. The father refused to pay it until his son had been released. He received his son's two severed ears.

In the weeks that followed, both Vespa and the French Consul in Harbin became convinced that the Japanese secret police were protecting the White Russian kidnappers – and obtained proof to that effect. But though the Japanese, because of the international attention the case attracted, were eventually forced to act against the actual White Russian kidnappers, who were shot dead, the Gendarmerie's role, which had been predominant, was never investigated. In early December 1933 Simeon Kaspe's hideously tortured body was found in a shallow grave outside Harbin.

Because all non-Japanese, foreign-owned businesses, even those run by privileged West European or American passport holders, were subject to constant racketeering, many sold out, at rockbottom prices, to Japanese businessmen. Vespa himself was dispossessed of most of his property. He fled to Shanghai in 1936, leaving his family behind in Harbin. A Chinese 'bandit' friend kidnapped several Japanese who were exchanged for Vespa's wife and child.

This was the kind of country Manchukuo was about to

become, and though Pu Yi could have had no knowledge of what the Japanese had in store, he must have known, from his earliest talks on Manchurian soil with Colonels Doihara and Itagaki, that these were ruthless men and that this might be the regime to expect. But as Pu Yi was to tell the International War Crimes Tribunal later, 'I had put my head in the tiger's mouth.' There was no going back now, though Empress Elizabeth did make one last, desperate bid for freedom.

CHAPTER SEVENTEEN

The day after the Lytton Commission arrived in Japan, a delegation of the 'All-Manchurian Assembly', a creation of Colonel Doihara's, which included Japanese masquerading as Manchurians and a few genuine Manchu opportunists, arrived in Port Arthur to 'beseech' Pu Yi to become Chief Executive of the new state. In traditional Chinese fashion, he 'refused modestly' the first time, accepting a few days later.

That night (24 February 1932) Colonel Itagaki gave an elaborate private banquet to celebrate Pu Yi's acceptance. It was a Japanese affair, attended by local geishas. All the Japanese present got very drunk, Pu Yi recalled later. Itagaki fondled the geishas on either side of him, joked constantly and had his Japanese guests in constant fits of laughter. One of the geishas, obviously inadequately briefed, cuddled up to Pu Yi and asked him: 'Are you a businessman?'

While Pu Yi was preparing to leave for the new Manchukuo capital, Changchun, the Lytton Commission was being fêted in Tokyo. But all the traditional Japanese festivities for honoured guests could not gloss over one shocking incident: the murder in Tokyo that week, on 5 March 1932, of Takumo Dan, the man appointed to become the Lytton Commission's Japanese assessor.

Baron Dan was the American-educated head of the Mitsui Bank, a man of considerable influence and integrity. Unlike most of the then Japanese establishment, he had a genuine liking for America and the West in general. He was internationally known in banking circles, and had a mind of his own. His assassin was a nationalist of the 'Blood Brotherhood', but his murder was seen as a warning to all Japanese, however eminent, to follow official Japanese policy as far as Manchuria was concerned, and steer clear of the League of Nations.

Though the palace could not be directly blamed for Baron Dan's death, the instigators of the crime had close ties with those with privileged palace connections, including as they did the sinister Okawa, head of Hirohito's secret Social Problems Research Institute, or 'University Lodging House'. The killing left a bad impression on the Lytton Commission, especially since Dan had attended a banquet for them the previous evening and made a moderate speech.

Pu Yi made his ceremonial entry into Changchun on 8 March accompanied by Elizabeth, his new Premier Cheng Hsiao-hsu, and his court, including the Japanese secret policeman Amakasu. The railway station reception had been carefully rehearsed. As Pu Yi described it later:

I saw Japanese gendarmes and rows of people wearing all sorts of clothes; some were in Chinese jackets and gowns, some in Western suits and some in traditional Japanese dress, and they were all holding small flags in their hands. I was thrilled and reflected that I was now seeing the scene I had missed at the harbour. As I walked past them Hsi Hsia [one of his new ministers] pointed out a line of dragon flags between Japanese ones and said that the men holding them were all

Manchu 'bannermen' who had been waiting for me to come for twenty years.

These words brought tears to my eyes, and I was more strongly convinced than ever that my future was very hopeful.

Pu Yi said he was 'too preoccupied with my hopes and hates' to notice the 'cold welcome that the Changchun citizens, silent from terror and hatred, were giving me'.

The cortège took the new Chief Executive and his suite to a hastily decorated mansion which served, for a month, as Pu Yi's headquarters. Later he was provided with a Russian-built mansion of truly hideous aspect that had previously housed the local Salt Tax Administration. Here in this vast brick building with pointed roofs, within a large compound surrounded by high walls, was where he would live for the next fourteen years, refusing to move to a larger, new 'palace' that was specially built for him.

Changchun, then and now, is itself an industrial city of considerable ugliness. Woodhead, who visited it for the first time in October–November 1932 on an assignment for the *Shanghai Evening Post and Mercury*, described it as 'a depressing place. . . really a railway junction' – the northern terminus of the Japanese-owned South Manchuria railroad, the southern terminus of the Soviet-owned Eastern railroad, and the western terminus of the locally-owned Manchurian railroad. Woodhead wrote that it was a 'large straggling town' and that the only attractive part of it was the Japanese Concession area, 'with broad streets, a beautiful park and imposing buildings'. The Chinese part of the town was 'a sad contrast', and the streets there became a quagmire whenever it rained, which was often. There was a golf course, but the weather was so bad that it could only be used for seven months of the year. There were few cars, the most common form of transportation being the Russian *droshky*, or pony cart.

'It seemed strange that Changchun with its inadequate accommodation should have been selected as capital in preference to Mukden,' Woodhead wrote. One reason given was that 'Mukden was one of three provincial Manchurian capitals, and that it was felt the other two would have felt snubbed had it been selected'. Another was that Mukden had been the fief of Chang Tso-lin and his son the Young Marshal, and that Pu Yi did not want to live in any palace previously occupied by them. 'I suspect, however,' Woodhead added, 'that one of the reasons. . . was that there was likely to be less open hostility on the part of the population.'

For all his personal friendship for Pu Yi, he noted that 'outside official circles, I met no Chinese who felt any enthusiasm for the new regime'. Harbin in particular, with its gangs of White Russian and Chinese gangsters doing Vespa's business, was 'lawless. . . even its main street unsafe after dark'. Woodhead was shocked that four armed White Russians were required to guard the Harbin Club night and day. The new Manchuria, he wrote, was 'very far from being the paradise which it is the avowed purpose of the Japanese to make it'.

Pu Yi's first official engagement, the day after his arrival in Changchun, was to take the oath of office, which he did in the reception hall of his temporary headquarters. He wore what he described as 'Western evening dress' – white tie and tails, along with his favourite Harold Lloyd spectacles. The ceremony was attended by his longtime court, those Manchu dignitaries whose personal loyalties to the House of Ching had made them the willing allies of the Japanese, and by a dozen top-ranking Japanese officers, including Itagaki. Pu Yi received his Chief Executive's seal, wrapped in yellow silk. A photograph taken that day shows him, solemn and pouting, staring fixedly at the camera and looking oddly Japanese himself.

There are no official pictures of Pu Yi with his 'First Lady'. Elizabeth showed her disapproval by refusing to take part in any state functions at all after her arrival in Changchun, a place she hated even more viscerally than any of Pu Yi's court. In any case, the Japanese aides around him were not at all keen to have her play any First Lady's role: they were well aware of her anti-Japanese sentiments, and of her growing opium habit. They kept her aloof from both the local press and any visiting reporters, who were simply told that Pu Yi's beautiful, shy wife wanted to remain in the background and spent all her time running the household and doing unspecified 'good works'.

The reality was somewhat different: bored to tears, Elizabeth spent her waking hours chain-smoking, reading what Chinese fashion and film magazines her servants could lay their hands on (postal services between China and Manchukuo remained disrupted for years) and in small talk with those servants she knew she could trust. But most of the domestic staff provided for Pu Yi and Elizabeth in Changchun were new, and, Elizabeth surmised, in the pay of the Japanese. She established a routine that made Pu Yi, at times, wonder whether he should not have her put away in some discreet clinic where she would not be an embarrassment to him. She stayed in bed most of the time, smoking opium in the afternoon, spending the rest of the day in an opium haze, avoiding Pu Yi as much as possible. Their quarrels in Tientsin had been embarrassing to witness. Now she no longer bothered to cross him in any way – though she sometimes made fun of him to trusted servants, behind his back. She would put on dark glasses – which he had started wearing at all times – and imitate his jerky, somewhat mincing walk, his mannerisms, the way he had of running his hair through his fingers. There was nothing affectionate about such behaviour: Elizabeth well knew that dark glasses – in Tientsin at least – were the outward badge of its tiny 'gay' minority. Pu Yi must have known this too, though surviving members of his court say he really was subject to eye strain and headaches from the sun's glare.

He was worried about Elizabeth's failure to cope with life in Changchun but he had not yet realized the extent of his own predicament: 'I was light-headed,' he wrote later. 'I thought: If I got along with the Japanese they might even help me recover my Imperial title. Looking on the bright side, being Chief Executive seemed to be not a humiliation but a step towards the Imperial throne.'

A *Corriere della Sera* reporter found Pu Yi elusive. 'I was unable to interview this pale, tired prince who doesn't like to talk, who is always plunged in his meditations and who maybe regrets his life as a simple, studious citizen,' he wrote. 'One can gather nothing behind his ivory countenance. He has a fixed stare behind his black-framed glasses. When we were introduced, he responded with a friendly nod. But his smile lasted only a second. We could only await the word of the Master of Ceremonies to give us permission to bow ourselves out. A Japanese colonel, our guide, showed us the triumphal arches, the electric light decorations and endless flags. But all this, say the shopkeepers, "is made in Osaka".'

They were right; the Peking-based Chinese League of Nations Society, in its April 1932 magazine, published the text of a cable sent on 20 February 1932 from the Japanese Import Co-operative Society in Mukden to the Co-operative Export Society in Osaka, ordering '300,000 flags of the [Manchukuo] state to be ready in four days'.

An Organic Law promulgated in March 1932 gave Pu Yi, as Chief Executive, formal powers to declare war, and supreme executive, legislative and judicial powers, though the Prime Minister's signature was required in certain matters. There was a parliament of sorts, not, of course, an elected one, but a gathering of notables from all over Manchuria, either coerced or bribed, themselves theoretically appointed by local 'committees for the preservation of peace and order', a Manchukuo 'independence movement' that had come into existence only after the Mukden Incident and was an exclusively Japanese creation.

As he was to find out very soon, the real process of government escaped Pu Yi entirely and was carried out by the 'General Affairs Office of the State Council' with six departments – planning, legislation, personnel, accounts, statistics and information – all of them staffed and headed by Japanese officials. 'This is the real director of policy and controller of all [Manchukuo] government activities,' wrote a London *Times* reporter in a Changchun-datelined story in December 1932. 'It appoints and dismisses officials, and prepares the budget.' The *Times* quoted a Japanese officer as saying it was 'the steel frame holding together the whole regime'.

According to the Japanese-run Information Department of the Manchukuo General Affairs Office, the new state 'was founded on 1 March, 1932 by the thirty million people of Manchukuo. . . who, by their efforts and the unfailing co-operation of their friendly neighbour, Japan, finally overcame all obstacles, both internal and external, and liberated themselves from the militarist regime from which they had suffered for many years'. Its founders were motivated by 'a sublime ambition to create a State dedicated to "the way of benevolent rule".' Its 'glorious advent', with the 'eyes of the world turned on it', constituted an 'epochal event of far-reaching consequence in world history, marking the birth of a new era in government, racial relations and other affairs of general interest. Never in the chronicles of the human race,' the article went on, with mounting hysteria, 'was any State born with such high ideals, and never has any State accomplished so much in such a brief space of its existence as Manchukuo.'

The Lytton Commission did not arrive in Manchukuo until 20 April. After Japan, its members spent six weeks in China. Wellington Koo, the once and future Chinese Foreign Minister, who was the commission's Chinese assessor, was refused permission by the Japanese to enter Manchukuo overland with the rest of the Lytton Commission. He joined them later, having flown to Mukden.

Japanese preparations for the Lytton Commission's reception in Manchukuo were a clear case of overkill. Yet another member of the 'eleven reliables' inner circle, Colonel Hisao Watari, was Japan's advance man. A former attaché at the Japanese Embassy in Washington, known as an Anglophile, Watari was the man to deal with Lord Lytton, himself the son of a Viceroy of India and grandson of the historian Bulwer-Lytton.

A month in advance of the commission's arrival, petitions were drawn up by local Japanese specialists and presented to a thousand Manchurian associations and businessmen's groups, who were asked to sign and submit them to the Lytton Commission. They knew that to refuse was to invite the full force of Japanese fury – a risk some of them were prepared to take. Those asked to appear before the Lytton Commission were carefully briefed on how to behave and what to say. The petitions submitted to the League of Nations commission were all, strangely, couched in the same language and made identical points: Manchukuo had come into existence as a result of the popular will; 'past military maladministration' had been a major reason for this sudden independence movement and a 'glorious future' would be that of the new regime. None of the submitted papers contained a word of reference to Japan's predominant role in setting up, and running, Manchukuo. Colonel Watari had carefully briefed all those liable to come into contact with the Lytton Commission, whose members included a German ex-colonial governor, Dr Heinrich Schnee, an Italian diplomat, Count Aldrovani, an American army officer, Major-General Frank Ross McCoy, and the French General Henri Claudel. Any awkward requests they might make were to be denied on 'security grounds'.

Neither Lord Lytton nor his associates were taken in by such tactics, which they had anticipated. Punch-drunk from Japanese-inspired propaganda, when the time came for them to meet Pu Yi they almost certainly knew they would get nothing out of him but the official Japanese line. Their session with him lasted a mere quarter of an hour.

They had only two questions, Pu Yi recalled later. 'How had I come to the North-East? and how had Manchuria been established?'

> Did I dare ask Lord Lytton to rescue me and take me back to London with him? I remembered how my tutor had said that the gates to London would always be open. Would he agree or not? But as soon as this idea swept into my mind I brushed it aside. I recalled that, seated next to me, were Itagaki and the Chief of Staff of the Kwangtung Army.

I looked at Itagaki's bluish-white face and felt compelled to repeat what he had 'reminded' me to tell the Commission, that 'the masses of people had begged me to come, that my stay here was absolutely voluntary and free.'

The members of the Commission all smiled and nodded. They did not ask for any more. Later we had our picture taken, drank champagne and toasted each other's health.

After it was all over, Itagaki congratulated Pu Yi. 'Your Excellency's manner was perfect; you spoke beautifully,' he said.

Amleto Vespa, the Italian 'double agent', witnessed the Japanese preparations for the commission's reception from the inside. 'A month before their arrival,' he wrote, 'all those suspected of wanting to tell Lord Lytton the truth were rounded up, and kept in jail until after its departure.' All local reception committees were made to learn their speeches, written for them by the Japanese, by heart, and warned that if they deviated from the prepared texts even by one word they were liable to 'pay with their lives' after it had left.

Because Japanese officials knew the Lytton Commission might ask to visit prisons and hospitals, 1,361 'unreliable' Chinese, Korean and Russian detainees, as well as nine Japanese suspected of trying to contact the Lytton Commission, were moved to a new, out-of-the-way detention centre. All ordinary prison detainees who could speak English or French were sent there too. Towns were 'sanitized' in all sorts of ways: beggars were removed from the streets, opium dens became 'social clubs' or 'cultural centres', and all along the commission's itinerary, Manchukuo flags and photographs of Pu Yi had to be displayed. The Japanese military police netted large sums selling them to the locals.

The Hotel Moderne in Harbin where the commission members stayed (whose owner's son was to be kidnapped and killed two years later) was, Vespa wrote,

. . . placed in a regular state of siege. Certain rooms near those to be occupied by its members were assigned to Japanese or Russian agents of the State Political Police, masquerading as ordinary hotel guests. Three policemen were placed as clerks, others as Chinese bellboys, waiters, roomboys, hall-boys and so forth. Three Japanese girls employed by the police acted as chambermaids. Dozens of agents were given posts in the dining-room, reading-room, reception-room and all around the hotel. . . In all stores, restaurants and theatres where the Japanese thought members of the Commission might go, they posted police spies. . .

Despite the security overkill, there were local citizens brave enough to make their views known to the Lytton Commission outside the 'official channels'. In his report, written later from his sickbed in the German Hospital in Peking, Lord Lytton wryly noted the Japanese security measures 'for fear of bandits':

The effect of the policy measures was to keep away witnesses. . . We had strong reason to believe that delegates representing public bodies and associations which left statements with us had previously obtained Japanese approval. In fact, in many cases, people who had done so informed us afterwards that they had been written or substantially revised by the Japanese and were not to be taken as an expression of their real feelings.

Many Chinese were frankly afraid of even meeting members of our staff. Interviews were therefore arranged with considerable difficulty and in secrecy, and many informed us it was too dangerous for them to meet us, even in this way. In spite of this, we were able to arrange private interviews with businessmen, bankers, teachers, doctors, police, tradesmen and others.

In all such cases, and from the 1,000 'private' letters smuggled to the commission's notice, Lytton noted the 'profound hostility' of all ranks of society to the Japanese 'occupation'. Their leitmotiv was: 'We don't want to become like the Koreans.'

The report also accurately summed up the tentacular hold on Manchukuo by Japanese 'advisers' and officials. The 'independence movement,' it added, 'was only made possible by the presence of Japanese troops.' It scarcely mentioned Pu Yi. The commission's conclusion, calling for the staged withdrawal of Japanese troops and some form of 'internationalization' of Manchuria, was anathema both to China and Japan.

A carbon copy of the report, intended to be released in Geneva on 25 September 1932, was sold to a Japanese agent in Peking by one of Lord Lytton's secretaries, and 'leaked' summaries appeared in Tokyo on 1 September. Needless to say, the Japanese government and press attacked its terms sharply: since Japan had no intention of withdrawing its troops or administrators from Manchuria, it was clear that, sooner or later, Japan would have to leave the League, which it did seven months later, in April 1933.

Pu Yi's own government issued a violent protest at the report's 'misleading assertions', and *The Voice of the People of Manchukuo*, a Manchukuo government publication, said that 'all the people of Manchukuo were deeply indignant'. The Lytton report, it said, had 'failed to devise any way of ascertaining the true desires or conditions of the people, but instead took up some 1,000 irresponsible odd letters of private and doubtful origin.' In turn, it published what it claimed were '103,005 signatures from 1,314 organizations including 3,300 letters to government departments' praising its new, 'benevolent' administration.

But the most damning piece of evidence was not in the Lytton Commission report, or even in Amleto Vespa's account of what happened before and during its visit to Manchuria. It is to be found in the lengthy, unpublished memoirs of Wellington Koo, which exist only on microfilm as part of the 'New York Times Oral History' series. Koo – like the rest of the commission – soon became aware of the blanket security measures to insulate him from the population. Two Chinese who tried to approach him in a restaurant were promptly arrested and frogmarched away by plain-clothes Japanese policemen who 'happened' to be there. Three men, one Chinese, one Russian and one Korean, were stationed immediately outside his room and followed him everywhere.

'One of my attendants used to be in the Peking police,' Koo reminisced. 'He said a representative of the imperial household in Changchun wanted to see me and had a confidential message for me. This person, in order to gain access, was to pose as a curio dealer.'

Because he trusted the ex-police officer, Koo said, he met the 'antique dealer'. 'We went out into the lobby and stopped on a corner. He told me he was sent by the Empress: she wanted me to help her escape from Changchun. He said she found life miserable there because she was surrounded in her house by Japanese maids. Every movement of hers was watched and reported.

'She knew that the Emperor could not get away, but if it was possible for her to flee she would be able to work for his escape.'

Koo said he was 'touched' by her story but 'couldn't do anything effective to help her'. The Japanese never found out about her trusted servant's mission. Did Pu Yi know? 'Not at the time, but later, yes,' Li Wenda, his ghostwriter, said. 'He told me about it, years later, in Peking.'

For the Empress, Koo's refusal to help, says Rong Qi her brother, was the 'final blow'. Soon afterwards, she became massively, suicidally, addicted to opium.

CHAPTER EIGHTEEN

Five months after the Lytton Commission left Manchukuo, Pu Yi gave his first interview to a foreign newsman – not unsurprisingly, to his old friend Woodhead, now an editor of the *Shanghai Evening Post and Mercury*. Whatever his innermost thoughts may have been on this occasion, he certainly put on a boldly confident front.

Woodhead reminded Pu Yi of the last time they had met – in 1931, the day before he had left Tientsin to take up his new, more lucrative appointment in Shanghai. Pu Yi had had him over for tea, and the two men had talked for hours. Pu Yi, Woodhead had written afterwards, had 'seemed reluctant to let me go'. On leaving, Woodhead had told Pu Yi that he hoped, the next time they met, that it might be in a more 'formal' setting. It had been a broad hint that Woodhead knew Pu Yi might up stakes and leave for Manchuria, and that he, like Johnston and other leading members of the British community in Tientsin, both approved and anticipated his move. Now Woodhead said his 1931 hopes seemed to have materialized. Pu Yi beamed.

The reasons why he had decided to 'accede to the people's wishes' and become Chief Executive, he said, were that in the past 'the people's welfare had been disregarded, China's relations with all foreign powers had worsened and the pledge of equality between [Chinese] races violated'.

Was he happy? Woodhead asked.

Yes, of course, Pu Yi answered.

Was he busy?

Not as much as in the beginning, Pu Yi said, 'but I devote a considerable proportion of the day to state business'.

Was he a free agent? Rumours were he had left Tientsin under duress, that he had been kidnapped.

'Kidnapped! Kidnapped! No! No!' Pu Yi 'emphatically dissented' from such allegations. On leaving Tientsin, he had left a letter with the Japanese Consul-General there asking him to 'look after the Empress' until it was safe for her to join him. She had done so, taking an ordinary passenger steamer, in due course.

'At no time,' wrote Woodhead, 'was [Pu Yi] ever under any restraint nor was any coercion applied.' Pu Yi looked around the room. Were there any Japanese present? Woodhead said he could not see any. 'Could I really believe,' Woodhead wrote, 'he was virtually a state prisoner under such conditions?'

Pu Yi told Woodhead he intended to govern Manchukuo 'in the Confucian spirit'. There would be no political parties. (There was soon, however, to be a 'Concordia Association' which became in effect the only authorized party in Manchuria.) He asked Woodhead 'nostalgic questions' about mutual foreign friends in Tientsin. 'Almost his last remark,' Woodhead wrote, 'was that perhaps I had been able to convince myself by now that he was perfectly happy in his present office.'

He probably was: despite intermittent doubts, Pu Yi still believed the Japanese might help him regain his imperial throne in the Forbidden City. The official Japanese policy regarding Manchuria was 'fear tempered by benevolence', and so far they had mainly shown their benevolent side, at least to Pu Yi. Also, while it was becoming clear that the Japanese were making all government decisions, Pu Yi still had a certain amount of rubber-stamping to carry out, which kept him busy, as he told Woodhead: putting his seal to Japanese-approved appointments, meeting his ministers and leading bureaucrats, receiving reports from his tiny 'embassy' in Japan. In September the Japanese had officially recognized Manchukuo as an independent state. (Costa Rica, San Salvador, Japanese-occupied Burma, Thailand, the 'free' government-in-exile of Indian nationalist Subhas Chandra Bhose, Italy, Germany and the Vatican were eventually to follow suit.)

Some of Pu Yi's more optimistic and naive advisers believed that Japan's recognition implied that it would soon step aside and give the Manchukuo government more freedom. In fact, Pu Yi had suffered his first major blow: the heroic General Ma, whose guerrillas had given the Japanese Kwangtung army such a bad time, had, surprisingly, 'rallied' to Manchukuo after intricate negotiations with Colonel Doihara. Ma had even accepted the portfolio of Defence Minister – and a cash prize of £1.5 million. It was all a ruse. Six months later, Ma decamped with the money, his troops, and large quantities of arms, crossing into the Soviet Union. General Ma was to use Siberia as a secure base from which to harass the Japanese, and the Manchukuo army, for years to come.

The Japanese by this time had stepped up their offensive against China in the north, occupying Jehol Province and Mongolia, and every time they won a major victory, Pu Yi dutifully conveyed his congratulations. To keep Pu Yi in a docile, hopeful frame of mind, there were constant Japanese hints that soon he would be recognized as Emperor of Manchukuo. In October 1933 the rumours became official: Pu Yi was to be proclaimed Emperor on 1 March 1934. 'I went wild with joy,' Pu Yi wrote. The Japanese decision did not really come as a surprise: all along, Colonel Doihara had told him to be patient. Emperor Hirohito, with his customary caution, had wanted to test

Pu Yi's docility and reliability, and he had passed the test. The decision proved the Japanese Emperor's good faith: it also bound Manchukuo much closer to Japan. Ties between emperors would be hard to sever, especially since the official Japanese line now being bandied about in Manchukuo, and soon repeated *ad nauseam* to Pu Yi by Doihara, Itagaki and other Japanese aides close to him, was that 'the Emperor is your father, and is represented in Manchukuo as the Kwangtung army which must be obeyed like a father'.

Pu Yi, at first at least, saw things differently. He sincerely believed his enthronement was a major step towards his restoration as Emperor of China, and immediately had his Imperial Dragon robes, last worn by prisoner-Emperor Kuang-hsu, smuggled into Changchun from Peking, where they had been kept in secret storage by relatives. The Japanese immediately stepped in. He was to be enthroned as Emperor of Manchukuo, not as Great Ching Emperor. He was not entitled to the robes, but would wear the uniform of Commander-in-Chief of the Manchukuo armed forces, a Gilbert-and-Sullivan ensemble with an orchid motif in gold braid on each sleeve, and a comic-opera plumed hat.

Premier Cheng Hsiao-hsu went back and forth, trying to get the Japanese to change their minds, finally negotiating a compromise: there would be one early-morning 'religious' ceremony – and Pu Yi would wear Imperial Dragon robes for it, but not those belonging to the late prisoner-Emperor. The second enthronement rites would take place in the afternoon, with Pu Yi in military uniform.

Woodhead once more travelled to Changchun, but this time was kept at arm's length. He was granted a more formal interview (Pu Yi insisted on speaking through an interpreter, whereas in 1932 he had spoken in English part of the time). Pu Yi intended to record, through Woodhead, a wireless 'message to the British people' but this never materialized. Neither Woodhead nor any other news reporter was allowed to attend either the religious enthronement ceremony, a dawn affair at a specially built 'Altar of Heaven' with symbolic sacrifices to heaven involving jade, silk, grain, wine, wood and a dead bullock, or the afternoon 'military' ceremony. According to Reuters, seventy per cent of those allowed to attend were Japanese, and all passes were issued by the Japanese army headquarters.

Many Japanese businessmen in Mukden had hoped that, once proclaimed Emperor, Pu Yi would move back to Mukden, the traditional Manchurian capital. But a Japanese newspaper, *Nippon Dempo*, said that keeping the new capital in Changchun was Japan's 'fundamental state policy'.

During the coronation ceremonies, and the subsequent visit of Emperor Hirohito's younger brother, Prince Chichibu, to present his congratulations and decorate Pu Yi with the Grand Cordon of the Order of the Chrysanthemum, Elizabeth, the Empress, was conspicuously absent. The Japanese spies inside the Salt Tax Palace, now renamed the Emperor's Palace (it could not be called 'Imperial' because this was Hirohito's privilege), said that Pu Yi had seriously considered having her sent under escort to Dalian and kept there under guard: she was becoming a serious embarrassment to him, not just because of her anti-Japanese sentiments, but because of her growing opium habit – and increasing unpredictability. But she dutifully showed up at Pu Yi's side when his father, Prince Chun, arrived by train from Peking on a visit. It was the only time she agreed to behave in public like a First Lady, and she only did so because no Japanese were involved.

Pu Yi was eager to show off: palace officials and a detachment of Pu Yi's own 'Imperial Guard' were on hand to greet Prince Chun on his arrival at the railway station – it was the kind of treatment a head of state might have expected. The royal couple met him at the entrance of the Salt Tax Palace. Pu Yi wore his Commander-in-Chief regalia, with Japanese, Manchukuo and Chinese decorations he had received as Emperor inside the Forbidden

City. Elizabeth was in traditional Chinese dress, and knelt before Prince Chun like a dutiful daughter-in-law. Pu Yi staged a huge banquet that night for his father, complete with a brass band playing outside.

Pu Yi's half-brother Pu Ren, sixteen at the time, who went to Changchun with Prince Chun, remembers the trip well. There were quite a lot of frank father-son arguments, some of them heated. 'Pu Yi was outwardly very polite, but he didn't have a lot of respect for his father's opinions,' said Pu Ren. Pu Yi 'badly wanted the whole family to stay in Changchun. He wanted me to be educated in Japan, but father was firmly opposed to the idea and I went back to Peking.' Pu Yi 'was still in pretty good spirits', Pu Ren recalled. 'He hadn't entirely given up the dream that the Japanese would restore him to the throne of China.' Prince Chun, for all his failings, knew better.

The following day the Japanese Ambassador reminded Pu Yi that Changchun railway station was a military zone under Japanese control, and that only Japanese soldiers could parade there. With icy courtesy, he insisted that the lapse should never be allowed to happen again.

Despite such pinpricks, and the fact that he was unable to leave his palace compound for unofficial strolls – the only time he did so, with Elizabeth, they were escorted back into their house and told never to go out again unescorted – Pu Yi was still amused by the pomp and circumstance of it all. He went on heavily guarded state visits to his three provinces; he presented his congratulations to the Japanese army headquarters on Hirohito's birthday; he paid tribute, on Japanese Memorial Day, to the souls of Japanese soldiers killed by 'bandits' in Manchuria. The ritual, in all cases, was Japanese.

So was the practice, introduced by the Japanese, of getting schoolchildren and Manchukuo soldiers to bow every morning, first in the direction of Tokyo, then to a portrait of the 'Manchukuo Emperor' in his Commander-in-Chief's uniform. Pu Yi found it all 'intoxicating'. He visited a coal mine and spoke a few words of good will to a Japanese foreman who, overcome with emotion, promptly burst into tears. 'The treatment I received,' he wrote, 'really went to my head.'

The outward pomp and circumstance made up for the grim home atmosphere in the Salt Tax Palace: the Empress had an apartment of her own on the first floor, and rarely left it except for meals. After a time, these were brought to her on a tray. When the time came for Pu Yi's reward for being a good boy – a state visit to Japan, in April 1935 – she remained in Changchun. Pu Yi was accompanied by hand-picked 'Manchukuo' ministers and a retinue of Japanese.

Premier Cheng Hsiao-hsu stayed home too. Long before Pu Yi himself started to have serious misgivings about the Japanese, Cheng was finding them increasingly difficult to deal with while at the same time keeping a modicum of self-respect. Almost alone of Pu Yi's entourage, he was a man of considerable, rigid integrity.

Pu Yi's state visit to Japan was immortalized in a handsomely bound book entitled *Epochal Journey to Nippon*, published by the Intelligence Bureau of the Manchukuo General Affairs Office of the State Council and distributed later to all diplomats in Tokyo, to their considerable hilarity. To capture its essence, one needs to imagine a hagiographic, book-length court circular written in the prose of North Korean propagandists extolling Kim Il Sung. Every platitudinous exchange between Pu Yi and his deferential Japanese hosts was recorded as though divinely inspired.

The 'epochal journey' began with a cortège through Dalian harbour to the carefully rehearsed acclamation of 20,000 marshalled citizens and a 21-gun salute from the Japanese warship *Hiei Maru* taking him to Yokohama. It was one of the oldest warships in the Japanese navy. The author of *Epochal Journey*, Kenjiro Hayashide, a Second Secretary of the Japanese Embassy in Changchun who was to act as Pu Yi's interpreter on the trip, accompanied Pu Yi on a tour of the ship. 'The Ruler observed the details of the ship with the utmost interest . . . Chief aide Chang and others frequently struck their heads on the overhead beams, the passages being so low. Concerned over the welfare of His Majesty, I suggested: 'Your Majesty, be careful not to strike your head.' His Majesty smilingly replied: 'You are of short stature and most suited for inspecting a warship.'

The fun did not last. Shortly after leaving harbour, 'the sea became very rough. When I visited His Majesty's quarters to enquire after His Majesty's health, His Majesty looked somewhat uncomfortable and said that he was a little seasick.' He remained abominably ill for two days, but, true to his reputation as a poet and calligraphist, bravely churned out a poem a day. The first one read:

Mirror-like is the ocean as the traveller embarks
On the long voyage to the Land of the Rising Sun!
Enduring is the handclasp between Japan and Manchukuo!
May the eternal peace in the far east be assured.

A fly-past of a hundred Japanese planes was cancelled because of the weather. It was staged four days later, just as Pu Yi arrived in Yokohama, with a guard of honour of fifty-five Japanese navy vessels. Prince Chichibu came aboard. By now Pu Yi had slightly recovered. *Epochal Journey* tells how 'the Ruler's great joy of seeing Their Majesties the Emperor and Empress of Japan . . . removed all thoughts of fatigue from the voyage.' Questions concerning the Manchurian Empress's health and absence were tactfully avoided.

Emperor Hirohito himself was at Tokyo railway station to greet Pu Yi. A newsreel exists of the Chaplinesque moment when Pu Yi, about to shake hands with him, suddenly became aware he was still wearing the white gloves that were part of his absurd Manchukuo Commander-in-Chief uniform. While Hirohito waited, he desperately attempted to remove the glove from his right hand. But it was a tight fit, and would not come off without embarrassing contortions.

According to the ineffable chronicler of Pu Yi's state visit, even the peacocks spread their tails and screeched in his honour, and the grace with which Pu Yi fulfilled his 'weighty mission . . . moved me to tears'. The ritual state visit functions – banquets, parades, civic receptions, kabuki theatre and museum inspections, tea with close relatives of the imperial family, visits to war memorials, army hospitals, schools and Shinto temples – unfolded with clockwork regularity, Japanese officials in morning coats scurrying around Pu Yi like deferential automats.

Emperor Hirohito – who attended a state banquet given by Pu Yi in his guest palace but failed to stage a similar one in return (it was hosted by the Japanese government) – was baffled by this gawky, dandified young man who could not speak a word of Japanese. For local press consumption, Japanese diplomats in Changchun had prepared a brief biography of Pu Yi, a booklet entitled 'a respectful record of His Majesty's virtues'. Love of literature, it said, was one of his major qualities ('he is hardly ever seen without a book in his hand'), as were his talents as painter, poet, calligraphist. He 'bathes regularly once a day', rose early, was a great connoisseur of horseflesh and was fond of riding 'to relax the Imperial body'. The Tartar sport of equestrian archery had no secrets for him. Emperor Hirohito's staff made the mistake of believing this claptrap – and one of the Emperor's gifts, after his coronation, consisted of two thoroughbreds from Japan's imperial stables.

It was naturally assumed that such a skilled horseman would want to show off his skills and review the huge army parade in his honour on horseback. In fact Pu Yi had a pathological horror of horses, and adamantly refused to do so. Protocol officials worked overnight to change the parade order. Both Emperors showed up in a carriage. More than anything else, the fact that this descendant of Tartar warriors could not even ride a horse filled Hirohito with contempt. He was, of course, also fully briefed on Pu Yi's opium-smoking Empress, and Pu Yi's own taste for inflicting, and witnessing, corporal punishment on his servants of both sexes.

The official part of Pu Yi's state visit ended on 15 April, but he stayed on another ten days as a private guest –

visiting the Meiji tombs, historic Nijo castle, Kyoto, Osaka, Kobe and where he boarded the *Hiei Maru* again to the lusty 'banzais' of its 620 crewmen.

It was not quite over yet. Pu Yi, overcoming his queasiness at sea, went by launch to watch 'tai' fishing off the Awashima coast. He was presented with some of the catch of these striking deep-water sea bream, which were placed, alive, in a tank for his perusal. 'Seeing them living, one cannot bring oneself to eat their flesh,' the author of *Epochal Journey* heard him say, adding: 'It is widely known that His Majesty is merciful, but as I heard these words, I was impressed anew with the virtues of this ruler.'

Pu Yi's proclamation, on his return, was caricaturally ecstatic: he had been overwhelmed by Japan's 'unsurpassed cordiality' and its demonstration of 'inseparable relations'. Manchukuo's 'colossal indebtedness' was a guarantee of the 'everlasting foundation' of 'eternal friendship' between the two countries.

The words were not entirely hollow. In his talks with the Emperor and his court, Pu Yi had not been able to sound them out. As the Japanese had intended, the ceremonies had been entirely formal: there had been no talk of restoration, of upgrading him from Manchukuo to Great Ching Emperor. Nevertheless, he had not given up hope. The Japanese would not have gone to so much trouble, Pu Yi thought, unless they intended making future use of him. Besides, in 1935, he was not yet appalled by the extent of Japanese control over Manchuria. Compared to China, it was an orderly, disciplined bastion of stability.

This was also the view of a minority of diehard British and French conservatives, who contrasted Manchukuo's stable regime and economic boom with the corrupt inefficiency – and economic stagnation – of the rest of China.

Pu Yi had his own public relations consultant in the United States, George Bronson Rea, a former railway engineer and Chinese expert. In 1935 he published *The Case for Manchukuo*, written in the florid style of a turn-of-the-century advocate pleading a somewhat weak case.

'I am the representative of Manchukuo in the U.S.,' he

wrote, 'I am its advocate. I am partisan in its defense. I believe that what has been done constitutes the one step that the people of the East have taken towards escape from the misery and misgovernment that have become theirs. Japan's protection is its only chance of happiness.'

Rea was an old China hand who claimed to have been an intimate friend of the late Dr Sun Yat-sen and to have reached his conclusions only after witnessing widespread corruption in Chiang Kai-chek's China. Japan had been condemned without a proper hearing, he claimed. 'It is entirely too early to question its good faith.'

He could not have used that argument for long. Predictably, the Japanese started tightening the screws almost immediately after Pu Yi's return from Japan.

Seeing the writing on the wall, Cheng Hsiao-hsu resigned. The Japanese 'advised' Pu Yi to replace him with Chang Ching-hui, a grossly corrupt, servile politician with an unsavoury drugs-dealing background.

Then came the Ling Sheng affair. Ling Sheng had been one of the Manchu aristocrats who felt that Pu Yi's return would protect Manchuria from the chaos engulfing the rest of China. A former adviser to Chang Tso-lin and, as a result of his lobbying for Manchukuo, one of the 'Founders of the Nation', he had been appointed Governor of Hsingan Province. One day, in 1936, Colonel Yoshioka, the Japanese staff officer who had known Pu Yi since the Tientsin days, and was not only his closet Japanese contact and eminence grise, but also the official Japanese attaché to the 'Imperial Manchukuo Court', told Pu Yi that the Governor was in trouble for complaining – at a Governors' Conference – of 'intolerable' Japanese interference in his work.

What kind of trouble? Pu Yi asked.

Actually, Yoshioka said, he was under arrest.

This was extremely bad news for Pu Yi, because one of Ling Sheng's sons was engaged to marry one of Pu Yi's younger sisters. Could nothing be done about it?

Yoshioka said it would be 'difficult'.

Pu Yi was wondering whether to bring the case to the

attention of the Japanese army commander in Manchukuo – the real ruler of the country – when the latter called on Pu Yi himself.

There had been an unfortunate case of treasonable subversion, he said. 'The criminal was an acquaintance of Your Majesty's.' He had been 'plotting rebellion and resistance to Japan in collusion with foreign powers'. Fortunately the case had been solved.

Solved? Pu Yi asked. In what way?

'A military tribunal has found him guilty of his crimes and he has been sentenced to death.'

Ling Sheng, and several of his subordinates, had been beheaded a few days before Yoshioka ever approached Pu Yi. It was, the Japanese army commander said, a 'necessary warning to others'. Pu Yi got the message.

On Yoshioka's advice, he ordered the engagement between his sister and Ling Sheng's son broken off at once.

Pu Yi's English interpreter suffered the same fate shortly afterwards. He was picked up by Japanese Gendarmes and mysteriously 'executed', also, allegedly, for 'plotting with foreign powers'.

Then there was the crisis caused by the marriage of Pu Yi's younger brother.

Considerable pressure had been put on Pu Chieh, now thoroughly assimilated after his years in Japan as student and cadet, to marry a Japanese girl. Photographs were submitted, discreet dinner parties arranged in Tokyo so that he could get a good look at suitable girls. Pu Chieh's choice fell on Hiro Saga, daughter of Marquis Saga and second cousin to Emperor Hirohito. The marriage took place on 3 April 1937 in Tokyo. Immediately afterwards, the Manchukuo Council of State passed a succession bill making Pu Chieh and his son the successors to the throne if Pu Yi died without male issue. By now the Japanese knew it was highly unlikely that Pu Yi and his Empress would have a child.

Understandably, Pu Yi saw it all as a plot against himself, and vowed he would never eat food prepared by his Japanese sister-in-law. She might poison him. Having been naively pro-Japanese immediately after his state visit to Tokyo, he now saw Japanese spies everywhere. He became convinced that his residence was bugged. Big Li, his servant who in 1935-6 was promoted to the rank of major-domo, thought not. The Japanese, he told me, 'didn't need to bug the place to know everything that went on there'.

Two months after Pu Chieh's wedding, some members of Pu Yi's 200-strong personal palace guard, a small élite corps of Manchus with officer status and the only unit in Manchukuo that did not come under the direct supervision of the Japanese, fell into a carefully prepared Japanese trap. An off-duty group became involved in a brawl with Japanese civilians who jumped the queue where they stood waiting for rowing boats on the lakeside of Changchun's Japanese park.

Out of nowhere, Japanese police with dogs closed in. The Manchus were beaten, stripped naked and forced to dance in front of the jeering plainclothesmen who took them off to prison. Later they were charged with 'anti-Manchukuo and anti-Japanese' activities. Those arrested were expelled from the country. The commander of the palace guard, one of the few Japanese-appointed officials Pu Yi felt he could trust, was removed. The remaining guards had their weapons taken away and were allowed to keep only small, largely ceremonial pistols. Throughout, Pu Yi had been powerless to either protect his men or prevent this series of humiliations. He had not even known about it until his men were in prison.

He at last began realizing the extent of his predicament. His new Prime Minister, Chang Ching-hui, a venal, cringing Japanese flunky, was constantly being held up as a model. It was all proof of Japanese contempt for him, Pu Yi now believed, and for Manchukuo. He now understood that his trip to Japan had been a cruel, coldly calculated joke. The Japanese had nothing in store for Manchukuo save short-term exploitation.

This picture was more accurate than Pu Yi realized: in 1935-6, the debate in Tokyo among Emperor Hirohito's advisers was at its peak over 'strike South' versus 'strike North' policy. Among advocates of the 'strike North' policy were those like Ishiwara (the mastermind behind the 1931 Mukden Incident and by now a major-general) who believed that Japan should turn Manchukuo into a truly model state – an example to the rest of the world, especially Asia – as a prerequisite for the conquest of those portions of Siberia, including Vladivostok, that had once been under Manchu rule. 'Strike South' advocates believed Japan need not bother with Manchukuo's welfare or prosperity. All that was required was to milk its industrial resources as brutally and as cheaply as possible as part of a general campaign of terror and intimidation of the rest of China.

Emperor Hirohito made his decision, and General Ishiwara found his promising career cut short, for all his past devoted service to Japan. On 8 July 1937, after two years of intermittent skirmishes, full-scale war between China and Japan began.

CHAPTER NINETEEN

Like the Mukden Incident which put Manchuria under Japanese control, the start of the full-scale war against China was carefully contrived.

On 9 July 1937, elements of the Japanese army garrisoned in Tientsin's Japanese Concession were on manoeuvres outside Peking, near the Marco Polo bridge. One of its soldiers went to urinate, and got lost. His company commander believed he had been captured by Chinese troops quartered nearby. He requested permission to search their barracks. When permission was refused, the senior Japanese officer present ordered the shelling of the Chinese unit – and the war began. With singular lack of imagination, the Japanese were to call the events that took place near the Marco Polo bridge the 'China incident'.

Long before the shelling started, the 'lost' soldier had rejoined his platoon. The whole scenario had in fact been devised a year before. It was the latest part of an overall Japanese master plan, which had begun with the 1931 Mukden Incident and was followed by the seizure of Jehol in 1933 and of Inner Mongolia in 1935.

With Manchuria and the provinces of Jehol and Inner Mongolia under their control, the Japanese might have held off from an official full-scale war had it not been for an unforeseen event. Dissatisfied by Chiang Kai-chek's leadership and charging that he underrated the Japanese menace, preferring to concentrate on his war with the communists, the Young Marshal had kidnapped Chiang and held him prisoner for several weeks in December 1935 until he agreed to a peace settlement and to a KMT-communist coalition against the Japanese. This had the effect of stepping up Japan's own blueprint for aggression.

The 'China incident' was the start of a co-ordinated Japanese invasion of eastern China. Peking fell to the Japanese in July 1937, Shanghai, after bitter fighting, in August. Pushing west along the Yangtse, crack Japanese troops laid siege to Nanking. Here Chiang Kai-chek was in personal command, and the Japanese advance got bogged down.

In an age when news dissemination was far from instant, and TV did not exist, it took some time for details of what happened in Nanking to reach the West. The fullest account of 'the rape of Nanking' was written by a German, General Albert Ernst von Falkenhausen, a Prussian Junker who later became famous for his participation in one of the army officers' anti-Hitler plots. Auden and Isherwood, in their account of their China travels in 1937, *Journey to a War*, describe him as looking 'more like a university professor than a Prussian officer. He wears a pince-nez, a gaunt grizzled man.'

Falkenhausen was in Nanking at the time the Japanese entered the city on 10 December 1937. He was a German military attaché accredited to Chiang Kai-chek, in fact one of his senior military advisers. When Chiang Kai-chek realized the situation in Nanking was hopeless, and his troops were caught in a three-pronged trap by the encircling Japanese troops, he fled (on 7 December 1937). Falkenhausen stayed behind. His record of events was one of several, but it was more detailed, more accurate, and more damning than any other precisely because it was a soldier's cold, factual account of a series of atrocities so chilling, as Falkenhausen noted, as to be 'almost indescribable for regular troops'.

The Japanese commander of the Nanking operations was General Iwane Matsui, a devout Buddhist who had been a personal friend of Dr Sun Yat-sen, but he was to have little control over the events that took place there after its fall. His orders were exemplary. Only a few Japanese battalions were needed to 'occupy' Nanking. 'No unit is to enter [Nanking] in a disorderly fashion,' he wrote. The occupation was to 'sparkle before the eyes of the Chinese and make them place their confidence in Japan'. The troops were to refrain from any form of plunder.

In the closing stages of the battle for Nanking, Emperor Hirohito sent his uncle, Prince Asaka, a professional army man, to supervise operations there. Prince Asaka's orders to the troops were very different. They were to 'kill all prisoners'.

Beginning on 15 December 1937 and lasting for nearly three months, Japanese troops in Nanking went berserk, especially the 6th and 16th divisions, the latter under the command of Lieutenant-General Kesago Nakajima, a former head of Japan's secret police, the dreaded *kempei*.

Many Chinese soldiers had shed their uniforms and fled to Nanking's European quarter. Japanese officers urged the Europeans to hand them over. They would be treated well, they promised. European and American community leaders started organizing transfers of prisoners. They were promptly taken away by the Japanese, then bayoneted, buried alive, or used as machine-gun practice.

In an orgy of rape, which did not spare grandmothers, pregnant women or small girls, Japanese soldiers, encouraged by their officers, rounded up all the women they could find. Hundreds were strapped to beds and used as army brothel fodder until they could be used no more and they either died or were murdered.

Army warehouses were filled with loot, inventoried in precise military detail. In a final, carefully coordinated operation, Japanese troops set fire to the districts they had looted, destroying one-third of the city.

At the 1946-7 Asian war crimes trial held in Tokyo, it was claimed that 200,000 Chinese men had been murdered in Nanking, and 20,000 women raped, in most cases repeatedly, between 15 December 1937 and 12 February 1938, when the last case of rape (a twelve-year-old girl) was recorded by the indefatigable General von Falkenhausen. Total civilian casualties during the battle itself had been 300.

Shortly after the rape of Nanking began, General Matsui was removed to Shanghai. Ironically, he was to become the scapegoat for the very events he deplored and had tried to prevent. Shortly before he was hanged as a war criminal, in 1948, he told his Buddhist confessor, 'I wept tears of anger. I told [my senior officers] everything had been lost in one moment through the brutalities of the soldiers. And, can you imagine it, the soldiers laughed at me.'

Matsui's hanging was the major miscarriage of justice to emerge from the verdicts of the International Military Tribunal for the Far East. The memories of Nanking were such, however, that for Matsui himself the sentence came as a kind of deliverance from shame. Half senile, babbling at the trial about Chinese-Japanese friendship, he paid the ultimate Japanese officer's tribute to his divine ruler.

The real culprits went scot-free: General Nakajima retired in 1939, a rich man from his Nanking loot; Prince Asaka was never called to the witness stand and, like Nakajima, died in his bed. Matsui effectively took the blame and punishment for everything.

Bergamini, author of *Japan's Imperial Conspiracy*, found it almost impossible to get eye-witness survivors to talk about the Nanking atrocity. Officially, Japanese army records showed, there had been only minor exactions. An unnamed officer had been punished (but who, and how, has never been revealed) and one Japanese NCO punished 'for stealing a Chinese lady's slipper'. Emperor Hirohito, after Prince Asaka's return to Tokyo, played golf with him, commended him for his Nanking service, and never showed his disapproval in any way.

For years, the reason for the organized rape of Nanking remained an enigma. If its real purpose was to frighten China into submission and oust Chiang Kai-chek so that a more pliable leader would be appointed with whom the Japanese could negotiate the 'peaceful' occupation of China, the plan misfired. Resistance to the Japanese intensified, and though most of China remained under Japanese occupation until the end of the Second World War, the Nanking horror galvanized 'free' China – in the east and south-east – to greater, and more effective, anti-Japanese activity.

I asked Pu Chieh how news of the rape of Nanking had affected Pu Yi, and his attitude towards the Japanese. 'We didn't hear about it until much later,' he said. 'At the time, it made no real impact.' For by now, the walls had really closed in on the pathetic Manchukuo court. New rules were in effect which so restricted the flow of information that Pu Yi and his entourage lived in a kind of vacuum. The press laws in force in Manchukuo (identical to those promulgated in other Japanese-occupied areas of China, where similar puppet regimes were installed) banned 'any mention of Chinese victories'. An official guidance manual required all those concerned with the media to develop the theme that 'Japanese soldiers are good people with pleasant manners' and that 'conditions in Manchukuo improve all the time and that the people there are very happy'. No bad or even mildly controversial news of any kind could be published, either in Manchukuo or in other areas under Japanese control.

In other parts of Japanese-occupied China, Chinese-language broadcasts from San Francisco and other long-range radio stations enabled the Chinese to keep abreast of events. But Pu Yi, inside his Salt Tax Palace, dared not listen to such broadcasts, for he knew he was being spied on, and feared for his life. It was only towards the very end of the Second World War that he started tuning in to US broadcasts, his nephews said. By that time he had to listen to Chinese-language stations beamed from San Francisco for he had forgotten most of his English.

Pu Yi was Manchukuo's Emperor for just over eleven years. During that time he went to Japan three times (the subsequent visits, in 1940 and 1943, were far lower-key than the initial state visit), but after 1938 he hardly ever stepped out of the hideous green-roofed former Salt Tax building. There was no point. The early euphoria was gone, and so were any hopes of becoming a restored Ching emperor: after the occupation of Peking in August 1937 the Japanese set up a puppet republic there with a handful of Chiang Kai-chek turncoats who gambled on a Japanese victory in the Second World War – and were duly executed by Chiang Kai-chek in 1945.

As months turned into years, with nothing to show for them but cupboards full of absurdly ornate uniforms, morning coats and top hats beloved of the Japanese for formal receptions, Pu Yi sank into a lethargy not so very different from his Empress's opium addiction. Significantly, in his autobiography, the whole Manchukuo experience is dismissed in 62 (out of 496) pages, and they are full of omissions.

Talking to survivors who shared Pu Yi's life in Changchun during the brief existence of the 'Empire of Manchukuo', it is difficult to get the 'feel' of those eleven years. They were interminable, in ghostwriter Li Wenda's words 'a kind of living death'. He too had difficulty in extracting from Pu Yi any coherent account of this particular period – whereas there were unending flows of words about both his Forbidden City experiences and his later prison experience in China. It was as if the shame of those Manchukuo years was such that he had wiped them from his mind.

After 1938, Pu Yi took his duties less and less seriously: he hardly ever left his palace compound, except on routine functions, – visits to hospitals, to factories, to housing developments – and the earlier thrill of performing 'royal' functions quickly palled. When his Japanese 'advisers' needed him to put his seal on a document, they just left it with him, collecting it a few days later. In this way, Pu Yi gave his official approval to expropriations of Manchu farmers and to various security laws giving the Japanese full powers in the maintenance of law and order. In theory, as 'Supreme Commander', he thus bore full responsibility for Japanese atrocities committed in his name on anti-Japanese 'bandits' and patriotic Chinese citizens.

Time and again he issued communiqués praising the Japanese war effort, first against China, then – after Pearl Harbor – against Japan's British and American enemies. All were in the style of *Epochal Voyage to Nippon*, that grotesque, risible prose so beloved of the Japanese. Pu Yi still had no idea of the extent of the rape of Manchukuo: all he saw of his country was what the Japanese wanted him to see. Yoshioka, his Japanese military adviser, briefed him on the state of Japan's war with China, then in the Pacific, but – at first at least – he said no more than the official Japanese communiqués.

The situation in Manchuria itself kept tens of thousands of Japanese and Japanese-officered Manchukuo troops busy. Peter Fleming describes (in *One's Company*) going out on operations with Japanese troops in Manchuria against 'bandits' – i.e. communist guerrillas, 'a soft-footed river of little slouching men in grey'. They marched and marched, but never made contact. It was, Fleming reported, what usually happened: the 'bandits' simply melted away – with the support of the local population. He had plenty of evidence of Japanese and Manchukuo brutality; he tells of arriving in a village to find 'two bandits tied to stakes and left exposed all day, knowing they would be executed that evening in front of the assembled population'. It was a routine means of terrorizing the people, and Fleming described the scene with a hard-boiled reporter's matter-of-factness.

The Manchukuo court was a self-contained, privileged little world, in the sense that its members were spared the shortages and privations which were the lot of ordinary Manchurians. But from servants and teachers (who came daily to give lessons to Pu Yi's pageboys and adolescent relatives) it was impossible to ignore entirely what was going on outside the palace walls. It was the knowledge that he was an object of hatred and derision that drove Pu Yi to the brink of madness.

He had always been unpredictable, subject to violent mood swings. Now he became downright vicious. Back in Tientsin, he had devised a series of 'house rules' to keep his court in order. 'Irresponsible conversations', embezzlement, profiteering, covering up for one another were all severely punished. Pu Yi did not administer the beatings himself, as a rule. The 'seniors' beat the 'juniors', but if he detected a 'senior' administering a fake beating, the beater was immediately beaten too. 'Take him downstairs' – where the flogging took place – was the dreaded phrase heard almost daily from 1938 onwards. Pu Yi wrote that everyone was flogged except for the Empress and members of his immediate family. Big Li, who had his share of beatings, said many were inflicted with wooden paddles. 'It got so that everyone was covertly watching Pu Yi all the time, to try and find out what mood he was in,' he told me. 'Pu Yi was completely paranoid: if you were caught eyeing him, he would bark: what's the matter? Why are you looking at me that way? But if one tried to look away, he would say: why are you avoiding me? What have you got to hide?'

As time went on, Pu Yi's daily routine became that of a *roi fainéant*: he did not get up until noon, lunched at two, and then promptly went back to bed for a siesta. He played tennis in the afternoon in summer, or table tennis indoors in winter, and rode a bicycle in the grounds of the small palace compound for exercise.

He would sometimes get behind the wheel of his official Buick, and drive it a few hundred yards round and round the palace. He was genuinely fond of Chinese music, and had a large collection of Chinese opera records, which he listened to for hours on end. Occasionally, the Japanese would arrange some formal entertainment for him: the palace reception room would be turned into a small theatre, and the whole court would watch ballet, kabuki or judo demonstrations. The visiting performers were invariably Japanese.

Following the 'old Buddha's' habit still, there were no fixed hours for meals. 'He would have dinner when he felt like it,' Big Li recalls. The evening meal was the only real meal of the day: Pu Yi's nephew Jui Lon, then a 'pageboy', told me that during the day they would have 'snacks' in the palace kitchen, but were invariably summoned to share Pu Yi's evening meal. He needed company then, and would make an effort to be sociable and 'relaxed'.

Towards the end, though, as his mood swings increased, along with a growing tendency towards mysticism, Pu Yi became a vegetarian, and insisted everyone else should become one too. He even had qualms about eating eggs and would bow low and pray to them before eating them, his nephew said. 'There were statues of Buddha everywhere, and he would spend hours in meditation before them. While this was happening, there had to be complete silence throughout the house. There were two Japanese cranes in the garden, and if they made a noise while he was meditating, the servants were fined. It got so they would get hold of the cranes and hit them every time they made a noise.'

His servants were not allowed to kill flies or mice, or any living thing. The cleanliness of the place, said a former pageboy, left a lot to be desired. But Pu Yi would fine the cook if he found an insect or a fly in his food, and – having nothing else to do – began examining palace accounts with obsessive attention. 'He became convinced that everyone was trying to cheat him,' says Jui Lon. But even this was something he tired of. 'His personal enthusiasms were like five-minute heatwaves. He would take up badminton, tennis, volleyball, calligraphy, sunbathing, body-building, and then lose all interest.'

Jui Lon, who came to Changchun in 1937 aged fourteen, was one of the many adolescent relatives sent by their families to serve at the Manchu court, half attendant, half companion. They were socially above the 'pageboy' category, but subject to Pu Yi's brutal whims in the same way as all the other servants. Jui Lon remembers that Pu Yi even had a few eunuchs from the Forbidden City join his court, and that when one of them fled to Peking he tried to get him arrested and returned to Changchun.

Pu Yi's court could at times be a place of real terror: one pageboy escaped, was dragged back and beaten so severely that he died. Pu Yi prayed endlessly for the soul of the dead boy, and had those who had beaten him to death severely punished.

The servants, eunuchs and pageboys inside the palace grounds numbered nearly a hundred, and they were constantly on short rations, because Pu Yi became increasingly mean, cutting back drastically on household expenses. It was, said Big Li, as though, miserable himself, he wanted everyone else to be miserable too. Only those relatives who dined regularly with Pu Yi escaped undernourishment. But at appropriate intervals – Chinese New Year, Pu Yi's birthday on 14 February, now a national Manchukuo holiday – there would be lavish banquets, and Pu Yi would insist that everyone should appear to be having a good time.

Jui Lon only caught occasional glimpses of Elizabeth: after 1937 she no longer appeared at the birthday or New Year parties. He remembers her as 'still beautiful, but thin as a rake, heavily rouged'. The sickly sweet smell of opium on her floor was overpowering. 'You could cut the atmosphere with a knife,' said her brother, Rong Qi, then a Japanese-trained lieutenant in the Manchukuo imperial guard.

From the Japanese butler-spy, the Japanese knew exactly the degree of her addiction. Between 10 July 1938 and 10 July 1939, he reported, she bought 740 ounces of 'ointment for the increase of longevity', as it was euphemistically called, along with the cheapest kind of pipes available on the market. That worked out to around two ounces of opium a day, a phenomenal, almost lethal quantity. She also smoked two packets of cigarettes a day, not 555s like Pu Yi but the cheapest, local brand. Because they no longer even talked to each other, Pu Yi found it convenient to give her a monthly allowance. He never made any effort to interfere with her opium habit, his nephew said. 'He felt there was nothing he could do about it.' As Elizabeth's state deteriorated, her own father stopped his visits to the palace. 'He loved her a lot,' says Rong Qi, 'and couldn't bear to face what she had become.'

Pu Chieh's return to Changchun with his Japanese bride had a temporarily stabilizing effect on Pu Yi. Hiro was a level-headed, highly intelligent young woman, who quickly assessed the extent of the crisis in Pu Yi's life. Though a Japanese aristocrat, she did her best to allay Pu Yi's fears, dressing in traditional Chinese dress, making it clear to him that she at least was no Japanese spy. Pu Chieh and Hiro did not live inside the palace compound. Their house was small, jerrybuilt, wretchedly cold in winter, and had no telephone. Slowly, relations between Pu Yi and his sister-in-law improved. He gave her a ruby-and diamond encrusted wristwatch as a wedding present, invited them to dinner, and even threw a party for them at which Elizabeth put in an unscheduled appearance. She was tall and graceful, Hiro recalled, her hair elaborately decorated with flowers and jewels. Afterwards Pu Yi said it was the first time in three years she had sat down to a meal with him. Pu Yi had not yet entered his vegetarian phase, and the cook had prepared a Western-style meal, with roast turkey. The only sign that night that Elizabeth was not entirely normal was that she ate ravenously, with her fingers. Her table manners, Hiro wrote later, were abominable, but her husband tried to turn it all into a huge joke, using his fingers too, urging everyone to tuck in like savages.

A year later, Hiro had a child. Pu Yi was relieved it was a girl, for had it been a boy he feared the Japanese might have been tempted to eliminate him in favour of his more worldly, Japanese-speaking brother. He even started behaving like an affectionate uncle, playing with his niece, showering her with specially imported Japanese-made toys.

Pu Yi's own sex life, Hiro wrote, in a random collection

of diary jottings that was eventually published in 1957 under the title *Wandering Princess*, was something of a mystery. Three weeks before her own marriage to Pu Chieh in April 1937, a sixteen-year-old girl called Jade Years (Tan Yu-ling) moved into the palace as Pu Yi's 'secondary consort', or concubine. She was a Manchu, a member of the Tatala tribe, and Pu Yi kept her in strict seclusion. She was not at the party attended by Elizabeth. Hiro went to see her after dinner, in her cottage in the grounds of the palace compound. There she noted Jade Years wore a string of Mikimoto pearls presented during Pu Yi's 1934 state visit to Japan as a gift to Elizabeth by the Japanese pearl industry.

Pu Yi, the surviving members of his Pirandello-like court recall, seems to have been genuinely fond of Jade Years. Whether they made love is not certain. In his memoirs, Pu Yi admits that none of the women in his life until then had been 'real wives – they were just there for show'. On the other hand Pu Yi gave the impression of badly wanting a male heir, complaining several times to his nephews that the Japanese must be doctoring his food to make him sterile. Again, Big Li feels this was all part of Pu Yi's paranoia.

It was during those interminable years in the Salt Tax Palace that rumours of Pu Yi's bisexuality spread, not just in Changchun but in Japan as well, where the reports from spies inside the palace household were scrutinized with considerable interest. They spoke of Pu Yi's increasing interest in youths of his own sex, of a whole stable of adolescents – half servants, half lovers – living in the palace compound. His sister-in-law, Hiro, was shocked to hear palace reports that Pu Yi had a pageboy lover.

'Of course I had heard rumours concerning such great men in our history,' she wrote later in her memoirs, 'but I never knew such things existed in the living world. Now however I learnt that the Emperor had an unnatural love for a pageboy. He was referred to as "the male concubine". Could these perverted habits, I wondered, have driven his wife to opium smoking?' Since the rest of her book is highly accurate, it is unlikely that this report is based on hearsay alone.

It is, however, the only reference in her book to Pu Yi's homosexuality, a subject his surviving relatives refuse to discuss, though Pu Chieh's admission to me that 'later on in life, he was found to be biologically incapable of reproduction' may have been a typically oblique, Chinese way of confirming his wife's allegations. The key to Pu Yi's sexuality remains locked away inside Japan's still classified secret service 'Manchukuo' archives.

In 1940 Pu Yi made his second trip to Japan. It was the 2600th anniversary of the establishment of the Japanese monarchy, and this time he was only one of several wellwishers paying tribute to Emperor Hirohito. Yoshioka, the liaison officer, had done his best to prepare Pu Yi for what was in store for him in Japan, hinting that the time had come for Manchukuo's 'filial' relationship with Hirohito to be taken a stage further. The Japanese plan was to compel Pu Yi to abandon Chinese ancestor-worship rites and Confucianism, and adopt Shintoism – the official Japanese religion – as Manchukuo's own.

Now in a special audience with the Emperor Hirohito, Pu Yi read out the speech that Yoshioka had prepared for him, asking to be allowed to worship the Shinto deity in Manchukuo. 'I must comply with your wishes,' said the Japanese Emperor, and gave him, as a sacred gift, three small objects symbolizing the Shinto religion: a curved piece of jade, a sword and a bronze mirror.

'I thought Peking antique shops were full of such objects,' Pu Yi wrote. 'Were these a great god? Were these my ancestors? I burst into tears on the drive back.'

The introduction of the Shinto religion as the official religion of Manchukuo followed Pu Yi's return to Changchun. It occurred against the advice of several Japanese officers who were familiar with Manchuria, who knew this was a sure way of alienating the population still further.

Shinto shrines were erected all over the country, and Manchurians had to bow in their direction whenever they walked past. Twice a month Pu Yi, flanked by his own officials and accompanying Japanese, including the Shinto High Priest for Manchukuo, Toranosuke Hashimoto (a former Japanese army provost-marshal), took part in Shinto ceremonies at the Changchun shrine. 'I would always kowtow to my own ancestors at home before going to the shrine,' Pu Yi wrote, 'and when bowing to the altar of the Japanese Sun Goddess, Ama-terasu-o-mi-Kami, I would say to myself: I am really bowing to the Palace of Earthly Peace in Peking.'

Praying at a Shinto shrine, Pu Yi wrote, was an even more shameful, nauseating experience for him than hearing the news of the profanation of the tombs of his Ching ancestors.

CHAPTER TWENTY

As the tide gradually turned against the Japanese in the Second World War, in ways some of Emperor Hirohito's more clear-sighted advisers had predicted, just about the only reassuring aspect of the worsening situation, for Pu Yi, was the fact that the USSR had signed a neutrality pact with Japan, also recognizing the territorial integrity of the 'Empire of Manchukuo'.

This meant that, despite Manchuria's close proximity to the Soviet Union, Pu Yi felt the Russians would not 'come and get him'. Otherwise, he had no realistic picture of the course of the war. Till the end, he was fed the same propaganda nonsense the Japanese censors determined was necessary to maintain morale. From little things – growing shortages of almost everything and pressing appeals for scrap metal of all kinds (Pu Yi donated some of the Orders bestowed on him as Emperor) – he was aware that the Japanese were on the run.

The sudden increase in 'Concordia' membership was a pointer. The 'Concordia Association', the fascist-style party that the Japanese had set up to control the Manchurian population through an intricate network of street and factory committees, all reporting upwards to Japanese security and intelligence units, suddenly showed a huge increase in members. The reason was not ideological – simply that with 'Concordia' membership came a free uniform, and Manchurians were going about in rags.

Having backed the wrong horse so early on in life, Pu Yi now belatedly hoped for an Allied victory. 'He desperately wanted America to win the war,' said nephew Jui Lon. 'When he thought it was safe,' said major-domo Big Li, 'he would sit at the piano and do a one-finger version of "Stars and Stripes".'

A question often comes to mind, why did Pu Yi never try to escape? Could he not have used his personal fortune (his stipend as Emperor was around £130,000 a year in current values) to bribe his way out, and escape the country? Ghostwriter Li Wenda asked him that very question. The answer was that even to ask it was to show no understanding of his predicament. In the first place, the Japanese were everywhere: under the guise of anti-bandit security, squads of dark-green-uniformed Japanese Gendarmerie had moved inside the palace compound, searched all cars going in and out and kept a close watch on its perimeter. They may have been venal in some ways, but theirs was a much feared SS-like organization that made the Salt Tax Palace no better than a prison. Also, after his return from the 1934 Japan state visit, Pu Yi had only limited access even to Japanese visitors. Yoshioka saw to it that he only came into contact with those needed to further his role as puppet Emperor. As Pu Yi was to tell the Tokyo International War Crimes Tribunal later, 'I couldn't even see my own ministers.'

The other reason why Pu Yi dismissed the escape option as 'absurd and futile' was that there was, literally, no place to go. Trains still ran between Manchukuo and Peking, but after 1937 Peking had been part of Japanese-occupied territory too, under the Japanese-controlled Wan Ching-wei puppet government. This meant that had Pu Yi managed to reach Peking, he would still have been at risk.

Prince Chun's Northern Mansion was under close Japanese surveillance. Besides, as his half-brother Pu Ren put it, 'after 1941 Pu Yi's father had written him off. He never visited Pu Yi after 1934. They rarely corresponded. All the news he got was through intermediaries, or occasional reports from Pu Yi's younger sisters, some of whom were allowed to see him.' Pu Yi sent his father a small monthly allowance – but Prince Chun, while accepting the money, had more or less disowned his son. In any case, all of Pu Yi's loyal restoration activists had followed Pu Yi to Changchun, and there was no one left in Peking he could really trust. His oldest adviser, Cheng Hsiao-hsu, was by now dead.

Pu Yi also knew that even if he did manage to escape from the Japanese, nobody in the Allied camp wanted him: he had issued too many slavishly pro-Japanese declarations during the war to be credible. Johnston's promised 'gate to London' was closed for ever. To Chiang Kai-chek he would have been a liability, even if he succeeded in avoiding treason charges. As for joining up with the (mostly communist) anti-Japanese guerrillas in Manchukuo itself, that was out of the question. Pu Yi believed they would have executed him at once. Yoshioka had inculcated in Pu Yi such a dread of communism that the thought hardly crossed his mind.

Was there no one, inside the palace itself, who could have galvanized Pu Yi into acts of passive resistance, like refusing to put his seal to Japanese-drafted laws? An anti-Japanese 'cell' probably existed inside the palace, for Pu Yi once came across a chalk-written inscription on the inside of the palace walls. It read: 'Haven't the Japanese humiliated you enough?' In his memoirs, Pu Yi deplored that during those dark years his only intimates were pageboys, young, inexperienced relatives, a hopelessly opium-addicted wife and a teenage concubine. There was no one Pu Yi respected intellectually whom he might have turned to. Since Johnston there had been no father-figure. Jade Years – sixteen in 1937 – was, Pu Yi later told the International Military Tribunal, a 'patriotic young Chinese woman' but she had neither stature nor influence within the court. 'You must remember,' his brother-in-law Rong Qi told me, 'that for all the absurdities and prison conditions that prevailed inside the Salt Tax Palace, there was still, in his immediate family circle and among his retainers, a feeling of blind loyalty to the Emperor. As the war went against Japan, a fatalistic mood took hold. The Emperor was going down, and we would go down with him.'

Temperamentally, Pu Yi was hardly a swashbuckling adventurer willing to take desperate risks. He became, after 1938, an increasingly devout Buddhist. He also became a hypochondriac, with nightly injections of vitamins and hormones (to combat sterility), also swallowing huge quantities of pills of all kinds. (In his aimless existence, he later wrote, he spent 'several hours a day' on medication.) He suffered from attacks of asthma and haemorrhoids, and occasionally could hardly walk.

As his puppet status became intolerable, so he retreated into the past. His nephew Jui Lon recalls that Pu Yi took a close interest in the private lessons given to the young relatives living with him. 'Two or three times a week, he would lecture us about the history of the glorious Ching dynasty,' he said. It was as if Pu Yi was masochistically contrasting the giant stature of some of his Ching ancestors with his own abject existence. Like the beatings he inflicted on his servants and pageboys, they were a manifestation of self-hatred.

He seems to have had at least some genuine affection and even love for Jade Years, for all his pageboy 'affair'. He wanted to upgrade her to Empress. During his 1940 trip to Japan, he informed Emperor Hirohito he intended to divorce Elizabeth. This the Emperor vetoed absolutely. An emperor, even a puppet emperor, could not divorce his empress. This too may have been the reason Pu Yi burst into tears after his 1940 meeting with Hirohito.

It was shortly after this second Tokyo trip that Pu Yi learned the appalling news: Elizabeth was pregnant, by one of his servants. In his memoirs, he skirts over the entire episode, only mentioning she 'behaved in a way I could not tolerate'. The man responsible was Pu Yi's driver, Li Tieh-yu, who had procured opium for her. They had smoked together, he had gradually become first her confidant, then her lover. Pu Yi behaved with a mixture of magnanimity and cowardice: he could have had Li killed, for his driver had perpetrated the ultimate crime as far as the Ching moral code was concerned. Instead, he slipped him £250 and told him to leave town. But when Elizabeth gave birth, a Japanese doctor killed the newborn baby girl with an injection before her mother's very eyes, and Pu Yi, aware of what the Japanese intended, did nothing to stop them.

The effect of this on Elizabeth can only be imagined, and indeed from that moment onwards she seems to have lived in a constant opium haze. The whole episode, discussed in hushed whispers behind Pu Yi's back, was so shameful that even Li Wenda could not get him to talk about it at any length.

Then, eighteen months later, in 1942, Jade Years died. As Pu Yi's sister-in-law Hiro tells it, she developed a fever, started drinking large quantities of water, and became delirious. A Chinese doctor diagnosed meningitis, and recommended glucose injections, but as Jade Years' health worsened, Yoshioka insisted that a Japanese medical team be called in. Pu Yi later became convinced that this team deliberately murdered her. As he later told the International Military Tribunal, 'the glucose injections were not administered. There was much to and fro activity that night, Japanese nurses and doctors speaking with Yoshioka, then going back to the sickroom.' By morning she was dead, at twenty-two, and when Pu Yi requested that she be buried in the Ching tombs in Mukden, Yoshioka dismissed his request out of hand. She had to be buried in Changchun, he said. (Her ashes remained inside the Changchun palace till after the war, and were eventually brought back to Peking.) As a profoundly significant talisman of his love and mourning, Pu Yi kept her nail clippings and a lock of hair in a tiny purse on his person throughout his later spells in Soviet and Chinese prisons.

A month after Jade Years' death, Yoshioka was pressing Pu Yi to choose a new concubine from a batch of photographs of teenage Japanese girls. Pu Yi refused.

But he did eventually marry again, after a fashion. A year later, in 1943, a twelve-year-old girl appeared at Pu Yi's side, Hiro wrote in *Wandering Princess*, but ran away three days later. Pu Yi made no effort to have her brought back. Instead, he finally succumbed to Yoshioka's pimping, insisting only that the new concubine be a local girl, not a Japanese. Jade Lute (Li Yu-chin), aged sixteen, reflected Pu Yi's diminished importance in Japanese eyes. She was a waiter's daughter. Hiro Saga wrote that she badly needed a bath – and delousing – when she first set foot inside the palace.

Her photograph shows a face with character, sternly handsome rather than pretty, and a boyish figure. Pu Yi treated her more like a pageboy than a concubine. Testifying before the International Military Tribunal, he explained that 'the reason I married a young Chinese girl was because, being young, she could be educated in the way I liked and not be assimilated or educated in the Japanese way'. It is more likely Pu Yi felt that at sixteen she would be impressionable and malleable enough to accept as the norm whatever he had in store for her. Many years later, he told one of his Chinese gaolers that 'I made her write out a list of rules and punishments, stipulating what would happen in case of disobedience or other faults. She signed this document. When I had reason to complain of her behaviour, I would produce it and tell her: read this. Then I would chastise her. Many's the beating I've given Jade Lute.'

They were presumably a prelude to, or substitution for, sex. Pu Yi acknowledged his dark side. Of his ill-treatment of pageboys, he wrote: 'These actions of mine go to show how cruel, mad, violent and unstable I was.' He implies, of course, that his 'madness' was the result of his upbringing and of his predicament as puppet Emperor.

The strains he suffered as the war went against Japan and he himself realized the full extent of his mistakes certainly aggravated his neurosis. But a whole series of behaviour patterns – the beatings, his attitude towards women in general – imply that his would have been a neurotic personality in any circumstances. While he bared his soul, years later, to his Chinese captors about almost everything else, often painting himself in an even blacker light than was necessary, he never really told them the truth about his peculiarly flawed sex drive – nor did they take any great pains to get him to talk about this side of his character.

While Pu Yi was behaving like a petty tyrant and lording it over his new teenage concubine, terrorizing his court with his paranoid mood swings, the Japanese were retreating in the Pacific and in Burma, and the first massive air raids began over Tokyo itself. The controlled Manchukuo press reported 'heroic sacrifices' of Japanese troops on all fronts, and all over Manchuria air-raid shelters and sandbags made their appearance. Overcoming his fear, Pu Yi started tuning in to Chinese-language broadcasts beamed from the US, and realized the end of the war was at hand. General Tomoyuki Yamashita, the Japanese Commander-in-Chief of all troops in Manchuria (and the man who had carried out the blitzkrieg on Singapore in 1942), was recalled to Japan and made a farewell courtesy call. 'Covering his nose and weeping, he said: this is our final parting. I shall never come back,' Pu Yi wrote.

The Japanese used him as a propaganda vehicle to the very end. Pu Yi described how, on a bleak sandstorm-swept day, he attended a Japanese army ceremony as guest of honour to 'dedicate' a handful of pathetic 'human bullets'. These were Japanese infantrymen who had 'volunteered' to become the ground equivalent of kamikaze pilots. 'The dozen or so victims were drawn up in a line in front of me and I read the speech Yoshioka had prepared,' wrote Pu Yi. 'Only then did I see the ashen grey of their faces and the tears flowing down their cheeks, and hear their sobbing.' After the ceremony had ended in the swirling dust, Yoshioka complimented him on his performance, and said they had shed 'manly Japanese tears' because Pu Yi 'had moved them so'.

Writing about the incident in his memoirs, Pu Yi said: 'I thought: you really are frightened, you know I've seen through the human bullets. Well, if you're frightened, I'm terrified.'

Surprisingly, there is not a single reference in Pu Yi's autobiography to the atom bombs dropped over Hiroshima (on 6 August 1945) and on Nagasaki (9 August) which precipitated the Japanese surrender. This was probably not, as I thought at first, a deliberate omission on his part to minimize US responsibility for the war and magnify the last-minute Soviet contribution to the war in the Pacific.

The Hiroshima bomb certainly, in the pithy words of Wisconsin's late Senator Alexander Wiley, 'blew Joey off the fence' even though the subsequent Soviet invasion of Manchuria – beginning 8 August – was entirely self-serving. Stalin's objective was to recapture Japanese-held territory seized after the 1904-5 Russo-Japanese War, dismantle Manchuria's industrial infrastructure for Soviet use, and deny a vital part of China to Chiang Kai-chek's forces, giving Mao's Eighth Route Army the opportunity of establishing communist control over what had been Manchukuo.

Neither Pu Chieh nor Rong Qi, who were with Pu Yi at the time, nor even ghostwriter Li Wenda, serving in Manchuria with the Eighth Route Army, recall any mention of Hiroshima and Nagasaki until some days after the war was actually over. 'It was the crossing of the border by Soviet troops that caused the excitement,' says Rong Qi. 'We only heard about Hiroshima while listening to the Hirohito surrender broadcast.'

It was not till 9 August (the very morning the bombing of Nagasaki took place) that General Yamata, the new Japanese Commander-in-Chief of Manchukuo, informed Pu Yi that Stalin had entered the war and Soviet troops had crossed the border. While he was assuring Pu Yi of his confidence in Japan's final victory, Changchun's first air-raid warning sounded, and the meeting continued in the Salt Tax Palace's new shelter. 'Before long bombs were exploding nearby and while I quietly invoked Buddha, the general was silent. He did not refer again to his confidence in victory after the all-clear,' Pu Yi wrote. A bomb had fallen on the Japanese-built prison immediately opposite Pu Yi's palace.

The next day General Yamata came to the palace to tell Pu Yi his army would 'hold the line' in southern Manchuria but that the capital would 'temporarily' be evacuated to Tunghua. 'We will leave today,' he said. Pu Yi told him he needed more time. He was concerned not only for his large household but also for his moveable assets – paintings, jewellery, jade – which, he hoped, would enable him to live in comfort for the rest of his life. ('He wasn't all that good an expert about jewellery,' his nephew Jui Lon told me, 'but he really knew about jade.') The Japanese were now really anxious to make the move. Yoshioka said: 'If you don't get out, you'll be the first to be murdered by Soviet troops.' One of the three Soviet armies sweeping into Manchuria was a Soviet-trained Mongol army, and this news struck fear in all concerned. By this time Pu Yi had learned ways of testing the real feelings of the Japanese, and was proficient in the empty, hypocritical professions of faith that had been expected of him for so long. He dressed up in the uniform of Commander-in-Chief of the Manchukuo army, whose troops were already on the run and shedding their uniforms as fast as they could, and summoned both his Prime Minister, the craven Chang Ching-hui, and the Japanese head of the General Affairs Office of the State Council, the real civilian ruler of Manchukuo.

'We must support the holy war of our Parental Country with all our strength, and must resist the Soviet armies to the end, to the very end,' he said solemnly – to test their reaction. Yoshioka fled the room, and shortly afterwards Japanese soldiers converged on the palace. For one awful moment, Pu Yi thought they had come to kill him. Still in uniform, he stood at the top of the main staircase, facing them. 'When the soldiers saw me,' Pu Yi wrote, 'they went away.' He tried to phone Yoshioka, but could not get through.

Another kind of fear gripped him. What if the Japanese were to leave without telling him? He phoned Yoshioka again, and this time the line was in order. Yoshioka said he was ill, but that the evacuation would take place on 11 August. Pu Yi summoned Big Li and said he was hungry. The palace staff had started deserting him. The cooks had all left. All Big Li could provide were some biscuits.

On the evening of 11 August Pu Chieh, his wife Hiro, and all Pu Yi's other relatives were taken by the Japanese to the railway station where they boarded a special train. By this time Pu Yi had sorted out his treasures, leaving behind the bulkier objects, but packing the most valuable bits and pieces in suitcases, hiding the most precious items in the false bottom of a cine camera case. Pu Yi was the last to leave the palace, with Yoshioka. Most of the Manchuria-based senior Japanese army staff, Hiro wrote, had already left by train for Korea.

To the very end, the formalities were observed: in the cortège taking Pu Yi to the station, the first car contained the 'sacred relics' of Shintoism Hirohito had given him, hand-carried by Manchukuo's Shinto High Priest, former Provost-Marshal Toranosuke Hashimoto. All Japanese bowed low before him as the slow procession made its way through Changchun's streets. As Pu Yi left the palace, he heard explosions: Japanese sappers were blowing up the Shinto 'National Foundation Shrine' at which Pu Yi had been compelled to worship according to Shinto rites.

Hiro noted in *Wandering Princess* that as they prepared to leave, Changchun's inhabitants were already preparing to greet the victors: women were busy putting together crude hammer-and-sickle flags. One Japanese official who behaved with exemplary calm throughout was secret policeman Amakasu, the man who had greeted Pu Yi on his arrival in Manchuria fourteen years previously and had since become head of Manchukuo's film industry. He paid out wages to his staff, reassuring everyone they would survive. Then, using a cyanide pill, he committed suicide.

The train bearing Pu Yi, his court, his ministers and a handful of Japanese officers steamed out of Changchun late that night, but never reached Tunghua. Because of Soviet air raids, the train was diverted to the mining town of Talitzou – an overnight journey. On the way, Pu Yi had ample opportunity to realize this really was the end of the Japanese dream: there were Japanese military convoys all heading south, 'and the men in them looked like a cross between soldiers and refugees'. Halfway to Talitzou, General Yamata boarded the train. 'He reported to me the Japanese army was winning and had destroyed large numbers of tanks and aircraft,' Pu Yi wrote, but at every station he could see for himself the Japanese were in full, panic-stricken retreat. Japanese civilians desperately tried to scramble aboard his train, 'weeping as they begged Japanese gendarmes to let them pass'. There were fights between Japanese soldiers and Gendarmes.

On the way, Pu Yi discussed his future with Yoshioka, who had other things on his mind but, professional liaison officer to the end, made polite conversation and even offered Pu Yi a choice of resorts. The plan now was to find a plane to take Pu Yi to Korea, not yet invaded by the Allies. From Korea the Japanese would try and fly him to Japan. Where would His Majesty like to live in Japan? Pu Yi said he did not know. Surely His Majesty remembered his 1934 state visit. Was there no place that attracted him? How about Kyoto? Kyoto would be fine, Pu Yi said.

Secretly, Pu Yi was relieved. He had taken the precaution of moving his personal funds from Changchun to a Japanese bank in Tokyo a few weeks before the Soviet entry into the war. He still had no knowledge of the A-bombs, and Yoshioka had assured him that a US military invasion of Japan would never take place, for it would take millions of American lives. But Yoshioka added that once Pu Yi had reached Japan, 'His Imperial Majesty cannot assume unconditional responsibility for Your Majesty's safety.'

On the night of 14 August the train arrived at Talitzou station, and Pu Yi and his entourage were taken to a wooden two-storey hostel belonging to a local mining company. Here, the following day, huddled around its wireless set, the assembled company listened to Hirohito's address to the Japanese people, announcing Japan's surrender. Speaking in the high-pitched, archaic style and language reserved for ceremonial occasions, and broadcasting to his subjects for the first time (electric power was turned on throughout the country so they could hear him), Hirohito embarked on the short speech he and his closest advisers had argued over for two days. 'We declared war on America and Britain,' Hirohito said, 'out of Our sincere desire to ensure Japan's self-preservation and stabilization of East Asia, it being far from Our thought either to infringe on the sovereignty of other nations or to embark on territorial aggrandizement . . .'

The address included a reference to the enemy's use of 'a new and cruel bomb, the power of which to do damage is indeed incalculable', as well as the understatement of the Second World War: 'the war situation had developed, not necessarily to our advantage'. It was over the word 'developed' that the state of war had been prolonged for two days. Hirohito had wanted to use the word 'deteriorated'. His advisers had objected.

Pu Chieh kept up a running translation as Hirohito spoke. Hiro wrote that afterwards the brothers clasped hands and wept.

Two days later, inside the hostel dining room, the largest room in the building, an almost surreal ceremony took place. Pu Yi formally renounced the throne of Manchukuo, also proclaiming the dissolution of its government, and its return to Chinese territory. A formal vote was held, all present voting in favour. Pu Yi affixed his seal one last time to give the edicts force of law. He read them out in a firm, emotionless voice, shaking hands with his ministers as they left the room one by one. In his autobiography, Pu Yi described the occasion as 'one more farce to be played out', with his ministers assembling before him as 'so many lost dogs', but no one present at the time questioned its solemnity. Hiro wrote that it was a 'simple but impressive ceremony'. Throughout, Pu Yi behaved with quiet dignity. He may secretly have been relieved that his ill-fated Manchukuo gamble was over thirteen years and five months after it had begun. There was an element of symbolism in the Talitzou ceremony. It was from here, three and a half centuries previously, that the Manchu tribal leader Nurhaci had begun raising his levies which were to challenge the Ming dynasty.

It was far too dangerous a place to stay in for long: the entire countryside was controlled by communist guerrillas, rapidly taking over the entire province. In something of a panic, the party split up. The train that had brought them there returned to Changchun, with former Manchukuo Premier Chang Ching-hui aboard. As a last, desperate compromise, he intended getting in radio touch with Chiang Kai-chek to turn Manchukuo formally over to him, thereby, he hoped, avoiding Soviet occupation. Chang Ching-hui's move came too late. The Soviets arrived before he was able to establish contact.

Pu Yi now told Yoshioka he had changed his mind. He wanted to go to Peking, and stay with his father. Yoshioka argued that while he might be able to find a plane to go to Korea and then Japan, no Japanese plane could be found to go to Peking, and an overland journey was out of the question. Pu Yi eventually agreed to the original plan.

The plane, Yoshioka said, would take off from Tunghua, and Pu Yi must choose who would accompany him, for it was very small. Pu Yi selected eight people in all, including Pu Chieh, Jui Lon, Big Li and his personal physician. Elizabeth, Jade Lute and Hiro were left behind.

This was Yoshioka's doing more than Pu Yi's. It was Pu Yi and his immediate entourage who risked arrest by the Russians, Yoshioka kept saying. The women in the group were in no such danger. Yoshioka reassuringly told them they would follow later, and all would meet up in Japan within a week. His relative lack of concern for them also reflected the traditional Japanese view of women as inferior beings. Pu Yi was in no position to argue. Besides, in the present crisis, both his drug-addicted wife and child-like concubine were embarrassments.

Jade Lute and Elizabeth started 'blubbering', Pu Yi wrote. Jade Lute said she wanted to go back to her family in Changchun. Hiro, ever the dutiful Japanese wife, immediately packed an overnight bag for her husband. Pu Chieh was in surprisingly high spirits. 'What do I need these things for?' he said. 'I'll be in Japan this time tomorrow.'

'Be sure and look after one another,' Pu Yi told those he was leaving behind. He took Hiro, the most responsible member of the group, aside. They should do their best to reach Korea as quickly as possible, he told her. If separated, they should try and make it to Japan individually. Once there, their troubles were over. There was enough money in the bank for everyone.

In one last forlorn little ceremony, the court members and servants left behind lined up along the station platform to see Pu Yi and his party leave by train. Pu Yi shook hands with every one. 'You have been of great service to me,' he said. 'I pray that you will lead healthy and happy lives.' Hiro noted he was crying when he climbed aboard the train.

To everyone's surprise, there was a small plane waiting for them in Tunghua which they boarded immediately. It was to take them as far as Mukden, where a larger aircraft was expected.

In Mukden, they waited for it to arrive. There was the sound of an approaching plane. Pu Yi and his party left the airport waiting room to go out on the tarmac. A whole fleet of aircraft landed and, as Pu Yi watched, they disgorged Soviet troops who immediately disarmed all the Japanese in sight and occupied the airport.

Almost as an afterthought they rounded up Pu Yi and his group, including Yoshioka. Kept under guard that night in the airport waiting room, they were made to board a Soviet plane the following morning. Somewhere between Mukden and Khabarovsk, their destination, it stopped to refuel and Pu Yi went up to the Soviet officer in charge. He was already working out a plan to disassociate himself from his erstwhile Japanese masters, conveniently shifting all the blame for Manchukuo onto their shoulders. 'We don't want to be on the same plane with Japanese war criminals,' he said, in as regal a tone of voice as he could command. Yoshioka was left behind.

CHAPTER TWENTY-ONE

As soon as Pu Yi's small group had left Talitzou, his court disintegrated for good. The few remaining Japanese and Manchukuo guards disappeared, and what was left of Pu Yi's family had to fend for itself. Though she had a baby daughter (her second child) to look after, Hiro took charge and at first all was well. It seemed her group might live on undetected in the mining hostel until the situation became clearer. Pu Yi had left them with plenty of cash and large quantities of valuable antiques.

By the third week of August the news came that Pu Yi had been captured by the Soviets, and everyone, including Hiro, broke down and wept. But it was not until 21 September that real trouble started: 'bandits' occupied the town, and began hunting down the Japanese. Hiro was stopped on the street. 'There's one,' a bandit said, pointing at her. 'No, no, she's my sister,' one of Pu Yi's younger sisters shouted, with commendable presence of mind – and they let her go. Hiro had left a trunkful of Manchurian currency in a strongroom in what had been the Talitzou Japanese Gendarmerie headquarters. The 'bandits' went through every Japanese-occupied house and barracks and confiscated the lot.

Soviet troops arrived a few days later. They too were looking for loot and women. Hiro cut her hair short and dressed in men's clothing, like most of the women in the group. The Soviets rounded up all the Japanese they could find and took them to Linchiang, a larger town. Hiro and her group followed. It would be safer, she thought, than fending off bandits.

A few weeks later, regular Chinese communist army units arrived, and while they were highly disciplined and looted only medical supplies, their presence put an end to any hopes of escape to Japan via Korea. The family's true identity was discovered.

Hiro's group was betrayed by one of its own members – the husband of one of Pu Yi's sisters and a grandson of the late 'reformer' Cheng Hsiao-hsu. Whether he wanted to ingratiate himself with the communists or simply get his own back on Pu Yi because of his exclusion from the original escape party, he turned them all in. A Chinese communist officer called on Hiro at the house they had rented. 'You are Madame Pu Chieh, are you not?' he said, and told her not to worry. As a former officer in the Manchukuo cavalry he had known, and liked, Pu Chieh. He would see to it they came to no harm.

He was as good as his word, but the renegade brother-in-law was out for revenge. He went to the communist military headquarters again, this time to draw their attention to the huge quantities of art treasures, some of them from the Forbidden City, in the family group's possession. This was 'national property', and the offence was serious. The entire group was rounded up, taken to Tunghua and held in a police station. It was now January 1946.

There was still the chance that the new communist powerholders might have treated the group leniently, but by now a new war had started – between Chiang Kai-chek and the communists. Chiang's troops advanced deep into Manchuria, with the support of some Japanese units that had escaped detention. A Japanese force attacked

Tunghua, retreating after bitter fighting. The Chinese communists retaliated by shooting some Japanese prisoners, and their attitude towards Hiro and her party hardened. They were left in the police station in the freezing cold.

By now, Elizabeth had used up her plentiful opium supply and started begging and screaming for more. Hiro bribed guards to help her replenish her stock. In April they were taken under guard back to Changchun, in preventive detention while the Chinese communists continued their slow investigation of the case. Hiro's spirits rose: they were not housed in prison, but in rented rooms above a restaurant.

Shortly afterwards, Jade Lute was released. She generously told Elizabeth she could come back to her home. She would look after her. But Jade Lute's mother, either to pay off old scores or ingratiate herself with the new powerholders, went to the local Communist Party bosses and denounced Pu Yi's whole family, Hiro included, as 'enemies of the people', alleging they had committed heinous crimes.

Once more the police rounded everyone up. This time, Hiro and Elizabeth were separated from the rest. They were taken to Kirin in the north and again locked up in a police station.

Here Elizabeth's final agony took place: there was no more opium to be had. Hiro wrote that she screamed so much that other prisoners kept yelling: 'Kill the noisy bitch!' Police, Party officials and ordinary townspeople came to watch her ravings, 'as if visiting a zoo'. Long lines of chuckling Chinese filed past her cell, gawking at the former Empress of China as she begged for opium or hallucinated that she was back in the Forbidden City. 'Boy!' she shouted, 'Bring me sandwiches!' 'I want a bath!' 'Where are my towels?' Hiro did her best to comfort her, trying to make her understand where she was – to no avail.

The Chiang Kai-chek offensive continued. Kirin was bombed, and all prisoners were moved again, this time east to Yenchi. Hiro and Elizabeth went by cart on which floated a banner inscribed: 'Traitors from the Manchukuo imperial family.' On arrival they were separated.

After a few days, Hiro managed to catch a glimpse of Elizabeth through her barred concrete cell window. She was stretched out on the floor, unconscious, in a pool of urine, excrement and vomit. Hiro begged a guard to take her something to eat. 'What! Go into that stinking room? Not on your life!' he said.

Hiro volunteered to wash the dying Elizabeth. A warder said he would think about it. The following day she was allowed to watch as a warder, wearing a mask, cleaned out the cell, bundling Elizabeth's dirty clothes into a bucket. Elizabeth, in her underwear, was now conscious, but still hallucinating. She again asked where her servants were, and why they had not run her a bath, or brought her clean clothes. The warder shrugged his shoulders. 'That one won't last long,' he said.

Hiro and her small daughter were moved again. Elizabeth, untransportable, stayed behind. She died of malnutrition and other effects of opium withdrawal in June 1946. She was forty years old.

A week later Hiro was set free, made her way to Peking, and from there was repatriated to Japan. While in Peking she called on Prince Chun and broke the news to him that both his sons were alive but Soviet prisoners.

While Hiro was on her long, adventurous trek, the Soviets were busy dismantling the industrial state the Japanese had so carefully built up. They plundered Manchuria's infrastructure, wrote Professor F. C. Jones in *Manchuria After 1931* 'in a highly selective, devastating fashion, wantonly destroying what they didn't remove'. US Reparations Commissioner Edwin Pauley, reporting to President Harry Truman in 1946, said: 'They didn't take everything, concentrating on certain categories of supplies, machinery and equipment. In addition to taking stockpiles and certain complete industrial installations, they took by far the larger of all functioning power generating and transforming equipment, electric motors, experimental plants, laboratories and hospitals. In machine tools, they took only the newest and best.' He assessed the loot at $858 million (in 1946 values). Despite what the Japanese had done in Manchuria, there were only isolated incidents of Chinese brutality towards the 850,000 Japanese immigrants: all but a few top officials and senior army officers were repatriated by 1947. Because of the way the Soviets behaved, Professor Jones reported, 'by 1946 the Russians were hated more than the Japanese'.

Pu Yi, while all this was happening, was living an eventless, boring life in a Russian spa hotel near Khabarovsk, half prisoner, half guest. His fellow-prisoners included leading Manchukuo ex-ministers, generals and officials. The Soviets, says Jui Lon, who was with Pu Yi in the first few months of his Soviet captivity, 'weren't sure how to treat him.' The food was good, the accommodation that of a luxury hotel, and the prisoners were left almost entirely to their own devices. Pu Yi was questioned a few times by a Soviet intelligence colonel, but never in depth.

The daily routine, Pu Chieh noted, was not unlike that of the Salt Tax Palace. Pu Yi prayed a lot, insisted on being treated with the deference due to an emperor, and had his servants punished for misdemeanours as in the past, except that they were not whipped; they had their faces slapped instead. Though the detainees listened to Soviet Chinese-language broadcasts, their news of the outside world was scrappy. Pu Yi knew that Chiang Kai-chek and Mao's armies were fighting it out, but the reports were vague: the civil war, Jui Lon recalled, was not a priority item on Soviet newscasts. There was no family news of any kind. Pu Yi was not to learn of Elizabeth's death for another five years.

Two months later, Pu Yi, under Soviet guard and in a Soviet plane, was on his way to Tokyo to appear before the International Military Tribunal for the Far East under the presidency of Sir William Webb, a formidable Australian High Court Justice. The Asian war crimes trial was to last two and a half years and lead to eight hangings among the twenty-eight accused of 'conspiracy to wage aggressive war' and 'crimes against humanity'. Among those sentenced to death were Kenji Doihara, the 'Lawrence of Manchuria', Seishiro Itagaki, who as colonel had negotiated Pu Yi's return to Manchukuo, and Hideki Tojo, who had served from 1935 to 1938 as head of the Japanese secret police and Gendarmerie in Manchuria, later becoming the most persistent advocate of the war against America, and Hirohito's Prime Minister during the war years.

The chief aide to US Chief Prosecutor Joseph Keenan was retired Major-General Tanaka, the elephantine exspy and lover of Eastern Jewel, who had been living in retirement since 1942 because he had opposed the policy of war with America and had bitterly clashed with Tojo over this.

The prosecution had insisted that Pu Yi be called as a prosecution witness. Newsreel footage shows an absurdly youthful-looking Pu Yi clasping a sheaf of handwritten notes, with long hair and the appearance of an unruly, somewhat dissolute student who has not done his homework and is distinctly nervous about his 'oral'. Although Sir William was clearly impatient to get Pu Yi's testimony over and done with as quickly as possible and proceed with other, more important witnesses, Pu Yi was to remain in the huge, packed, Klieg-lit courtroom, formerly the dark-panelled auditorium of the Japanese Military Academy, for ten uncomfortable days.

It was Prosecutor Keenan's task to make Pu Yi out to be the innocent victim of the Japanese militarists who had placed him on the Manchukuo throne. It was the objective of the conscientious British, American and Japanese defence counsel to prove that Pu Yi had been a willing collaborator and was consistently lying about his role as Manchukuo Emperor. In the lengthy list of prosecution witnesses, Pu Yi was small fry, but if one witness could be utterly discredited, the testimony of other, more important witnesses might also, inferentially, be questioned.

So, from the moment the witness officially described as Henry Pu Yi began his testimony ('I was born in Peking. My name is Pu Yi, and the Manchurian last name is Aisin Goro. I was born in 1906, enthroned as Chinese emperor

272

in 1909. In 1911 revolution started in China . . .'), he came under withering cross-examination which he was clearly unprepared for, though he rapidly overcame his initial confusion, even, at times, trading sarcasm for sarcasm. As Arnold C. Brackman was to write in *The Other Nuremberg, the Untold Story of the Tokyo War Crimes Trials*, (William Morrow, 1987), 'Pu Yi's performance in the box was bravura. Until his first public appearance, he had been derided by observers as slow-witted, if not mentally retarded, a cardboard figure. On the stand, however, Pu Yi proved himself wily, the master of cunning, guile and downright deceit. He outduelled Sir William Webb, Joseph Keenan and both the Japanese and American defense. He alternately infuriated them and teased them, and, in the end, got them fighting one another. If Pu Yi had been a free man, his performance would have been impressive. But given the peculiar circumstances in which he found himself, his performance was truly remarkable.'

His first hurdle was over the notes he held on his lap, which were disallowed. They were, Pu Yi told the court, merely references to 'simple dates and months, no detailed documents'.

Step by step, in answer to Keenan's questions, he gave a chronological account of his life, from his childhood in the Forbidden City to his days as Manchukuo puppet Emperor, and at every step, as Pu Yi told it, only the Japanese were to blame.

He had initially taken refuge in the Japanese Consulate-General in Peking, he said, because 'the British Embassy was too small'. He interjected comments of his own. 'Dr Sun Yat-sen was a great man . . . At the time, the officials of the Chinese Imperial Court were very corrupt.' Sir William told him to stick to the facts of his own life.

In his version of his meeting with Itagaki, Pu Yi said 'refused' the Japanese offer to head the new Manchukuo 'state because Itagaki demanded that as soon as it was set up, we should employ Japanese as Manchu officials'. He had been 'forced' to leave Tientsin 'under the compulsion of the Japanese garrison commander of Tientsin . . .

Itagaki said that if I refused they would adopt drastic action against me. My advisers told me that unless I acceded to his proposition there would be danger against my life.' Itagaki had adopted 'a very stern and forceful attitude'.

From the moment he set foot in Manchuria, Pu Yi said, 'I did not have my hand, I did not have my mouth . . . If I had told Lord Lytton the truth, I would have been murdered right after the commission had left Manchuria.'

Keenan asked him about Jade Years. 'My wife – my late wife – was deeply in love with me,' said Pu Yi. 'She was twenty-three years old when she contracted a kind of disease. She was a very patriotic Chinese. She always comforted me by saying that I had to be patient for a time. Then we can recover the lost territories. But she was poisoned by the Japanese. Who was the man who poisoned her? It was General Yoshioka.'

Pu Yi claimed he had set up his personal palace guard with a view to 'connect up with the Chinese Army . . . My idea was to have some sort of an army so that at some future date I might have a chance of joining up with the Chinese Army to resist the Japanese.'

Sir William Webb sat through all this with growing impatience 'We are not trying this witness, but we are concerned about his credit,' he said. 'Danger to life, fear of death does not excuse cowardice or desertion on the battlefield. Neither does it excuse treason anywhere. All day long we have listened to excuses by this man as to why he collaborated with the Japanese. I think we have heard enough.'

But the defence was determined to have its say. By far the most effective defence counsel was the U.S. Army Legal Department's Major Ben Blakeney. Johnston's book was to play an important part in the exchanges.

BLAKENEY: I want to ask you whether it is not true that after you did leave the Forbidden City in 1924, after you ceased to receive the treatment due to royalty, after your pension had not been paid in full, did you not feel, quite naturally, that the Republic had violated its contract with you in almost every particular?

PU YI: My feeling then was that I would rather move out of the Forbidden City because the circumstances there were not wholesome at all. This situation was fully recorded in Mr Johnston's *Twilight in the Forbidden City* from which you can understand my feeling and my situation.

BLAKENEY: Then we may assume, may we, that Sir Reginald Johnston's book correctly expresses your viewpoint?

PU YI: Yes, rather correctly.

Soon, Blakeney was exploiting this admission.

BLAKENEY: I should like you to tell us just what his (Johnston's) position was.

PU YI: He was my English tutor.

BLAKENEY: Did he serve you for a good many years?

PU YI: Yes.

BLAKENEY: In addition to being your tutor, was he also your friend and adviser?

PU YI: He was merely a tutor of mine.

BLAKENEY: Was he quite familiar with all the details of your life and your opinions during the period he was with you?

PU YI: For ordinary times, he knew a little bit about me. But after I went to Manchuria he didn't know anything about me.

BLAKENEY: I believe you stated that in his book he correctly stated the circumstances of that part of your life?

PU YI: In that book there were many sections . . . I never had the occasion to read the whole book . . . . as far as the section describing my life in Tientsin, I didn't know what he was writing about.

BLAKENEY: When was the last time you saw Sir Reginald Johnston?

PU YI: The last time I saw him was in Manchuria.

BLAKENEY: When was that?

PU YI: I cannot recall the date or the year.

BLAKENEY: When was the last time you saw him before leaving Tientsin?

PU YI: To tell you frankly, I cannot recall these dates. Since I cannot recall, I cannot tell you.

BLAKENEY: Did you see him within about a month before the time you left Tientsin for Port Arthur?

PU YI: I cannot recall.

BLAKENEY: Did you write a preface to his book?

PU YI: I cannot recall that.

Blakeney immediately produced a copy of *Twilight* and began reading Pu Yi's preface, which referred to the events in Tientsin in 1931 ('no one has a more intimate knowledge than he of the disasters and hardships of that critical period') which had provoked his departure. Pu Yi scrutinized it.

PU YI: This was written by Cheng Hsiao-hsu. It was not written by me.

BLAKENEY: Do you mean that the calligraphy is not by you or the words are not yours?

PU YI: I have never seen this.

A procedural wrangle followed, with Prosecutor Keenan objecting to the use of the book as evidence on the grounds that Johnston was dead. 'We know nothing about the author, and he is not a recognized authority as far as I am aware.' Sir William sided with Keenan, to Blakeney's evident chagrin. But he was able to cite one passage of *Twilight* because, he argued, it affected Pu Yi's credibility as a witness. It referred to Johnston's last conversation with Pu Yi, just before he left Tientsin for Manchuria. Was that, Blakeney asked, a correct statement of the facts?

PU YI: At that time Johnston was, as a matter of fact, in Tientsin. But there was no such conversation. Johnston wrote this book with a commercial end in view. He wants to sell this book for money. Hitler has written a

world-famous book by the name of *Mein Kampf* . . . I
have not finished my answer yet.
SIR WILLIAM: Well, don't finish it.

That was bad enough. But Pu Yi's statements about his
interview with Henry Woodhead after becoming Chief
Executive made an even worse impression. He had made
all statements to Woodhead in the presence of Japanese, or
of interpreters he could not trust, he claimed. In any case,
'I had to adopt a hypocritical, pretensive attitude, otherwise I couldn't obtain the confidence of the Japanese . . .
I can't remember my remarks to Woodhead. They should
be regarded as a kind of counter-propaganda.' As for statements made on his behalf by Cheng Hsiao-hsu, 'I have no
way of knowing about his personal activities. I had
nothing to do with his personal beliefs.'

Japanese defence counsel produced a copy of the *Epochal
Journey to Nippon* and began quoting his daily poems, on
the grounds they expressed his 'intimate feelings'.

PU YI: When I composed these poems it was but a kind of
    entertainment . . . I had to write something just to
    make them happy. It cannot be taken seriously. I don't
    blame you, being counsel for the defence, of course you
    would like me to distort the truth as much as you wish.
    I don't want to argue with you.
SIR WILLIAM: I have already warned you, witness, that you
    must be satisfied to answer questions, simply, and that
    you must not make these discursive statements.

As the cross-examination entered its second week, Sir
William did his best to bring Pu Yi's testimony to a close.
But the Japanese lawyers were not about to give up with-
out a struggle.

T. OKAMOTO (defence counsel for Itagaki): Have you ever
    asked the Japanese Government to make you
    Emperor . . . to assist you to become Emperor again?
PU YI: No.
T. OKAMOTO: It seems today you are greatly dissatisfied

with the Japanese Government. Is that not because Japan did not assist you in attaining this so-called heavenly mission?

Pu Yi: This is all a fabricated story.

T. Okamoto: You have stated that in order to deceive the Japanese Government you made various false statements while you were Emperor, that you even wrote poems honouring Japan, but were not these honours also because of your desire to regain the Forbidden City?

Pu Yi: I have already replied to you, no.

Sir William had had enough. 'The real question is whether the witness was an emperor in substance or a mere shadow for the Japanese,' he said. 'We have already heard enough to make up our minds one way or another about that.' The question, he said, was 'whether the witness was really a puppet. It is beside the question whether he was a willing or an unwilling puppet.'

Using his prerogative as President, Sir William told the court that by terminating cross-examination 'it does not necessarily follow that it will be because we believe the witness. We may have open minds about that. It will be because we think that further cross-examination is utterly useless.'

Pu Yi was led out of the courtroom back into the custody of his Soviet guards. He was not required to appear in court again.

His game plan, from the moment of his arrest by Soviet parachutists in 1945 in Mukden, had always been to shift all the blame for what had happened to him between 1931 and 1945 onto the shoulders of the Japanese. He was partially successful in Tokyo, because he was lucky: only a few lines of *Twilight in the Forbidden City* and none of Woodhead's articles had been allowed as evidence; neither Sir Reginald Johnston (because he was dead) nor Woodhead (because he could not be found in time) were there to state their version of the facts. Pu Yi was quick to exploit this, showing himself to be a consistent, self-assured liar, prepared to go to any lengths to save his skin.

He also proved that his barren fourteen years inside the Salt Tax Palace had not affected either his intellect or his power of reasoning. After the first disastrous day, his self-confidence returned: he realized that, with the exception of Major Blakeney, no one in court had read either Johnston's *Twilight* or Woodhead's articles.

Back in Khabarovsk, a Manchurian guard told him that a Chiang Kai-chek mission had flown to Moscow to demand his extradition to China. Pu Yi prepared for the worst, for he knew Chiang Kai-chek would certainly have him executed as a traitor after a show trial.

But the Soviets were not about to surrender such a valuable prize to a shaky, anti-communist government. They were confident that Mao would win the war in China. Then, and only then, would they hand him back.

CHAPTER TWENTY-TWO

Not all the several hundred Japanese and Manchukuo war criminals in Soviet hands immediately after the war shared Pu Yi's luxury detention. Many of them experienced the Soviet 'gulag'. Only the older, and more senior, prisoners shared Pu Yi's comfortable routine, first in a spa hotel, then in a converted school near Khabarovsk, known as Detention Centre No. 45.

Rong Qi, Elizabeth's brother, was one of those who found himself overnight in a Soviet labour camp, along with most of Pu Yi's nephews – and Big Li.

They became hardened to privations, used to labour camp discipline and acquired a different perspective during those years (1947-50). Some of them, like Rong Qi, worked as slave labourers in factories or on collective farms, living in undernourished, brutally disciplined gangs. The lucky ones became hospital attendants.

They turned into survivors, as any 'gulag' inmate must. Also, away from the stifling atmosphere of the court, they began to reflect on the series of events that had brought them to the USSR in the first place. The traditional personal and family ties that had made them Pu Yi's loyal bondsmen became, if not severed, at any rate seriously frayed, during those years apart.

Though deprived of most of his court, Pu Yi's own lifestyle was not markedly changed by his spell in Soviet custody. Detention Centre No. 45 for Manchukuo and Japanese VIPs was staffed by Japanese and Manchurian orderlies who looked after the detainees' wants. Pu Yi's former emperor status afforded him considerable privileges still. He never had to make his bed, empty slops or do any work. The orderlies looked after everything. His father-in-law, Jung Kuan, who was not in Pu Yi's original 'escape' party but had been rounded up separately, ended up in Pu Yi's detention centre – and immediately took over the duties of major-domo. Replacing Big Li, he was the one who now looked after Pu Yi's clothes, possessions and considerable store of jewellery.

Surprising though it may seem, the inmates of the special camp were never searched by their Soviet gaolers, never really treated like prisoners. They were 'temporary detainees'. Sending the more physically able ones to tough detention camps was not punishment – that would be China's prerogative – but simply a cost-effective way of disposing of them while waiting for Mao's final victory.

So, along with some privileged Japanese generals and elderly Manchukuo ex-ministers, Pu Yi prayed to Buddha, played mah-jong, ate three ample meals a day and watched two films a week. The Japanese generals listened endlessly to their limited stock of Japanese records in their upstairs quarters. After his return from Tokyo, Pu Yi wrote that he was overcome with guilt and tried to atone for his shame in his prayers: he knew he had not only lied, but sullied the memory of one of the few people he respected – the late Sir Reginald Johnston.

Before his relatives and Big Li dispersed, Pu Yi took stock of his assets. He hoped, quite irrationally, that the Soviets might allow him a 'dignified' exile in a country other than China. Even the USSR itself would be preferable, and Pu

Yi wrote twice, asking for permanent asylum in the USSR. He received no reply.

If the Soviets allowed him to leave, Pu Yi knew that he had enough gold and jewellery left in his possession to live comfortably for the rest of his life. In fact, there was too much to carry: of his own accord he handed over some two hundred pieces of jewellery to the detention centre authorities and simply got rid of some of the less valuable items, hiding them on the premises, burying them in the school grounds. Later, he was to learn that the Soviets handed these treasures back to China – this was still a time of Soviet-Chinese friendship. The most valuable items, which he kept in his room, fitted inside his cine camera case.

Pu Yi's contacts with his Soviet guards were few and far between. For gossip he depended on the Manchurian camp orderlies, who did not know what was going on but gave themselves important airs. One told him he had nothing to worry about: the Russians would probably keep him in Siberia for the rest of his life, for 'this is the part of the world you come from'. Another piece of gossip, which he did not really believe, except in his wildest dreams, was that the Soviets intended restoring him to the Manchurian throne, this time as a Soviet puppet. When he did meet Soviet officers, they were polite, reassuring and noncommittal.

The war between Chiang Kai-chek and the Chinese communists – at first almost entirely ignored in the Soviet media – gradually became front-page news as Chiang Kai-chek's forces went from defeat to defeat. A Soviet staff interpreter translated Soviet newspapers to the assembled detainees, and a Chinese-language news bulletin was distributed daily after 1947. Pu Yi learned of Shanghai's fall to the communists in 1948 the week it occurred.

Gradually, Pu Yi came to understand that the Soviets were simply keeping him on ice, waiting for Mao Tse-tung to establish a communist regime in China. As soon as this happened, he would be sent home.

It was a nightmare that he gradually came to terms with.

At first, the prospect was so appalling he could think of nothing else: he became more religious than ever. In time, however, the notion that one day he would be handed over to the communists became a familiar fear, as familiar as the fear of dying. Death, too, was inevitable. His one hope was that it would be a speedy one at the communists' hands.

Pu Yi's knowledge of communism in general, and of Chinese communism in particular, was confined to what he had learned as a boy from Johnston, from Cheng Hsiao-hsu and – later – from his Japanese advisers. Yoshioka, in the closing stages of the war, had hinted several times that the Chinese communists were not ordinary 'bandits', that their egalitarianism and military skills made them a formidable force. Pu Yi would have liked to have discussed this with him now, but he was not around. Unknown to Pu Yi, Yoshioka had commited suicide shortly after falling into Soviet hands.

Neither the Japanese nor any of Pu Yi's co-detainees had any real understanding of the nature of Chinese communism. In particular, no one in Pu Yi's entourage was aware that its judicial and penitentiary system was entirely different from that of pre-revolutionary China. Not that it was less brutal: the huge numbers of people – landlords, kulaks, capitalists and 'traitors' of all kinds – executed in the wake of the Chinese communist takeover testify to the contrary.

The difference lay in the overall approach of those in authority to all those accused of any kind of 'crime'. As Jean Pasqualini, author of *Prisoner of Mao*, a uniquely insightful analysis of the Chinese penitentiary system based on his own prison and labour camp experiences, put it: 'Prison is not prison, but a school for learning about one's mistakes.' Chinese prisons were places 'where the prisoners reform the prisoners'.

The interrogation techniques used by the Chinese communists, which Pasqualini anatomized so skilfully, were not like those in force in the non-communist world. The intention was not to extract, from an alleged criminal, evidence which could be used against him in a court of law. Rather it was a religious process, a technique used in bygone days by Inquisition specialists not only to convince suspects of their guilt but to get them to accept it – an extraordinarily effective form of brainwashing.

As Pasqualini wrote, the aim was 'not so much to make you invent nonexistent crimes, but to make you accept your ordinary life, as you led it, as rotten and sinful and worthy of punishment.' In the Chinese judicial system, the accused is himself the most effective prosecutor, for 'self-accusation is one of the masterpieces of the penal system . . . the prisoner takes care to build the case against himself as skilfully as he can . . . When a prisoner has finally produced a satisfactory statement the government holds a document with which, depending on emphasis of interpretation, it can sentence him to virtually any desired number of years. It is the prosecutor's dream.'

The system was also surprisingly flexible: some of those accused of the most serious crimes, in Pasqualini's experience, were treated, at one time or another, with great leniency. Spies and 'saboteurs' had been given three meals a day and plenty of reading material while others, like Pasqualini himself, accused of lesser crimes, were kept on the brink of starvation. The prisons themselves varied enormously in quality: some were showcases, others were abominably overcrowded, cruelly and callously run. This was no accident: in the Chinese approach to the redemption of criminals, kindness too could become a weapon – at times an extraordinarily effective one.

In Pu Yi's case, the straightforward way would have been to confront him with the atrocities perpetrated in Manchukuo, assess his responsibility both in the assumption of power and during his spell as puppet ruler, and sentence him accordingly. This was what had happened to the Japanese accused at the Tokyo-based Asian war crimes trial. At best he could plead, as he had in Tokyo, that he had been a puppet, manipulated at all times by the Japanese. In his own mind he was half-convinced that the trial would be a summary one, that after a brief, perfunctory session he would be taken out and shot.

This might have been Chiang Kai-chek's way of dealing with Pu Yi. It certainly was not Mao's. Just as, in China, a prisoner had not only to repent (Pasqualini never once came across a single detainee who questioned the grounds for his arrest) but be seen to repent, so Pu Yi and his former court had to be made to serve the new society as object-lessons of the old.

This required special handling, special techniques, special people – and also special incentives. The prisoners would be exposed to Chinese communism at its most virtuous best, in a very special environment. In the eyes of Mao and other Chinese communist leaders, Pu Yi, the last Emperor, was the epitome of all that had been evil in old Chinese society. If he could be shown to have undergone sincere, permanent change, what hope was there for the most diehard counter-revolutionary? The more over-whelming the guilt, the more spectacular the redemption – and the greater glory of the Chinese Communist Party.

There was an additional reason for treating Pu Yi and his court with particular care: the transformation of Pu Yi into an exemplary communist citizen would demonstrate the superiority of Chinese revolutionary justice over the Soviet system. Shortly after the Soviet revolution, the Tsarist family had been brutally murdered. Not even Lenin had succeeded in turning the last Tsar into a communist!

For all these reasons, the rehabilitation of Pu Yi and his court became a top priority for Chinese communist leadership after their assumption of power in 1949. It was of special interest to Prime Minister Chou En-lai, who negotiated their return from the Soviet Union. Chou En-lai had another reason for hoping that the detainees would become 'new men': some of the prisoners who would share the process of 'rehabilitation' with Pu Yi were former KMT generals who had once been Chou En-lai's students at the Whampoa Academy. In his schoolmasterly way, Chou En-lai intended to have the last word.

Pu Yi knew nothing of all this when the time came for him to leave the Soviet Union and return to China in the summer of 1950. By this time Big Li and Pu Yi's nephews and half-brother had moved back to Detention Centre No. 45. One day the inmates – all of them except Pu Yi carrying their belongings – were put on a train, under Soviet guard, and taken to the border.

It was like old times again. Pu Yi's nephews were as deferential as ever. Everyone, including Big Li, seemed genuinely glad to see him. Pu Yi took their mood for granted. He was oddly calm and even jaunty as he boarded the train, a raincoat on his arm and a walking stick in his hand. He travelled in a separate compartment – the only prisoner among several sweet-chewing, beer-drinking, tobacco smoking Soviet officers.

In his heart of hearts he was convinced he was heading for a firing squad. During the night the officers slept, but 'I lay with my eyes wide open, kept awake by the fear of death'. Pu Yi prayed, thought he heard the tramp of marching army boots, looked out of the window. The platform was deserted. The officers had done their best to reassure him, thought Pu Yi, but that had been a trick to keep him docile. 'My life will last no longer than the dew on the outside of the windowpane, and there you are, sleeping like logs.'

In the morning Pu Yi was taken to another compartment where two Chinese were waiting for him. One was wearing a blue 'Mao suit', the other army uniform. The civilian looked Pu Yi up and down, and said: 'I have come to receive you on the orders of Premier Chou En-lai. You have now returned to the Motherland.' Pu Yi wrote that he waited for a soldier to put handcuffs on him, and when none were produced, thought: 'He knows I can't run away.' An hour later, the train drew up in a small station on the Russo-Chinese border. There were two lines of armed soldiers – Chinese on one side, Soviet on the other. Pu Yi walked between them and boarded a train waiting on another platform. As he approached this train, Pu Yi noted that his party, and other Manchukuo ex-VIPs, were all already inside this train, 'and none were manacled or bound'. The windows of his compartment were papered over. 'My heart sank. Surely this meant we were on our way to execution.' At this very early stage Pu Yi had already assumed his guilt. 'The faces of the criminals around me,' he wrote, 'were deathly pale.' From now on, in his book, he was to refer to his co-detainees as 'war criminals'.

The re-education process had, in fact, already started: from the beginning of the journey, Pu Yi and his party were overwhelmed by kindness, concern and constant instances of virtuous behaviour on the part of his guards. An officer came by, welcoming them home, telling them 'you have nothing to worry about'. There was a doctor on the train in case anyone needed medical attention. The prisoners ate a filling Chinese breakfast of pickled vege-tables, salted eggs and rice congee. When their guards saw that congee was a popular item, they gave them more – from their own rations. Pu Yi believed this must be because they wanted to keep the prisoners happy for the short period left before they died.

He chose to engage one of his guards in conversation – the young soldier sitting opposite. 'I had to have someone to talk to, to make my escorts know I ought not to be killed,' he wrote. For the first time in his life, he used the polite form of address ('nin' instead of 'ni'). 'You are a member of the People's Liberation Army,' he said. 'That's good, very good. I myself am a Buddhist, and in the Buddhist scriptures the theme of liberation often comes up. Buddha is compassionate, sworn to liberate all things . . .'

The soldier stared at him in wide-eyed incomprehen-sion. Pu Yi faltered, and gave up. Embarrassed, he rose and made his way to the toilet.

On his way back to his seat, he heard conversation in another compartment. One of his nephews, Little Hsiu, was talking about 'democracy' and 'monarchy' in front of the guards. Pu Yi, from the compartment doorway, interrupted, for the guard's benefit: 'Still talking about monarchy? If anyone thinks democracy is bad I'll fight him.' Everyone looked up. 'Don't worry,' Pu Yi shouted, 'I'm the only one they'll put in front of a firing squad.' A soldier urged him to go back to his seat. Pu Yi told him: 'That's my nephew. He has bad ideas. He's against democracy. The other one there's Chao. He used to be an officer. He said many bad things about the Soviet Union.'

The train stopped the following morning. Pu Yi could not see where they were but heard the guard say Changchun. 'So this was the place I was to die, since I had been Emperor here,' he thought. But the train had only stopped to take food aboard.

There was another stop, hours later, at Mukden. Death in the land of his ancestors must be at hand. A civilian went through the train, holding a list. Those whose names he called out (Pu Yi's was among them) were entitled to leave the train for a rest in a guesthouse. This, Pu Yi was convinced, must be a device to get those sentenced to death off the train.

They boarded a bus and were taken to a large house on the outskirts of town. It was guarded by more PLA soldiers. Pu Yi's anxiety must have been evident, for the civilian leading them said: 'What are you afraid of? Didn't I tell you you were coming here for a rest?'

In a room upstairs, tea, cakes and fruit were laid out, as for a party. 'This must be the banquet for condemned men,' Pu Yi thought, and grabbed an apple. When he had finished eating it, he turned to a soldier and said: 'All right. Let's go!'

'Don't be in such a hurry,' said the civilian. 'You'll have plenty of time to do your studying in Fushun.' Still convinced he was about to be executed, Pu Yi asked to see the list of names called out earlier. He was sure it must be a list of those destined for the firing squad.

Just then, Pu Yi wrote, another batch of 'war criminals' entered the room. They included Little Chang, the son of Manchukuo puppet Premier Chang Ching-hui. He had been in China for some time, he told Pu Yi. They would be heading for Fushun together. Only then did Pu Yi relax. 'When we heard that the earlier group were all alive, that our families were all right and that the children were either studying or working, our faces lit up. Tears came to my eyes.'

Back on the train, the prisoners' mood was now one of elation. 'We spoke of the fear we had experienced earlier and roared with laughter,' Pu Yi wrote. The group was now convinced that the worst was over. Soon they would be going home, 'after reading communist books a few days'. But armed guards took them by truck to a high-walled compound with watchtowers. Inside were rows of one-storey buildings. All windows were barred. Pu Yi had arrived at his destination – Fushun prison.

He was stripped, searched, and taken to a cell full of former Manchukuo generals. They stood to attention, not knowing how to react to Pu Yi's presence. Then the cell door opened again and Pu Yi was taken out – to another cell with familiar, reassuring faces. These cellmates were 'family': his father-in-law Jung Kuan, his brother Pu Chieh, and three of his nephews.

Their hopes of freedom had been dashed, but things could be worse. They were together, and fears of execution receded again. Pu Yi's terror returned, however, after dinner. The evening meal had been so good that it might well be their last, a special 'execution banquet'. Jung Kuan disagreed. They would not have been issued with toothbrushes, soap and towels, he said, if death were imminent. The next meal was just as good, but what finally convinced Pu Yi that his gaolers intended him to live was the detailed medical examination he underwent the following day. The prison doctor asked him whether he required any special foods. He was issued with prison uniform and cigarettes.

Pu Yi and his cell inmates settled down to prison routine: a thirty-minute exercise period in the yard, three meals a day, use of a common room at certain fixed hours to hear radio news bulletins and listen to music. What impressed everyone was the apparent cordiality and good humour of the warders who brought them hot water for bathing. None of them behaved like traditional gaolers in the 'old society'. No one spoke brutally or cursed them. One of the nephews tried to give a warder his watch. It was politely refused.

It fell to Jung Kuan to tell them the facts of prison life. As the oldest, most worldly-wise member of the group, the others looked up to him and he was gradually assuming the role of leader. The warder must have refused the watch, he explained, because someone else was observing him. Jung reached for his cigarettes. 'Damn!' he said. 'I left them on a windowledge during the exercise period. The warders all smoke. I've made them a present for nothing.' It was the last pack of a carton of expensive cigarettes he had bought at the stopover in Mukden.

The cell door opened. 'Anyone lost some cigarettes in the yard?' the warder asked. He handed them back to Jung. Another object-lesson in Chinese virtue had been learned. Rehabilitation was under way.

CHAPTER TWENTY-THREE

As a Harbin schoolboy, Jin Yuan had kowtowed every morning, first in the direction of Tokyo, then to Pu Yi, Emperor of Manchukuo. He remembered lining the Harbin streets for hours, with the rest of his school, clasping the Manchukuo flag, waiting for the Emperor to drive by. In 1940, he had been part of a school delegation welcoming Pu Yi back from his second visit to Japan. Every time he went to the cinema, as a child, there were newsreels of Pu Yi visiting factories, greeting dignitaries, or comforting wounded Japanese soldiers in hospital.

After the Japanese had murdered his brother, Jin Yuan's family, always anti-Manchukuo, began hating the regime even more. Jin Yuan himself stayed away from school – he could not bring himself to kowtow to Hirohito any more – and in 1945, at nineteen, he joined the People's Liberation Army and became a communist. In 1950 he entered Manchuria's Public Security Bureau, and was a junior member of the staff of Fushun prison when Pu Yi arrived there with his relatives, his former court, and Manchukuo and Japanese 'war criminals'. One of the reasons he was assigned to Fushun prison was that he spoke fluent Japanese, learned at his Harbin school. Yuan was one of the first prison officials Pu Yi saw, bringing him books and newspapers, advising him on prison behaviour.

Fushun prison had been built by the Japanese in 1936 to house Manchuria's many political prisoners. After the end of the Second World War, when Chiang Kai-chek's men moved back to Fushun, it became, briefly, a cavalry barracks. In 1950 Chou En-lai instructed the Manchurian Public Security Bureau to repair the now abandoned building, install central heating and ready it as a special prison for Manchukuo and Japanese war criminals. Jin Yuan was selected by his local superiors to be one of its staff. Ironically, one of its earliest occupants was to be its former Governor under the Manchukuo Emperor.

'I didn't welcome the idea at all,' Jin Yuan told me. 'I tried to get another posting. I wanted nothing to do with those who had been responsible for my older brother's death and my family's suffering during the Manchukuo years. I wondered how I could ever bear to be in their company.'

Now retired and living in Peking, Jin Yuan is a burly man in his sixties with the features of a benevolent Chinese Otto Preminger. He was to remain in Fushun prison till 1975 – first as warden, then as Deputy Governor, and, after 1960, as Governor. Pu Yi, from the start, became his special responsibility. Bertolucci gave Jin Yuan a cameo role in his film *The Last Emperor*. He is the 'Party boss' who hands Pu Yi his pardon and rehabilitation papers.

From the start, Jin Yuan played a key role in the process that was to turn Pu Yi (prisoner no. 981) into a loyal citizen of China. Though twenty years younger than Pu Yi, he became a kind of father-figure – the first since Johnston. From 1950 onwards, with only a brief interruption in 1952, Jin Yuan was to be in daily touch with Pu Yi, even teaching him to play poker. In the course of his nine years in prison, and afterwards, Pu Yi came to depend on him in the same way a patient depends on his analyst after years of therapy.

In many respects, Jin Yuan owes his distinguished career in the Public Security Bureau to Pu Yi. His success in transforming Pu Yi from Emperor to citizen came to the attention of Mao himself, who wrote him a personal congratulatory note. Pu Yi's case history has been used ever since as a model for other Public Security Bureau officials to follow.

Without in any way belittling Jin Yuan's success, one should bear in mind that from the day Fushun prison received its first war criminals it remained under the close scrutiny of Chou En-lai himself. This was an enormous advantage. Unlike another 'showcase' prison, Peking's 'Number One prison', often visited by foreigners, it did not have to operate as a factory producing goods and meeting quotas with non-specialized labour and antiquated machinery; it did not have a varied, 'difficult' prison population: all inmates were of the same type – Manchukuo and Japanese war criminals who were joined, in 1956, by former generals from Chiang Kai-chek's armies. Its staff could spend unusually large sums on its upkeep and on the prisoners' welfare. Food was always in abundant supply, medical care the best China could offer, its staff hand-picked. Even when the entire prison population was moved from Fushun to Harbin for two years because of fears that the advancing American forces might overrun the town during the Korean War, most of the staff moved too.

Pu Yi was to write about his prison experiences at enormous length, but such was his desire to please his gaolers – and ingratiate himself with his eventual readers – that his account of his 'remoulding' sounds at times irritatingly smug, almost too good to be true. Even taking the special circumstances of his incarceration into account, one longs in vain for just one reference to a less-than-perfect warder, or a single account of unjust or less than ideal treatment of prisoners: in Pu Yi's prison environment, all those in authority seem to have been saints.

Clashes did occur. In 1952, Jin Yuan told me, the Japanese ex-generals 'mutinied': they could not understand why, so long after the war, they should be compelled to go through the experience of endlessly rewriting confessions of their wartime and pre-war crimes. There must have been some fairly stubborn cases among the former KMT generals too, for the Japanese prisoners were released in 1964, the last of the Manchukuo inmates by 1965 – but the last KMT generals did not leave Fushun till 1975, more than thirty-five years after their arrest.

It took nine years for Pu Yi to go from Emperor to citizen. By Chinese prison standards, this was a comparatively short time. The reason, Jin Yuan readily admits, is that the Public Security Bureau had instructions to bring about his 'remoulding' as quickly as possible: 'they wanted him to live a normal life for a while, they didn't want him to be too old to do so,' he said. In other words, from the start, and perhaps understandably so, the Chinese Party leaders intended to use Pu Yi's 'born again' conversion for ideological purposes.

It was a gamble just the same, for no one could be certain how Pu Yi would react to prison life and the 'remoulding process'. It so happened that Jin Yuan, despite his earlier experiences, not only 'came to like Pu Yi quite a bit', as he put it, but also, very early on, had to protect him from the jibes and torments of his former court. For without the remnants of a court or the traditional privileges of his old environment, Pu Yi was the weakest, most helpless of all the inmates inside Fushun prison – and without the help and protection of Jin Yuan he might not have survived their teasing and ideologically inspired criticism.

Even in the cosy family atmosphere of his cell, tensions quickly arose. Big Li soon turned against his former master. Little Hsiu had not forgiven Pu Yi his outburst on the train; he refused to act as his servant. Pu Yi had to rely on another nephew, Little Jui, who washed his clothes and socks and made his bed. In those first few days together, Pu Yi still had a certain vestigial authority as head of the family: out of Little Hsiu's earshot he warned the rest of them to be very careful and circumspect. Pu Yi, having denounced his nephew during the train journey, feared that he might do the same to them. He also gave little homilies about the strength of family and tribal loyalty ties.

His spell in the 'family' cell only lasted ten days. He was moved again. This time the other inmates were all strangers, and Pu Yi felt hopelessly lost. The prison rule was that conversation was restricted to one's own cell. Pu Yi asked the prison Governor for special permission to see his family every day. It was granted, and Little Jui continued to mend his socks and wash his clothes.

For the first time, though, Pu Yi was treated like any other prisoner, and he found it a galling experience. All his life he had been waited on hand and foot. 'I had never even washed my own feet or tied my shoes.' Now, 'when other people were already washing in the morning I would only just have got into my clothes . . . When I put my tooth-brush in my mouth I would find there was no tooth-powder on it, and when I had finished cleaning my teeth the others would be almost through with their breakfast.'

He became the butt of his cellmates' jokes. They were all former Manchukuo officers 'who would never have dared to raise their heads in my presence in the old days'. Now they sniggered behind his back. Pu Yi had to take his turn emptying the communal toilet, and this he simply could not do. 'I thought I would be humiliating my ancestors.'

On parade, he was such a mess that the prison Governor, 'in a kindly voice', singled him out in front of the others and told him to get cleaned up. Pu Yi did not take kindly to this. 'All my life I had been surrounded by walls, but in the past I had been treated with respect.'

The Korean War did not improve matters: a few months after arriving in Fushun, prisoners and staff were taken by train to Harbin where conditions were much tougher. The Harbin prison, also built by the Japanese, had not been refurbished: it was less comfortable and colder, and morale plummeted. The war became a constant conversation topic among the prisoners. No one believed the newspaper reports, and when these, for a brief few weeks, were no longer available, all the prisoners believed the reason was that China was experiencing a series of defeats. The official reason for the ban on newspapers, Pu Yi learned later, was that the prison authorities had not wanted their charges to read articles about 'counter-revolutionary legislation' then being introduced, lest it affect their morale.

The inmates were divided in their attitudes towards the war: some ex-officers believed the United States was bound to crush China; the pessimists – Pu Yi among them – were convinced that if such a victory were near, they would all be shot. This rumour spread with such intensity that the Harbin prison security chief assembled all prisoners and harangued them for an hour, assuring them their lives were not in danger.

It was on this occasion that, for the first time, Pu Yi realized he was in for a long haul. The prison Governor spoke last. 'Perhaps you will say that if we are not going to kill you, it would be a good idea to let you go,' he told the assembled prisoners. 'No, it wouldn't. If we were to release you before you were remoulded, you might commit other crimes. Anyhow, the people would not approve and would not forgive you when they saw you.'

It was the first clear indication of what was expected of Pu Yi, but he was not prepared for the consequences. He had established himself, along with his family and Big Li, as a key witness of past events, a system of defence which he thought he had used to some effect at the War Crimes Tribunal hearing. So when, in Harbin, the time came for him to write about past events in his life 'as part of your thought reform' (and as all prisoners in Chinese prisons must), he stuck to his Tokyo version of the facts: from the time he left the Forbidden City, he claimed, he had been an unwilling victim of the Japanese.

At the same time, he was trying to become a model prisoner: as untidy as ever, and still dependent on Little Jui to keep his clothes clean, he took his turn as cell orderly, but so clumsy was he that he was exempted from serving the food – he invariably spilled it.

He was determined to show, in a spectacular way, his loyalty to the new regime. In his possession was a priceless jade carving of the Chien-lung period, three interlocking seals crafted from a single piece of jade. One day, while a senior visiting official was inspecting his cell, he ceremonially presented the seals, bowing low and begging to 'present this object of mine to the People's Republic'.

To his surprise, the visitor did not accept the gift. 'Aren't you Pu Yi? You'd better discuss this with the authorities,' he said. Pu Yi handed the seals over to Jin Yuan. The impact was not what he had hoped. The prison Governor told him casually: 'We have your seals, and your letter. We also have what you gave to the Soviet authorities. But what matters to the people is men, remoulded men.'

The process was going to be more complicated than Pu Yi had thought. The trouble was that all around him loyalties were shifting. Jung Kuan, who might have remained loyal to him, died while they were in Harbin. Though Pu Yi failed to realize it at the time, he had lost the support of his group even before the Harbin move – and the biggest change of all was in Big Li, his personal servant for the past thirty-two years.

In the jargon of Chinese public security, there are two kinds of individuals – the toothpaste prisoner and the watertap prisoner. Pu Yi's 'remoulding' process occurred piecemeal – it was like squeezing a toothpaste tube, a little came out at a time – but Big Li was a watertap man. 'It didn't take more than a month,' said Jin Yuan, 'for it all to pour out.'

Jin attributed Big Li's 'progress' to his 'poor family background . . . after learning about the feudal system he realized he had been working for the biggest landlord of all'. But what undoubtedly fuelled the change even more was Big Li's discovery that he was in prison through no fault of his own, but simply because he had had the misfortune to become Pu Yi's servant in the first place. 'Big Li had committed no crime,' Jin Yuan admitted. 'He was in gaol because he was Pu Yi's personal servant, and it was thought Pu Yi was so helpless that he could not have survived without him.' The first sign of Big Li's change of heart, Pu Yi recalled, was when he refused to mend Pu Yi's spectacles. The first revolt was a horrible moment for Pu Yi, because Big Li knew everything about the flight from Tientsin, the jewels in the camera case, the way Pu Yi had behaved towards the pageboys. If Big Li told the prison authorities all he knew, Pu Yi's carefully written prison confession would be shown up as a pack of lies. It was not easy for Pu Yi to talk to Big Li since they were in different cells. He tried to use a nephew to relay a message. But even the nephews were becoming less responsive to him.

This became obvious to Pu Yi the day the inmates put on a series of sketches about their life in prison. Such practices are common occurrences in China – and valuable pointers to the inmates' progress. There was a sketch poking fun at a former Manchukuo justice minister who invariably tried to ingratiate himself with the warders by reading communist literature at the top of his voice when warders came into earshot. There was a sketch, too, about Pu Yi, ridiculing his habit of praying to Buddha and refusing to kill flies. All but Little Jui took part in the sketches. And Little Jui himself was 'criticized' in another sketch which ridiculed him for slavishly acting as another prisoner's servant. Shortly after the sketches were performed, Little Jui refused to look after Pu Yi's laundry, and was soon behaving in a downright hostile manner.

Pu Yi understood why as soon as he received a note from him, urging him to make a clean breast of things and hand back all the jewellery he was hoarding in his camera case. Now it was clear to Pu Yi that, behind his back, his relatives were telling the authorities all about his hoard. After thinking things over for a week, Pu Yi decided he had better hand them back voluntarily.

In fact, the prison authorities had been playing cat and mouse with Pu Yi ever since his arrival. 'They knew what was in the camera case,' one of his relatives who was with him in Harbin at the time told me. 'They merely wanted to see how long Pu Yi would hold out.'

The prison Governor gave him a receipt for the 468 pieces of jewellery he handed over. The gesture was seen as Pu Yi's first 'sincere act of repentance'. It was also an important lesson in prison behaviour: when he returned to his cell after surrendering the jewellery, his formerly standoffish cellmates congratulated him, and started calling him 'Old Pu'. For the first time, they were neither ignoring him nor treating him with contempt. It had been a wise and timely gesture, said 'Old Yuan', a former Manchukuo ambassador to Japan. 'Remember, the government knows about things you forgot years ago.'

The return of the jewels was just the beginning of Pu Yi's 'remoulding' process. When the prisoners were asked to compile lists of Japanese crimes in Manchuria, Pu Yi now realized that his earlier confession would not be at all consistent. Guilt over his past behaviour opened a floodgate of remorseful self-accusations. Just as important, perhaps, was that Pu Yi realized 'that I was up against an irresistible force that would not rest until it had found out everything'.

'I must confess my guilt to the people,' Pu Yi told the prison Governor. 'I couldn't atone for it even if I were to die ten thousand times.' He asked one of his cellmates if he should refer to his own 'crimes' in his essay on Japanese behaviour in Manchuria. 'Of course,' was the answer. 'In any case, the government has got so much material on us that it is much better to speak up.'

Pu Yi started writing, making nonsense of his earlier confession, telling the facts as he remembered them of his spell in Tientsin and the circumstances of his departure to Manchuria. It was the turning-point in his life, and the first major step in his 'remoulding' process.

Ghostwriter Li Wenda, who was to read the confessions in the process of helping Pu Yi with his published memoirs, says they were an abject record of cowardice and lack of moral fibre, showing that all his life he had been haunted by fear and guilt. Pu Yi was now embarked on an 'autocritique' that was to continue for the rest of his life.

What was it that caused the floodgates to open? Was his 'remoulding' – as Pu Yi himself believed – the result of reflections on the nature of his own absurd, and absurdly privileged, fate? Or was this spectacular conversion merely the last of a series of devices designed to extricate himself, as in the past, from the consequences of his acts? Big Li, to this day, believes that his former master was neither as humble, nor as innocent, as he seemed. It is almost irresistible to believe that the same low cunning Pu Yi showed at the Tokyo war crimes trial could also – in these new circumstances – be put to good use and lead to skilful self-criticism as a means of redemption in Chinese communist society. He certainly learned the jargon fast enough. By the time he returned to Fushun, in 1954, he was well on the way to becoming China's most famous prisoner.

CHAPTER TWENTY-FOUR

One of the main differences between China's penitentiary system and that of the rest of the world is that in China a prisoner's behaviour is constantly monitored without electronic surveillance of any kind. The wardens are immediately aware of an inmate's mood change, or of a sudden fit of temper. Even what the prisoner mutters in his sleep usually comes to their attention.

The reason is that in a Chinese prison everyone informs on everyone else, and every inmate in turn assumes the role of prosecutor. In group sessions, they accuse each other of sloth, hypocrisy and anti-state behaviour – and the way everyone reacts determines how real their ideological 'progress' is. Prisoners immediately become aware that their freedom depends not so much on the length of their sentence – like Pu Yi, they may never come to court at all – but on tangible evidence of 'remoulding'.

Such evidence comes to the authorities' attention in a number of ways. The written 'autocritique' is an essential element without which an inmate can never hope to leave prison. But the Chinese are a practical people, and the 'autocritique' alone is never enough: what matters just as much is the prisoner's day-to-day behaviour, on his own and within his cell group. And while wardens cannot be in constant attendance, even in a special prison environment like Fushun (there were, after all, Japanese and KMT 'war criminals' to 'remould' as well), nothing occurred in prison without their knowledge because prisoners knew that nothing could or should be concealed from them and that the franker they were about each other's faults and behaviour quirks, the better it was for them all.

In most prisons, informants are looked down on as stool pigeons, and stool pigeons get murdered. In China, this was not so: an inmate who did not report even the most insignificant events and pettiest clashes within his cell to his warden discovered that his cellmates held it against him. Such non-cooperation never lasted long, because he quickly realized he was a minority of one.

A Chinese prison cell, especially in the years Pu Yi was in Fushun (1950–9), was a twenty-four-hour Marxist-Leninist-Maoist encounter group, and even if a warden was not present during its interminable sessions (a refusal to take part in 'discussion groups' being itself evidence of anti-social behaviour) he knew all about them on a day-to-day basis. For their own protection, and in order to draw attention to their 'remoulding' process, prisoners told the wardens everything that went on around them from the time they got up in the morning to the moment they fell asleep. Everything said, every apparently meaningless little exchange or quirk of behaviour was offered up for comment, analysis and self-criticism.

Of course there were ways to beat the system. Since ideology – in Mao's China, at least – conditioned all human behaviour, it was important to behave, and 'confess', in ideologically acceptable terms. A prisoner's mistake, even if it concerned something trivial, like breaking a windowpane, could be forgiven (but never forgotten) if the written 'confession' followed the proper semantic pattern. It could, on the contrary, lead to severe penalties if improperly penned, or if the prisoner gave the impression of trying to outsmart the authorities through excuses considered either perfunctory or glib. In all circumstances, humility and frank admission of guilt were *de rigueur*.

Pu Yi's understanding of the system undoubtedly hastened his 'remoulding' process. Humility became his stock-in-trade. It was not all that simple. Many of his fellow-prisoners, for instance, made the mistake of turning on Pu Yi, 'denouncing' him not only as China's 'biggest landlord' but also for being such a helpless booby in prison; they failed to realize that the prison authorities interpreted such behaviour as a transfer of guilt, as minimizing their own crimes. It failed to win them any points, and may have delayed their release by months, possibly even years. Someone like Big Li, however, who early on provided the authorities with a factual record of Pu Yi's real behaviour from 1924 onwards, and never allowed his personal resentment of him to spill over into abuse, was clearly 'progressive'. Big Li was released in 1956, as were some of Pu Yi's nephews who informed Jin Yuan about Pu Yi's cache of Forbidden City treasures. In fact, Pu Yi never did become aware that from the day he entered Fushun prison, Jin Yuan knew almost everything about him.

The other prisoners' harassment of Pu Yi took many forms, and the way he dealt with them was closely observed. While in Harbin, for instance, the inmates were given manual work to do. It was not the back-breaking factory work most prisoners in China must become proficient at or forfeit their rations: in Fushun they merely had to glue cardboard strips together, making them into cardboard boxes to package pencils from a Harbin pencil factory. Needless to say, Pu Yi was clumsy. The boxes he turned out at first were rejects. For this, one of his cellmates, a bullying former Manchukuo high official, constantly abused him, accusing him of 'acting like a stinking emperor still', and adding prissily that his remarks were all for Pu Yi's own good.

Pu Yi's response was a 'school solution' answer in Chinese penitentiary terms. 'Look,' he said patiently, 'I'm stupider than you, I'm not good at talking or making things, and I was born that way. Will that do?'

The bullying made him ill, and he was taken to hospital with a fever. It was, Pu Yi wrote, a period of intense thought and stock-taking. 'Whenever I had been laughed at or been shown up as incompetent I had bitterly resented it, hating those who found fault with me and the People's Government that had locked me up. Now I saw this was wrong of me. I really was laughable, incapable and ignorant.' The responsibility for his current state lay, he now saw, in the way he had been brought up.

The prison Governer praised him for his new awareness. 'You have recognized the source of your incompetence,' he said. It was a step in the right direction, 'but you ought to ask yourself why those princes and court officials brought you up that way.'

Because it was in their own interest, Pu Yi said.

Things were not that simple, the Governor said. Had those who brought him up to be Emperor deliberately meant to harm him? Pu Yi did not know what to answer. 'Think about it carefully,' he was told. 'If you can find an answer, your illness will have been worth while.'

What the Governor meant – but intended Pu Yi to discover for himself – was that it was the system which had been at fault, not the individuals implementing it. It was another lesson Pu Yi was quick to learn. Those truly responsible for his plight were not individuals at all, but abstractions: imperialism, feudalism, capitalism. It was both reassuring and conducive to growing self-respect.

'Remoulding' had barely started: in March 1954 Pu Yi and the rest of the war criminals returned to Fushun, and here the serious process began, with an exhaustive cataloguing of Japanese and Manchukuo war crimes, the Japanese inmates fulfilling twin roles – as witnesses and accused seeking forgiveness. More 'confessions' had to be written, but this time – since they were to be far more detailed and the inmates were expected to incriminate each other – the security measures taken to prevent anyone from concocting a story with the co-operation of others were drastic. How on earth, I asked Jin Yuan, was it possible to ensure that they did not get together and fabricate a version that would clear them of blame? Easy, he said, looking for a moment as threatening as the late Otto Preminger. 'We kept them all in solitary confinement.'

It took Pu Yi months to complete his report, and this time he was cross-examined by two outsiders from the Public Security Bureau, who went through it line by line. They were, Pu Yi wrote later, incredibly knowledgeable. They knew how much rice, soya bean and opium had been grown in Manchuria, year by year. They had records of Japanese imports from Manchukuo, were aware of the details of the food rationing system introduced by the Japanese, and each time they came to a figure in Pu Yi's lengthy statement, they asked him what his source had been, unerringly discovering how much was fact, how much hearsay – and to what extent Pu Yi had relied on past conversations with his cellmates.

Now the 'autocritiques' of the individual members of Fushun Prison were blended into an orchestral whole: the Japanese 'war criminals', previously segregated, were brought into play. They too had been through the same 'remoulding' process, and were ready to play their part. One of the Japanese prisoners, Tadayuki Furumi, a former head of Manchukuo's General Affairs Office of the State Council, lectured the assembled Manchukuo inmates on Japanese crimes in the region, tirelessly spelling out Japan's opium policy, its systematic plundering of Manchurian resources.

A former Japanese Gendarmerie officer told the assembled prisoners how he had conducted mass executions and rounded up civilians for slave labour. 'All the atrocities,' Pu Yi noted, 'had been carried out in my name.'

The next step was to provide evidence of Japanese and Manchukuo torture and cruelty from the victims themselves. Written testimony from certain selected survivors, who had defied the Japanese and Manchukuo authorities and paid for their resistance through torture, was now read out. Each ended with a call for retribution. 'The Japanese and Chinese traitors must repay their blood debt. Avenge our murdered families!'

The intended lesson was this: Pu Yi had invariably excused his past actions on the grounds that there was no way he could have opposed the Japanese. Now here were humble Manchurian workers, farmers, housewives and children who *had* dared defy the Japanese and Manchukuo oppressors. His guilt was now overwhelming, as his gaolers meant it to be. Pu Yi wrote: 'You can never escape the consequences of your sins.' By 1955 he was a changed man. When the prison Governor asked him how he envisaged his future, Pu Yi bowed his head and said, 'I could only wait for my punishment.'

Though he did not yet know it, he was already becoming an object-lesson for the 'masses'. Early in 1955 a Chinese camera unit came to Fushun prison, and the inmates were filmed playing volleyball and ping-pong in the yard. Pu Yi was the focus of their special attention, but such was the resentment of the others towards him that no prisoner wanted to be filmed standing next to him.

In March a group of China's most senior generals – the famous Marshal Chuh Teh among them, though Pu Yi did not know this – visited the prison and talked to Pu Yi and his younger brother Pu Chieh. One of them told Pu Yi to keep studying. 'One day you will be able to see the building of socialism with your own eyes.' This could only mean, one of Pu Yi's cellmates said, that they meant to let him out eventually. 'This cheered everybody up,' Pu Yi wrote. 'If the number one traitor was safe, that meant there was hope for them too.'

He was still a below-average prisoner in many ways: he now washed his own clothes, but remained hopelessly untidy; he was always forgetting to turn off the tap after use, wasting the prison's water; he still had an aversion against killing flies (1955 was China's 'fly eradication campaign' year and inmates were expected to kill fifty a day with specially issued flyswatters) and though he had long stopped being a vegetarian, he still prayed. The other prisoners treated him with a mixture of contempt and impatience. Pu Yi was now thoroughly imbued with a sense of his own worthlessness, and was pathetically grateful whenever he was singled out for praise. Without fully realizing the extent of the change, he was well on the way to becoming a model worker – humble, zealous, self-deprecating. He admired the prison Governor and Jin Yuan for their wisdom and forbearance, recognizing the superiority of his former servant, Big Li, over him. He was ripe for the final stage of 'remoulding'.

This took the form of guided tours of what had once been Manchukuo and meetings with some of the former victims of his own puppet rule. Dressed up in Mao suits, the prisoners were taken to the former sites of Japanese atrocities. Pu Yi talked to the woman survivor of a mass execution. 'Her amazing forgiveness,' Pu Yi wrote, 'struck the Japanese war criminals dumb for a while, and then they began to weep for shame and kneel before her, asking the Chinese Government to punish them.'

In a rural commune, he confessed his identity to a farmer's wife whose family had all but starved to death during the Manchukuo years. Instead of cursing him, she said: 'It's all over now, let's not talk about it,' and Pu Yi broke down in tears. Everywhere he went, he found evidence of a new prosperity and self-respect among the once 'downtrodden masses'. In coal mines, steelworks and power stations, the captive audience of former Manchukuo and Japanese war criminals was overwhelmed by the welcome they received. The circle was almost complete. Now Pu Yi was ready to be displayed to a larger audience. He was unlikely to forget his lines.

His first visitor was an unexpected one: Jade Lute, the concubine he had left behind in 1945, brought him a pen and a pair of shoes. She was pregnant, but Jin Yuan told her not to tell Pu Yi. It would only upset him. Although her meeting with Jin Yuan was brief, he got her to talk, 'off the record', about her life – and the identity of the father of her child. Shortly afterwards, this man was sent to a labour camp for 'having an affair with a married

307

woman', and the child was given for adoption to a childless couple.

Jade Lute was to return to the prison twice – in 1957 and 1958 – but Pu Yi never mentioned any of her visits in his autobiography, probably because they failed to live up to the rosy picture of his new life he was now intent on conveying.

Instead, he preferred to recall another visit, which he describes as his first: on 10 March 1956, a formal family reunion took place: Pu Yi, Pu Chieh, two brothers-in-law and two nephews were summoned to the Governor's office, and found Pu Yi's uncle, Tsai Tao, and two of his younger sisters waiting for them.

It was not a complete surprise: the Manchukuo war criminals' families had been allowed to correspond with the inmates since 1955. Pu Yi knew that most of his family was well, and had adjusted to the new regime. Significantly, there is no mention in his book of the circumstances of the death of Elizabeth, merely a passing reference to the fact that she had died 'long ago'. He also failed to mention the circumstances of his father's death in 1951, perhaps because right up to the moment he died Prince Chun, unable to obtain any news about them, still believed they were Soviet prisoners.

Prince Chun had survived the Japanese occupation, and the ensuing civil war, in straitened circumstances. He and a son, Pu Ren, had opened a private school. When this was closed down they became schoolteachers in a government school. In the last few months of his life he sold Northern Mansion to the new Chinese government, and the family's money problems had eased somewhat. In his memoirs Pu Yi wrote tirelessly, however, about the ideological progress of other relatives: Uncle Tsai Tao, who had never been tainted by collaboration, was now a member of the National People's Congress representing the Manchu minority – and had recently met Mao. It was Mao who had authorized the family reunion in Fushun prison.

Pu Yi's other sisters had also, voluntarily, 'remoulded' themselves. Two were schoolteachers, one a seamstress, another a 'social activist' and street committee member. Recalling how they had all been idle children, waited on hand and foot, the prison inmates could not believe the change. 'Do you really sew? Do you really ride a bicycle?' a brother-in-law asked 'sister number three'.

To his surprise, Pu Yi discovered that not only his sisters but also the younger generation family members were doing well under the new regime. All were either students or in jobs. None had been penalized for their blood ties with Pu Yi. His gratitude to the new regime was compounded, and after this meeting with his family his description of prison life takes on a positively elegiac tone. He went on more tours of Manchuria's factories and farms, marvelling at the progress made since the communist takeover; he seems to have been unaware of the errors that turned the 'Great Leap Forward' – which began while he was still in prison – into a devastating agricultural and industrial setback for China. He was called to testify as a witness at the trial of some Japanese war criminals in Mukden, and did so with relish: he was now a firm believer in revolutionary justice. He wrote:

> My thoughts went back to the International Military Tribunal in Tokyo. There the Japanese war criminals had used lawyers to make trouble and attack the witnesses. In the hope of lightening their sentences they had used every conceivable method to cover up their crimes. But at this court all the war criminals admitted their guilt and submitted to punishment.

He started giving interviews – between ten and twenty a year from 1956 onwards, says Jin Yuan. 'His manner with the press was very good.'

The most memorable moment of his last years in prison, however, was his star role in a series of plays written and performed by the Manchukuo inmates for their Japanese and KMT fellow-prisoners. In the past Pu Yi had never been asked to take part. The organizers thought him too shy, and too clumsy, to perform. But beginning in 1956, he not only sang in the chorus, but also had speaking parts. The theme of his first play was the 1956 Suez expedition. It was called The Defeat of the Aggressors. One of the Manchukuo ex-ministers ('because he had a big nose') played the part of British Foreign Secretary Selwyn Lloyd. Pu Yi played a left-wing MP who attacks Selwyn Lloyd in parliament for Britain's 'disgraceful' behaviour.

He dressed up in the same dark blue suit he had worn at the Tokyo trial. When the cringing Selwyn Lloyd tries to justify Britain's policy, Pu Yi challenges him. Some of his forgotten English returned and he *ad libbed*. 'No, no, no,' he shouted. 'It won't do! Get out! Leave this House!' His performance was enthusiastically applauded. It was one of the proudest days in Pu Yi's life. He soon became fond of theatricals, and also played the part of a Japanese war criminal at the court of the Manchukuo puppet.

Another play – written by Pu Chieh – was about Manchukuo. It was crudely dramatized history: a couple of Chinese 'traitors' first collaborate with the Japanese, then try and contact Chiang Kai-chek to hand over the country to him. They are caught and 'remoulded'.

It was the stuff of conventional Chinese films of the fifties and of the later, officially approved, Peking operas. Though 'nothing wonderful in itself,' Pu Yi wrote, 'all of us war criminals could see ourselves in it. It reminded us of our past, held our attention and made us feel more and more ashamed of ourselves.'

One aspect of the play was poignantly tragi-comic: every time the two 'traitors' entered their office, they kowtowed in the direction of the 'Imperial Image' of the Manchukuo Emperor – a photograph of Pu Yi in full regalia – while the real Emperor watched the play among the prison audience. He experienced no irony, only disgust, writing that the portrait the actors bowed to was 'the filthiest thing in the world'.

One person had not fully come to terms with Pu Yi's transformation. Jade Lute, his concubine, put in another appearance. She stayed two days, sharing Pu Yi's cell (he now had his own quarters, moving within the prison compound almost like a free man). She must have thought she might at last start benefiting from her association with him.

She questioned Jin Yuan closely about their prospects. When would he be set free? What was her share of his property? What had happened to his personal jade collection? Wasn't she entitled to part of it?

Jin Yuan, sensing her predatory nature, was noncommittal. He had no idea when Pu Yi would be freed, he said, and in any case everything he had ever owned now belonged to the state. A few weeks later, she began divorce proceedings, on the grounds that hers had been an arranged marriage, without her initial consent.

Pu Yi endured one last 'struggle' session with his former Manchukuo ministers and generals. They could not believe that Pu Yi had not known about the transfer of Manchukuo's exchequer – £20 million – which had taken place a few weeks before the end of the Second World War. Pu Yi at the time had only ordered his own personal funds transferred, and, with unaccustomed stubbornness, indignantly protested his innocence. When he realized the prison authorities had believed his own version of events all along, he 'burst into tears'.

The ultimate proof of Pu Yi's 'remoulding' came one day in 1959. China was in the throes of a nationwide anti-rodent campaign. Every child had to produce the corpse of at least one mouse. Pu Yi wrote he was able to overcome his 'superstitious' Buddhist aversion to taking life after listening to a warden's 'tales of suffering' under the Manchukuo tyranny. 'The guidance of Warder Chang,' he wrote, 'enabled me to kill six mice.'

In September 1959, to celebrate the tenth anniversary of the establishment of the People's Republic, Mao Tse-tung proposed a special amnesty for certain categories of prisoners, including war criminals who had 'truly reformed themselves from an evil past to a virtuous present'. The Party's Central Committee duly approved it, and in Fushun prison the news was given a rapturous reception.

Jin Yuan asked Pu Yi how he felt about it. He was happier than he had ever been, and healthier, he said, from 'voluntary labour' – tending the prison vegetable garden and moving coal. He was now one of the prison's hospital assistants, wore a white coat, and the Japanese war criminals called him 'doctor'. 'I will be the last to go,' Pu Yi said modestly, 'that is, if I can ever remould myself.'

What if Pu Yi's name was included in the next batch of 'remoulded' prisoners to be released?

' "It's out of the question," I replied, laughing.'

The next day an official from the Supreme People's Court read out a 'notice of special pardon' at a meeting of assembled prisoners. 'The war criminal Pu Yi, 54, of Manchu nationality, and from Peking, has now served nine years' detention,' it said. 'As a result of remoulding through labour and ideological education he has shown that he has genuinely reformed. In accordance with clause one of the Special Pardon Order he is therefore to be released.'

Once more, Pu Yi broke down and wept.

CHAPTER TWENTY-FIVE

Half-brother Pu Ren was at Peking's main railroad station on 9 December 1959 to meet Pu Yi. He barely recognized him. 'I hadn't seen him since 1934 in Changchun,' he recalled. 'He had then seemed immensely tall. Now I was almost as big as he was. He was stooped, and looked old as well as frail.'

Pu Ren took him to the home of one of his married sisters. They talked far into the night. Pu Yi displayed a gossipy curiosity about all the members of his family, wanting to know who was married, what each one was doing, how many grandchildren he now had. He had assumed the *persona* of the benevolent family patriarch. He was to maintain this 'big brother' attitude towards his family for the rest of his life.

'He was naïve and curiously childlike,' said Pu Ren, 'and he had a certain amount of difficulty adjusting to day-to-day life in a big city.' In those early days of freedom, living in his sister's tiny apartment, he helped with domestic chores to the best of his ability; but she wished he would not – he was as clumsy as ever, still breaking and spilling things.

All Chinese residents are responsible for the cleanliness of the streets where they live. Pu Yi insisted on taking his turn sweeping the area outside his sister's apartment block – and promptly got lost. Wandering about in his neighbourhood with his broom, he finally asked for directions.

'I'm Pu Yi,' he said, 'the last Emperor of the Ching dynasty. I'm staying with my relatives and can't find my way home.'

He had taken Mao's dictum, 'Serve the People', caricaturally to heart: whenever he took a bus, he would not get on till the last person had boarded; this meant he was frequently left behind. In restaurants, he made embarrassing little homilies to waitresses. 'You should not be serving me,' he would say, rising and bowing his head, 'I should be serving you.'

He was more absent-minded than ever, and seemed to revel in this trait. 'The first time I saw him,' says ghost-writer Li Wenda, 'he was desperately gripping a shoulder bag containing his notes, his spectacles, his medicine, his watch and his wallet. Going out with Pu Yi, one was guaranteed at least one major crisis, for he lost everything.'

His personal habits could also be irritating, Li Wenda recalled. In hotel rooms, Pu Yi 'invariably forgot to close doors behind him, forgot to flush the toilet, forgot to turn the tap off after washing his hands, had a genius for creating an instant, disorderly mess around him'. Clearly, the habit of being waited on for half a lifetime had not been altered by nearly fifteen years in prison. Perhaps he even cultivated his absent-mindedness, discovering it was an endearing characteristic. In his early years in Fushun prison, his inmates had treated him like a buffoon. Now he may have become one by choice.

'He never mastered the "ticket" system in restaurants,' said Li Wenda. In all but tourist eating places in China, customers buy cigarette-paper-thin tokens in advance for the food they will eat. 'He never got used to this, or to adding up what the different dishes cost.' He was hopeless about money. 'When he started work he would spend his pay packet in the first week, and then rely on the generosity of others.'

He corresponded assiduously with Jin Yuan, promoted, shortly after Pu Yi's departure, to Governor of Fushun prison, giving him a day-by-day account of his 'progress'. When Jin Yuan came to Peking, Pu Yi called on him, sometimes late at night, always without warning, and talked interminably about his efforts, and shortcomings, in becoming a completely 'remoulded' communist.

He was privileged to remain idle for months with his family in Peking, visiting museums, reading, drinking tea with relatives. In contrast, Big Li, immediately after his release, was assigned to breaking stones in a roadbuilding 'team' in Peking, and Pu Yi's nephews to backbreaking work in state farms thirty kilometres from Peking.

Pu Yi was constantly amazed by the honesty of ordinary people: he left his wallet and gold watch behind in countless restaurants, canteens and libraries, but always had them returned. The watch had immense sentimental value: evading his father's spies, he had bought it in a shop in the Legation Quarter in Johnston's company in 1924 the day he left the Northern Mansion to take refuge, first in the German Hospital, then in the Japanese Legation. 'It was on that day,' Pu Yi wrote, 'that my disgraceful record began.'

It was the only valuable object left from the cache of treasures he had handed back to the State while in Fushun. The day before he left prison, the Governor formally presented the watch to him. Pu Yi refused the gift at first, saying it had been bought with money 'derived from exploitation'. The Governor made him take it. Whatever its origins, he said with contained impatience, it was now 'a gift from the people of China'.

Pu Yi returned to the Forbidden City, for the first time since 1924, in the company of other released KMT and Manchukuo prisoners, as part of a 'familiarization tour' of Peking. Pu Yi was their guide, and marvelled at its transformation. It had been a desolate, broken-down place then. Now it was a fully restored museum, full of visitors.

He recognized on exhibit a number of items he had himself removed from the Forbidden City and later returned to the state.

With Li Wenda, he later wrote an article in the Chinese travel magazine *Luyou* (Travel) describing his impressions on returning there for the first time in thirty-two years.

He sought out the handful of still living, elderly mandarin scholars who had been his advisers in his early life. One of them, Chang Yen-ying, had loyally followed Pu Yi first to Tientsin, then to Changchun, until the Japanese tutelage became too oppressive for him. He was now in his eighties, bedridden and almost dying. 'When you are better we will serve the people together,' Pu Yi told him. 'I'll always go along with you,' the old man said. 'I'm going along with the Communist Party,' Pu Yi said piously.

Shortly after Pu Yi's release, he and a few former KMT generals called on Chou En-lai. The Chinese Premier was perhaps the busiest man in China, but he talked to them at length – and his remarks were surprisingly free of ideological jargon.

They should all remember they were now members of one country, adjust to the change around them and banish any nostalgia for the 'old society', Chou said. They must be careful not to offend members of their family, and remember that in the 'new society' women were men's equals, held down important jobs, and were no longer men's domestic slaves. Speaking from personal experience, Chou En-lai told them, he knew how much he owed to his own wife.

Turning to the KMT generals, Chou En-lai said he recognized several of his former Whampoa Academy pupils among them.

'I couldn't have been a very good teacher, or you wouldn't have taken the path you did and fought the communists,' Chou En-lai said with a grin. 'Either that or you were pretty awful students.' But he spoke, he said, as an 'old friend', not as someone intent on reviving old wounds, and they could always come to him with their problems. His door was always open.

Addressing Pu Yi, Chou said he could not be blamed for anything in his life that had happened in his childhood.

'You weren't responsible for becoming Emperor at the age of three or for the 1917 attempted restoration coup,' he said. 'But you were fully to blame for what happened later. You knew perfectly well what you were doing when you took refuge in the Legation Quarter, when you travelled under Japanese protection to Tientsin and when you agreed to become Manchukuo Chief Executive.'

Pu Yi bowed his head. Humble as ever, he told Chou En-lai that even in childhood he should have known better.

In March 1960 Pu Yi was finally given a job. He became a part-time assistant at the Botanical Gardens, itself an offshoot of the Chinese Academy of Science's Botanical Institute. He also, with Li Wenda, started writing his autobiography, *From Emperor to Citizen*.

The suggestion came from Chou En-lai himself at one of their meetings shortly after Pu Yi's release, and Li Wenda is unable to say whether the idea came to Chou En-lai suddenly, or whether the proposal was carefully contrived. Pu Yi reacted with enthusiasm. He proudly told the Chinese Premier that he already had most of the material at hand, in his prison 'confessions'. Chou En-lai told him to get to work.

Contrary to the legend that had him tending roses in Peking's gardens, Pu Yi never became a skilled gardener. He transplanted seedlings and cleaned hot-houses, but the job was in fact a sinecure. He lived in a spartan single room in the worker's hostel there, and after a morning's light work, he and Li Wenda would retire to the nearby Fragrant Hills Hotel, where they lunched and worked all afternoon on his memoirs. The expenses for this were met by Chou En-lai's office, and Chou himself frequently enquired about its progress.

Chou En-lai, himself the revolutionary offspring of an aristocratic family with several mandarin ancestors, had from the start showed a special interest in Pu Yi and the 'remoulded' Aisin Goro clan. That first Chinese New Year after Pu Yi's release, he invited him and several members of his family to an informal meal in his house; every subsequent Chinese New Year, right up to the Cultural Revolution, the invitation would be repeated. Chou En-lai's fascination for Pu Yi stemmed in part from the latter's quite extraordinary ideological volte-face. If communism could turn someone like Pu Yi into this kind of man, he used to say, there was nothing it could not achieve.

When work started on *From Emperor to Citizen*, Li Wenda thought they would only need to edit Pu Yi's lengthy 'autocritique', written in prison, and that the whole process would not take more than three months. Reading it, however, he realized they would have to start afresh. The 'autocritique' was not factual enough; its language was stilted; on almost every page there were emotional confessions to hosts of sins. For the book to gain a wide Chinese and international readership, as Chou En-lai intended, it would have to be entirely rewritten.

It took them four years, and for the last three Pu Yi was no longer working in the Botanical Gardens, but in the archives of the China People's Political and Consultative Committee (CPPCC). By this time (November 1962) he had become a full citizen again, with voter's rights. It had been, he wrote, 'the proudest day of my life'.

Pu Yi and Li Wenda worked in libraries, conducted interviews with survivors of the Forbidden City and talked to those who had known him during his Tientsin years. Pu Yi sought out eunuchs, to ask them about conditions inside the Forbidden City, and Li Wenda went back to Manchuria for several weeks.

Pu Yi even talked to Li Tieh-yu, his former driver, the man who had fathered Empress Elizabeth's child in Changchun. As Li Wenda recalled, it was a chance meeting: they came face to face one day on a crowded Peking street. Pu Yi recognized Li, and said they must have a little chat. Li Tieh-yu was embarrassed, and wanted to say no, but Pu Yi told him he had nothing to worry about: he only wanted to know about conditions in the servants' quarters inside the Salt Tax Palace, for the book he was writing. He never once referred to Li's affair with Elizabeth. On parting, he gave Li all the money he had on him – about seven pounds.

In 1962 Pu Yi remarried – for the fifth time. Li Shu-hsien was a hospital nurse, in her forties, a relative of one of the former KMT generals imprisoned with Pu Yi, who introduced them. They were given a tiny two-room apartment in the centre of Peking. Li Shu-hsien kept her job, but found that looking after Pu Yi could be a maddening experience. She had a sharp, nagging tongue. 'Pu Yi was kinder to her,' says Li Wenda, 'than she was to him.' From various accounts, she seems to have been a shrew. But Pu Yi bore his new misfortune with equanimity.

Was this, too, part of his saintly new *persona*, or had he really changed? Younger brother Pu Chieh is convinced Pu Yi's transformation was genuine: 'Gaol was like a school for him,' he said. 'All his life, until 1945, everyone around him had convinced him he was special, almost divine. Because of this, his attitude towards others had never been normal. Only in Fushun did he become aware of people as people.'

'One of his earlier characteristics,' says nephew Jui Lon, 'was his utter selfishness. Even in gaol he hoarded his cigarettes, and would never give any away, even though he was not a heavy smoker. When I saw him in Peking after his release he was a changed man. In his family, he started to care for people for the first time in his life.'

He certainly started showing a genuine concern for others: riding a bicycle one day, he knocked down an old woman who had to be admitted to hospital. Pu Yi visited her every day until she recovered. While working at the Fragrant Hills Hotel with Li Wenda, he always asked a nephew, who worked on a farm nearby, to join them for lunch. This was the height of the 'Great Leap Forward', and food was desperately short, except in luxury hotels.

His new orthodoxy made Pu Yi at times intolerant. When Pu Chieh (released in 1960) and his Japanese wife

Hiro wanted to live together again (Hiro had been in Japan all these years), Pu Yi did everything possible to prevent her from returning to China. Pu Chieh appealed to Chou En-lai who told Pu Yi to show more understanding. 'The war's over, you know,' he said. 'You don't have to carry this national hatred over into your own family.' It is difficult to avoid the impression that Pu Yi, in an effort to prove himself a 'remoulded' man, displayed the same craven attitude towards the powerholders of the new China that he had shown in Manchukuo towards the Japanese.

I asked Rong Qi about this. 'Of course the survival instinct is very strong in all of us,' he said with considerable insight. 'Nevertheless, his change was real. He came to see that imperialism and feudalism didn't really work, that communism was the only way to save China.'

The trouble is that since 1949, there have been several communist Chinas. The euphoria of the early fifties quickly gave way to a form of totalitarian personality cult rarely seen in history. The more fulsome, cliché-ridden chapters in *From Emperor to Citizen*, dealing with Pu Yi's prison experiences and written at the height of the Mao personality cult, give the impression of well-learned, regurgitated lessons. The style of them was *de rigueur* in 1964. Today, they have a faintly archaic air.

These days, all Chinese historians recognize the appalling consequences of the 'Great Leap Forward' and deplore the repression that followed the 'Let a hundred flowers bloom' movement. Neither is mentioned in Pu Yi's book, nor was it possible to begin doing so anywhere in China without risking arrest until the dark years of the Cultural Revolution and of the 'Gang of Four' were over.

There are some absurdities in Pu Yi's book, too, that today's Chinese readers find difficult to accept. Everyone in China is today aware that it was the Soviets, and not Chiang Kai-chek, as Pu Yi wrote, who dismantled Manchuria's factories in 1945; and the unreservedly rosy picture of prison life causes a certain amount of mirth among those – and they number millions – who experienced Chinese prisons, labour camps, or voluntary farm work in remote rural areas during the Cultural Revolution years.

The reason is that *From Emperor to Citizen* is now read in the light of the Cultural Revolution, and awareness of what happened during those years has generated scepticism over what occurred *before* it broke out. There is a far greater awareness of the excesses generated by the Mao personality cult during those years (1960–4) when Pu Yi was writing his autobiography, and far greater scepticism. The younger generation of Chinese knows, even if their elders do not, that during those years vast areas of China became 'Potemkin Villages' bearing no relationship with reality: some of the farms and factories Pu Yi visited during his final 'remoulding' years in prison may themselves have been 'Potemkin Villages'. Maybe they were real – Manchuria, after all, is a rich Chinese province – but the after-effects of the Cultural Revolution are such that the kind of prose Pu Yi used to describe his experiences will never be believed wholeheartedly by post-Cultural Revolution readers.

This form of scepticism will last until the last trace of Mao-worship gives way to a frank, realistic assessment of him in the light of his appalling 'Let a hundred flowers bloom' repression, his half-baked 'Great Leap Forward' and the ruthless destruction of his own Party apparatus during the Cultural Revolution. It is a source of wonder for those who knew China at its Maoist apogee to see how China has undergone 'de-Maoization' while at the same time continuing to pay lip service to him. By rights, as Simon Leys in *The Burning Forest* has pointed out, the much vilified Gang of Four which brought such chaos and misery to China should be called the Gang of Five, for without Mao it would never have established itself as a ruling group in the first place. Pu Yi, however, belongs to the era when the cosy, narrow Maoist line was still unquestioned, and not yet brought into terminal disrepute by the Red Guards and the Gang of Four.

Given the enormously powerful Maoist propaganda

machine of the fifties and early sixties, were Pu Yi's later conditioned responses any more genuine than those of his Manchukuo years? Was not his whole later life the reflection of a weak, neurotic and profoundly flawed personality?

Here, it is essential to remember that Pu Yi was not alone in undergoing such successful 'remoulding'. Tough KMT generals, and even tougher Japanese generals, brought up in the samurai tradition and the 'bushido' cult which glorifies death in battle and sacrifice to martial Japan, became, in Fushun, just as devout in their support of communist ideals as Pu Yi. A whole literature exists about these Japanese conversions, and a few Japanese graduates of Fushun prison have themselves written just as fulsomely as Pu Yi about their 'remoulding'. A good example is *A War Criminal Returns from China*, the autobiography of Saburo Shimamura, a former Japanese Gendarmerie general released shortly after Pu Yi. The book was written in 1975, never published in Japan, and only published in China in 1984.

There is a case for saying that Pu Yi underwent a truly 'Pauline' conversion, and that only after spending forty-one years in a series of gilded prisons did he find true freedom in a real prison, embracing Maoism naïvely but sincerely.

There is another analysis of the Pu Yi saga, held, among others, by Big Li: that all his life, Pu Yi was a professional survivor, bending to the wind, and that his 'remoulding' was as contrived as his ostentatious humility in the last few years of his life. Big Li, who had been at Pu Yi's constant beck and call since 1924, is one of those who believes the new Pu Yi *persona* was as calculated as the old. 'His book, *From Emperor to Citizen*, doesn't correspond to the truth,' he says. 'Out of self-abasement, Pu Yi made himself out to be worse, and more helpless, than he actually was.'

Big Li recalled that Pu Yi once came to see him in Peking after his release, and 'with humble gestures brushed some dust off my coat. It was all for show. He wanted everyone to believe he had changed, but was consciously play-acting all the time.'

Ironically, Big Li does not begrudge those years in Fushun prison, where he learned to read and write. It is his earlier, 'wasted life' that he cannot forgive Pu Yi. Today, Big Li lives in a small Peking apartment surrounded by his family, including several grandchildren. He is reluctant to talk about Pu Yi, but when he does, the hostility is immediately apparent.

Real or contrived, Pu Yi's repentance cannot disguise the fact that the leniency shown to him was remarkable, even if it derived from a conscious decision to exploit his 'remoulding' for propaganda purposes.

Treason on Pu Yi's scale is, in most countries, a capital offence. Many major Second World War criminals were treated with surprising laxity, but the pro-Nazi Anglo-Irish radio propagandist 'Lord Haw-Haw' was hanged: in the West, prejudices against quislings are very strong indeed. There is a very good case for saying that had Pu Yi come before a Western court, he too would have been executed. In contrast to the many French and Italian collaborators summarily executed by the Resistance, Pu Yi fared very well indeed.

The reason was, I believe, not only that Chou En-lai wished to use him for propaganda purposes; paradoxically, the communist takeover in 1949 lessened the strength of the charges against him. In a society where all landlord and 'capitalist-roaders' were evil incarnate, it did not matter so much that Pu Yi was also a traitor to his country: he was, in the eyes of communist ideologues, only behaving true to type. If all capitalists and landlords were, by their very nature, traitors, it was only logical that Pu Yi, the biggest landlord, should also be the biggest traitor. And, in the last resort, Pu Yi was far more valuable alive than dead.

In 1963, a year before his book was published, Pu Yi gave a press conference. He announced he was working on his memoirs, and answered questions with a kind of sad dignity. A Western diplomat present recalls that 'he never smiled once'. At the time, China's diplomatic isolation was almost complete, the regulatory hold of the Party on Chinese lives was rigid and all-encompassing, and the event was interpreted, by the diplomatic corps, as a sign that Mao's government was relaxing its hold a little.

From Emperor to Citizen, published in 1964, had relatively small sales in China (30,000) on first printing. It did, however, turn Pu Yi, almost overnight, into a media personality. He gave few interviews, but became a much sought-after figure among the diplomatic community. The book was translated into several foreign languages, and in his diffident way he became quite a celebrity. He was now working on the historical committee of the China People's Political and Consultative Committee, going through the Forbidden City archives and writing regularly about pre-republican days: China's authorities had realized that people like Pu Yi and his family were repositories of fascinating information about the past. Not only Pu Yi, but also his brothers and sisters contributed their reminiscences to government archives.

'There's no doubt,' says Li Wenda, 'that had events taken their normal course, Pu Yi himself would have become a member of the CPPCC.' Pu Chieh took his seat on the CPPCC in 1980 – a seat Pu Yi would almost certainly have occupied had he lived. As retired prison Governor Jin Yuan says, with a trace of envy: 'These people now enjoy a higher rank than I do.'

Pu Yi's cancer pains began in 1964. He had an operation in 1965, another in 1966, and was taken to the Capital Hospital, a dying man, in 1967. His communist faith, says nephew Jui Lon, 'enabled him to face death with equanimity. It was perhaps the biggest change in him. In earlier years, in Changchun, we had despised him as a coward, who would do anything to save his own life.'

As Pu Yi lay dying, the China of his dreams, which had never really existed except in his own mind, collapsed in a welter of Cultural Revolution violence. Thanks to Chou En-lai, his younger brother Pu Chieh lived through those dark days unscathed, as did his half-brother Pu Ren, the schoolmaster. 'They only raided my home and took away some books,' he says. 'I was lucky.' But the damage done to China's intellectual and administrative infrastructure was incalculable. It led to the deaths, in agony, of some of China's most prestigious leaders, including its President, Liu Shao-chi, and some of the leading heroes of the 1936 'Long March'. Marshal Chuh Teh, its real hero, who had visited Pu Yi in Fushun, died after repeated humiliation at the hands of the Red Guards.

Today, almost every Chinese family bears the scars of the Cultural Revolution, through deaths, deportations, maimings or through wasted years spent in the country-side on meaningless farm work. Many Chinese students taking part in *The Last Emperor* as film extras were in their mid-thirties. They had missed out on ten years of educa-tion. Chinese Leader Teng Hsiao-ping's own son was thrown out of a three-storey window by Red Guards who left him in agony for hours. He is today a wheelchair-bound paraplegic.

Those who had helped in Pu Yi's 'remoulding' were not spared: prison Governor Jin Yuan found himself a prisoner of the Red Guards in his own gaol for several years. Years later, he still flushes with rage as he recalls the indignity of it all. Li Wenda spent seven years in solitary confinement, branded as a 'counter-revolutionary' because of his work as Pu Yi's ghostwriter. The Red Guards disapproved of Pu Yi's book, not because it was not fulsome enough in its praise of Mao, but because it had been translated into foreign languages – and anything foreign was anathema to them, as it had been to the Boxer rebels and, indeed, to the 'Old Buddha' herself.

Nephew Jui Lon had just finished a ten-year stint on a communal farm and returned to Peking to perfect himself as a calligraphist when the Cultural Revolution broke out: he spent another nine years on another farm, in Manchuria this time. He now works full-time as a calligraphist in one of Peking's largest art galleries. Talking to him, one can only wonder at the resilience of the Chinese. Looking like a sunburnt, Chinese Charles Aznavour, he talks about the past without any trace of bitterness. Yet he too went to Fushun prison merely because he was part of Pu Yi's court, and only since 1979 has he been able to practise his calligraphist's craft, which he excels in, as a professional.

In the end, the Red Guards themselves became the victims: they were eventually rounded up by the People's Liberation Army and deported to the countryside.

With the end of the Cultural Revolution, and in the aftermath of Mao's death in 1976, books other than Mao's 'little red book' were published once more. A second edition of *From Emperor to Citizen* sold 1,300,000 copies in 1979. But Li Wenda admits that the new generation of Chinese, who did not experience the Cultural Revolution, find it almost incomprehensible in its present form: they are baffled by the early chapters describing his royal antecedents, and they find his description of his years in prison boring as well as hard to credit. The Cultural Revolution has made all Chinese much more sceptical of this kind of 'remoulding'.

But Chou En-lai's goal has been respected: Pu Yi is already part of China's pantheon of heroes, the perfect example of 'remoulded' man. Fushun Prison has become a museum. Pu Yi's letters to Jin Yuan are on display there, under glass. In Changchun, the Salt Tax Palace is now a geology school, but Pu Yi's reception room, complete with throne, where he held court, is also a small museum.

As he lay dying, Pu Yi could not have known that, one day, he would become an exemplary figure of Chinese communism, and that films would be made about his life. He alone could tell us whether his 'remoulding' was as thorough as he made out, and whether the film corresponds to the truth. We can only guess.

But his story is a heartbreaking one whether we regard him as a true convert or as a skilled, play-acting opportunist to the last. He was profoundly human, faced with impossible choices, made to live out the consequences of his mistakes for an agonizingly long time. His story takes place on several levels: on one it is the strange saga of a traitor who became a posthumous hero, without fully deserving either the earlier obloquy or the halo of communist sainthood. On another, it is the story of two young people caught up in a world they neither understood nor controlled. One died, a hopeless drug addict, the other survived, at huge personal cost to himself and others. In an attempt to find atonement for his real and imagined sins, the survivor could see nothing but evil in his early life.

Weak he may have been, and a coward most of his life. But he was also an innocent. In his later years, Pu Yi wanted posterity to see him as a solemn, 'remoulded' communist in a totalitarian paradise.

We have another vision of him: he is the tiny boy staring at us from his absurdly high throne, the teenager racing through the Forbidden City on a bicycle with his beautiful bride, the dandy ordering suits at Whiteway and Laidlaw's in Tientsin, the puppet emperor fumbling with his gloves before Hirohito.

In his youth he was unaware of his appallingly bleak future, or of the changes he would undergo in order to survive. Later, he plumbed his soul to the very depths, carrying an almost unbearable burden of guilt that had been inculcated into him by masters of their craft.

No wonder, when I saw him, he wore that wan, sad smile.

BIBLIOGRAPHY

Books

AUDEN, W. H. and ISHERWOOD, C.: *Journey to a War*, Faber and Faber, London 1939

BERGAMINI, David: *Japan's Imperial Conspiracy*, William Morrow, New York 1971

BLAND and BACKHOUSE: *China under the Empress Dowager*, Heinemann, London 1910

BRACKMAN, Arnold C.: *The Other Nuremberg – the Untold Story of the Tokyo War Crimes Trial*, William Morrow, New York 1987

CHEN, Jerome: *Yuan Shih-kai*, Stanford University Press, 1961

CHOU, Eric: *The Dragon and the Phoenix*, Corgi Books, London 1973

CLEMENTS, Paul: *The Boxer Rebellion*, AMS Press Ltd., New York 1967

FLEMING, Peter: *The Siege of Peking*, Rupert Hart Davies, London 1959; *One's Company*, Jonathan Cape, London 1934; *News From Tartary*, Jonathan Cape, London 1936

HAYASHIDE, Kenjiro: *Epochal Journey to Nippon*, Government of Manchukuo Publications (no date)

HIBBERT, Christopher: *The Dragon Wakes*, Longman, London 1970

JOHNSTON, Reginald: *Twilight in the Forbidden City*, Gollancz, London 1934

JONES, F. C.: *Manchuria After 1931*, Royal Institute of International Affairs, London 1963

KOO, Wellington: *Memoirs*, New York Times Oral History series, 1978

LEYS, Simon: *The Burning Forest*, Holt, Rinehart and Winston, New York 1986

MCALEAVY, David: *A Dream of Tartary*, George Allen and Unwin, London 1963

PASQUALINI, Jean: *Prisoner of Mao*, Howard McCann and Geoghegan, New York 1973

PEARL, Cyril: *Morrison of Peking*, Angus and Robertson, London 1967

PU YI: *From Emperor to Citizen*, Foreign Languages Press, Beijing 1964

REA, George Bronson: *The Case for Manchukuo*, D. Appletone Century Company, New York 1935

SALISBURY, Harrison T.: *The Long March*, Harper and Row, New York 1985

SNOW, Edgar: *Battle for Asia*, Random House, New York 1941

TAYLOR, George E.: *Japanese-sponsored Regimes in Northern China*, Garland Publishing Inc., New York and London 1980

TE-LING: *Two Years in the Forbidden City*, Dodd, Mead, New York 1924

VARE, Daniele: *Laughing Diplomat*, John Murray, London 1938

VESPA, Amleto: *Secret Agent of Japan*, Little Brown and Co., New York 1938

WARNER, Marina: *The Dragon Empress*, Weidenfeld and Nicolson, London 1971

WOODHEAD, Henry: *Adventures in Far Eastern Journalism*, Hokuseido Press, Tokyo 1935

YOUNG, Ernest P.: *Politics in the Aftermath of Revolution: The Era of Yuan Shih-kai* (publication details not available)

Documents and Periodicals

Peking and Tientsin Times
Shanghai Evening Post and Mercury
The Times
Corriere della Sera
Contemporary Manchuria, 1939
Manchuria Yearbook, 1933–9, Chinese League of Nations Society publications, 1932
Proceedings of the International Military Tribunal for the Far East, 1946–7, held by the National War Memorial, Canberra

Interviews with:
Pu Chieh, Rong Qi, Jui Lon (Aisin Goro family)
Li Wenda (co-author of *From Emperor to Citizen*)
Jin Yuan (former Governor of Fushun prison)
Big Li (Pu Yi's servant, 1924–57)

INDEX

China 165–6; Ishiwara on 171; in Manchuria 201; Gen Ma operates from 226; neutrality pact with Japan 252; invades Manchuria 259; supports Mao 259, 278–9; takes PY and family 265–6, 268, 278–82; dismantles Manchurian industry 270–71
Russians, White 140–41, 155–6, 162, 180, 202–3, 208, 210, 215

Saga, Hiro (Mme Pu Chieh) 16, 235, 248; *Wandering Princess* 248–50, 257, 263; evacuated 261, 264–5, 267–70; rejoins Pu Chieh 319–20
San Tao 115–16
Semenov, Gen 162
Shanghai 198, 239
Shao Ying 127, 130
Shimamura, Saburo 16, 322
Shintoism 250–51, 261
Snow, Edgar 14, 139–40, 204, 206
Soong, Mei-lin (Mme Chiang Kai-chek) 12–13, 166, 167, 168
Soong, T. V. 13, 185–6
Su, Prince (Eastern Jewel's father) 187–8
Su, Prince (PY's father-in-law) *see* Jung Kuan
Summer Palace 35–6, 42, 44, 96, 125–7
Sun Fo 196
Sun Yat-sen, Dr 12, 66–7, 68–9, 89, 136, 139, 145
Sun Yat-sen, Mme 13, 133

Taiping rebellion 11, 43–4, 46
Takemoto, Col 16, 148
Tanaka, Gi-ichi (PM of Japan) 16, 164, 165
Tanaka, Maj-Gen Takayoshi 16, 180, 186, 189, 196, 272
Teh-hing 13, 38, 39
Teng Hsiao-ping 325

Tientsin 50–51, 86, 155–7, 192; *see also* Pu Yi
Times, The 111, 205; *see also* Morrison
Timperly, H. J. 206
Tojo, Hideki 142, 272
tombs, Ching 185, 251
Tsai Tao 308
Tsao Kun, President 130
Tuan, Prince 55, 58
Tuan Chijui, Marshal 144–5
Tung-chih, Emp. 13, 43, 46–7
Tzu-hsi, Empress 9, 12, 13, 37–9, 41–2, 57, 117; Empress Dowager 44–51; and foreigners 46, 49–51, 54–7, 58–9; and 'hundred days' 53–4; imprisons Kuang-hsu 54; and Boxers 54–7; returns from exile 57–9; rule until death 59–61; and succession to Kuang-hsu 60, 61; death 61, 64–5; tomb 167

United States of America 36–7, 56–7, 137–8, 204

Vespa, Amleto 14, 206–10

Wan Ching-wei 253–4
Wan Jung, Empress 13, 108, 115, 326–7; marriage 108, 111–14; relations with PY 19, 20, 95, 114–16, 175–7, 196, 247–8, 255–6; and Feng takeover 133; in Japanese Legation 157–8; opium addiction 175–8, 215–16, 247–8; to Manchuria 186, 188–9, 190, 195–6; in Manchukuo 195–6, 215–16, 223, 228, 230, 247–8; PY wants divorce 255; illegitimate child 12, 255; evacuated 261, 264–5; death 269–70; PY and news of 271, 308
Wang, Mrs 63, 64, 65, 66
war, Chinese civil 17, 268–9, 278–9, 282